STONE
MAIDENS

STONE MAIDENS

MAIDENS

Lloyd Devereux Richards

Published by Thomas and Mercer
P.O. Box 400818
Las Vegas, NV 89140

ISBN-13: 9781612186054
ISBN-10: 161218605X

To Ritie, in loving memory.

PROLOGUE

It was late summer, and he was seventeen. It was hot. He liked that, even though he worked on a farm and spent long hours stacking hay. He was laying up bales for the winter in a three-story loft. From the open bay where the chain pulley swung to hoist the pallet, he saw her—the nubile young daughter of a neighbor farmer in a flower-print dress that flowed prettily. The tight-fitting bodice showed off her slim waist. The way her body moved inside the frock sent him tumbling down the wooden steps and out into the hazy August air.

She wandered into a cornfield, slapping the long green leaves of a second planting tasseled out, and disappeared down a row, taking a shortcut home. He followed her into the corn as if pulled by a ring in his nose, pushing aside the leaves and thick stalks in the fading heat of the day, his work boots sinking into the loamy soil. Walking faster, two rows over, he caught glimpses of her flowery dress. For several minutes he trolled behind, waiting till she was farther along into the maize. Gradually, he drifted deeper into the sweet-smelling crop. The bees buzzing from tassel to tassel made a loud, persistent hum.

His skin began to crawl as if covered in a swarm of ants. The droning of the bees penetrated directly into his skull. Breathing shallowly, he dropped to one knee, and everything went dark. He scratched at the ground, as if searching for his lost sight there, heaving on all fours with his face in the soil, sucking up dirt. Then slowly, slowly the light had returned—and with it a new craving.

CHAPTER ONE

The air had a film in it like her eyes did upon first waking. By mid-morning the Fourth of July heat pressed in, almost choking her. Missy Hooper tapped END, dropped her cell phone into her purse, and closed the bag with a sigh. A second later she double-checked to make sure she'd turned the clasp all the way. The amusement park was jam-packed, and it would be easy to get pickpocketed if she wasn't careful.

Now what? Glenna had gone in to cover for a waitress who'd called in sick at the diner where they both worked, and couldn't meet her as planned. What a drag. Wandering around alone in a park full of so many people her own age out on dates was not her idea of fun. Damn Glenna. Why couldn't she have just told Rickie no? Missy sighed again. Glenna let people take advantage of her. She needed to learn to stick up for herself better.

A tattooed carny drifted her way, holding out three baseballs with a toothy grin. "Whaddya say to a game of chance, little lady? Got some nifty prizes for a purty girl like you. Three balls for a dollar."

Missy turned to avoid him and ran smack into a wiry young man with sandy-brown hair and bright-blue eyes.

"Whoa! It's the bottles you're supposed to knock over, not the other patrons." He smiled and ran his hand through his crew cut.

Missy took a step back. "I'm sorry," she stammered. "I guess I wasn't watching where I was going."

"No problem. What's your poison: bulldogs or monkeys? One of those prizes would look mighty good sitting on your bedroom shelf." He leaned in closer. "It's on me." He gave the carny a five-dollar bill and got handed back four ones from the man's change bib.

"Beg your pardon?" Missy said, blushing. "Are you speaking to me?" The young man had the weather-beaten appearance of someone who worked outdoors, like both of her brothers, and his face was strangely familiar though she couldn't recall from where.

"Sure am." He bowed from the waist, clothed in paint-spattered jeans and a red T-shirt. His orange Timberland work boots were flecked with paint stains. "Just point out the prize you want," he boasted, his arms akimbo, "and it's yours."

Missy tugged at the front of her blue tank top, which immediately rode back up, exposing her belly button. She squinted up at the stuffed animals that hung from hooks. "That bulldog looks kind of cute."

"Wish me luck then." He winked.

Missy giggled. "Good luck." She watched him collect the first baseball from the carny and palm it lightly, judging the target's distance. He turned toward Missy and gave her a confident grin.

The shriek of a girl mid-drop on a roller coaster spun Missy around just as the coaster banked steeply and disappeared behind a high-topped tent.

Thwack! The sound of the bottles toppling spun her back again.

"Darn if you aren't the best of me!" The young man pumped a fist, obviously pleased with himself. "Now ain't it just true that faith moves mountains?" He winked at Missy again. "Yours sure did."

Missy awkwardly rode the outsides of her sneakers—the young man's addressing her so forthrightly embarrassed and flattered her at the same time. A moment later her arms were full of the bright-blue bulldog, which was as awkward to carry as a bale of hay.

"Got a car to put that thing in?"

She rolled her eyes. "I wish. A friend dropped me off. Someone else was supposed to meet me here."

"Not a problem. You can leave it in my truck if you'd like." Before she could respond, he blurted, "Say, are you hungry?" He stepped up to a concession booth and then turned his head back to her. "Want a Coke with your elephant ear?"

She was suddenly aware of the smell of fried dough and sugar permeating the air. Her stomach, as if on cue, gurgled loudly. "Sure."

She decided she liked being waited on better than being the waitress. Even his doing all the talking felt nice, like he was taking care of her. He returned with the drinks and two fried elephant ears, each wrapped in wax paper. She rested the prize on the ground between her legs.

"Thanks. I can pay you back."

"Your money's no good here," he said. The words were overly gracious, but his tone was self-mocking. He was funny, Missy decided, and cute in an odd, scraggy sort of way.

"Thank you," she said. "My name is Missy."

"Glad to meet you, Missy. I go by Jasper. On account of I like carving rocks in my spare time. Shall we go drop your prize in the truck then?"

They finished their fried dough and drinks and then walked out the park entrance.

"Say, if you'd like, I can drive you home." He climbed in the driver's side, leaned over the bench seat, and shoved open the passenger door, adding, "I'd be more than grateful to do you the honors, Missy."

The thought of having to call and ask one of her brothers to come get her made her cringe. It would be a hot, sweaty wait, with

Jimmy at his coed bowling league and Dean over in Odon at his girlfriend's house. "Sure. I guess that'd be all right."

"Spilt some paint in the back bed. It's still a bit messy," he said. "Why don't you put the bulldog up front?" He gestured toward the passenger seat.

Missy pushed the bulky prize across the seat then climbed in herself. The bulldog caught on cracks in the vinyl covering; yellowed foam padding protruded, and an acrid, salty smell hit her in the face.

He goosed the engine and shoved the vent window out all the way, told her to do the same. The road wound through a state forest. Although the amusement park was only a couple of miles away, it felt like they were in another world entirely. Everything here was quiet. Peaceful. Splintering sunlight shot between the trees.

"Ever been to Clear Creek before?" he said across the rush of incoming air.

She glanced at him over the stuffed animal. "You mean that swimming place?"

He shook his head. "Nah. Different place. I suspect it's about as sweet a spot as you could find." Jasper turned to look at her and smiled, almost shyly. "I'd like to show it to you if I could."

They were on State Road 67. Her house was only five miles farther south. He seemed polite. "How far did you say it is?" she said, squinting in the sunlight that blazed through the side window.

"We're almost nearly there."

She nodded. "All right then, I guess." She looked over at him again, trying to place him. The man was working something around in his mouth, and the edge of something glistened between his teeth.

"Got any more?" she said. "Of those candies you're sucking?"

He lifted his lips. A dark sliver jutted out, glistening and wet. "Not what you think." It slid back into the pocket of his cheek. "Didn't your mother ever tell you sugar's bad for your teeth?"

"OK. Well, what is it then?"

"Ever since I was a kid I always liked cutting stone. Carving small things, you know, like faces, animal shapes. Even cut some people out of rock. It's tricky." He slid a quick glance her way and then looked out the windshield. "Easy to break the stone in two if you aren't real careful doing it."

Missy grew quiet and gazed out her side window, not exactly sure how to respond. The truck passed familiar landscape. She could see a friend's farmhouse on a ridgeline opposite the road. She was about to ask him to stop the truck and say that she just remembered she was supposed to drop by her friend's house this afternoon when the man extended an open palm near her lap.

"See?" he said. "I finished this one yesterday. Hand carved from chert, a variety of jasper." He smiled at her. "Like my name."

Missy stared at the reddish stone still wet from being in the man's mouth. It was about the size of a chess piece. At one end, a distinct head and face were carved. Grooves along the small stone outlined arms and legs.

"I bet that takes you a long time."

"Yup." The man closed his palm and pocketed the charm.

"So where do you work, Jasper?" Missy asked, changing the subject. "I bet it's outdoors, on account of your tan."

"Well, aren't you a smart young lady," he said, nodding slowly. "I sign paint different places, business establishments. Some people think hand-painted signs are old-fashioned. I guess I'm what you call a throwback." He grinned and flicked the tips of his fingers gently against her bare shoulder.

She started at the casually intimate touch.

"A regular artist I am. Do my best work when I'm left alone, know what I mean?"

She glanced down at his spattered jeans. "Yeah. But it kind of looks like you work for the fairground people, painting clowns."

He chuckled, shaking his head. "That's a funny one. Truth is, the damn Sweet Lick Resort can't buy near enough of me. I get worn out working so much."

"You mean that fancy golf course place?" she asked. "My friend's uncle is a groundskeeper there. His name is Lonnie Wallace. Ever hear of him?"

"No, I don't think I've ever met the man. But then..." He arched his brow and hesitated as if pondering her question. "I'm not apt to talk to anyone when I'm on the job. Better to concentrate." He fidgeted his hands over the top of the steering wheel, twisting his grip. "Like throwing that baseball, winning you this prize." He tugged one of the stuffed animal's ears. "It truly was worth all the tea in China meeting you like this, Missy."

The truck jounced over a bump. Missy rocked forward and pushed back her hair away from her face. He winked both his eyes at her, and Missy laughed right on cue. He told her how earlier in the year he'd been put in charge of a painting crew renovating a Chicago museum—a hundred men working under his watchful eye repainted primitive exhibits, ones that displayed spear-wielding cannibals in their native jungle habitats.

"Really? That must have been amazing."

"I fib you not." She felt his eyes brush over her and smiled self-consciously. "I'm only the greatest damn sign painter on the whole darn planet, you know? No splash-and-dash operation, no ma'am."

"Well, yeah. Sure." It puzzled her—his saying first how he worked solo most of the time and then right afterward saying a hundred men had worked under him in a museum renovation. She chalked it up to male insecurity—his needing to boast so much. Besides, he was funny and sweet in his own way. And she'd finally figured out why he looked so familiar.

He slowed the truck and pulled off under a high canopy of evergreens. The air was a full ten degrees cooler than the fairgrounds and smelled piney sweet.

She leaned an elbow over the stuffed bulldog, rubbing one of its ears between her fingers. "Know why I really came along with you?" A coy smile broke across her face.

"I suspect you wanted to see Clear Creek."

"You don't remember me, do you?" she said, dipping her chin shyly. "Science class junior year?" She looked straight into his eyes. "Weaversville High?"

He hesitated. "If you say so."

"Come on. Really, don't you remember? You were the only one too afraid to cut open that cow's eye." Nodding, feeling more certain of herself, she said, "You walked out of class too grossed out to even touch it."

He scratched hard behind one ear. "You sure got a memory for things, I'll say that." He opened the truck door and hopped out.

Missy followed him around to the hood, hands tucked in her back jeans pockets. "You were so shy back then. What happened?"

"I guess"—he covered his face, peeking out between his fingers—"because I started playing hide-and-seek so damn much! Better run and hide before I count to ten," he yelled.

Like a lit firecracker, Missy took off. She plunged down the wooded bank like a kid half her age would, sparked by Jasper's boyish charm and his clear interest in her. There was nothing but the petticoat rustle of leaves and the nutty smells of the forest telling her that this was one of those rare occasions in life when wishes might just come true. When finally, finally you met someone meant just for you. Like magic, it was happening exactly the way it was supposed to, the way her mother had met Missy's father and had known in that instant he was the man for her.

The grade slanted steeply. Missy took choppier steps and had to grab hold of slender saplings to keep from falling. Far below, she caught glimpses of water sparkling between the trees.

She deftly slalomed in and out of a mixed grove of beeches and oaks, then dropped onto the sandy bottom of a partially dry creek bed. Beyond were standing pools of water. She crouched behind a massive overturned sycamore, giddy with expectation. Peering up the wooded ravine she'd just descended, she listened intently for his footfalls over her rapid heartbeats but could hear nothing.

She registered a dull thud behind her, across the creek. How could he be there already? Missy bolted away from the sound across the deep, damp basin, each step slowed by the sucking sand. Something wasn't right.

From behind, she heard him splashing through a deep pool. "You sure are...fast on your feet," he panted. His voice sounded taunting somehow, not charming at all, and a sharp bolt of fear ripped through her chest.

Scattered sunlight glinted on the water. Instinctively, Missy's eyes scanned what lay ahead, searching for an exit. Her eyes picked out a line of escape: a patch of harder ground that veered back up along the edge of the woods. She swung her arms for added speed, unnerved that she hadn't heard him coming through the forest. She hadn't heard a damn thing until he had dropped down from the opposite bank.

She ran while looking behind her and plowed straight into a fallen tree, sending her sprawling to the ground. Frantically, she clawed at the bark, tumbled back down the sandy bank, and tore her shirt in the process. Tendrils of panic worked their way into her brain, nearly sending her headfirst into a deep pool. The collision with the tree had left a nasty gash on her left kneecap, and blood was trickling down her shin.

The sound of a semi downshifting nearby brought her struggle to a standstill. She could just make out the moving hulk's flickering shadow in breaks between the trees that rimmed the steep ravine high above her. A coal carrier chugged by with a full load from the Lincoln Mines in Blackie, where her father worked. Her dad's kind, weathered face flashed through her brain. The slow-moving truck was only a football field's distance away as the crow flies, but deadfall formed a near-insurmountable barrier.

Missy suddenly realized it wasn't her own breathing growing louder, but her chaser's, from directly above her on the bank. She looked up, blinked.

"Thought I'd lost you for a minute."

Confusion spun the contents of Missy's mind as she tried to make sense of what she was seeing. The man was reclining, arms crossed and utterly relaxed, on the fallen tree that had sent her flying to the ground. His face was covered by an elaborate feathered mask.

He tucked the mask back over the top of his head and gazed at her sympathetically. "Got a little hung up, didn't you?" His hand flopped over the side of the trunk, pointing out her torn shirt. A stone of some kind dangled from his neck.

She crossed her arms over her ripped shirtfront and stepped backward into the cool water, warily maintaining eye contact with him. She'd lost her sneaker during her mad dash, and her one bare foot slipped on creek stones coated with algae. She had been badly mistaken. Jasper wasn't the name of the student from science class, and the face gazing down at her wasn't anything like that of the shy boy she'd known in high school.

CHAPTER TWO

A knock came at the door. A slim woman with gray hair pulled primly back poked her head in. "Christine, they're waiting."

"Just a sec, Margaret," said Christine Prusik, chief forensic anthropologist of the FBI's Midwest Forensic Sciences Laboratory. Its jurisdictional responsibilities took in most of the central corridor from the Great Lakes to the borders of the Gulf Coast states, which were handled by New Orleans forensics teams.

Prusik tucked her short chestnut hair behind her ears, revealing two gold studs—the only piece of female hardware on the special agent—and continued to scan her field notes with practiced eyes. Of medium height and well proportioned from years of swimming the backstroke—she'd been a county champion when she was in her early teens—she was adept at rebuffing the advances of men who hadn't correctly read what she tried to make eminently clear through her body language: Hands Off.

Her mammoth desk—a fortress of piles, with no surface free on which to jot even a note—was still insufficient a space to display all the materials she needed to ponder a case and its possible permutations. On the floor wreathing around her desk were open field notebooks, forensic-ruled photographs, and postmortem summaries underscored and starred with Magic Marker blues and pinks. Prusik's dynamic intelligence at once focused in on the most diminutive detail and nuance of trace evidence and panned out to the wide screen, factoring in the significance of geographic location, crime scene patterns, and any similarities and differences with other potentially linked cases.

To Prusik, working a case meant all information had to be at hand, to be positioned or repositioned on the floor as she stood hunched over, scanning downward like some bird of prey on patrol, intently searching for a telltale sign, something—anything—odd or out of place or deliberately wrong.

Wind buffeted the building. Slanted streaks of rain raced across the large-paned windows of her sixteenth-floor office overlooking downtown Chicago. Prusik leaned back in her chair, holding a color slide up to the light. Hurriedly she skimmed the stack sent by overnight courier, looking for one in particular, the angle shot of the neck. She preferred holding actual slides to toggling through an array of digital images on a flat screen. To her, a photographic positive was crisper on close-ups than on the digital counterparts from the new Canons most field agents preferred.

She propped a brown, crepe-soled oxford shoe on the edge of her desk. Her free hand tugged a tuft of her hair, snagging loose a few strands in the process, as she mulled one particular close-up of a gaping purple wound—a vicious cut—that perversely mimicked the contours of an open mouth along the abdominal cavity. Just then an itchy panic took hold of her, and the photographic slide slipped from her fingers onto the floor.

Prusik fumbled open the desk drawer and grabbed the small pewter pillbox she kept there. Many years ago it had belonged to her grandmother, and Christine had wondered what pills her mother's mother would have kept in it. Swallowing one Xanax tablet dry, she lofted the Bose headset over her ears and flipped the lever of the CD player on the credenza. She closed her eyes in the hunt for calm, waiting for the near-trance-inducing chords of Bach's Partita for Keyboard no. 1 to return things to order. She tightened her right fist, squeezing her pinkie against her palm. Pills couldn't erase the fact things were getting worse.

Within a few minutes, the combination effect had worked—the modern miracle of neurochemistry acting in consort with Bach's genius. Her breathing had slowed; her heart rate no longer frightened her.

The office phone rang, destroying her peace and startling her forward in the chair. It was Margaret, her secretary, nudging her again. But she wasn't ready yet. She refocused on the short stack of slides in front of her and hunted for any forensic anomaly that might cast light on the killer. The pictures had been taken the preceding day, July 27. Three whole months had gone by since the first corpse had turned up—nearly three whole months without delivering a positive ID of the killer or even one iota of incriminating evidence. The body of the first victim, a teenage runaway named Betsy Ryan, was found in water, near Lake Michigan and protected shore lands. Very private, with no residences nearby housing someone who might have heard her cries for help had she made any.

This latest victim, a Jane Doe, had been found two hundred and fifty miles south of Chicago in Blackie, Indiana, a coal-mining district southwest of Indianapolis, a region dominated by dense forests and steep-sided ravines. The victim's body had been discovered partially exposed under some leaves near a creek bank; she wasn't a floater or submerged like Betsy Ryan had been. Ryan's body had surfaced in the third week of April, snagged on the anchor line of an outgoing skiff on the Little Calumet in Gary, Indiana—practically Prusik's doorstep. The Ryan girl had been washed clean; nipping minnows and crustaceans had made sure that no foreign DNA had been left behind. But one thing remained that no amount of washing could erase, and it tied the first crime irrefutably to the second—a vicious ventral slit running the length of the left side of the victim's abdomen. All the internal organs had been removed, leaving the bodies literally eviscerated. And both killings had occurred near water.

The office door cracked open again.

Without looking up, Prusik said to her secretary, "Yes, Margaret, I know." Christine's boss's plane to Washington would be leaving in one hour, his car to the airport in fifteen minutes.

"No, you don't know," Margaret scolded in a stern whisper. Margaret eased herself all the way into the office. "It's Thorne. He's calling again." She paused for emphasis, though none was needed. "He's got a plane to catch."

"Tell him to keep his shirt on for chrissakes." In her ten years with the bureau, Prusik had acquired a reputation for gruff impatience, which she exhibited at inopportune times with superiors and subordinates alike. Driven by high expectations of herself, she had little room for work or effort that was, in her opinion, second rate.

Prusik took a deep breath. "You can tell Mr. Thorne—"

Their eyes met, calculating the possibilities and silently rejecting most of them. Calmer now, Prusik said, "Thank you, Margaret. Tell him I'm on the way."

Christine watched as her secretary's face relaxed and she left the room, carefully avoiding focusing on any of the gruesome photographs pinned to the corkboard behind the desk. The blow-ups of Betsy Ryan, the first victim, looked more like color abstractions than the barely recognizable remains of a young human. Ryan was a fifteen-year-old runaway who'd been living with an aunt in Cleveland. The girl's trail had gone cold shortly after she had hitched a ride on March 30 with an Allied Van Lines mover. The driver had let her off at a Portage, Indiana, truck stop. His fuel receipt checked out. So did the absence of any incriminating forensic evidence in the cab of his truck. Three weeks later, on April 21, her body had been recovered off the boat anchor, cruelly hooked through the man-made pocket along the victim's left side, not far from the Indiana Dunes National Lakeshore, where the killer would have been able to savage her with plenty of cover. Cellular analysis disclosed that the remains had likely been underwater several weeks, which Prusik figured meant her attacker had probably spotted her shortly after the driver—the last known eyewitness—had dropped the girl off at the truck stop.

She fingered another slide from the Blackie crime scene. This one showed a man's boot print, approximately size nine. The local police had found it in the mud beside the creek and made a quick-dry plaster kit impression. The killer liked to do his cutting by water. She swallowed hard. Time was ticking.

Damp weather had inundated the Midwest for most of the spring and early summer—conditions appalling for the preservation of evidence, accelerating the decomposition of flesh. Prusik knew that it was unlikely she'd find anything worthwhile on the latest victim's body or in the area surrounding the crime scene. The Blackie woods, a great stomach of damp forest, had surely already digested her case, eating with it whatever evidence the killer might have left behind.

Tucking the slides into her lab-coat pocket, she stepped quickly around the desk, resolving not to let the case get away from her. She hustled past her secretary's partition and walked briskly down the hall. "Back soon," she called over her shoulder as an afterthought.

Outside the lecture room, Prusik's hand froze on the doorknob at the unmistakable sound of Roger Thorne clearing his throat a few feet behind her.

She turned and met Managing Director Thorne's piercing gaze over his tortoiseshell glasses. His fine navy-blue suit made Prusik feel frumpy in her so-so stretch knit, which had more than a few tired sags and stains from stooping and studying remains in situ. Its last excursion had been to another field agent's crime scene, where a local deputy had done a miserable job fending off the weather with an umbrella, letting the small of her back become a nice rain catch.

"Christine, may I speak to you for a moment?" Thorne's tone was studied, formal. He bent his forearm, purposely displaying the gleaming new chronograph watch he was so proud of—a

Montblanc, the same brand as the smart-looking fountain pen clipped to his shirt breast pocket. He tapped the watch crystal.

"It's getting late." Thorne straightened his cuff back over the shiny chronometer, then arranged the jacket he frequently wore for his Washington trips, the chosen type of garment of all men who sat behind desks behind doors with brass name placards at the FBI. "I just got off the phone with headquarters. Told them about the *second* one, we think."

She nodded. "I'm on my way to update the team. There are important forensic similarities between both cases. The forensics *will* yield us results, I am confident."

Thorne smiled into her eyes. "Good, good. I'm confident you will succeed, Christine. It's why I assigned you these cases in the first place. Stick-to-itiveness is one of your finer qualities." He squeezed her shoulder. She stiffened at his touch, and he dropped his hand. "You are an astute scientist, one of our best. You know how much I respect your able observational skills. I doubt there's another managing director in the agency whose forensic unit is superior."

She returned his smile, pleased by the compliment yet expecting to hear a "but" coming next. "Thank you for saying so, Roger." Christine always appreciated hearing his praise. Thorne's sincerity in acknowledging her accomplishments as a forensic scientist was unquestionable. That, his good looks, and sharp dressing style were all it had taken for her to fall in love with him.

His straw-colored eyebrows rose a notch higher over the tops of his glasses. "So, now that you're in charge, I can speak frankly." His eyebrows lifted again. "I'd be remiss if I didn't tell you that they're a bit concerned I let you take the lead on such a high-profile case." He put up his palm before she could respond. "Hear me out. You've been a prominent head of the forensic lab, doing a damn fine job for ten years—until now, that is. It's your first lead, and their concerns are understandable given that you have no demonstrated experience managing all aspects of a case: the logistics, directing personnel from different offices, interfacing with local police and political officials. You know what I'm talking about, Christine."

Let me take the lead? She bit her lip, trying to remind herself that Thorne was only doing his job. Still, she knit her brow and spoke defensively. "You know I've put together the best team. They're working around the clock on this. No one has slipped up unless you count the local and state police foul-ups."

"So is that it then—police foul-ups?" Thorne clearly wanted some significant news. "I need progress to report, Christine. Progress is what gets noticed. I know your team is diligently processing fragmentary information, looking for clues. Give me something to prove to Washington I made the right decision putting you in charge of this case. Management needs to be kept informed of a case's progress and be assured that appropriate assets are being committed to bring about an effective resolution. Believe it or not, Christine, a cost-benefit analysis figures into everything we do."

"I believe it." Budgetary cutbacks in 2010 meant Prusik's lab had had to take on more responsibility in 2011 while receiving no increase in resources. It seemed that Management 101 for the FBI mirrored the strategy that private enterprise, stymied by the severe economic downturn, was employing: make your people do more with less, then expect miracles.

"Roger," she fought to keep the frustration out of her voice, "let me put it this way. The body found in Blackie bears the killer's trademark. It's most definitely the same perpetrator, most certainly a man, given the sheer physicality of the crime, the strength involved in the nature of the killing. Unfortunately, judging from the slides, the body's state of decomposition suggests exposure to the elements for at least a month."

Thorne nodded once, almost imperceptibly. "What do you make of this profile so far?"

She found it easier to focus on Thorne's perfectly knotted tie than on those mustard-brown eyes that still disarmed her. His undeniable good looks and the memory of the intimacy they had shared caused her face to flush. She hoped he didn't notice.

"He travels. Picks his victims carefully. The first was a runaway. This Jane Doe we think may be a local, a young woman who went missing from an amusement park a couple of miles away over the Fourth of July. We'll be taking dental impressions and an X-ray set of her jaw tomorrow, of course. Tell headquarters the suspect is very likely in his early twenties, fit, living alone or staying by himself most of the time, perhaps odd-jobbing. He's private, a good site planner. Doesn't tolerate the prospect of interference, which explains why the victims aren't found soon after. Both bodies were located well away from any neighborhoods where someone might accidentally intrude. He needs time for what he does to them."

"And what exactly is that?" Thorne cupped an elbow, listening intently to what she was saying.

"You've already read my detailed report on the condition of Betsy Ryan's corpse. The Blackie victim was strangled, similarly cut open—a single slash wound longitudinal and ventral. The internal organs were completely removed, and there was no recovery of them, according to the local coroner's report."

Their eyes met. His mouth cinched shut. The tendons on either side of his neck tightened. She whiffed Thorne's cologne, and her breathing momentarily stopped. After a couple of months of lunchtime rendezvous, their affair had abruptly ended, nearly six months earlier. Prusik had grown uneasy; she couldn't take the intimacy and had broken it off with him. Thorne had wasted no time in retreating to a marriage that he had intimated to her was at most a comfortable truce. All these months later she was mostly over it, but sometimes she still missed their charged encounters, the feel of his gaze on her body. And he had a discerning mind, even if he did sometimes buy into the Washington bullshit. She missed talking over the puzzling details of a case in the lazy aftermath of lovemaking.

In a softer voice, Prusik said, "My team is doing everything humanly possible to identify this perpetrator. They're waiting for me right now." She glanced back at the door.

"One more thing," Thorne said, clearing his throat. "Check with Bruce Howard on these profile particulars you've developed. I assume Howard will be leading the field technicians to the Blackie site? Frankly, he's got excellent leadership qualities with a team, Christine. Knows how things should be handled. Hits the ground running, you know what I mean. You're going to need his help. This is a much larger area of focus now." Thorne peered over his tortoiseshell rims. "Cooperation and teamwork are the keys to success in this organization—in any soundly run organization."

Christine felt the sharp slap of his words on her face. "I have Mr. Howard and the field unit well in hand, sir," she said tightly.

Thorne glanced at his watch, then looked back at her, making no move to leave. "There's nothing more you can tell me, Christine?"

She blushed under his intent gaze and was irritated with herself for doing so. "The killer is quite sophisticated with a knife, sir. What he does to his victims is highly invasive. He's a repeater, suggesting a ritualistic pattern of some kind. The predilection for gutting is quite extraordinary, unlike that of any felon we've so far checked on any of the interstate violent persons' data banks. The blood around the incisions appears minimal, not coagulated. Meaning he cleans them shortly after death. I'll know better tomorrow." Almost subconsciously, Prusik picked polite code for the unspeakable truth, in deference to Thorne's vulnerability. He detested gory forensic details.

"Ritualistic, did you say?"

"Neither victim appears to have been sexually assaulted," she explained. "He does not tamper with their faces. The victim's cranium in each case is intact. I'd say that catching them is an intensely personal experience for him." Prusik looked directly into Thorne's eyes.

He blinked twice. "I suppose that *is* something significant to report."

He made as if to leave. Held out his hand to shake hers, hesitated, and gave her shoulder another light squeeze. It was their gesture, the one they used to use at work to acknowledge their relationship, and something about using it now seemed cheap to Christine. It hadn't been her fears alone that had ended the relationship. After a few months, she couldn't ignore Thorne's hesitation and her growing sense that they wouldn't be going any further than their noontime trysts because he'd never leave his wife. The shoulder squeeze somehow belied all that.

"Very good work, Christine." He hurried down the hall, his leather soles slapping against the marble floor. "And good work by your team. Tell them for me, will you?" He waved, without turning, and made his way toward the flight that would take him to Washington.

CHAPTER THREE

Prusik stood quietly at the lecture-room door, regaining her composure. She wasn't sure whether it was the physical contact with Thorne or his intimations about Bruce Howard's role in the case that had flustered her more.

What had gotten her this far was not her ability to manage a case but her aptitude for science and her combination of uncannily accurate hunches and careful deciphering of wounds. Her PhD was in physical anthropology, the evolution and science of man, with a subspecialty in the darker, dirtier deeds: murders involving aberrant mutilations of the body, committed either pre- or postmortem. The shapes and types of marks told her of the instruments used to turn the perfect-working processes of life into rotting flesh. To Prusik, what turned a criminal to violence was as interesting as the mortal wounds.

Her forensic skills were legendary at the FBI. In the decade she'd worked in the Midwest office, she'd made her mark with a combination of imaginative intuition and determination. Brian Eisen and Leeds Hughes, who were working with her on this case and who were two of her most astute technicians, had also worked with her on the high-profile Roman Mantowski case, which she had cracked by profiling the killer's family in astonishingly accurate detail from a pitiful few forensic details.

Mantowski had bludgeoned his victims and smashed the backs of their hands, always breaking every bone of every digit.

With the tip of each victim's broken forefinger dipped in his or her own blood, he had drawn a cross and beneath it spelled out CLEANLINESS IS NEXT TO GODLINESS.

Reading the chilling message for the first time, Prusik had started to piece together the theory of the killer's family structure around a painful cleanliness and a strict religious practice. Extreme cleanliness was a well-known Eastern European custom among many immigrant families, Prusik's own included. Noting the distinctive odor of polishing wax that had adhered to several of Mantowski's victims, Prusik had profiled him as the only child of an elderly couple, perhaps newly immigrated, who had raised him in a very orderly house. Nothing would be out of place in that house without serious consequences, she theorized.

Inside of a month the killer was caught buying Band-Aids, sterile gauze, and adhesive tape in a drugstore less than a mile from the bodies of a family of four who'd suffered at his hands. Mantowski's own knuckles were a dead giveaway to an observant pharmacist. He had spotted the killer's right hand—as swollen and battered as those of the victims in photographs released by Prusik's team to area store owners on the basis of her hunch. Mantowski had beaten himself after every attack, just as Prusik had theorized, re-creating and ritualizing the childhood punishment that had been meted out to him for as minor an infraction as scuffing the floors with his rubber-soled shoes. His grandparents, who had raised him, were stern practitioners of an especially strict sect of Lutheranism, and they had routinely forced him to go before a pastor for admonishment after his transgressions. But the admonishments were never enough, and after each holy meeting, they would rap the boy's knuckles repeatedly with a bronze-wire cleaning brush till his hands were bloody.

Mantowski's remarkable capture had elevated Prusik to the position of senior forensic scientist, but never before had she functioned as the lead on a major investigation.

She entered the lecture room and marched down the aisle between rows of folding chairs to the easel set up beside a projection screen.

"Sorry for being late. Shall we get started?"

Seated to one side of an overhead projector was her core forensic team: five specialists skilled in the world of death, decomposition, and everything found near or clinging to a corpse. Like her, the men wore lab coats and ID badges. They were experts in chemical and materials analysis, DNA testing, latent prints, fiber identification, and computer technologies, and all of them were married to their work. Leeds Hughes and Brian Eisen were in their early thirties, contemporaries of Prusik's. Leroy Burgess and Pernell Wyckoff, both gray and balding, had grandchildren and were within spitting distance of retirement but showed no signs of letting up. The last face was that of Paul Higgins, new to her team, a next-generation Internet ace whom Eisen, Prusik's chief technician, had coaxed her into bringing on board. Prusik eyed the young man suspiciously. Right off, his long hair didn't please her.

"Gentlemen, things are happening fast." She looked directly at each of them. "It appears we have a serial killer. The Blackie Jane Doe's death resulted from strangulation, a severe break of the third and fourth cervical vertebrae. Opposing clench marks across the throat are similar in size and degree to those on the Ryan girl.

"A cursory inspection of these slides"—she patted her lab-coat pocket—"leaves little doubt it's the same man's work. This man has strong hands. Calluses are built up over his medial finger pads, meaning he's likely a farmhand, gas station attendant, or regular laborer of some kind. The job allows him to move around freely. He is efficient, gentlemen. No one's reported seeing him yet. No one's spotted a struggle."

Prusik's eyes landed on the greenhorn recruit. "Any computer matches, Higgins?"

The young man sat up straight. A long lock of dark hair fell across one eye. Tucking it back behind an ear, he skimmed through a pile of printouts.

"Including assaults with mutilations involving women and all known assailants from ages eighteen to forty-five, forty-one hits came back for the Midwest corridor between Chicago and New Orleans. Thirteen are confirmed incarcerated, leaving twenty-eight."

"Yes, I know what forty-one minus thirteen equals, Mr. Higgins." Prusik folded her arms across her chest. "What of the unaccounted?"

He glanced up from his laptop. "Who? Me?"

"Come on, Mr. Higgins." Prusik motioned for him to continue.

Higgins clicked open a series of spreadsheets, one leg wiggling tensely. Eisen had warned him to be prepared. "I haven't received confirmations on their whereabouts during the dates in question. Only four have existing last-known addresses in Indiana and Illinois."

"And?"

Leroy Burgess cleared his throat loudly. Prusik glanced over at the chemist and the fiber expert, Pernell Wyckoff, sitting next to him. What they lacked in communication skills they usually made up for in delivering the goods on trace elements and identification of the finer grades of wool, cotton, and polyester fibers from various clothing manufacturers. So far this time, though, they had not come up with much more than metallic grit, possibly rust from a vehicle trunk or truck bed.

She looked back at the new guy. "And?" she repeated.

"Still waiting to hear back from local authorities on those, ma'am," Higgins said. "No current or outstanding warrants are showing."

She approached the man. "Higgins, you're new here?"

"Eighteen months with the bureau, ma'am." It was the wrong answer.

"But you transferred to forensics only last week, right?"

"Yes, ma'am."

"Deciphering evidence in your case depends on programming ability, knowing your way around Internet access codes. But you're only good to me if you can produce results. Eisen here says you can. Can you?"

"Yes, ma'am."

"When I report in from the field or, say, update you on a breaking development, I need to know you're going to take that information and run with it. That means initiate without my asking," she said in a lower voice. "Got it?"

Higgins nodded, his lips pursed uncomfortably.

"He's been staying late, Christine," Eisen underscored softly. "Like the rest of us."

"Late is not good enough." Without taking her eyes off Higgins, Prusik said, "It's all about science with a sense of *urgency*, gentlemen. I work late. You work late. But we can't afford to have our results be late. I am in charge of investigating this case. As long as my ass is in a sling, so are yours. Understand?"

"Yes, sir." Color flooded Higgins's cheeks and throat. "I mean ma'am."

"He likes creeks, gentlemen." She capped the pen and faced the room. "So he can clean up after. They say it's a gift when a complete stranger knows how to find his way quickly into a young girl's heart. This guy has charm in spades. He's not skirmishing with them out in the open. This isn't a boorish thug. His victims offer little or no resistance. They go willingly to their deaths in well-concealed places near water."

Prusik glanced at Eisen. "Lights please, Brian."

Eisen went to the light switch by the door while Prusik arranged the slides on the glass surface of the special overhead projector, which had 30X magnification capabilities. "These were taken yesterday by the local coroner's office in Blackie, Indiana."

Eisen flicked off the lights. The projector lamp flooded bright white against the screen, which transformed a second later into the nasty purple streaks of a ruptured throat. An abraded cheek showed partially under a browned oak leaf.

"He's right-handed," Prusik said, displaying the next slide, which showed the second victim's abdomen. "He cuts while lying over them, which may explain the trace paint fragments recovered on the chest and lower abdomen. I'll know more tomorrow."

Prusik's collecting team, led by Bruce Howard, would retrieve whatever clues they could find at and around the crime scene, including the leaf foundation surrounding the area in which the body had lain, as requested by Leeds Hughes, Prusik's DNA expert. But she realized that with the body's removal might have gone useful DNA evidence. Though genetic analysis was a rapidly advancing and sophisticated science, DNA was easily contaminated by rain or ungloved tampering. If Prusik's team was lucky enough to uncover any uncontaminated DNA substance, it would be checked against those in the national indexing system, which included samples from most convicted felons. Following the postmortem examination, Prusik would intervene by federal preemption, taking jurisdiction from the local police, who had few resources for investigating the bizarre killings that now stretched over half of Indiana.

"Same abdominal technique?" Eisen asked, removing large-framed glasses too big for his pudgy face. He breathed on each lens and wiped them clear on his lab coat. Two horizontal purple dents scored his cheeks where the rims had rested.

"Yes." She used a laser pointer. "Judging from the decomposition, it's likely the girl was killed the same day she was abducted, making it around the Fourth of July. Entomology suggests he killed her where we found her and didn't move the body. I'll get to that a bit later. Notice the clench marks along the neck."

Murmurs arose among the team. The next slide was taken from directly above the unclothed torso. The dazzle of leaf color looked tarnished next to the vividness of the remains. It hushed the room. Following it was a side view of the torso that would have required the cameraman to lie prostrate at close range. Prusik dialed in 10X magnification along the long knife cut, which shimmered iridescently.

"What do you think, Pernell?" She upped the magnification thirty times, the maximum, and focused the lens on one particular organism. A nifty striped millimeter rule ran along the bottom edge of the frame to better gauge scale.

"Family of Calliphoridae for sure—its Latin binomial is *Lucilia sericata*—the green bottle fly, a common variety of blowflies that oviposit or lay their eggs under shade and next to running water. In July heat, it's likely adult females would lay eggs within twenty-four hours of death, with pupae hatching maybe eight or nine days after. The larva there has darkened already, an advanced pupa stage, and looks to be around nine millimeters in length, which means it's been anywhere from eighteen to twenty-six days since the adult female oviposited. Of course, until we take it back to the lab, it's only a best guess."

"Thank you, Pernell," Prusik said. "So clocking the time of death by the stage of larval development of these maggots found feeding on the corpse puts it sometime during the first week of July, as I suspected."

The next slide showed a mix of adult green bottle flies and larvae that were feeding along a gaping seam in the victim's left side. The flies were gathered in a feeding frenzy as if they had been glued in place. The slit ran from the eleventh rib straight down to the hip bone.

Prusik ran the laser light over one fuzzy patch of nearly transparent larvae caught in the act of voraciously gobbling the cadaver—the fuzziness came from the fury of their motion.

"Blowflies have a remarkable appetite for human flesh, but so does our killer, which doesn't leave the flies much to feast on inside." Prusik displayed the next picture taken nearer the cut.

Higgins's clipboard hit the floor. A muffled heaving was clearly audible. The young computer jock bumped into a few folding chairs before wrenching open the back door and disappearing down the hall.

In the dark, a small grin perversely made its way across Prusik's face.

"Have you any better close-ups of the tissue around the neck lacerations?" Eisen poked his glasses up, concentrating. He was the best digital analyzer of crime photographs that Prusik knew. Eisen would digitally convert the images, overlaying any latent fingerprint or partial pattern retrieved against those in the FBI's vast data banks. From the size of a clear thumbprint he had developed an ingenious technique to extrapolate the approximate height of a perp, often accurate to within a few centimeters. So far, no thumbprints had been lifted in this case.

"One is coming up," she said. "I knew you'd be asking."

The anthropologist's eyes followed a series of deep contusions along the victim's contorted neck that had resulted from an ugly wrenching. As everyone in the room studied the cruel markings, Prusik became aware of a throbbing in her palm. She took a breath and willed herself to relax her fist, clenched so tightly that two of her fingers were spasming. Then, abruptly, she flicked on the lights and returned to the front of the room.

Tapping a pencil against his front teeth, Eisen spoke first. "Stains along the incision on Betsy Ryan suggest the perp used a carbon steel blade."

Higgins returned to the room and took a seat near the door.

"Should we be checking morticians, their helpers?" Hughes asked, vigorously rubbing the bridge of his nose.

"I assumed Higgins was," Prusik responded. "Check morgue workers at area hospitals, too, Mr. Higgins."

The computer jock stirred in his seat. "Yes, ma'am." He cleared his throat. "What do you think he's doing with their organs?"

Prusik shaded a hand over her eyes. "Good to have you back among the living, Higgins. In answer to your question, I don't know. The utter absence of any internal organs at the crime scene is dramatic, suggesting he is removing them from the site. Water is nearby. It enables him to wash up. I believe that our killer's fascination with their internal organs goes further. That his removal of them completes some inward process." Prusik yearned to know what.

"In both cases, judging from the distance of the victims' bodies from any road or point of easy access, I believe he is luring them, coaxing them to ride in a vehicle with him to a safer, preferred place. The police crime report from Blackie describes a trail of disturbed leaf piles down a steep-sided wooded ravine. I believe a key part of our man's rules of engagement is in the chase, some kind of game he plays. Check psych records of felons released in the last five years with any history of cruelty to children or caught stalking them." In a low, steady voice, Prusik continued, "In nature, the chase is a striking characteristic among predators. A mother cheetah always leaves her nearly full-grown adolescent cub to fend for itself. At first, the young cheetah is unable to kill. Why do you suppose that is, Higgins?"

Higgins's head rocked loosely backward, revealing a glistening forehead. "In—inexperience...I guess?"

"The baby Thomson's gazelle must run first. Running triggers the big cat. The kill instinct is tied to the run. The young cheetah must wait for the frightened gazelle to make its move before it can finish the job."

She stopped a few feet short of the new transferee. "The gazelle must gather enough courage to make a mad dash for it. When it does, the cheetah will stop it with a biting hold. So long as the Tommy stays put, the big cat is stalemated. It *can't* kill unless the Tommy runs. And maybe, just maybe, neither can our perp, Higgins. Maybe he needs them to run to kill. It's what ignites him."

Standing in the middle of the room, she clasped her hands as if in prayer, touching her fingertips to her lips, her eyes shut, envisioning it in an almost trancelike state. Then she looked up.

"Make no mistake, gentlemen. Our killer exploits human frailty. Cunning always does. He is gaining their trust. There is no better, more efficient way for a stranger to do that with a child than through the art of deception—by projecting something that looks like tenderness, anything that appeals to a young mind, something irresistible. They must fall for it—the affection, kindness, or an enticement of some kind."

Prusik dug down hard on her pinkie. "The point is these girls are very likely walking off the road willingly, without a struggle that would draw unwanted attention to our killer. He selects well and then fools them. A vulnerable target is necessarily alone."

Prusik paused. "If there are no further questions, gentlemen, let's get back to work. I don't need to remind you that the pressure is on, and I imagine it will get worse before it gets better."

She left the lecture room and returned to her office, fantasizing about carving backstrokes through warm water in the dimly lit aquamarine lap pool at her club, her nostrils invaded by the sharp smell of the chlorine, her body relaxed by the nice buzz the swim would yield afterward.

A knock came at the door. Margaret's head poked in. "Bruce Howard's on line one. He says it's important." She rolled her eyes.

Prusik took a breath, picked up the phone, and forced good nature into her voice. "Hi, Bruce. What can I do for you?"

CHAPTER FOUR

He tucked in behind a Dumpster at the Wilksboro Clinic and switched off the truck's ignition. The southern Indiana air smelled sweet after a week of soaking rains. The clinic was on the outskirts of Weaversville, the county seat located in the so-called toe of the state of Indiana, near the confluence of the great Ohio and Wabash Rivers, and equidistant between St. Louis and Chicago—a traveler could reach either of those cities in less than three hours' driving time.

David Claremont's scheduled appointment was at seven o'clock. He had skipped dinner with his parents, his appetite decidedly off. He took a breath and knocked on an office door with a plaque: IRWIN WALSTEIN, MD.

The doctor greeted Claremont and motioned him to sit down in a cushioned chair in front of the large mahogany desk. Dr. Walstein opened a folder. "So, has the prescription been helping you to sleep any better?"

"Yes. But I wake up so late. I don't even hear my alarm. My mother has to pound on my door and she gets mad."

"OK, try taking only one of the fifty-milligram Mellaril tablets a half hour before bedtime. See how that works. Keep up with the amitriptyline, one tab before each meal."

Claremont noticed a strange little painting on the shelf behind the psychiatrist's desk he hadn't seen before, an abstract of a darkened face looking down. The face in the painting wasn't complete. Not all the way filled in. It made the young man uncomfortable.

Walstein came around to the front of the desk and sat opposite Claremont in a leather armchair. "What about the daydreams?
Any more of them since…July fourth, was it?"

"No. Nothing to speak of, really." He started wiggling his leg.

Claremont uncapped a tube of ChapStick and smeared it
across his lips. More than three weeks had passed since the sun
had borne down on his shoulders as he weeded a row of toma-
toes in his mother's garden. Three weeks since that indescribable
moment when the raised hoe he was holding froze in position on
the upswing while he stared down at clumps of earth, the dirt
moving as if invisibly sculpted. One damp tip of compacted soil
had protruded upward—a tongue sticking partway out, with the
rest of the face fast forming, resembling someone. Just thinking
about the strange transformation sent his heart pounding. There
he was again, transported to a ravine filled with oaks and the nutty
smell of last year's leaves. A ravine like that carved down through
the woods beyond his father's planting fields outside Weaversville.
All at once he saw her—the dirt had configured itself into a face
that let go a scream—a girl's—and wrenching upward out of the
dirt came her large doe eyes, growing wider, deer panic in them,
and the sensation of his teeth bouncing against hers, his hand
probing her ribs lower down.

"You seem apprehensive." Walstein picked up a gold ballpoint, rotating it between finger and thumb. "What's on your
mind, David? We didn't talk much about July fourth last time."

"No, we didn't." Claremont swallowed hard and did his best to
wrench himself out of the dreadful vision.

"Talk to me, David. Talk can't hurt. Only silence kills."

"It might not hurt, but does it really help?" Claremont made
brief eye contact with the doctor before glancing back at the portrait on the shelf. He shrugged. "It didn't help that woman who
just left."

"I see." Walstein smiled slightly, nodding. "Now you're a mind
reader."

"Whatever. She sure as hell didn't look cured."

He quickly scanned the small room again: the desk, the floor, the carpet. Checking and rechecking, familiarizing himself with the truth of the office—that it existed separate from him and that whatever simmered in his head did not somehow lie waiting in the shadows behind Dr. Walstein's desk to sabotage him. But checking didn't bring any comfort. If the earth in his mother's garden could move, so could the furniture, the rugs, and even the walls.

"So." The doctor clapped his palms on his thighs. "The medicine seems to be working—the bad daydreams seem to have stopped for now. That's a good start. Sounds like you're making progress."

"It means nothing. Nothing. It will keep happening. Like it did in March. Like I told you the last time." Claremont looked down and noticed his foot was tapping a rapid beat.

"OK then, David. Help me to understand better. I can't help if you aren't willing to discuss what's terrifying you. Everyone has dreams and daydreams. Yours are very important." Walstein leaned forward. "Dreams are as much a part of us as, say, driving a car is, or having a baby, or going to work. Even more, dreams say something unique about each one of us, and if we can decode their language, they can give us valuable information."

Claremont closed his eyes. He didn't want to make the doctor mad. He wanted the doctor's *help*. He'd always been a private person, but lately he'd been longing for companionship. Only trouble was he feared his suffering would peg him as unstable, too weird for any girl to want to go out with or take seriously. He especially longed for the affections of Bonnie Morton, the lovely neighbor's daughter he used to chase with such glee as a child, playing hide-and-seek. Bonnie's recognizing him in downtown Weaversville the week before, saying hi and waving, flashing him her big smile, had given him something to hang on to. Hope. For days he had mentally reviewed their brief encounter, pretending her little hi and wave had meant something more, that she really did like him and wanted him to call on her.

"Hello?" Walstein was gently tapping his leg. "David? You're daydreaming again."

"Sorry." Claremont straightened in his chair. "I sort of was."

"Ever hear the expression 'It's only a dream'?" Walstein's eyes were kindly, but his words didn't make David feel any better.

"But even in daytime?" Claremont fired back, forgetting the momentary image of Bonnie waving. "What if I'm driving a car, and then all of a sudden…it's as if I'm not?" He studied the floor. "Be barely able to pull over and stop the truck even."

The doctor nodded. "That must be hard."

"I smell things—actual things, awful things—the real deal, Doctor. You've got to believe me. You've got to help me."

Walstein ruminated over Claremont's words, rotating the tip of the gold ballpoint between his teeth. "That seems vivid. I can see that it is very upsetting to you." The doctor leaned forward and touched David's knee. "Can you share with me what exactly it is that you see and smell, David?"

"I couldn't have," Claremont said in a raspy voice not clear enough for the doctor to know whether it was a question or an admission. "There's no way I would ever…"

"What's that you say?" Walstein said, training his eyes on Claremont. "What is it exactly that you are imagining, David?"

Claremont nodded vaguely, transported to some remote forest floor, the rush of water filling his ears.

The Simplex electric on the doctor's office wall read eight o'clock. They'd gone ten minutes over, and he'd be late picking up his ten-year-old daughter at his ex-wife's house. Was Claremont in any immediate danger? Hard to say. He didn't think so. "I'm sorry, David," he said, "but this will have to be our stopping point. Let's save this for next time?"

Walstein removed a small calendar scheduler from his shirt breast pocket. "I think it would be a good idea for you to come in again later this week. How about, say, Thursday, seven o'clock?"

"What if I can't make it to Thursday?" The troubled man's head hung lower. "What if—"

"Absolutely call me sooner if you have to, David. I'll be here." Walstein wrote down his cell phone number on his business card and handed it to him. "If you have any more upsetting visions, call my cell number anytime, day or night, and I'll get right back to you. See you Thursday at seven."

CHAPTER FIVE

The town of Crosshaven was situated dead center in southern Indiana's hill district. The limestone caves honeycombed the forested ravines and kept an even fifty-four degrees Fahrenheit throughout the year, cool enough to store meat for days. A break in the July heat wave had brought a mass of unseasonably mild air down from Canada and, with it, an exhilarating drop in the humidity.

Julie Heath's sandals slapped down her friend Daisy Rhinelander's steep driveway onto the sidewalk of Old Shed Road. The fourteen-year-old had spent most of the afternoon lazing around her friend's bedroom listening to a Taylor Swift CD.

It was Thursday, which meant her younger sister, Maddy, had Brownies. Their mother would be driving her, and the house would be empty when Julie got home. She considered taking the shortcut through the woods. The weather was perfect for it. At the bottom of the ravine the sandy creek eventually led to an area below her house. She cut across the road and into the fringe of forest. A branch poked through her sandal, hurting the arch of her foot. She reconsidered and crossed back to the sidewalk, content to walk along the road.

A cool breeze blew Julie's frizzy blonde hair into her mouth and lifted her neon-green skirt, exposing her knobby knees. With the Taylor Swift tune "You Belong with Me" stuck in her head for company, Julie half walked, half danced down the sidewalk.

"I'm the one who makes you laugh when you know you're 'bout to cry..."

Around the bend an old truck was pulled over sloppily, abandoned as if it had broken down. Instinctively she glanced around and then resumed humming the melody more softly as she passed by the vehicle.

She heard a voice and stopped singing. There was someone close by. At the foot of a large oak not fifty feet away, a young man was kneeling, bathed in a shaft of sunlight. The stranger had on a one-piece coverall, the kind garagemen wear. He was holding something cupped in his hands close to his face, talking to it, crooning. He didn't seem to have noticed her.

Julie rested her cheek against a smooth-barked beech for a better look. The man was gently petting the thing in his hand, talking in a soothing voice. How sweet, she thought. The truck must be his. Maybe he had stopped suddenly for a baby animal crossing the road. Squirrels and rabbits were always making mad dashes in front of cars. How many times had her mother slammed on the brakes, muttering to herself? But she'd never gotten out and comforted a poor creature like this guy was doing—stopping to save it from harm, walking it into the woods to set it safely free.

The man brought his cupped hands close to his chest, tenderly nestling the frightened creature.

"Excuse me, mister?" She cleared her throat and spoke a little louder. "What are you holding?" She stepped through ankle-deep leaves a few feet closer. "Is it hurt?"

He pivoted his head her way, smiled pleasantly. Julie walked closer.

"What have you got there?" A small turtle, Julie could see it now. She liked turtles, especially the way they stretched their necks out to check if the coast was clear before trundling off.

"Was it crossing the road?" she said, guessing what had happened.

He held up his palm, nodding. "You can say that again. Nearly a goner, this one was. The guy in front of me swerved on purpose. Know what I mean? Shocking, man's cruelty to animals. We're all God's children. Am I right?"

Julie nodded, feeling more at ease by his mentioning God. Raised a Baptist, she and her family went to church most Sundays.

"He's lost his way." The man examined the turtle at eye level. "I believe he's got a brother down near that creek." He motioned with his head farther down the wooded ravine.

Julie noticed the man's clothes were heavily stained, spattered with layers of paint.

"My name's Julie. Julie Heath," she said, stopping ten feet from him.

"This here's Snappy." He held the turtle close to his face again, marveling. "Because he ain't told me his real name yet."

Julie could see the creature had a steeply ridged shell. "Oh, it's a baby snapping turtle," she said with a smile.

"Yeah, I guess that'd be right, a young whippersnapper." The man glanced up at her, then returned his full attention to the reptile.

Julie cut the distance between them in half, more slowly this time. "Is that why you stopped your truck all crooked, to save it?"

"She's got a head on them shoulders," he said to the turtle. "Makes you feel good, don't it, Snappy, when someone else cares so much?" He showcased the turtle on his upturned palm. "Would you like this nice girl to hold you some? Take you for a sip of nice water? You would?"

The man didn't look up at Julie this time. He kept his eyes glued on the turtle. When he finally did glance, the girl was standing an arm's length away.

He offered the turtle. "Here, you hold him." Only the end of the small snapper's snout protruded.

"Thank you," Julie said in a hushed voice.

The man craned his hand over to meet hers. Julie carefully lifted the turtle by the top of its shell. Its head, legs, and tail stayed neatly tucked in.

The man got quickly to his feet and started down the slope without another word. Julie stood still, watching him go. He descended the sheer bank until all she could see was the top of his head. She started down, watching her footing as she went. The bank quickly became steeper. She checked behind her but couldn't see the road anymore. She wiped her brow with the back of her wrist.

The turtle poked its head out. Its eyes glistened. When Julie looked up again, the man was stooped in front of her with his hands braced on his knees, waiting. She hesitated, caught by a crosscurrent of feelings. The turtle could make it fine if she let it go here. It didn't need to be put down beside the creek. Turtles knew how to find water on their own. She could faintly make out a trickling sound. The creek was nearby.

A crawling sensation—the creature nearly scrambled out of her hand. She curled her fingers around its shell and whispered, "It's OK. I'm going to let you go. Don't you want some water?" Her own throat was dry; she craved a drink in the late summer heat.

The man ambled ahead, wading through leaves with his hands in his pockets. Julie followed slowly over the leaves that crunched below her feet, not wanting to upset the turtle. For fun, she and Maddy would often jump into the deep leaf piles—as cushioning as comforters—in the woods behind their house.

The stranger ranged farther ahead. Julie could glimpse the sparkle of water. Then suddenly the man was gone. Nothing but a ravine riddled with tree trunks and an ocean of leaves lay between her and the creek. The turtle frantically clawed at her hand.

A swarm of grackles rushed overhead. The frenzy of their calls and whistles filled a nearby tree. Her throat felt grainy. She turned uphill back toward the road. An amphitheater of pillared oaks surrounded her. She rotated full circle, her eyes darting from tree to tree to tree.

Where is he?

Her eyes locked on some quivering feathers that stuck out from behind a large oak at head height, directly in front of her. She squinted in disbelief. Through two holes in the feathers, two dark irises were riveted on her. "Peekaboo," he said, his voice suddenly changed.

The sight of him made her drop the turtle. Julie charged back up the hill. She heard him close behind her and gaining, trampling through the leaves and calling out her name. Her own heavy breathing filled her ears, and then his did, too, and then she was twelve feet from safety at the top of the hill, eight feet, six feet.

He grabbed her ankle and pulled her to the ground, chuckling. "I was just toyin' with you, Julie honey," he said softly. "You didn't really think I was going to let you get away, did ya? Nah." He gripped her ankle so tightly she cried out in pain. Movement out of the corner of her eye—the turtle crossing into view. It stopped, drew its neck full out, staring her way. It blinked once and then hurried away over the forest leaves.

He pulled himself on top of her and grasped her jaw. "I got other plans for you, little Julie. Special plans."

She focused on the ridged shell of the turtle, her eyes blurry with tears. She couldn't scream; she couldn't move. All she could do was watch as the creature noiselessly made a clean getaway.

* * *

An hour after Julie Heath had walked alone down Old Shed Road, Joey Templeton was riding home from summer band practice on his shiny blue Schwinn. The unwieldy trombone case strapped to his back shifted from side to side, making the bike's front tire wobble. The boy was small for his age, shorter than most of the kids in the sixth grade, and his thick glasses magnified two eyes staring out at a big scary world. The weight of his lenses caused him to constantly shove them back into place.

He rounded a steep curve then stopped pedaling when he spotted the crookedly parked pickup truck. The boy swerved, nearly colliding with the opposite curb. A strange man was leaning into the back of the truck, stuffing something into it. The man straightened up quickly, staring at Joey. His coveralls were filthy and stained.

Coasting by, Joey gawked uneasily at the stranger, whose eyes were too deep set to see clearly. The man's sullen face suddenly broke into a wide smile and he nodded and waved. But Joey wasn't buying it—the man had not been happy to see him. And seeing someone unfamiliar so unexpectedly on the loneliest stretch of road between band practice and home unnerved him. It wasn't the way taken by most other kids leaving band, either. Joey always pedaled hardest through this forested area.

Joey reached home all out of breath. "Gran, Gran!" he yelled, racing into the kitchen. No Gran. That was what he called his grandfather, Elmer Templeton, who, four years earlier, had come to live with Joey and his older brother, Mike. It happened after the boys' parents had been caught in a deluge and had driven onto an unmarked railroad crossing as a freight train sped through, killing them both instantly.

A truck door slammed. Joey bounded off the porch and ran pell-mell around to the side yard. At the turn of the hedgerow, there he was—the kindest man in the universe—Gran, shuffling slowly on stiff legs toward the boy.

Joey grabbed Elmer's leathery hand, nearly toppling the old man. He drew his grandfather's hand close to his cheek, smelling the nutty residue of the Corn Huskers that had spilled out of the large square bottle the night before. Elmer had rubbed the excess goo on Joey's soft white hands.

"What's with you, son?" The old man stooped down in his faded denim bib overalls. Clean shaven, Elmer had a thin build like Joey's.

"Gran, all right, I know how you think I go around blabbing all the time. And I know Mike does," Joey said. "But I saw this really strange man, I mean he was weird. What he was doing in a creepy old truck like that God only knows. He wasn't from around here, no way." Joey stopped to take a breath, his chest heaving. "He gave me a mean look, Gran, real mean, then smiled right after so I wouldn't think anything was wrong about his creepy face. He didn't fool me one bit. I'm not biking home that way anymore!"

"Slow down. What are you talking about?" Elmer cupped the boy's shoulder. "Did someone bother you? Was the man minding his own business?" Joey's grandfather was used to his grandson's tendency to exaggerate, but the lad's pained face seemed more serious than usual. Together they walked up the porch steps to sit on the glider. Elmer dearly wanted to see the boy overcome his fears, to get over the awful dread his life had been full of ever since that day on the railroad tracks when his parents had been crushed to death.

"You got to believe me, Gran. Honest, he was up to no good. He had an old truck, real rough, way badder than yours, parked all crooked by the woods, nowhere near anyplace. You know that long way I sometimes bike?" Joey crinkled his forehead, staring into Elmer's watery eyes. "Where there aren't any houses for a long ways? Old Shed Road?"

Elmer nodded. "I know it."

"He was there covering something in the back of his truck. He didn't want me to see. But I did see, Gran."

"What'd you see?"

"It was…" Joey studied the porch floor as if spotting something creeping toward him. "Something he was trying to hide." Joey looked up at the old man. "He didn't want me to see it. That's for sure. It ticked him off that I did."

Elmer bobbed his head, assessing things. "I think what we need to do is go collect Mike and get something to eat at Shermie's Diner."

"The truck was parked real crooked," Joey repeated himself, the flesh on his forehead bunched with worry. "And his clothes were real dirty, like he'd been digging or something in the woods. Now why would he be doing that? Why, Gran?" The boy shuddered, seeing the man's hostile glare again in his mind's eye. "Something was wrong, Gran, something really, really bad."

CHAPTER SIX

"It's a steep wood. Her body was nowhere near the road. I'd esti-mate a good quarter mile and maybe three hundred feet verti-cally below the highway grade. Victim placement was literally drowning in downed leaves, nearly impossible to discern much of anything around the grave site." Bruce Howard's end-of-day call reporting in to Prusik was strictly factual. "We've scooped thirty-seven bags of environmental sampling surrounding the grave site. That's pretty much it. No forensics to speak of really."

Prusik stood up from her desk, examining an eight-by-ten blowup of the victim in situ. Tentatively, the Jane Doe was believed to be nineteen-year-old Missy Hooper, the local who had gone missing about a month ago.

"So the locals didn't corrupt things too much?" Prusik made an effort to match Howard's level tone, although her mind raced. It was hard to remain patient when it appeared that no clues were to be forthcoming.

"It's hard to tell, Christine. Like I said, difficult terrain. It's easy to stumble on a damn root hidden beneath the leaves," Howard said as if he had done just that. "I'm sure it wasn't easy removing the body. Hard to imagine there wasn't some contamination by the locals. Tough break, huh?"

She mulled over the crime scene conditions—the chaotic trampling by local enforcement, and now Howard and his team stumbling over hidden roots. All of which could only obfuscate matters further and make it even less likely that she might find another piece of the puzzle. All of which conspired against the remains of whatever cordiality she could muster with Howard over the phone.

"Can you at least confirm that the body is protected, Bruce?" Howard's cell phone had an irritating echo, feeding back Prusik's own voice each time she spoke. "You've been to the coroner's office?"

"I wouldn't exactly describe it as a coroner's office, not in any normal—"

"Yes, I get it. But is she properly bagged and in a cooler?"

"Look here, Christine, I've got a field unit on site. My orders are to secure the crime scene and collect evidence," he responded crisply. "I assumed you'd be inspecting the body, personally. After all, that is your expertise."

Christine's jaw dropped at her subordinate's reply. She forced herself to take a breath. "You're absolutely right, Special Agent. I will be. And I'm sure I needn't remind you this operation *does* require teamwork—in the lab and in the field." The snap in her voice doubled back through her phone with a metallic reverb. "What's with your phone, Bruce? Did it fall in the creek?" She clicked off, not waiting for his response, and unbuttoned the top of her shirt collar.

Bruce Howard had transferred in from the Boston office only four months earlier. A front-office man, he was good with a hand-shake in a gathering of troopers, a real man's man—something there was no shortage of at the bureau. She had already witnessed Howard's natural inclination to go directly to Thorne instead of following the chain of command through her—very likely Howard was unaccustomed to reporting to a woman—and she had noticed that Thorne hadn't made a point of discouraging that behavior.

Prusik took a breath, relaxed her fist, and considered whether or not she might have handled things differently on the phone. Howard's team had not recovered any physical evidence unless inadvertently gathered inside one of the sampling bags. The intactness of the victim's body was of paramount importance, and the concern she expressed with Howard *was* correct. She had been right to ask him about it. And the urgency in her voice had been appropriate, and the snap, too. This was their first assignment working together and already it was becoming a turf war, with Howard looking at his individual piece of the puzzle only and not seeing the larger whole. His ego and pride were unmistakable. Even with the poor quality of the cell reception, it was clear that Howard displayed not a single straw's worth of team spirit, nor did he recognize the fact she was in charge, like it or not. But she couldn't allow her frustration with him to cloud the larger issue: it was essential that they uncover more information about the killer. Soon. Immediately.

Her desk phone rang.

"Christine?"

"Well, who else?" She combed her fingers through her short hair. "Sorry, Brian, don't mind me. What have you got?"

"I think you had better come down to the lab and see for yourself."

She barely took the time to say "I'll be right there" before racing out of her office.

Prusik took the elevator three floors down and passed her CASI identity card through the lab door's magnetic reader. Eisen was stooped over a large stainless-steel examination table. He wore protective lenses over his eyeglasses.

"Christine." Eisen gave her a big grin, carefully showcasing a large curved piece of glass between his gloved forefinger and thumb. "We've recovered a partial thumbprint."

"From?"

"Remember we did a drift analysis for Betsy Ryan to locate the crime scene?"

Since the actual location of Ryan's murder was never discovered, Prusik had acquiesced to Eisen's using a math whiz friend to see whether a time and movement study could establish the corpse's origination point, factoring in the current and local weather conditions, to help target the crime scene. But nothing had been discovered.

"I thought that was a no-go," she said.

"Max, my guy who's good with numbers, hadn't calculated the late ice melt along the lakeshore this year. An unusual surface current changed the calculation, too, resulting in a sweep zone along the beachhead more than a mile farther back from our first check. Not far from the shore we found it—a patch of disturbed sand and this piece of smashed glass jar with a partial print."

"You're not telling me everything, Brian." She leaned closer, studying the fragment. "A partial print is forensically questionable evidence at best."

"OK, yes, you're correct. But what you should be asking is how I can connect the broken glass with the murder." Eisen beamed. "The inner surface of the jar, where I lifted the partial, is coated with the vic's DNA." Eisen beamed.

Prusik looked puzzled. "Are you certain?"

"Yeah, I know you're thinking: Why the glass? What's it doing there?" he said. "I don't think he used it as a weapon, though. No DNA was recovered from along its broken edge, so it doesn't appear to have been used to cut or tear through her flesh."

Eisen held up the evidence along its edges so Prusik could see more easily. "And, yes, I do mean a 'he.' The width of the print falls within the normal range of an adult male."

"That's a public beach, Brian," she reminded him. "It could have been picked up by a passerby."

He nodded, already expecting the challenge. "Yeah, true. But the print was preserved in some sort of secretion—presumably the victim's—while it was still impressionable, meaning at or near the time of her death. And another thing, the partial was protected from the elements on the inside of the jar." Eisen removed the protective lenses. "It was a very isolated spot, Christine. Low among the beach dunes, well out of sight of the waterfront or the park road. We never would have found it without refactoring the drift equation. An isolated place indeed," Eisen underscored.

Christine's heart started to gallop and her breathing became ragged. She sat down and gripped the chair arms. Another remote forest landscape came into her mind's view—very isolated and very far from home—one filled with ear-deafening insects that were nowhere near Lake Michigan's waterfront dunes. For a moment she thought she might pass out. Where was the damn antianxiety medicine when she needed it?

"Christine, is it something I said?" Eisen said half jokingly. "Are you OK?"

"I'm fine, Brian. Fine." Prusik stood up too quickly, fighting dizziness and an irrational impulse to run out of the lab. "Great work. Anything come up on the prints?"

"We're running the partial print through AFIS right now," Eisen said, referring to the Automated Fingerprint Identification System.

Prusik's pinkie pulsed with pain. She hadn't realized she'd been clenching her right hand, squeezing her small finger tightly the whole time. "Good work, Brian, really. Excellent. Please let me know what you find." She strode through the laboratory door, glancing backward, seeing Eisen still standing where she'd left him, looking her way, perplexed, until the door clicked shut.

Christine returned to her office, picked up her purse and car keys, and took the elevator down to the parking garage en route to her athletic club and the calming waters of the pool. The other lanes would be quiet now. Only the drone of her own flutter kick would fill her ears and her rhythmic taking in of a lungful of air with each spiraling pull of her strong arms.

* * *

"Crosshaven Sheriff's Department." Mary Carter, the police dispatch operator, spoke in a calm voice. A natural at police work, Mary had been on the force for ten years. She wore a wide bullet belt and a leather gun holster that chafed every time she rocked forward in her chair, which was frequently, as she rarely left the sheriff's office on street duty.

"Your daughter's late coming home, Karen? I understand. Julie's fourteen, right? And she has frizzy blonde hair." The dispatcher typed the entries onto a missing persons screen, reading a list of questions off the computer monitor to Karen Heath, the missing girl's mother. Mary's police-issue black polymer eyeglasses were designed to take abuse in the field. Mary mainly needed them for reading crime thrillers. The most active duty they saw was slipping off her desk when she wiped the bridge of her nose with a Wet-Nap towelette. She loved the lemony scent of the foil-wrapped wipes, which usually made an appearance right after she'd polished off two glazed crullers from Libby's Kitchen.

"Where'd you say Julie was earlier?" Mary typed in *Daisy Rhinelander, 6 Old Shed Road, phone number 426-9807.*

"Has she any notable identifying features or disfigurements?"

Small scar on right elbow from falling out of tree, Mary recorded, after winnowing out that information from a response that included Karen's frustration with the pace of the phone call and her complaint that Mary stop delaying and call Sheriff McFaron immediately.

The dispatcher patiently stayed on the line. "I'm sorry, Karen, I didn't get that." She adjusted her headset. "How long has Julie been missing? Several hours, I see. You've checked with Mrs. Rhinelander twice. Your daughter left there at approximately three p.m."

Mary knew that unless exigent circumstances existed, a missing person report usually couldn't be filed with the state police network until twenty-four hours had passed, but she had Karen stay on the line while she contacted the sheriff by radio.

"Sheriff, Mary here. Over."

"What's doing?" Sheriff Joe McFaron said into the mike, stretching the coil its full length out the window of his 1996 Ford Bronco truck—the model four-wheeler that he favored. At that moment he was standing next to a culvert at the Beecham farm several miles south of town, eyeing Mr. Beecham, pale and sitting on the ground next to his tractor. The farmer appeared to have suffered a mild heart attack. McFaron was waiting for the ambulance to arrive.

"I've got Karen Heath on the line. She's pretty worried, wants you to send out a missing child APB. Her girl's been gone three, maybe four hours, she says. Evidently, there's no sign of her whereabouts. Over."

The sheriff shoved back the brim of his trooper-style hat and rubbed a palm across his brow. He knew Karen Heath could be a bundle of nerves. Even in high school, he'd never forgotten how she'd fainted when Henry Small, a lineman on his high school varsity team, had gotten his leg caught between two tackling players. The hollow crunching sound of Small's leg bone had dropped Karen Heath straightaway on the sidelines.

"Put through a radio call to the Staties," he said. "I should be back to the office within the hour. Did you say it was Julie or Maddy Heath missing?"

"Julie."

"If she turns up, you'll have to call the state boys back quick or they'll have a conniption over my jumping the gun on this. Between you and me, Karen Heath's always been a borderline nervous wreck, God bless her soul. Over."

Mary issued the bulletin to the state police district office ten miles north of Crosshaven and then leaned back, chewing thoughtfully on a fresh hot cider doughnut. It was small enough to pop into her mouth whole, and just the thing to fill the lonely silences between dispatch radio calls.

Mary released the mute button and told Karen Heath that she'd notified the sheriff and put out a bulletin, then said, "Karen, if Julie turns up, I'd appreciate a call back. Anything we hear, I'll be in touch right away."

Karen Heath didn't reply. Mary thought it must have finally struck home: filing a missing persons report on her child.

"Karen, you still there?" Mary's voice was softer this time, less businesslike.

"I hear you."

"We'll be in touch, Karen. You try to get yourself some rest." Mary hung up the phone and shook her head. Julie was a nice young girl, responsible. She'd know better than to get herself in trouble. It's probably nothing, Mary thought, reaching for another doughnut. Then she changed her mind and closed the box up tight.

* * *

The boys and Elmer took seats at a table away from all the smoke that roosted over a huddle of men on stools facing the open griddle. Shermie Dutcher, the owner of the diner, looked up from the grill, mumbled something to Karla—the only waitress in the place—and then went back to cooking, his skinny arms flailing away.

Karla placed three paper napkins tightly rolled around dinnerware in front of Elmer and the boys.

"Hey, Karla," Elmer said. "How are you today?"

"Fine," she said. "What's wrong with junior here? Seen a ghost?"

Mike snorted. "Kind of."

Joey glared at his older brother. "I didn't see a ghost, but I *did* see something."

Sixteen-year-old Mike clamped his strong hand down on his brother's arm. "Button it, Joey." His dark eyes drilled into the eleven-year-old's. He'd warned Joey plenty of times about jumping to conclusions about people and spreading rumors.

Seeing the younger boy's wounded face, Elmer said, "OK, OK, Mike. Let Joey be. He and I have got some serious fishing to do tomorrow morning early. Right, Joey?"

"Fishing" was their code for sitting and talking a spell. Joey desperately needed the old man for that. He depended on his grandfather, the only living person on the planet who would let him ramble on and listen to it all. Mike wouldn't.

Joey rubbed his eyes. Those paralyzing seconds coasting by the truck on Old Shed Road replayed in his head. He looked up at Karla and blurted, "I saw this guy—"

"Joey, what'd I tell you?" Mike spoke over his younger brother's voice. "You don't know that guy from Friday. You have got to stop making up stories about people."

Mike jabbed a finger on the table and leaned closer to Joey so Karla wouldn't hear. "Last spring it was what's-his-name—Johnny Shannon, that punk who had you all in a tizzy at school? So don't go spreading rumors about people you don't know. I'm warning you for the last time."

"OK," Elmer said. "You made your point, Mike. We came here to eat supper, not to heap troubles on your brother here. The boy's done no harm."

They all ordered the dinner special—meat loaf, fried potatoes, and onion rings.

Joey's eyes locked on a man sitting at the counter, dressed in the same one-piece bibs as Elmer, only where Elmer's hung slack from his lean body this man's spilled over with rolls of fat. The heavy man rotated on his stool and looked straight Joey's way.

"You got a grip on them boys, Elmer?" The fat man's body jiggled when he laughed. "Karla tells me that boy's seen a ghost."

Realizing the fat man was poking fun, Joey raised his chin angrily. "It's no ghost. I never said that!" He faced the other way, hurt. "It was the truth, Gran."

Elmer rapped his great brown knuckles on the table. "I know you're not fibbing, son. Don't pay attention to Mr. Barnes. Mike's right as far as showing your hand to others. They know how to get you going, joking and kidding around like they do."

Joey was sick and tired of hearing it all. He took off his glasses and rubbed his eyes deeply with his dirty hands. "I'm going to the bathroom." At least nobody would be scolding him or laughing at him there.

Slowly rubbing the grainy bar of soap between his hands, Joey listened to the diner talk through the thin paneling. The fat man who'd laughed at him was snickering like the bullies at school did. Joey hated that. The thought of Johnny Shannon—his nemesis in the hallways—wrestling him to the ground and kneeing him in the groin while Shannon's punk crew chuckled was too much to bear.

Joey leaned his forearms against the sink. The smell of Lava soap and greasy home fries mingled. Someone entered the diner in a hurry, a man puffing.

"Say, boys, Julie Heath's been reported missing. Just heard it on the scanner. An APB's out for her already. She plum disappeared without a trace a few hours ago. After visiting a friend at the Rhinelander place on Old Shed Road. No one's seen her up at Libby's, Harris's Grocery, or anywhere else. Police report said she's wearing a green skirt and a white button-down shirt."

Joey dropped the soap, his hands foaming white. He looked at himself in the heavily etched mirror hanging over the sink and remembered seeing something. Like polka dots. He fought to calm himself, the way Mike always said to. He placed his glasses between the faucet handles and splashed cold water on his face. He had to be sure. He blinked to clear the water, then refitted his glasses.

The old truck had been pulled over as if parked in a hurry, one wheel over the curbstone. That look the man first gave Joey when he rode by—he could never forget it. It was right afterward he saw, when the man turned to shove something in the back of the truck.

Without drying, he turned and grabbed the door handle. The man who mentioned the police report was standing next to the heavy man on the stool.

Interrupting them, Joey said, "Hey, mister, did you say Julie Heath?"

The man stared down at the boy. So did the other men at the counter.

Fat Fred Barnes noticed Joey's dripping hands. "Boy, you forgot to dry off your mitts, didn't you?" He laughed, making a sound like a tuba.

Joey paid no attention. He wiped his hands on his pants, still looking at the man standing by Barnes. In an unfaltering voice Joey said, "She goes home the same way I go. Same place I saw this strange man on Old Shed Road."

He swallowed hard, not worrying anymore about Mike getting angry or anything other than what the actions of the glaring stranger had to mean. What they could only mean.

"He was stuffing something in the back of his truck. He didn't want me to see." He rode his glasses back up his nose. "But I did see. A painter's tarp, like it was covered with polka dots. Red ones."

The room grew quiet. Everyone heard the words. It was one of those odd moments people would recollect later, something taken out of time, words that floated out, hardly skipping a beat. The room stayed silent until the man who'd said Julie was missing stooped beside Joey and said, "Boy, you sure about this?"

Barnes hopped off his stool, too, breathing hard. The other men crowded around. Joey could hear Mike cussing behind them, then his grandfather's voice rising, saying, "Just a minute, Mike!" Another man went to a pay phone by the door. Joey heard a coin drop into the phone. The men standing in front of him were blocking Elmer and Mike from getting through. Others asked questions too fast, one on top of the other.

Elmer's face poked over their heads and shoulders, and then he sidled through. "Excuse me, please," he said. "Let me through to my boy."

With Elmer's hand on his shoulder, Joey looked straight into the eyes of the man stooped beside him, and said, "I'm sure. I am very, very sure."

This time not a breath could be heard; not even Funny Bones Barnes moved a muscle. The words didn't break the spell, they added to it, almost as if Joey was a silence conductor, and the diner patrons, his orchestra, were playing out the chords. But theirs was the music of hushed breathing, only the sound of so much hushed breathing.

CHAPTER SEVEN

Sheriff Joe McFaron gunned the motor of his cream-colored Ford Bronco. The cell phone trilled on its base mount over the transmission hump. McFaron picked up the small black portable.

"Joe here," he said in a deep voice.

"Sheriff, seems there's a commotion over at Shermie's Diner. Evidently, Joey Templeton knows something about Julie Heath." Mary rocked back in her chair, revealing to an empty office the full extent of her paunch. Her barrel chest was little different from that of a heavyset man. The police uniform gave Mary a distinctly androgynous quality, masking the purely female desire she secretly harbored for the sheriff. She leaned forward in her seat, reaching for the keyboard, then tapped open a screen of daily report details while she conversed with McFaron.

"I'm two minutes from there. I'll head on over," McFaron said. "Over and out."

McFaron unbuttoned his collar. Out his side window he saw a combine make a wide turn, swallowing a whole row of feed corn. Crows were cawing and swooping behind it. The angle of the late afternoon sun had suddenly cast a rich sepia tone over everything. He always liked how the light at the end of the day softened the edges of the trees and fields. Late afternoon in high school he would run the bleachers after everyone else had gone home, run till the sky turned rosy, then take a seat in the stands.

The soothing effect was closer to worship than anything he'd ever experienced at a church service.

McFaron pulled up in front of the diner and got out. A full six foot two and handsome as a cowboy, the sheriff had a chest size that was still several inches larger than his waist. At thirty-five, he had a full head of wavy dark hair that was covered most of the time by his wide-brimmed trooper hat. Often, late at night, he would fall asleep on the office couch with the hat on.

McFaron opened the diner door, and the commotion inside quieted momentarily. "Hey, Joe," Shermie said. "Wilson here claims Julie Heath's gone missing?"

"Yeah, that's right," the sheriff said, his face serious. "So listen up." He cleared his throat. "Julie's fourteen, five four, thin, has long frizzy blonde hair, and is wearing a green skirt. She was last seen leaving Daisy Rhinelander's place on Old Shed Road around two forty-five today," McFaron continued. "Her mother, Karen, called it in. Look, men, keep a sharp eye out. She could be hurt beside the road or in a ditch. Give the station a call right away if you see or hear anything."

"Joey here saw something," a loud voice called out. Immediately the room started to buzz with the sound of hushed voices.

"Give me a minute, will you, fellas?" McFaron walked over to the table where Joey Templeton was seated with his brother and grandfather.

The sheriff touched the boy's head. "What did you see, son?"

Joey's eyes locked on McFaron's the way they always did on his grandfather's, with complete trust. "A real creep. I saw him when I was biking home."

McFaron nodded. "Where was this?"

"Riding my bike the back way from band practice, a little after three thirty. The road that starts by the end of the school field?"

"I know it. Old Shed Road." McFaron shoved up the brim of his hat. "What happened next?"

"I saw this truck parked real crooked, and he was standing there. Behind it. Right near that broken telephone pole with the new one fastened to it."

"You mean the one damaged by last year's ice storm?"

Joey nodded. "He didn't like me seeing him, Sheriff." The boy's eyes narrowed.

"Can you describe him for me?"

Joey stared into the dark space beneath a table, conjuring a more vivid image, seeing it all over again. He looked into the sheriff's strong tan face.

"He was covering something up in the back of his truck. He didn't want me to see it." The boy swallowed hard. "His clothes were awful dirty."

McFaron recalled seeing Joey at a birthday party held out at Echo Lake State Park earlier in the summer. The boy had become excitable over a minor teasing incident. A smart aleck had poked fun at him for playing with the girls. Luckily, the boy's grandfather had been there to console him and had taken him for a walk to cool down.

"Did you see the man's face?" The sheriff sat down opposite Joey and removed his hat. "Can you describe him?"

A hush fell over the diner. Karla put down her tray, and Shermie stepped away from the grill.

"He was sort of young. I've never seen him before in my life. He was wearing one of those one-piece suits that mechanics wear. Real dingy and splattered down the front. It looked wet."

"Describe his build for me," McFaron said. "What'd he look like?"

"Not real tall, pretty thin. His eyebrows were thick—it was hard to see his eyes. Honest, Sheriff, I think Julie was stuffed in the back of that truck."

"Why do you think that?" McFaron observed the boy closely. The sighting was significant. The timing of it, too. Joey was obviously shaken, shredding his paper napkin under the table.

Joey's eyes welled up suddenly and his voice grew softer when he added, "What else could those splatters mean, Sheriff?"

Mike cleared his throat forcefully but otherwise remained quiet. Joey didn't care about the scolding Mike would surely hand out on the way home. What Joey had seen mattered more—and what he was doing wasn't the same thing as whining about the bullies or teasers at school. It wasn't about his being unable to fight back against the Johnny Shannons of the world. He had seen something. He was telling the truth.

McFaron scratched the short hairs below the haircut line on his neck. "Describe the truck if you can. What color was it?"

Joey took a deep breath and concentrated. "Stained and real rusty, sort of grayish paint, I guess. Old, I'm sure of that. The wheel wells were big humps. It had a dark-painted grille and a big rusty bumper that stuck way out." The boy made an S motion with his hand.

"Good, son, you're doing real good. Suppose I show you a picture book of trucks. Think you could pick it out?"

"Yeah, I'm sure." Joey had a good memory and had been able to recite without a hitch the first and last names of all the US presidents and vice presidents in history class this past spring.

Joey glanced at the men standing by the counter. Their faces all looked the same: their mouths sagged open. Now Fred Barnes looked like *he'd* seen a ghost.

McFaron's mind was assessing: the stranger Joey had seen was on the same road as the Rhinelanders' house, where Julie Heath had been visiting. Joey's report of seeing something suspicious had the ring of truth about it, and his description of the truck sounded real enough. Yet he was known to be an overexcitable, fearful kid, one with an overactive imagination. The sheriff would have Mary check to see whether anyone living on Old Shed Road had had a painter or workman at their house earlier in the day.

The portable radio on McFaron's belt blared, followed by a woman's voice.

"Go ahead, Mary. Over," he said into the unit, turning down the volume as much as he could.

"Bob Heath just called in," she said. "Wants you to contact him ASAP. Over."

McFaron glanced around the diner. "I'll call back in a minute. Over."

He patted Joey's head. "Son, you've been a great help noticing the things you did." He glanced up at Elmer. "I'll drop a truck book by a little later, Mr. Templeton, unless the Heath girl turns up first." He looked back at Joey. "Can you help someone draw a picture of this man?"

"Yes, sir, I can." The sheriff's belief in him made Joey stand up taller.

"That'll be fine," Elmer said to McFaron. "We'll be waiting for you."

McFaron stood and reminded the others to report any sighting of the girl immediately to him. Then he headed out to his truck, where he called Mary on the cell phone and related Joey's story.

McFaron started backing up the Bronco when Joey Templeton and his brother, Mike, stepped out of the diner with their grandfather. He admired the old man. Elmer reminded the sheriff of his own grandfather, who had been the first Crosshaven sheriff in the family. When his son, Joe's father, dropped dead of a heart attack, he'd taken the sixteen-year-old McFaron in. No amount of work could clear the hurt of being robbed so young. Had Maddy Heath been robbed young, too, he wondered? Robbed of a sister? And had Julie herself been robbed of more than that?

CHAPTER EIGHT

Roadside dust swirled with the changing weather front. Prusik quickly paid the cabdriver and leaned into a headwind, squinting. A well-defined anvil—a cumulonimbus cloud—loomed several miles in the distance, topping out somewhere high above the cruising altitude of a commercial jetliner. It was oppressively muggy, and thunderstorms were forecast. She'd flown from Chicago to the small Blackie Airport on United Express—a commuter offshoot swallowed by the major carrier to service the spread-out tracts of farmland and huge hardwood forests that blanketed the middle of America for hundreds of miles, bounded by the Mississippi two hundred miles to the west and the Gulf of Mexico nearly five hundred miles to the south.

She stepped inside the FBI's rolling laboratory, base for Bruce Howard and the team responsible for collecting and identifying forensic material recovered from the site where the body had been found.

"Stuart Brewster. Nice to meet you, ma'am." The field agent stood up from his small desk, where a laptop computer displayed a series of plot lines on a topographical grid demarcating the crime scene.

Prusik put down her briefcase and forensic bag and shook the man's hand. "Nice to meet you, Agent Brewster. Where is Mr. Howard?"

"He's been down below at the scene with three other agents since this morning. They're reconnoitering, looking for forensic evidence we may have overlooked yesterday." Brewster was heavyset and short legged. He leaned his head out the doorway and studied the encroaching storm clouds. "Before things start to open up and turn the ravine into an erosion gully."

Good, she thought, Howard was being thorough. Prusik did not know this man, Brewster. He was relatively new to the Midwest office of the bureau. Thorne had given Howard the leeway to bring in a few agents to build his field team. Brewster withdrew a cotton handkerchief from his back pocket and sneezed, briefly turning his face and neck crimson.

She glanced back at the storage area inside the vehicle. Puffy collection bags filled with detritus removed from the crime scene lined the shelves, each tagged and cataloged. Hopefully, she thought, a clue lay trapped in the leaf mold.

She heard a muffled shout coming from somewhere down the steep wooded ravine. Prusik stepped outside and walked to the edge of the road, sheltered under the natural awning of several large hemlocks. Two men were methodically scanning the slope filled with dead leaves from the oak, beech, ash, and yellowwood trees that were interspersed with dark groves of cedar and hemlock. They were sweeping the area using a photosensitive ultraviolet lamp and a magnetometer to detect any metal object or other forensic clue that may lie beneath the leaves or near to the surface.

Another man shouted. She recognized the voice as Howard's: dictatorial, almost like Managing Director Thorne's. One of the men scanning turned to face his boss. Prusik could not see Howard, but she heard him give the agent instructions on where to search with the device. She stayed by the road, not wanting to interfere.

Howard's head appeared, bobbing from side to side as he climbed the steep embankment. A fine sheen of sweat coated his forehead. He shoved his aviator glasses up the bridge of his nose. "Hello, Bruce. How's it going?" she called out as he neared.

Prusik quickly assessed the field agent's features. He looked strained. The crease between his eyebrows was deep, and his eyes looked tired. The case was getting to him too, no doubt.

"Have you been here long?" he said, picking up his pace to greet her. They shook hands.

"I just arrived." A clap of loud thunder sounded nearby, and the sky grew suddenly darker. "Good thing you got an early start today," she said. "I guess we shouldn't stand so near tall trees."

He nodded and allowed the corners of his mouth to turn up into a half smile. "Guess not."

"Anything to report since we last talked?"

"I'm not sure really. You've probably seen the quantity we've scooped and bagged," he said, removing his sunglasses and wiping his brow. "Did Brewster show you the feather we found?"

"Feather?"

"It was stuck in the bark of a fallen bough just above where the body was discovered."

Prusik waited for him to say more. When he didn't, she asked, "What makes you think it's relevant? Connected to the crime?"

"I don't know that it is. You're the forensic anthropologist," he said with a twinge of defensiveness. "It may be nothing. There certainly are plenty of birds in the vicinity."

"I'm sure, Bruce, you wouldn't bring it to my attention unless there was some reason to?"

"Again, I'm no bird expert. But in the last two days I've not seen a single bird with blue-green feathers fly overhead or perch anywhere near here."

Prusik cleared her throat. "That's very interesting, Bruce. I'd like to see that feather now if you wouldn't mind."

Inside the RV, Prusik angled the clear plastic evidence sleeve containing the feather under a high-intensity halogen lamp. The shaft appeared to be a wing feather cut and shaped on one end.

Not what she would've expected to find had it fallen from a bird's wing midflight. Also, it was slightly bent in the opposite direction of its natural camber for flight. From a struggle? she wondered. And of most interest, it was bright blue-green. What kind of bright-blue-green bird flew over southern Indiana?

A line of sweat trickled down her temple. She wiped it away with her sleeve.

Blue-green plumage: she had read once that some farmers kept peafowl near chicken coops and sheep pens to warn of the presence of foxes and other predators. Peacocks had a very loud call that could be heard from miles away. Their prized tail feathers were an iridescent blue-green color. But there were no farmyards anywhere nearby, and this wasn't long enough to be a peacock feather. The fact of its placement next to the crime scene deep down a wooded ravine was extremely significant.

"No outward appearance of any blood is visible," she said, pondering the implications. Prusik would have Eisen swab it for human DNA anyway.

"Under the ultraviolet scope we picked up nothing either," Howard replied. "It's certainly out of place down there. Not what I would have expected."

"I agree, Bruce. It is quite significant." Beneath the small examining bench, and quite out of Howard's sight, Prusik balled her fist and flexed her pinkie hard.

Her cell phone rang. "Good afternoon, sir." It was Thorne wanting a progress report. Howard stepped outside and Stuart Brewster followed.

"Yes, yes, how is it going, Christine? Is it the same killer we're dealing with?"

"Howard's team has collected a large sampling from the scene, including an atypical bird's feather—not of a type you'd expect to find in an Indiana forest."

"How does it tie in, Christine?" The same cell phone distortion she experienced talking with Howard on the previous day marred her call with Thorne, whose voice wafted in and out as if he were speaking through an elongated tube.

"I don't know, sir. We'll need to run lab tests back in Chicago. I've yet to examine the victim's body."

"Call me when you have any solid news to report." Thorne clicked off.

Immediately Christine retrieved her pewter pillbox from her purse. She held the small metal container in her hand for a moment, deliberating. She'd been relying more heavily on her Xanax ever since the discovery of the first victim's body. It wasn't a good sign, to say the least. But she needed to manage her anxiety if she had any prayer of keeping her thinking clear. At least that's what she told herself. She removed a small tablet and swallowed it dry.

The wind buffeted the mobile unit violently, spraying road grit against the outer paneling. A few large raindrops darkened the pavement. Stuart Brewster was nowhere in sight. Howard paced outside the RV's side door, oblivious to the approaching bad weather. He was talking into his cell phone, and Prusik thought she heard him laugh. She distinctly made out the words "she just arrived" followed by more laughter. *What the hell was so funny?*

A flash of lightning followed by a roll of thunder cleared her mind of the thought. The rain started to come harder. She had a body to examine, a case to solve. Prusik stepped into the darkening landscape and prepared herself for whatever was next.

* * *

Ever since he was a young boy, David Claremont had shown a penchant for carving wood. A set of shelves in his room displayed a vast assortment of wild animals, some carved from pictures in books, some from memory. Resting on the fireplace mantel downstairs was a matching pair of tigers that his mother loved, two of his finest creations. The image of the big cats had been imprinted indelibly in his mind when his father took him to see a traveling circus years ago. A showman had stood in a cage between the two tigers, who were balanced on barrels, with only a bullwhip separating him from ivory teeth that looked ready to bite. The bullwhip cracked again and again. One beast had tensed, flattening its whiskered face, and then suddenly it had lunged skyward, hissing, sending a paw the size of a catcher's mitt against the cage wire.

Shortly after his twenty-second birthday six months ago, Claremont's interest had abruptly changed to carving rock. One morning he had imagined himself wandering a cavernous hall in which great columns rose high into the overhead shadows, not unlike Ely Jacob's cave down the road, which was open to visitors. But in Claremont's dream he wasn't stumbling down rickety wooden steps in the dark. The great hallway was made of slab-smooth marble. Voices echoed off a domed ceiling as high as a cathedral. When he tried to remember what it was about the dream that was so riveting to him, all he could see in his mind's eye was a series of small figurines carved of garnet, jade, and tourmaline.

Claremont had begun carving stone the very next day. He spent hours on collecting forays along the creek bottoms that ran through the ravines past his father's fields. Sometimes he'd drive to better spots he knew. Obsessively he tumbled the stones in coffee cans filled with sand, rolling them down the driveway to smooth the chert, eventually turning out a finger-size figurine that his mother said was good enough for a chess set. Claremont hardly gave chess a thought. He didn't like playing games. He liked carrying the carved stone around in his front jeans pocket. He considered it a lucky charm, like a rabbit's foot, though he couldn't exactly say why.

"David?" Lawrence Claremont's raspy voice intruded. "You coming?"

A flutter came from high above in the old barn's rafters, where an owl was napping. His father's voice had disturbed it. David vigorously ran the ribbed steel file back and forth between his fingers, not having to look. He knew from feel how much stone to remove. He had nearly finished another piece.

His father shuffled over the straw-covered floorboards toward David's hobby-room door.

"David? Did you hear me, son? Your mother's set to go."

"I'll be right there." David held the stone up to the workbench light—a lovely translucent purple amethyst he'd unearthed from a nearby gravel pit.

"Come on, son. Her blood sugar's on the fritz. You know that." The old man slapped a barn post. "If we don't get going to Beltson's right this minute, she'll be off the backseat after those blasted orange-slice candies she keeps hidden in the kitchen."

David placed the carved stone on the workroom shelf, flipped off the light switch, and followed his father out to the double-cab pickup idling in the turnaround drive. His mother was fidgeting in the backseat, waving them on.

The road looked practically desolate. Lawrence stared out his side window over a great expanse of corn that reached to the horizon. The sun broke free of a low-lying cloud layer. Angling shafts of sunlight struck the windshield.

"Damn!" The old man scowled. "Flip your visor over, will you, son?"

David heeded his father, but a minute later blazing sunlight had found Lawrence's face again. Hilda hunched forward, tidying her son's collar.

"Now remember, David," she spoke close to his ear. "If they ask you anything in the serving line about how you're doing, always remember to smile. It's the courteous thing to do. Even if they don't seem pleasant." This last was in reference to the fact that everyone in town knew he was having "trouble" and needed to go see a head doctor for it.

"You needn't answer them if you don't want," she added. "No one expects you to carry on a conversation." She patted his shoulder like a corner coach in a boxing match between rounds.

No one expects a crazy person to be able to do anything right. That was what his mother was thinking but hadn't said. David turned his head sideways to acknowledge her, catching sight of the crease of concern between her eyebrows. Mostly, she was completely foreign to him, doting in ways he couldn't really understand.

"Don't let them bother you. You're only looking to eat dinner like everyone else." She folded her arms across her large midriff. "Don't mind the looks. There's always going to be some spoilsport trying to get a rise." She meant that everyone in town would be thinking, *There goes the crazy man who collapsed on the pie-contest table at the Fourth of July farm show.*

"Oh, Hildy, don't get the boy all wrought up!" Lawrence put in. "The bastards can whisper all they want to. The boy's done nothing wrong. Besides, he's seeing that doctor."

Lawrence's heavy hand came down on David's thigh. "After dinner we'll get back in plenty of time to finish chores, son. Probably be enough time to get back to that carving of yours, too."

More of Weaversville appeared: a hodgepodge of sundry stores, an auto parts place. David's chest heaved under his Windbreaker. The struggle to keep his anxiety in check worsened at the sight of downtown. Beltson's Cafeteria was in the middle of an old block of brick-fronted buildings that showed their waterlines from the flooding of previous years. It was a pick-and-choose buffet-style restaurant, his mother's favorite.

As they approached the restaurant, itchy heat built under David's collar. His hands began to jitter. The ringing in his ears intensified.

His father parked on an angle, bumping the curbstone gently. Hilda shoved against the back of David's seat, wanting out.

"Come on, come on," she said. "I need something to eat."

David stumbled out into late afternoon sun too bright for his eyes. That was a bad sign. The edges of buildings and cars, even the people sitting in the big front window eating, appeared to shimmer. His breathing became uneven. Another vision was coming. Or was it his conscience not letting him off the hook? Increasingly, he feared that he was leading a double life and that others would notice him out of sorts, put two and two together, and that would be the beginning of the end. But what could he do?

"Are you all right, dear?" Hilda's clammy hand touched the back of his neck. "Why, David, you're burning up."

"I'm fine." He cringed from her touch, from the whole world that suddenly pressed in on him. "Not that hungry." He leaned against the side of the truck fender, almost sounding convincing.

The old man scooted ahead to hold the door for Hilda. Inside, she brushed past a waitress carrying a tray, nearly upsetting it. She quickly dropped her jacket over the back of a seat and made for the waiting bins of hot food with the urgency of a kid needing to pee.

David fell into a chair, cowering under the full press of another siege, his sense of sight draining into so many swirls and dots. The people will see! What could he do but take a seat?

"Pick up a tray and get some green beans," his father bent over and whispered. "They'll settle your stomach."

David stood up, off balance. Someone behind him was murmuring; he glanced sideways at the blurring shadows of two women huddled at the next table. The murmuring stopped. They were staring. He was a spectacle already—proof that he was mad!

He followed the old man to the serving line. It was all he could do to navigate between tables without bumping into people. Hilda was at the far end already, happily facing an assortment of desserts, instructing a female server to ladle up an extra scoop of apple crisp.

It made him dizzy to look down. His tray began warping in and out. Someone said, "May I help you?" and sounded a mile away.

Hot flashes made his skin tingle. A revving heart sent him sucking for air. Everything was happening at once. He was descending a ravine again, chasing a screaming girl at a full run—with no say in the matter with this raging maniac inside his head.

The face of a girl, her mouth open in a high-pitched scream, hammered him back into an empty seat. A high-speed camera was rolling in his head, yanking him into the middle of a chase scene that wove through oaks and a dark grove of hemlock amid non-stop shrieking. *Damn!* He'd left his prescription pills inside the glove box of his truck after making the run to Crosshaven earlier.

A woman at a nearby table took in a mouthful of meat loaf. David glanced down at his own tray, which was now covered in a carpet of oak leaves. An awful ripping sound made him gag. Noises skittered from left to right as if his head were wired with special stereo made solely for his ears. The sweat wouldn't stop rolling down his cheeks.

Trembling, he glanced back at the woman eating meat loaf. The fork in her hand had morphed into a rubbery hose that glistened red. David gasped in disbelief. *Not at Beltson's!* She bit off a chunk of the ribbed hose, snapping it between her teeth like a piece of red Twizzlers candy.

David staggered down the serving line, forcing himself not to look back at the woman, but his mind couldn't stop the picture show running, filling his head. A ladleful of green beans jumped out at him: pure green screaming, bright green under sprays of red, and now there was the distinct sensation of a warm limpness convulsing beneath him.

David's exhaling couldn't keep up with his inhaling. Inside him, the demon was taking charge. He no longer could keep the full-bore vision from consuming him. In the line ahead, his father mumbled something, pointing to a vegetable dish under a protective hood. The surface of his palms prickled as if his hands had fallen asleep. Deadened. The tray hit first. Then the lights went out.

CHAPTER NINE

Sheriff McFaron turned onto Old Shed Road under a flaming red sky. Shreds of daylight dimmed as they passed through the oak and hemlock groves. Slowing, McFaron flicked on his high beams and swung the Bronco's side-mounted light along the sidewalk, illuminating the dark shadow of the double telephone pole. He pulled over.

He replayed the eyewitness's story in his head. Joey Templeton had said that he saw a flash of something red. Like polka dots, the boy had said. Karen Heath had reported to his dispatcher that Julie was visiting Daisy Rhinelander's house on Old Shed Road. McFaron retrieved his cell phone from the Bronco and clipped it to his belt, then shone the Maglite along the curbstones, looking for tire marks, anything. The boy had mentioned that one of the truck's front tires was over the curb.

He projected the light back and forth along each side of the buttressed phone pole. On the lip of the sidewalk he spotted a grayish mark about six inches wide. It looked recent, the right placement and width of a truck tire. McFaron angled the flashlight and made out a tread pattern.

So the boy had been telling the truth about the truck. A faint cross-hatching was visible in the centerline of the tread, which meant the tire might have been bald on the outside. McFaron reached into the backseat and grabbed the Polaroid he used for accidents. There were still seven frames on the roll from Henry Beecham's tractor mishap.

The sheriff snapped an overhead shot and then took several more from the side. In the blaze of the flash, a spot of deep red caught his eye a couple of sidewalk sectionals over. He traced the Maglite's beam over a line of red drops that vanished into the leaf litter, then knelt for a closer look. Unquestionably blood spatter, but there were no footprints, no smudge marks of any kind.

A high-pitched screech jerked him upright. McFaron shone the light across the road. Retinal glows fluoresced back from the upper branches of a large oak. Blackbirds roosting—he'd disturbed them. Spooked, the sheriff aimed the light chest-high around the perimeter of the forest; he saw nothing. Satisfied that the birds were the only onlookers, McFaron returned to the blood, trying to imagine what had happened, what it meant. The surface of the largest drop appeared tacky.

McFaron punched in Doc Henegar's number on his cell phone. The local general physician, who'd been practicing in Crosshaven for at least thirty years, did double duty as the part-time county coroner.

"Doc?" McFaron said. He could hear Henegar chewing a mouthful of food.

"What's up, Joe?"

"Julie Heath, a ninth grader, went missing today. Last seen leaving the Rhinelander place on Old Shed Road."

He filled in the doctor on the Templeton boy's sighting. McFaron paused, gazing at the blood illuminated by the Maglite.

"The reason I'm telling you all this, Doc, is because I've found some blood along Old Shed Road about a quarter mile up from the main intersection. The shortcut kids sometimes take leaving school. Know the place?"

"I do," Henegar said. "Need some medical assistance?"

"Might be foul play," McFaron said. "And, Doc..."

"Hmmm?"

"Keep this private. The last thing I need is for Karen or Bob Heath to go jumping to any conclusions."

"I'll bring my kit in a jiffy," Henegar said.

McFaron shoved the cell phone into the slash pocket of his Windbreaker. If Julie Heath had been badly injured, why wasn't there any sign of a scuffle? It didn't make sense.

A few minutes later, an old Ford Granada's headlights glowed dully against the forest near a bend in the road. Doc glided to a stop behind the sheriff's Bronco just as his car motor quit. The driver's door creaked loudly. Birds in the nearby trees cackled and flapped, disturbed by the commotion.

McFaron yelled into the dark, "Doesn't Sparky have a decent used car you can trade up to?"

"What, get rid of a perfectly good car?" Dr. Henegar's stocky hulk emerged from the gloom. Only his heavy eyebrows and beard were visible. "I don't like it when the coroner part of my job involves young girls."

The sheriff grunted and directed the doctor's flashlight down. "The spot's over here. And let's not go assuming it's a done deal already. The girl's only been reported missing."

Henegar placed his doctor's bag on the curb. McFaron trained his Maglite on the blood spatter.

"Joey Templeton said there was a man standing by a truck parked near the pole." McFaron shone the light quickly on the tire smudge. "Evidently, this guy was stuffing something in the back bed. The boy also claims he saw red polka dots on the man's clothing and face."

"Just missing, huh?" Henegar said, shaking his head and ducking closer to inspect the blood. "Sounds more like a done deal to me."

"Hey, you're the doc," McFaron said. "Let me be the cop."

Henegar reached into his medical bag. "Shine your light over here, will you, Joe?" He took out a plastic container, which held a blood recovery kit like the kind used by paramedics for insurance applicants. He swabbed a few blood spots onto two circled areas of absorbent material for DNA and blood-typing.

"This ought to do the trick. Her family doctor should have Julie Heath's blood type on file. If not, siblings' and parents' blood can determine consanguinity." Henegar grunted as he stood.

"Hold on a minute," McFaron said. "There's no need for you to go calling Dr. Simington just yet. First off, what does this look like to you?" The sheriff flashed the light over the evidence.

"Blood—what else?"

"Obviously, Doc. I mean the way it's sprayed, like a squirt mark. No scrapes, no scuffs, no smudges, not even a single footprint or sign of any scuffle. Just this jet of blood." McFaron stepped closer to Henegar. "To be honest, I'm not sure what we've got here."

"Maybe she bit the attacker on the wrist, cutting an artery?" Henegar said. "Deep-red spatter usually indicates arterial blood."

"Do you really think a kid's bite is likely to yield that much blood?"

Henegar threw up his hands. "You asked. I answered. Look, I've collected a decent enough sample. We'll know something more definitive after the crime lab analysis. I assume you've photographed it already?"

"I have," McFaron said. Then he cautioned, "This stays between you and me till further orders."

"If it's confirmed human," Henegar said, giving the sheriff a sober look, "you know I'll need to get the girl's blood type, Joe, or they'll take away my coroner's license."

"No one's quarreling with your statutory duties. I'm only asking that you check with me first before contacting anyone." So far, there were more questions than answers, and the sheriff didn't want to heap any unnecessary anguish on the Heath family.

"And, just so you know," Henegar reminded the sheriff, "if the girl doesn't turn up for some reason, I'll probably need to take blood samples from the whole Heath family for DNA matches to compare against this sample, too."

McFaron faced the doctor. "How long before you'll know the results?"

"You want to drive it up? It'll save a day," the doctor said. "Blood-typing results should be back in less than twenty-four hours. The DNA analysis will take longer, a week maybe."

"I'll drive it up," McFaron said.

Henegar handed him the sample in its double-secure plastic case. McFaron's cell phoned trilled in his pocket. It was Mary, wanting to know when he'd be going over to the Heaths'. He said right away.

"Any other thoughts?" McFaron asked. Doc Henegar stood with his bag, ready to leave.

"Only ones you don't need to hear if you're going to see the Heaths right now." Henegar lowered himself into the front seat of his decrepit vehicle. The starter wheezed like a croupy baby.

The sheriff walked over. "Appreciate your coming so quick, Doc." The dim glow of the dash illuminated Henegar's bearded face.

"Don't bother giving my best to Karen and Bob. My heart and prayers go out to them tonight." He saluted McFaron and drove off.

McFaron watched the taillights of the doctor's car disappear around the bend. "Oh, Lordy," he said aloud, and then he unfurled a roll of police tape, twisting it several times around two orange traffic cones marking off the site.

* * *

Although Julie had been missing only four hours, the discovery of blood gave McFaron the ammunition he needed to request that the state police send all available personnel, including off-duty troopers, ASAP to commence a dusk-to-dawn search of the wooded areas between the school and the Heath girl's home. They'd gather at the state police post for a briefing in one hour. Driving to the Heaths', the sheriff mulled over what he might tell them. He would reiterate the obvious: that everything possible was being done to find Julie, that she might have gotten lost in the woods taking a shortcut home. Kids frequently got into trouble doing the silliest things.

And it was all nothing but lies. In his gut, he knew Julie had been harmed, or worse.

Acknowledgment of what was sure to be a fact strengthened his resolve. He had never been a quitter, although some had accused him of it. Twelve years ago he'd left law school after the first year and run for sheriff of his hometown county, frustrated at how easily defendants got off on technicalities and at the lack of quality law enforcement in his rural jurisdiction. It had been disgust that had pushed McFaron out of the classroom, and a desire to do good; quitting had nothing to do with it. As it turned out, though, resolving disputes between feuding landowners, keeping perennially drunken drivers off the streets, and intervening in petty domestic quarrels formed the bulk of his police work.

He slowed the Bronco at the turn to the Heaths' driveway. Heat built along the ridge of his spine. It always had during big moments, all the way back to when winning football games had been his most important goal. Don't fail the fans. They're depending on you. Don't fail Julie or the Heaths. But tonight he had no magical play in his repertoire to keep from coming up empty. He drove in and parked.

Above the Heaths' front door a cluster of PAR38 outdoor lights blazed. McFaron checked himself in his rearview mirror, steadying his gaze, making sure he only conveyed concern and gave away nothing that might fuel an outburst from Karen Heath. Keep it simple. The girl had gone missing, nothing else. He would assure them, but most of all he would listen. That much he owed the Heaths.

McFaron gently shut the door of the Bronco and took in a long slug of night air, unsure what he'd say first. The only thing he was certain about was that he wouldn't breathe a word about the blood. Not until it was identified.

Bob Heath cleared his throat, surprising him. The man had silently slipped out the front door and stood waiting for the sheriff.

"Hey, Bob." McFaron tipped the brim of his trooper hat.

"Any word?" Heath stopped short, sensing no good news. His hands stayed jammed in the front pockets of his pants. "Thing is, Sheriff...it's Karen..." He spoke in a strangled voice, as if even talking was too much of an effort.

"I'm afraid not, Bob. We got an APB out. State troopers and I are starting a sweep of the area as soon as I leave here. She'll turn up."

Heath's brow creased. "What's that supposed to mean—she'll turn up?"

"In all likelihood she's lost somewhere. We'll find her, Bob."

Heath shook his head, gazing downward.

"Bob, listen to me." McFaron spoke in a softer voice. "She probably cut through the woods coming home from Daisy's. Maybe she fell, twisted her ankle. Believe me, we'll find her. It's where I'm headed right now." The sheriff refrained from mentioning Methuselah, Clyde Harmstead's bloodhound, whom they'd use if Julie didn't surface by the next morning.

"Karen's given a good description to Mary." McFaron stopped short of assuring Bob that he'd bring her home alive. "I won't rest till she comes home or we find her. You know I won't."

"I want to join the search party."

The sheriff gently rested his hand on the father's broad shoulder. "As hard as it is, Bob, I'm asking you to stay home and take care of Karen and Maddy. They need you here with them."

Heath shook his head; his lower lip pushed out. McFaron was thankful for having to deal only with Bob. Facing down Karen would have been harder with the blood evidence looming.

"I need to be going now. I'm on it full time, Bob. I'll call as soon as I hear anything."

McFaron got in his truck, waiting for Heath to go inside. Standing by a window next to the front door was the Heaths' younger daughter, Maddy. Her face was plastered against the glass, staring at the sheriff. It was easy to see she'd been crying.

McFaron backed out of the drive. A mile farther down the road he veered onto the state highway, taking it north to Monroeville to the regional crime lab. He called his office on his cell. Mary was still there. McFaron told her he was headed straight for the lab, and then the briefing, and wouldn't get to the Templetons' till morning with the truck identification book. Mary said she'd notify Mr. Templeton and that she'd stay as late as he needed her to. Tonight he didn't discourage her from the overtime.

The STATE POLICE POST sign appeared a quarter mile before the exit. McFaron took the turn and parked near the crime lab annex, which was a one-story gray building attached to the police barracks. The lab was well equipped for blood-typing, fingerprinting, and preparing samples to be sent to the main lab in Indianapolis for DNA testing, and McFaron had been there plenty of times before. Always with fingerprints though. Never with blood.

Missy Hooper, the girl who'd gone missing from Paragon Amusement Park, flashed through McFaron's mind. Her decomposing body had just been found less than forty-five miles from here. It felt like a bad sign—and the blood sample riding on the seat beside him didn't seem to promise anything good, either.

CHAPTER TEN

The ceiling lights in the narrow fuselage flickered as the Saab 340 turboprop commuter plane banked aloft, leaving behind the small Indiana airfield but not Prusik's unsettled nerves. She checked her digital watch—7:30 p.m.—and adjusted the collar of the navy-blue polyester suit she preferred to wear to crime scenes and postmortems. She had spent a long day leaning over a decomposed body in a stuffy back room of a Blackie, Indiana, general medical practitioner's office, blowflies constantly strafing her face mask in the makeshift morgue. Zippered in with the body as maggots, the pesky flies had emerged undaunted by an overnight stay in the cooler. The decaying flesh couldn't disguise the ruthlessness of the young girl's end.

Afterglow from the sunset came flooding through the porthole windows, coloring the cabin orange pink. In an hour a driver would pick her up at Chicago O'Hare and deliver her downtown to headquarters to face a barrage of questions from Brian Eisen and the rest of her team. Roger Thorne was impatient to see progress. Already stacked up on her new wireless PDA were three incoming messages from him since noon, wanting an update. Although she knew keeping him informed was part of her job heading up an investigation on a high-profile case, she was in no mood to talk to Thorne about Washington's expectations. She needed clear air to think.

The fiery sky faded into a hazy charcoal gloom. The dead girl had a name: Missy Hooper. Dental records would confirm what the girl's distraught parents already had. She'd been reported missing on July 4, close to a month ago, having last been seen by a friend, who'd dropped her at a local amusement park in Paragon, Indiana. From there, she'd placed a cell phone call to Glenna Posner, her best friend, a waitress who was supposed to meet her at the park but who'd canceled at the last minute. Posner's feelings of guilt were so profound she had little to offer except one important piece of information: there was no boyfriend in Missy's life, nor anyone Missy'd had a crush on, even from a distance. Whoever she'd left with, therefore, was most likely someone she'd just met. Interviews of park employees by Indiana state police officers had turned up nothing out of the ordinary. The Hooper family had recently moved from Weaversville, a city one hundred miles farther south, to Paragon, one town over from Blackie, where Mr. Hooper worked as a coal separator in a strip mine.

During the postmortem exam, Prusik had had to endure the plaintive wails of a distraught child in the doctor's outer office. Between swatting flies and having to listen to the sobbing girl, whose mother kept calling her a crybaby for not cooperating, Prusik had nearly dropped the forceps more than once to rush out, dressed in mask and stained gown, and demand that the mother leave the office. But each time she had bitten her lip as she delicately lifted the dead girl's fingers, carefully scraping and bagging the grit from under each grimy nail before taking a miserably gooey set of fingerprint impressions.

A sweltering heat wave had accelerated decomposition and jellified the flesh. Prusik had confirmed the estimated time of death: approximately twenty-four days ago. Larva hatchlings collected from the corpse were definitely second generation, meaning the body had been decomposing in humid heat since shortly after Missy Hooper's visit to the amusement park. It disturbed

Prusik to see so many larvae squirming beneath the tissue, giving a weird life to the face.

What disturbed her more, though, was the startling discovery she'd made near the end of the exam. Her mind had started reeling with the bizarre connections the discovery forced her to make and then just as quickly discard. She had recovered her composure enough to complete the exam, but it had cost her. One Xanax, to be precise.

As Prusik had finished her job, the drama in the outer office had continued unabated. A nurse, now the mother's coconspirator, kept repeating that the booster shot wouldn't hurt a bit, promising the girl a cherry sucker when it was all over. Prusik shook her head in disgust. She hated it when people lied, and she especially hated it when they lied to children.

Too much had gone wrong before she got to Blackie. Police had crudely raked aside all the leaves at the crime scene, looking for a weapon, when it was perfectly obvious the girl's neck had been broken. She wondered how long the site had remained unprotected and not taped off. How many onlookers had wandered down to see where it had happened? Prusik didn't believe the local police's assurances that no one had. How many unauthorized pictures had been snapped of the slain girl and sold already to the highest-bidding tabloid? The snafus were driving her crazy.

From her limited perusal of the crime scene, she doubted Howard's field unit would have much success documenting which way the victim had fled through the woods, which might have led to the location of vital evidence. Howard had done the best job possible with a contaminated site, she had no doubt about that; he was nothing if not thorough. The business with the feather bothered her—why had he doled the information out so stingily when it was such a significant finding?—but she realized that she had to stop feeling threatened by him. Howard had his own fears and insecurities, no doubt. Alienating him now would do her no good;

she would only lose any insights he might be able to provide. The cases were spread over a wide geographic area. And if she wanted to succeed, she was going to need all the help she could get.

The plane bucked wildly, tossing Prusik's briefcase onto the floor in the aisle. The seat belt light flashed on and the captain announced that they were in for a little turbulence. Her tongue was throbbing, and she tasted coppery blood. She'd accidentally bitten herself.

"Ma'am, are you OK?" A heavyset man in a business suit leaned across the aisle and handed her the briefcase.

"Fine," she muttered in a funny voice, favoring her tongue.

It took hitting an air pocket to know she wasn't fine at all. With her heart at a canter, the uncomfortable sinking feeling was taking hold again. She sucked for air, just as she had in the makeshift morgue with her arm buried up to the elbow in pulpy remains. When her hand had touched Missy Hooper's torn windpipe, she had found something hard wedged tightly there. Pinching the object between a rubber-gloved finger and thumb had sent ten-year-old adrenaline shooting through Prusik's veins.

Her eyes floated in and out of focus on the seat back in front of her. The past is never done with us, she thought. She had so successfully concealed it from everyone at the bureau all these years, but all it took was one little thing. *One little thing?* She interrupted herself. *One little thing? This was not a little thing.* She clenched her right fist, burying the pinkie nail into her heavily callused palm.

Furtively Prusik checked around the cabin. No passengers were looking. She flipped open the end clasps of her briefcase. Papers spilled from file folders onto her lap. A hard plastic vial rolled loose over the top, tumbling to her feet. Prusik quickly scooped it off the floor, ripping a jacket seam in the process.

She pressed her forehead against the small porthole glass. Blackness met her gaze. The vial in her hand had taken her straight back to the heat, the water, the terror.

Eleven years earlier, she'd been sitting cross-legged between the shelves in the graduate library stacks at the University of Chicago when she had come across a thin sleeve of hand-bound notes. They were research notes typed in the field by Marcel Beaumont, a graduate student in physical anthropology, her own department, in the early sixties.

Beaumont had done fieldwork two springs in a row in the highlands of Papua New Guinea. In May 1962, when he was scheduled to return home from Port Moresby, PNG's capital, word had come back that the young researcher had vanished in the vast reaches of the Katori rain forest. One possible explanation for his disappearance Prusik had gleaned from the riveting final passages of his prior summer's typed field notes. He had been in pursuit of an infamous highland clan known as the Ga-Bong Ga-Bong. Though forbidden by law, the Ga-Bong men continued the practice of cannibalism with depraved indifference. There appeared to be no social or kinship explanation for their behavior, nor could it be attributed to internecine fighting—the well-documented practice of ritual wars between tribal villages. Most ritual wars, as Prusik understood, were more a matter of economic shoring up, resetting the balance, a give-and-take between villages, not the wreaking of unholy violence as the Ga-Bongs did. Their attacks were haphazard, with no relationship to debts owed or reciprocal exchanges expected. No witnesses ever came forward, so feared were these nomadic kinsmen.

To Prusik it was too fantastic—a serial-killer family in the wilds of New Guinea. She read and reread the savage tale of Maleek Ga-Bong Ga-Bong, each time drawn to the tantalizing conclusion Beaumont himself had speculated upon—that the Ga-Bong men suffered from an inborn predilection to murder. Were the Ga-Bong Ga-Bongs proof that psychopaths existed among primitive peoples? Or that the drive to kill was not just cultural, but hereditary?

The Ga-Bongs always stuffed a charm or magic stone inside their victims' remains, a ritual taken from an earlier age, usually out of respect for a deceased victim's ancestors. But the Ga-Bongs could hardly consider inserting the sacred stones a virtuous act, Prusik thought.

Beaumont's bizarre story struck a chord in Prusik. From his passages on the Ga-Bong clan, she devised her own thesis proposal: to study deviant behaviors among reformed highland villages in New Guinea where cannibalism was officially outlawed in modern times. She was dying to learn whether any Ga-Bong clansmen still roamed the Katori rain forest. Six months after her first avid reading of Beaumont's field notes, Prusik stepped off a 747 into the blazing heat of the Turama River basin.

Prusik closed her eyes. Gooseflesh tightened the skin over both her forearms. With her right hand she felt along her left side, below the ribs, tracing her fingertips along the length of the ridged scar that ran nearly to her hip. Years later, during her short-lived affair with Roger Thorne, when he'd asked her about the scar, she'd lied to him, said it was from a freak accident at college, walking through a plate glass door.

She was certain the lie had affected their relationship. He'd never doubted her word, but she felt the gulf between them every time he touched the scar.

The pitch of the plane's engines shifted, rattling the paneling overhead. The commuter plane began its descent, causing her ears to pop. She gazed out the porthole window. In the distance, the shimmering lights of Chicago's tallest buildings jutted upward like a phosphorescent reef against the dark horizon. A patchwork of streetlights suddenly materialized beneath the wing, apparently as orderly as an integrated circuit board. Yet that was so far from the truth. Chaos reigned everywhere, it seemed. The *Tribune* and *Herald* only tapped the surface, reporting the latest homicide, drug deal, gang shoot-out, or abuse scandal. For Prusik, all of it was wallpaper, a noisy backdrop to her own current part of the bedlam. And her unshakable past.

The pilot's voice came over the intercom, announcing that they'd be landing at O'Hare shortly. Prusik clutched her briefcase. She closed her eyes, craving the quiet of the lap pool. She could almost smell the chlorine-soaked warm air of the dim-lit amphitheater of the downtown club where she swam, often well after midnight. The late-night sessions were her favorite, when she had the pool to herself, swimming lap after lap until she'd lose count. Losing count was best.

The United Express's tires chirped down on tarmac, and air brakes squealed as it came to a halt. The pilot cut the engines. Prusik opened her eyes, tasting her fillings; she hadn't eaten since breakfast. Her mind suddenly flashed on the girl's body—the sharp, deep cut running the length of her side. There had been no hesitation in the execution. She'd been gutted and left as empty as a stolen purse. Except for the carved stone deliberately placed by the killer in her windpipe. The carved stone that was now tucked away in a vial in Prusik's briefcase.

She stepped off the commuter plane and quickly moved past a queue of incoming passengers that stretched all the way out through the automatic doors that led to the street. Outside the terminal, exhaust from a dozen idling buses washed across her face. Prusik scurried past a line of waiting taxis parked bumper to bumper along the concourse. The FBI sedan with white government plates was straight ahead.

Prusik slipped across the backseat and greeted the driver, Bill, with a weary nod.

"Tough day, Special Agent Prusik?"

"You don't know the half of it, Bill. How's Millicent?"

"Oh, she's coming along. She's coming along." Millicent, the driver's wife of thirty-one years, had still been working at the bureau as a secretary in the communications department when Christine had started there. She had retired early, two years ago, only to be diagnosed with lung cancer six months later. She'd never even smoked.

"Please tell her I was asking after her."

"That I will. She's a big fan of yours, you know. She knows what it takes for a woman to get ahead in this organization. And I guess I do, too, since she's always telling me."

They both laughed, and Christine felt somehow lighter. She keyed AUTO DIAL on her cell phone for Brian Eisen.

"Brian?" Prusik's voice was all business again when she heard Eisen pick up. "It's our man, all right. She was in an awful state. The epidermis practically slipped off just heaving her onto the examining table. Second-generation maggots were pupating in the body bag. Adult flies emerged all over the place after I unzipped her." A huge airliner rocketed down the runway parallel to the exit ramp, drowning out all other sound. "What was it you said, Brian?"

"Rather unexpectedly it showed up," he repeated.

"What exactly?" She leaned her cheek against the cool glass of the side window. Outside, the traffic on the interstate whizzed by, careening toward downtown.

"A misplaced evidence bag…"

Eisen's deliberate hesitation, she realized with a start, was his expecting to be chastised by her. Not good. It wasn't the kind of leader she wanted to be. She modulated her voice. "Continue, Brian."

"It contained fragmentary evidence recovered from the first victim. Embedded in Betsy Ryan's hair—minute flecks of gilt paint. This guy could be a painter, or at the very least had been painting recently."

Eisen sounded cautiously optimistic. Prusik could hear the tapping noise that meant he was striking a pencil against his front teeth. A good sign that meant he had something important to share. Ryan's body had been underwater for nearly a month. Paint would have had to be fresh to stay stuck to her hair for that long.

"What checks have you run?"

"Here's the good part," he said. "Wyckoff's gas chromatograph reading detected some very unique chemical properties."

"Translation?"

"When he applied the electrode to the sample, it yielded a higher than expected presence of gold and silver. I'm pretty sure this paint is a specialty brand used for fancy sign painting."

"Good, Brian. Have Higgins run checks on every high-end paint store in the area right away. As in now."

"He's been on it for the last four hours, Christine," Eisen said, not bothering to hide his annoyance.

"I have something important, too." She described the forensic exam and her discovery of the intricately carved stone figurine wedged inside Missy Hooper's esophagus.

"The bastard's decorating them, Brian. He's using the stone as a marker, letting us know it's him. We'll need to exhume Betsy Ryan to check her windpipe for abrasions to the esophageal tissue. My money says the stone fell out of her body while she was submerged."

She paused. "Brian?"

"I'm here."

"About this stone business."

The stone wedged in the torn throat of a Midwest girl—what could New Guinea highland rituals possibly have to do with these Indiana deaths? It was inexplicable, pure craziness to even think it was anything but coincidence. Yet...

"Yes? You were saying about this stone?" Eisen said, matter-of-fact.

Prusik exhaled a breath she didn't know she'd been holding. "Never mind. Later. That seed expert from the museum? Has she called back with her findings?"

"Not yet. Oh, and you'll want to know we picked up another missing person report on a girl from Crosshaven, Indiana. Apparently she disappeared while walking home from a friend's house. Her name's Julie Heath. It's probably nothing, but given the proximity to Blackie, I thought—"

"Jesus, Brian! You could have called sooner, left a message on my voice mail. That's less than an hour's drive from Blackie, for crying out loud!"

Prusik pounded the padded car ceiling with her free hand. Bill turned his head. She shrugged her shoulders, then drew her fingers through her hair, which had lost its mousse-tousled effect hours ago.

"The bastard." She felt certain the killer had struck again, adding queasiness to the empty pit of her stomach. "OK, OK. Where'd you say that report was filed? The missing person report?"

"Crosshaven Sheriff's Department reported it," Eisen said. "A state police barracks is not too far away. Do you want me to follow up?"

"Yes…no." She thought of the foul-ups by the Blackie police. "I don't want local law enforcement involved any more than necessary unless there's a damn good reason. You're right—most missing children do eventually turn up. Sorry I jumped down your throat. I'll be at the office in a half hour," she said as the Chicago traffic suddenly slowed.

Prusik clicked off her cell. She couldn't just swim her way out of this one. Maybe that was her problem—no lap-pool victory lay in sight.

She gently rocked forward as the car came to a halt in three-lane traffic on the expressway. Up ahead she could see flashing blue lights against the high buildings along the lake. She was relieved for the moment to be stalled in traffic. Out the left side window a sudden gap in the lights appeared and grew into a vast plain of darkness stretching in all directions: the great lake. A few ship lights twinkled on the horizon of Lake Michigan's western shore.

Her cell phone trilled. "Special Agent Prusik."

"Hi, Christine. It's me."

Thorne's voice sounded soft and cozy against background chatter and clinking glasses—one of his wife's social events in the ritzy North Shore suburb of Lake Forest, no doubt. It bugged Prusik the way he still acted casually intimate with her. And tugged at her heart, too.

"Hi, Roger. Just got off my flight. I'm going to the office right now."

"I was curious to learn what you found down in Indiana. Anything to report yet? From Blackie, is it?"

"Without a doubt, it's his latest victim, the same calling card. Gutted the same way." Prusik divulged what she knew as thoroughly as she could. "It's too early to say whether we can pick up any trace DNA, nab him on CODIS."

The Combined DNA Index System, or CODIS, was a nationwide database of more than six hundred and fifty thousand convicted offender DNA profiles and nearly thirty thousand forensic samples to match against any recovered biological material.

"I see."

"She's been exposed to the elements for over a month," Prusik said. "A lot of rain has fallen in the Blackie area. She was practically mulched in with the leaves. I did find some paint particles. And Pernell Wyckoff recovered paint fragments embedded in Betsy Ryan's hair."

She didn't mention Eisen's latest news about another missing girl report. It could be nothing.

"Paint chips are pretty common stuff," Thorne said. "It's been nearly four months, Christine. Washington isn't going to sit still for much longer on little more than paint fragments at this stage of things."

Someone interrupted him, and he covered the phone with his hand. Prusik listened intently, trying to hear what Thorne was clumsily attempting to block.

"Say, listen," Thorne said, "I'm really sorry about the other day. I would like us to get along better. But I will need more than paint chips by the Wednesday conference call. Washington already has a team prepared to fly out and take over. Sorry to be breaking it to you like this."

In the shadows of the backseat, Prusik's face registered shock. "But we're close, Roger. I've gathered crucial evidence linking the victims. By Wednesday we should have more details." She hesitated. "And I've got something else—something I'm not completely ready to brief you on. It will satisfy Washington that I am qualified to handle this case."

Prusik stopped for a breath. Thorne remained silent. A hot flush shot down the front of her neck between her breasts. How could he so casually drop the bombshell that Washington had another team waiting in the wings? Surely he understood how crucial collecting little bits of evidence was to nailing a killer. It was practically everything.

"Still there?" Thorne said in his best just-back-from-Washington voice.

"Still here," she replied. She composed herself. "As I said, I do have something more to report. I'm just not prepared to give you a thorough analysis from the backseat of the car."

"Come, come. Let me hear what you have, Christine." More laughter from the partygoers. Thorne covered the mouthpiece and replied in a muffled voice to someone calling out his name.

Prusik knew her job was on the line. At the same time, she was furious at the blasé way Thorne was handling her call while guests partied around him. Couldn't he have picked a quieter place to call her from, someplace free of such lighthearted distractions? Or had he deliberately called her from the party to give her fair notice before she got back to the lab to find Howard in charge and her team shut out?

"Sorry, I'm being called back to the table. My wife's giving a speech," he said.

"Would you rather wait on it till morning?" Prusik asked.

"Good idea," he said. "I'll look forward to your report first thing tomorrow."

Thorne's apparent disinterest in her new evidence was not a good sign. It implied that her command of the case was past being in jeopardy. "I think you should know that I've uncovered another apparently ritualistic aspect," she blurted. "It's pivotal information, Roger. The killer inserted a carved stone into the torn esophagus of the Blackie victim. It's his calling card. It opens up a whole new avenue of inquiry."

"Carved stone, did you say?" Thorne's voice was interested again.

"A little over three centimeters in height, about the size and shape of a chess piece. Hand carved," she said. "Quite good work."

"Fascinating. Better check with Howard on this. Confirm your observations with him when he and the field unit get back from Blackie."

Prusik bit her lip. "Sorry?" she said. "There's a bad accident out my window. It's hard to hear." Was Thorne suggesting that she, the forensic anthropologist, should check out the meaning of her observations with Howard, *a paper pusher*?

"It's late, Christine. Get some sleep. You did good. I'll look forward to your complete report in the morning."

"But, Roger, I did research—"

The phone clicked off before she could say "in New Guinea."

Reflexively, she tightened her fist in her lap, bearing down on her pinkie. Not now, Christine. Don't. Christine groaned in frustration over the conversation just concluded. She didn't know whether she was more upset by the professional disregard or the personal one. The way Roger flipped back and forth between the soft and intimate "It's me" on the phone and the patronizing "Better check with Howard on this" kept her off balance. She wondered what she meant to him at this point, if anything. Certainly it couldn't be much or he'd stand up for her in Washington a little more.

Oh, grow up, Christine, she chided herself. So he was your first lover in years, so you trusted him, so you thought he loved you. Enough already. It's time to move on. She gazed out the car window at the Chicago night. Traffic from the accident was starting to clear. Ten more minutes and she'd be back at the office.

If she were taken off the case as lead investigator, so be it. She wasn't a man's man and she couldn't play politics, but she could get to the bottom of these murders. If Howard took over her job, she would still do her best to help him bring the killer in. If he and Thorne didn't appreciate her contributions, she would make the contributions anyway.

But she wouldn't give up her role without a fight. She needed to solve this case. It was in her body now. It was in her bones. It was in her throat.

CHAPTER ELEVEN

He couldn't keep blood hidden for long—at any moment someone might spot the police tape on Old Shed Road. McFaron figured he had an hour or two at most before Bob Heath would come
demanding to know why the area was roped off. He would counsel the man in his best police voice, keeping a stiff upper lip all the
way; he'd have to. The last thing he wanted was the whole town
flying off half cocked. He needed more time.

It was seven o'clock. McFaron drove toward the Templetons'
with the truck identification book. The road dipped sharply,
enshrouding the sheriff's Bronco in mist. He turned on the wipers. The Templetons' mailbox appeared in the dull yellow of his
headlights.

"It's a rotten morning to be out and about, Sheriff," Elmer
Templeton welcomed McFaron from the porch.

"Joey up yet?" McFaron rubbed his hands together, the truck
book tucked under his arm.

"Brushing his teeth." Elmer motioned with his head, then said
in a hushed voice, "Any word on the Heath girl?" His tired eyes
searched McFaron's face.

McFaron hesitated. The all-night search had yielded nothing,
but the sheriff didn't feel comfortable talking about that with anyone but the Heaths. Not yet. "No," he said simply.

"My lands, Joey!" Elmer said as the boy raced downstairs and onto the porch. "You keep on like that and you'll run out of gas before the day gets going."

Joey stuck out his hand and the sheriff shook it. "I *thought* that might be your truck out the window," Joey said, shoving his glasses into place.

"I've got the book I said I'd bring by, son."

Joey gulped. His two upper teeth protruded. "I'm ready."

The old man led the way into the kitchen, where Mike was fixing breakfast. "I've marked several pages of older truck styles. Maybe you'll recognize the one."

"Hi, Sheriff," Mike said, taking a bite of toast.

McFaron tipped his hat. "Your brother here may be our best ticket to finding Julie quick."

Mike shot a meaningful look at Joey, who shrugged and sat down at the table, his lower lip sticking out.

The sheriff placed the book on the table and opened it to a page marked with a torn piece of paper. "Here are some classic trucks of the fifties. Take a close look."

The boy peered at each view of the models. The front grilles were hard to see clearly from a side angle. It was the rusted bumper he kept seeing in his mind, but these pictures were all of shiny new trucks.

"See any trucks the same color? You mentioned it might be gray before."

"I'm not sure. These all look so new. This one was real old. It didn't have any chrome on it. There wasn't anything shiny about it."

"Take your time."

The sheriff turned to another marked page of older models. Joey ducked his head lower, examining the grillwork, but none matched.

After ten more minutes, the sheriff said, "I'll leave you with the book. If you see one that rings a bell, give my office a call right away."

"You bet I will, Sheriff," Joey said.

"By the way, you mentioned yesterday in the diner that you saw polka dots? Across the man's chest?" McFaron wiped his finger across his chest, indicating the area the boy had mentioned.

Joey swallowed hard enough for the sheriff to hear. "Yeah, he was tucking something in the back bed." The boy's voice dropped so low it was hard to hear. "Could it have been blood, Sheriff?"

"You said the man was wearing a dirty garage mechanic's coverall, right?"

"It was real dirty. With dark blotches, I think."

Elmer rested his hand gently on Joey's shoulder.

"You think you already know who it might be?" Joey looked hopeful.

"No, son. But what you can describe is definitely helpful." McFaron made a move to stand.

The boy's head sank. "I'm sorry, Sheriff." He looked up at Elmer. "Do you think I could do better if I was hypnotized? I read about it in science class." He turned to the sheriff. "It can bring things back that you've forgotten."

McFaron smiled. "You've been a lot of help already, Joey. We'll hold off on the hypnotist for now."

The sound of a car pulling up caught their attention. Mike led a state trooper through the entry. Another man with him was holding a large pad of paper and supplies.

"Hi there, Sheriff," the trooper said, holding his hat in one hand. "This here is Floyd Walters, the state police artist. Your dispatcher said it would be all right to drive him over. Said you might be here."

McFaron looked at Joey. "You ready to describe that man you saw to Mr. Walters?"

"No problem, Sheriff. I couldn't forget that creep's face if I tried."

Walters opened the sketch pad next to a window in the living room for better light, then asked Joey to sit beside him.

"Nice seeing you, Sheriff," Mike said from the landing. "Gran, I'm off to work now."

How much the older boy's attitude reminded McFaron of his own quiet way and serious manner growing up. McFaron's father had been like that, too. Carrying the weight of living inside him. It was an art not to show much, to keep it all in, one his father had nearly perfected till his heart gave out. Was that McFaron's fate, too, to be a silent, brave hero until his body couldn't take it any-more? Night after night falling asleep on the couch at home with his boots on—the holding pattern he'd mastered since returning to Crosshaven to become sheriff. Waiting for something more in life.

"Your boy has the best evidence yet," said McFaron to Elmer. "If we get a good description of the man out early, we'll nab him. You can be sure of that."

Walters asked Joey to close his eyes and picture himself on his bicycle. He knew young minds often imagined things better with eyes closed.

Joey described approaching the truck, seeing the man's stony stare. The artist asked him to freeze the exact moment he was opposite the vehicle. Was the man's head above or below the cab roof? In shadow or light? Was he clean shaven or scruffy? Hair scraggly or cut short? Did his hairline come down his forehead or was he balding? The police artist worked as Joey answered. Afterward, he had the boy sit next to him while he made further refinements to the suspect's face.

In the kitchen McFaron and Elmer sipped coffee, McFaron occasionally glancing into the living room, where he could see Walters's arm moving behind his pad. The sheriff itched to see how the sketch was coming along. Finally, unable to resist any longer, he walked into the room and peered over the artist's shoulder. Walters was busily working on the mouth, a pencil and eraser held in the same hand. Blurry strokes from erasure marks narrowed the width of the man's head, and a prominent nose emerged between two narrow-set eyes.

Back at the kitchen table, the sheriff raised his eyebrows. "He's got a ways to go, I guess." The drawing didn't look like anyone he'd ever seen.

"Joey's an alert child," Elmer said. "Quick, sensitive, and he has good recall. But like any boy, his mind can conjure up all kinds of evil things."

"The boy's comments are consistent." McFaron flashed on the blood on the sidewalk. "A good police sketch ought to get a reaction."

He could hardly wait to send it out over the police fax to the state police post. It would circulate throughout Indiana and the rest of the country's law enforcement agencies immediately.

"His chin," the two men heard Joey say. The boy feathered his own between forefinger and thumb. "It came down more."

The artist manipulated the pencil lead, deftly exchanging it with the eraser, polishing the drawing until Joey said, in a voice that brought McFaron and Elmer to their feet, "That's him, all right! That's the man!"

* * *

David quietly shook in his mother's Taurus on the ride over, the way his old dog Pepper had on that last ride to the vet's when he was twelve. Pepper had known. Staring up at him from his lap, trembling uncontrollably, she had known. He'd held the old dog the whole way, absorbing her shakes. And now it was his turn, with no one to absorb his.

Hilda Claremont parked the car by the door of the Wilksboro Clinic and they went inside.

"We've got a two p.m. appointment," she said, leaning over the receptionist's desk. "Dr. Walstein's expecting us."

Hilda patted her son's arm and bent her face nearer his. "I'll be coming in for the beginning part. The doctor said I could." She searched his face for confirmation. "The doctor needs to know. It's to help you, David."

He took a seat, unable to answer her, already in surrender mode. His eyes caught the curious looks of an elderly couple sitting in the waiting room.

"Dr. Walstein said yes to my coming in. You know I have your best interests at heart."

Why won't she let it go?

"Your father and I only want what's best," she said.

"OK, OK, please drop it."

But David knew his parents weren't to blame for the fact that here he was a grown man sitting with his mother in this depressing place waiting for a useless psychiatrist. The incident a few nights ago, followed by the one yesterday morning, had forced their hands. Early yesterday he had blacked out while riding his father's favorite 1953 Ford tractor and had driven it straight into a ditch. Thrown clear, he'd been saved from serious injury. The tractor had gone upside down, though, snapping off the seat and severely bending the steering shaft. It was the last straw. His father could spend the rest of his golden years going to farm auctions looking for a decent '53 steering shaft. David had come to in the weeds and had seen his father standing motionless on a nearby embankment, staring as if his whole life had gone down into that ditch. In the old man's gaze David could see that he had given up. While his mother fussed over David, rubbing her hot hands over his head and soaking wet back, David watched his father slowly pace back to the house without so much as a word. Shutting David out was the worst possible chastisement.

Why couldn't he hack life on the farm? Make his father proud? Carry on the Claremont name and tradition? It wasn't his fault and yet it was.

"Mrs. Claremont? David?" Dr. Walstein's shiny tasseled loafers were pressed close together. "Please come in."

"Thank you for seeing me, Doctor," Hilda said, "and on such short notice." The old couple, their heads turning in unison, stared as David, his mother, and the doctor walked out of the room.

The doctor escorted them into his office. Walstein retreated behind his desk and gestured for them to sit in two high-backed leather chairs.

"What would you like to discuss then, Mrs. Claremont?" He glanced down at his watch.

Hilda addressed her son. "In the bathroom the other night…" Her voice sounded pinched. "You say you don't remember, but I don't know how that's possible. You were talking loud enough to wake the dead. It was nearly two a.m. You scared me out of bed, David. Thank goodness your father's too deaf to wake."

"And what did he say, Mrs. Claremont?" The doctor sat lightly, bridging his hands over his elbows.

David felt both sets of eyes bearing down on him. *Why is she doing this?*

"You practically bellowed at me when I called to you." The woman's powdered forehead crinkled indignantly down the middle. "As if I were the one to blame."

Her crinkle line deepened. "'Over my dead body,' you said, like you meant it."

David sighed. "I was walking in my sleep. I was only having a bad dream."

"You weren't asleep at all. You looked me straight in the eye and said, 'But, Mother, I don't have to go. I don't have to pee anymore!' I never heard such a thing."

Hilda's hands frantically polished the knurled ends of her chair arms.

"I don't remember. I can't." David stroked the top of his head. "I didn't mean anything by it."

"Soiling yourself, the sheets, soaking the floor all wet, too? You deliberately missed the toilet, David. You missed on purpose." Hilda held a clenched fist to her mouth. "You're a grown man, not an eight-year-old. And you've no right to speak to me that way. No right."

The doctor leaned back in his chair, tapping his toe. "Is there anything you'd like to say, David?"

Keep a cool head, David told himself. But the deck was stacked against him. His father's tractor lay ruined, his mother's bed linen was soiled, and he'd disgraced himself in front of her.

"How are you feeling today?" Walstein asked him.

David made tentative eye contact. "Fine. I guess."

"Yes, fine now," Hilda carped. "But you weren't at all fine the other night." Flustered, she leaned closer to him over the chair arm. "Accusing me of saying no woman would marry a man who always wet his bed," she said, her tone acerbic. "I've never said such a thing in my life. Never heard such a thing!"

The doctor drummed his fingers on the desk. "OK then. I do think it's very important that we keep things in perspective. David and I have only just begun the process. Sometimes things may seem a lot worse than they really are, once they are exposed in the clear light of day."

David buried a fist in his lap, squeezing it tightly. How could he explain the demon inside that was devouring him, eating up the good David and replacing him with a monster? Walstein wouldn't believe him. His mother wouldn't understand. He didn't understand himself. Were his visions, his blackouts, portents of worse things to come, horrifying acts that hadn't yet happened because he wasn't quite crazy enough to pull them off?

He looked at Hilda, tears building in his eyes. "I'm sorry. I meant nothing by it. Honest, I didn't. I…I don't know what got into me."

"And the other morning?" Hilda withdrew something from her purse. David could feel another accusation building. His head began to pound.

"You left the house at the crack of dawn?" Hilda looked directly at Dr. Walstein as she spoke. "I asked you where you were going. When I poked my head out the bedroom door, I heard you distinctly say, 'On an errand.'" Hilda thumbed a ripped ticket stub and handed it to the psychiatrist.

"I did, yes." David's hands were tremulous.

Hilda stood, accosting David full-on while looking directly at Dr. Walstein. "Then why does he buy a bus ticket to Chicago? I found it in your jeans pocket, David. What were you doing in Chicago?"

"I…I went to the museum. An exhibit there. I wanted to see it. Is that such a crime?"

"Don't raise your voice to me!"

"I didn't raise—"

"Why did you lie?" Hilda wailed. "Why say to me that you're running an errand and then go sneaking off to Chicago? It's not like you, David."

David's leg began to wiggle violently. "My interest in carving. I…I can't explain it." He turned his palms up quickly and then rubbed them across the tops of his thighs. "I'm sorry."

"Why didn't you say so in the first place?" Hilda said, an octave lower. "You came home so late, David. We were so worried about you."

Walstein clapped his hands. "Well, you've certainly given David and me a lot to discuss, Mrs. Claremont."

Hilda halfheartedly hugged her son about the shoulders. The doctor followed her to the door and closed it behind her.

"By the way, on the phone this morning your father said you came home late several times last week." Walstein faced David. "Running more errands?"

"It was only a little after dark," David said. "Not so late."

"He's concerned about this erratic behavior, David." Walstein gazed at him sympathetically. "Talk to me, David. I need to hear it from you. What's going on? You know what I'm referring to— your visions?"

"I...I can't."

"I can't help unless you're willing to talk."

"It won't change anything," David said, exasperated. "Nothing stops him from coming."

"Stops who from coming?"

David focused on the Oriental rug pattern, his eyes racing over and over its zigzag designs.

"Who? You said 'him.'"

"I don't know who! Some two-faced bastard." David scrubbed a hand through his hair. "If I did know, I'd tell you."

Dr. Walstein was unfazed. "Two-faced? That's an interesting choice of words. It implies a person who has another side to him."

A line of sweat traced down David's temple. He could hardly contain the urge to run. "The visions. It's what I call him."

Walstein nodded. "Tell me more about this two-faced bastard."

David's face muscles grew taut. "No, I can't. I haven't really anything to say. It makes no sense."

"I can see that he troubles your conscience, David. What else does he do?"

"That's just the point, Doctor." David shook his head. "He controls everything. I have no choice. It happens and...and then I'm not trusted. By my father, mother, probably even you."

"David, the healing process can only begin if we establish trust, if you are willing to speak openly about these matters. You know the difference between right and wrong, between what's real and what isn't. You hold the key."

The doctor leaned forward in his chair. "I can help. I can see that these visions torment you and are triggering your fears."

Suddenly the ache was looming—phantom pains David had known for much longer than the recurring visions. The uneasiness grew; the ache was advancing.

"Something's bothering you right now," the doctor said. "I can see that it is. Tell me. Is he hurting you now?"

David fought to keep the ache at bay. "I…I don't know…"

It raced through him. Closed his eyes for him. Every ounce of David strained to hold on. A sensation of bumping heads nearly collapsed him to the floor. He fought against it with all his strength.

"Come now." Dr. Walstein removed his jacket, folding it neatly and draping it over his chair. The doctor sat beside David. "What's happening inside you?"

The muscles in David's jaw tightened a notch. "I told you. I have trouble seeing things straight sometimes." He met Walstein's gaze. "But it's not me. You have to believe me. I'm not the one doing it."

"I believe you."

David nodded, drained. "I…I black out. That's all I know." A trickle slid down his cheek. "I've done nothing wrong." He swallowed uncomfortably. "Seeing things isn't a crime."

"That's the second time you've mentioned the word 'crime.' Do you feel that you're doing something wrong?"

"No!"

"I think it's your conscience eating away at you that's causing these problems," said Walstein softly. "We need to talk more about that." A cell phone on the doctor's desk blotter vibrated. "Tomorrow then. At seven."

David walked out the clinic door, feeling drained and defeated. The visions had been getting worse. More vivid, more out of control, and now, according to his mother, he, David, was saying things and doing things that he himself could not remember or explain or understand. Seeing his mother patiently waiting for him in the car, he wondered how much longer he could hold it together. Then he had a frightening thought: If they are not visions, but real events, what unspeakable acts might happen next?

CHAPTER TWELVE

Prusik hurried up the steps to the Chicago Museum of Natural History with trepidation. It had been almost five months since she'd embarrassed herself on the podium at the opening night gala celebrating completion of the second floor's exhibit renovations. She shuddered involuntarily. Embarrassed wasn't strong enough a word, really. Humiliated was more like it.

The evening had started out smoothly enough. Normally Christine was uncomfortable making idle chitchat with the kind of people attending the gala—überwealthy patrons of the museum decked out in all their conspicuous finery—but for some reason, on that night she hadn't felt self-conscious at all. Maybe it was because it was a Tuesday night, the weeknight traditionally open to the public free of charge, and so there were plenty of "normal" people mixed in with the tuxedo and gown crowd. Maybe it was that she was wearing heels and a lovely gray-green dress that matched her eyes, instead of the slacks and sensible oxfords that her job seemed to require, and she actually felt attractive. Or maybe it was just that she was getting more accustomed to speaking in public.

She had been flattered to have been asked to speak about the museum's formative influence on her, and it hadn't been difficult for her to come up with an enthusiastic speech. But she never got to give it. Thirty seconds into her talk she had turned to gesture, with a flourish, to a display case behind the podium. And she had frozen.

The case contained a life-size tableau of the sort the museum was so famous for. This one was a jungle scene set in Papua New Guinea, fitting for the reopening of the Oceania exhibit. Discernible, now, in the lush vegetation, was something she had not been able to see when she had been waiting in the wings to be introduced—a well-muscled warrior wearing a brilliant blue-green feather mask. Around his neck hung a carved stone amulet, gleaming under the bright casement lights.

The warrior, the mask, and the charm stone had taken her straight back to the Turama River basin and immobilized her in her tracks. Moments passed. When she turned around again to address the audience, Christine had found she was unable to speak. Eventually, she had made her way off the stage to haphazard and bewildered applause.

Now she was late for her ten o'clock appointment with Nona MacGowan, the institution's resident botanist, who had sounded so young on the phone that Prusik had wondered if she'd called the botanist's home number and gotten her daughter by accident. MacGowan was an expert on Midwest flora and a principal adviser to the University of Chicago's arboretum collection. Christine hoped she hadn't heard about the opening night fiasco in April, or worse yet, hadn't been one of the puzzled people in the audience. She took a breath and brought her attention back to the case.

It was late August already and she was still mucking around with seeds and flecks of paint. The kinds of things you do when a case has gone cold—that's what Thorne had said. While she was grabbing a sandwich yesterday, he'd gone into her office and stuck a red Post-it to her desk lamp, flawlessly written with his Montblanc nib: "Christine: Still expecting your report. Thx, Roger."

What had happened to being a cop in the field? There wasn't time enough for anything *but* writing up damn reports—a distraction from maximizing her efforts on the case. Too much time was wasted worrying how it might play out with the higher-ups.

Christine sighed. She would push herself harder. Thorne hadn't taken the case away from her, but she had a sense that it was only a matter of time before he did.

MacGowan had said for her to go all the way to the end of the south wing, past the *Rise of Mammals* and *Dawn of Man* exhibits. Her office door was next to a large alabaster crouching lion.

Dim light filtered down from skylights. Prusik knocked on a frosted glass door marked BOTANICALS: AUTHORIZED PERSONNEL ONLY.

"Special Agent Christine Prusik." She held out her hand to the woman who opened the door.

"Call me Nona." The woman took Prusik's hand in both of hers. She was dressed in brown work pants and a tweedy jacket that went with her outdoorsy face, which creased in all the right places when she smiled.

"Please call me Christine," said Prusik, smiling in return in spite of herself.

"I've something to show you," said Nona. She opened an inner office door and flicked on a bank of overhead fluorescent lights. Large wooden collecting cases lined the room from floor to ceiling, their drawers labeled with Latin binomials.

"Brian has spoken so highly of you," Prusik said. Eisen had earlier supplied the botanist with several seeds taken from the Blackie victim's clothing.

"Bless his heart." Nona withdrew some samples in glassine. "As I told Mr. Eisen, I help set up the museum displays so specimens of elk are properly mounted next to bear grass or Western sage, for example."

"So—what have you found?" Prusik asked, taking a chair.

The botanist held one of the sample bags up to the light. Small green pearls gathered along its bottom crease. "None of these seeds is a forest species per se."

Nona took out a notebook with a yellow pencil clipped under a thick rubber band that held the book closed.

"They're members of the mallow family, a big one. This particular variety grows quite tall, even in poor soil conditions along dirt roads or gravel driveways. It likes lots of sun. It's not the sort of thing you ordinarily find in dense forest."

Nona glanced down at her notes. "I understand from Mr. Eisen that this sample came from a rural farming district. This species is a fairly common variety in the Midwest. It frequently grows next to farmhouses and barns."

Prusik imagined a painter whitewashing a barn, trampling over mallow plants, seeds sticking to him. "Something that might readily stick to a painter's clothing?"

"Yes, that would be very likely, especially in summertime when the seeds are ready to disperse. They have a tendency to cling to clothing. They act very much like Velcro."

"But you say it wouldn't be the kind of plant found in a forest?" Prusik tugged at the gold stud in her right earlobe.

"No, of that I'm quite sure. This species prefers open spaces, plenty of direct sunlight. Unfortunately, it *is* quite common. You'll even find it growing in many abandoned city lots here." Nona stared down at the floor as if a mallow shrub might sprout up right there.

Prusik pondered the point. Betsy Ryan's body had been found near the Little Calumet River. That was practically in Chicago.

Nona flicked the second sample bag with her fingernail. "This one's an *entirely* different story." The weathered lines around her eyes curved up. "Absolutely no relation to mallow."

"What are they?" Prusik leaned forward, studying the tiny brown bits.

"*Rosaceae multiflora*, a species native to Asia but widely distributed in North America for centuries." Nona circled the name in her notebook. "Sticky wicket, *multiflora*. You don't go wandering into it willy-nilly without getting horrifically entangled."

Prusik thought of Missy Hooper's blackened, writhing corpse. She'd recovered a thorn off the girl's sock. "Where does this *multiflora* like to grow?"

"This particular species you mainly find along the edges of fields—it's the bane of farmers. Years and years ago they were planted as hedgerows to keep herd stock from wandering off. The thorns like the mineral-rich soils of the Midwest and spread easily, sending runners everywhere. It's become quite a problem. Fields have been inundated. When livestock wander into the thorns, their necks get entangled, choking them to death. It wouldn't be a surprise to find it growing near mallow. Thornbushes grow right up to fences, around barnyards, too."

Prusik fished the vial out of her briefcase. "I realize your expertise is—"

"The charm stone!" Nona blurted out. "Where'd you find it?"

"Beg your pardon?"

Nona rotated her chair and leaned over. She removed a portable lamp from its metal carrying case.

"Shortwave UV. May I see that vial?" She switched on the lamp and passed the ultraviolet beam close over the glass vial. "Can you see it?"

Under the intense beam a green strip of light glowed on the yellowish rock. "What is it?" Prusik said.

"Invisible to the naked eye. We'll need high-power magnification to read the micro-etch security lettering," Nona said. "I'm sure it's one of the charm stones that went missing during renovations last winter. Museums worldwide have had good luck retrieving stolen artifacts from the secondary collectors' market using this identification technique."

"These thefts were reported?" Prusik asked, frowning. "I don't remember hearing anything about them."

Nona nodded. "Oh yes, they were most certainly reported, though we did try to keep it all under the radar. Everyone on staff was interviewed by investigating officers, then reinterviewed by the museum's administration. All of the exhibit halls on the second floor—including the one that housed the Oceania collection, where the thefts occurred—were undergoing major renovations last February and March. The floor was crawling with painters and sanders and construction contractors for two full months. The police figured it had to have been someone from one of the contractors' crews."

"How many stones were taken?"

"Five."

Christine's mind was whirring. Five stones. Two dead girls. One with a charm stone in her throat.

"And the thefts were discovered when, exactly?"

"The third week of March, as the work was being completed. The administration considered postponing the formal reopening, but ultimately decided to go ahead as planned. Less bad publicity that way." Her voice took on a sardonic tone. "We wouldn't want to discourage any potential donors."

"Right. Anything else?"

"Oddly, nothing," Nona said. "Only the charm stones. Oh yes, and the feather mask from the mannequin in the same Oceania display. A pity to lose that gorgeous mask. We've substituted another one in, but it's not quite as vivid. I helped with background flora in the exhibit."

The iridescent feather fragment recovered by Howard from the Blackie crime scene flashed through Prusik's mind. "Could you show me?"

They left Nona's office. The upstairs hallway teemed with grade-schoolers.

"All these exhibits"—Nona extended her arm to include the whole exhibit room, which included many Indonesian artifacts in display cases—"are now wired with electronic security."

Prusik's eyes locked on a spotlighted feather mask. Its iridescent shimmer sent her heart skipping, and she realized she'd averted her gaze too late. Christine looked back at the botanist and met a Papuan clansman's bold dark stare. Tattooed cheek lines under wild-looking eyes displaced Nona's kind, weathered features.

"I...need to go." Dizzy waves distorted her voice. A hard pulse throbbed in her head. She couldn't shake the image of her attacker's black eyes staring through his mask of iridescent blue-green feathers, the lanyard around his neck, the stone hanging from it braced between his teeth. With both her hands gripping his knife hand with all her might, she hadn't been able to prevent the assailant from stabbing the blade's tip in just below her ribs, slicing downward to her hip.

Though she was standing in a dimly lit room, intense sunlight now warmed her shoulders. The sound of a hard rain now filled her ears. She couldn't control it. Wet leaves and broken branches suddenly matted across the marble floor at her feet.

Prusik took a step back, breathing too fast, and heard Nona ask if she was OK. But the forensic anthropologist was caught in the coffee-colored Turama River again, choking, water rushing up her nose and sinuses, pummeling her ears, momentarily blurring her vision. At each turn, the river's currents did everything possible to sweep her into the advancing clutches of her frenzied attacker. The Turama had been an obstacle course from hell; it had nearly owned her, and so had he.

"Christine?" someone said, stroking her hand. "Christine, are you all right?"

Prusik felt cold marble beneath her back. She forced her eyes open and looked up, seeking the woman's face that went with the gentle voice. Nona helped her to her feet and guided her to a bench along the hallway. With difficulty, Christine pulled herself back into the present and rummaged clumsily through the contents of her purse on the bench, spilling half of the items onto the floor. She pried open the pewter pillbox and downed two tablets dry. Antianxiety medication took time her heart didn't have. She inhaled, counting to five, and exhaled, counting back down to zero. Then she noticed the throbbing in her pinkie and released her clenched fist.

Maybe things were getting too personal. Maybe she should let Thorne take her off the case or—better yet—she should recuse herself. That would stump him. No, what she needed was her own forensic anthropologist to watch over her—a guiding spirit to steer her out of harm's way. But she *had* survived New Guinea. Why wouldn't it leave her alone then? Her ability to carve through the Turama's churning waters had been her salvation. She had saved herself with her powerful swimming stroke. But still her heart beat too fast. *Come on, drug!*

Children in single file headed her way. A few minutes later a paramedic appeared in a fluorescent yellow jacket. She refused a stretcher but, in compromise, agreed to be escorted down to the ambulance, not wanting to make more of a scene than she already had.

The emergency vehicle was idling at the bottom of the grand staircase that led to the museum's main entrance. She sat on the tailgate of the ambulance, between the open rear doors, answering the medic's questions. Christine closed her eyes, thankful that neither Thorne nor Howard—nor any of her lab team, for that matter—had been present to observe firsthand another chink in her armor. Only Nona MacGowan had witnessed it, and she had left puzzled as to what it was all about.

After she flashed her badge and repeated that she was not in need of transport to the emergency room, the paramedics made her sign a release form, then left.

In the quiet of the car, Prusik traced her fingers over her blouse along the scar ridge beneath her ribs. In the frenzy of heat, mud, and battle, she'd slipped free from her attacker's grip and dived into the churning mountain waters of the Turama. How had she survived? The wound had been more than a superficial cut, yet the flesh had held together, her life-sustaining fluids intact. The knife hadn't punctured any of her organs. The wound hadn't become infected. She hadn't drowned in the river. Her fluids hadn't been imbibed because of the Ga-Bong lust for blood, or in the reenactment of some ancient Papuan highland ritual to bring male and female into balance, or whatever her bird-of-paradise-feather-masked assailant had had for a reason.

She moaned softly. When would it ever leave her, this panic, this sense of doom? Telling herself again and again that she must have survived against all odds for some reason had done nothing to dispel the awful memories that followed her in and out of motels, down hallways, at her office, and into the woods while she was trying to do her job. It was always the same: death on the ground, death on the examination table, and death whispering into her head that it would find a way in. Finish the job.

Had it finally found its way in?

And the question that was plaguing her during her long workdays and at night in her dreams remained: How could slit-open Indiana girls with charm stones lodged in their lifeless throats be part of all that?

CHAPTER THIRTEEN

Clouds were moving fast as the front pushed through. Only a few errant drops struck the windshield. He steered down the dirt two-track that led up to the large weathered barn, the site of his painting job. He waited, just as the man had said to do. Spanning the tired-looking asphalt shingles was a faded testimonial for Sweet Boy chewing tobacco from an era gone by. Annexed to the barn stood a one-story outbuilding in the same worn condition.

He kept the engine running. The WTWN announcer was finishing the 7 a.m. farm report. Corn futures were up on the Chicago Mercantile Exchange. After an ad came the local weather report. Overnight rains should lead to clearing skies by midmorning. Good.

The hourly news report followed: "State Police Post Nine outside Crosshaven is continuing the search in Patrick State Forest for Julie Heath, age fourteen, who went missing four weeks ago on July twenty-eighth. Those who wish to volunteer to be part of the search party should contact—"

He clicked off the broadcast. A short man in one-piece bib overalls was approaching fast, holding down the front brim of his straw hat. He got out before the farmer reached the bed of the truck.

"You've come early," the man said. They shook hands. "Fred Stanger. Glad to meet you. Lonnie Wallace at the Sweet Lick Resort said you were the man to get. A damn fast painter, he said."

The farmer turned and surveyed his buildings. "Not much to look at. What do you guess?"

"Still a bit wet," the painter said, kneading his hands.

"Nah, not for staining. It'll be OK to get started. There's a good breeze. Them upper boards are damn near dry enough. I'm just looking for a once-over. Nothing fancy."

Stanger leaned sideways to see into the truck bed. "Got enough stain?"

The painter nodded. "Plenty for the job."

"Like I said, five hundred dollars for the whole deal. Half now, half when you finish. Sound all right with you, Jasper? It's Jasper, right?" Stanger noticed that the painter's wrist was bandaged. "Cut yourself?"

"Just a scratch." The painter pulled his sleeve down.

"Wife's a retired nurse. You might want her to give it a look, make sure it's not infected. Looks like your bandage could use changing."

Jasper said nothing. He removed the triple-tier aluminum ladder he'd borrowed from the Sweet Lick Resort garage bay and one of the gallon tins from the bed.

Stanger stepped closer. "Would you like some help carrying—"

The painter swung his ladder, blocking the man from getting any closer to the truck. "It's OK."

"You're forgetting something, aren't you?" The farmer held out a wad of folded bills.

The painter balanced the stain on the top rail of the bed long enough to slip the cash from the farmer's hand.

Stanger eyed him for a moment before nodding. "I'll have the wife bring you down some iced tea around noon."

"Don't bother." Jasper didn't raise his voice. "Carry my own thermos with me."

"Suit yourself then." The farmer turned and headed for the small farmhouse across the road.

Jasper rested the ladder against the barn side and roped up the sectionals, then fully extended the ladder to within a few feet of the eaves. He watched the farmer cross the road and go up the gentle slope of high grass between some pruned-back apple trees. He removed a portable radio from the front seat of his truck, then climbed the full length of the ladder, hooking the radio to the cradle opposite the stain can.

The farmer had been right. The boards up high were dry enough to start on. An hour later, he had finished the top story of an entire broadside. The news report came at a good time to break. The dial in the truck was tuned to the same station. He unscrewed his thermos and savored the first sip.

"According to state police authorities, fourteen-year-old Julie Heath was last seen shortly after three o'clock on July twenty-eighth, walking home from a friend's house on the Old Shed Road in Crosshaven." The broadcast repeated a description of the girl and what she had been wearing then and the phone numbers to contact. There had been no new developments.

The drink refreshed him. He yanked a full can of stain out of the truck that sat next to a rolled, heavily blotched painter's tarp. He lost himself in work. By two the sun began showing itself in and out of the clouds. By three the sky was completely clear and he had gone through six gallons, staining three complete sides of the barn and the entire annex. He was working the last section on the barn's far side when the sound of joyful screaming snapped his head around. Another young voice joined in with the first.

He quickly finished the section and then put down his brush, his right hand drenched in stain from seven hours of its dripping down the handle. He determined that the shouts were coming from near the fruit trees across the road. He clambered down the ladder and jogged to the corner of the barn. He couldn't quite see over the tall weeds, but they made for good cover. He fidgeted with the stones in his right front pocket.

"Say there!" Stanger was walking under the eaves of the barn straight toward him, inspecting what the painter had done.

"You sure do quick work." Stanger wore a wide grin, obviously pleased. "Lonnie was right. Say, listen, would you be interested in some indoor painting over to the farmhouse? The wife wants the upstairs—"

He shook his head. "I only work outdoors."

"I'll make it worth your while. You sure?"

"As sure as eggs is eggs."

Jasper headed for his truck, which was parked around front. Stanger's presence made him uneasy. He yearned to hear the spirited young shouts again.

"Suit yourself." Stanger trailed after him. "As long as I'm out here, I'll pay you the rest."

He took the money without another word. Stanger didn't linger this time. The painter clenched his fists, cracking the dried stain over his knuckles. The interruption had spoiled things. Barely half an hour of staining was left to do—the double doors and the transom beneath the pulley and chain where a hay-lift claw hung rusted in the open position. It looked ready to snatch him. He didn't know whether he could manage—his stomach was in such knots, his need was still so urgent. He was feeling a great, unfilled void. Over the last days the pangs had been getting worse.

He reached through his truck window, collected the nearly empty thermos, and upended it, yearning for the very last drop. He missed those young voices in the field so much it stung.

* * *

Over Labor Day weekend, a coon hunter was out walking the Patrick State Forest, a shotgun slung over his shoulder. The hunter's German shorthaired pointer had gone sniffing ahead, crisscrossing, homing in on something only its nose could detect.

A crow flapped off a fallen bough, a small morsel threading its beak. The man marveled at the bird's ability to avoid crashing into trees as it accelerated out of sight down a ravine riddled with oak trunks. Sunlight suddenly flooded the forest, bathing it in a sweet wine-colored light.

Movement in the ravine caught his attention—three deer bounding off in graceful arcs with hardly a noise, their white tails flashing. None had antlers. It wasn't deer season, either. A doe's head appeared farther down the slope, its sleek neck erect. The animal looked the hunter's way intently, then disappeared behind a broken branch. The man waded through shin-deep leaves to where the doe had vanished.

Beneath a steep overhanging ledge of limestone, his dog let out a plaintive yowl. Its head hung low, pointing to something tucked under the rocky outcrop. With some difficulty, the hunter traversed the steep wooded terrain across to the spot drawing the pointer's attention.

"What is it, Zeke? Coon got your tongue, boy?" A disturbed leaf pile drew the man's attention. He squinted, trying to discern the meaning of a strange-looking mushroom shape poking up through the leaves.

"Almighty God!"

The hunter recoiled, and the ridge of his boot heel caught on a branch, sending him and his gun flying apart. The weapon discharged with a loud crack, and a handful of blackbirds materialized out of the trees, flapping their way to safety wildly.

Now the pointer's whining sounded nearly human as it gazed down at its master. Regaining composure, the hunter approached the spot. A stiffened forearm stuck out; purple-blue fingers projected upward like a decomposing blossom, still attached to a body that lay somewhere beneath the leaves.

He reconnoitered, memorizing the spot, then wreathed the tree closest to the body with red plastic ribbon. It was what he used for marking trunks when his dog treed a coon too high up for buckshot and he had to go retrieve his rifle. Before leaving, he said a small prayer, then turned to get help.

It was September 2, and the hunt for Julie's killer was about to officially begin.

CHAPTER FOURTEEN

The fourth day of September broke smoky. Wisps of gray sky brushed the treetops. A chilly dampness roosted over yellowed pipes of cut corn.

McFaron rose from bed to the sound of the portable phone— Mary calling. A tireless servant, the dispatcher was always there electronically by McFaron's side. She'd taken plenty of hits for him lately, while he was so involved in the search for Julie Heath. Last week a farmer had come barreling into the office, pissed off and saying he wouldn't budge from McFaron's desk till the sheriff showed up. It was no contest for Mary, who had stuck her thumbs through the top of her bullet belt, flashed her .38 Special in its leather holster, and gotten right in his face. The farmer had taken a corner chair by the door without another word.

"Sorry to be bothering you so early, Joe. Bob Heath phoned. Wants you to call him right away. Over."

"I'll give him a call on the way in."

"Copy that, Sheriff."

McFaron put his feet on the floor and scratched his head fiercely. An image of Karen Heath retching on her hands and knees after he'd given her the news yesterday shot through his head. He'd driven the distraught mother to the home construction site where her husband was working. The disappearance of his child had already been a huge drain on Bob Heath; it was obvious to McFaron that over the past month, the work on the house had hardly progressed. The sheriff had stayed long enough to tell Bob the news, told it to a face already fearing the worst. Hearing the brief facts of his daughter's death, Bob shuffled off toward his truck and sat down on the tailgate. He didn't even notice his wife, who didn't seem to notice her husband, either. She stayed seated in the sheriff's truck, her forehead resting against the dash. The sheriff's last act before leaving had been to lead Karen from his truck into the passenger side of Bob's vehicle. As he'd driven off, McFaron had checked his rearview. Julie's mother was slumped forward in her seat. Her father remained unmoving on the tailgate.

What could he do for Karen and Bob and little Maddy now? He was unable to shake Karen's eyes: they were lost, no matter what he did. Her grief was his grief, too.

It was too early to start beating himself up. On his way to the crime scene, he radioed Mary from the Bronco. "I'm expecting the FBI today."

"FBI?" Mary said. "Were you planning to fill me in? Over."

"I wasn't exactly consulted in advance," McFaron said with an edge to his voice. "As county coroner, Doc Henegar had to report the murder to the feds. Don't repeat that, please. Evidently it's very similar to two other killings the FBI is investigating." Suddenly he saw again Doc inserting the spatula through the purple slit along Julie Heath's side. She was filleted like a fish; the perp took her insides out and left her empty—what kind of creep could do that? The whole thing seemed unreal, like a scene from a movie he'd rented about an alien monster that bored through its victims.

"And just when is this agent going to be arriving?"

"I have no idea. Doc said she'll be flying in from Chicago, a female anthropologist of some kind."

"A female agent?" Surprise registered in her voice. "Can we assume she'll be on the eleven o'clock incoming? And do we need to arrange for someone to meet her?"

McFaron thought he detected a twinge of indignation in Mary's tone. "Yes, yes, and no. We can assume she'll be arriving at eleven, but we don't know for sure. She'll have to arrange her own transportation. Right now I'm off to take another look at the crime scene," he said, feeling pressure to find crucial evidence before the FBI hit town.

"Aren't you forgetting something?"

"To call Bob Heath, I know."

"What about your coffee?" she said in a muffled voice. "It's already brewed and waiting, nice and hot." She swallowed some of her Swiss Miss hot chocolate. "You won't last ten minutes scrounging around the wet forest without caffeine and a fresh cruller."

"Save me one. Over and out."

McFaron rode the brakes as the grade steepened; fog engulfed the Bronco in an early morning whiteout. Houses and trees suddenly vanished. Fine droplets silently dotted the windshield. When an especially nasty shred of fog erased all traces of the road in front of him, McFaron pulled off to the side of the road. He closed his eyes, hoping to get a few moments' rest, but the image of young Julie's desecrated body was right there every time he lowered his eyelids.

* * *

A black limo with government plates idled in a parking space outside O'Hare. Prusik's driver pulled into the empty space beside it. For a moment she bristled, imagining that Bruce Howard had ridden in to catch the same flight to Crosshaven, beating her to the punch. Then she realized the absurdity of her thinking. Howard was driving down with the forensics field unit in the RV. Only a lone driver sat waiting in the limo.

She grabbed her bags and hustled through the terminal's automatic doors. She had left instructions for Brian Eisen and Paul Higgins to track down each and every member of the painting crews who were doing renovations at the Museum of Natural History the previous March. The museum thefts and the special gilt paint flecks found in one of the victims' hair might prove to be linked and to show that the killer had deeper connections with the greater Chicago area. Under a high-powered bioscope Eisen had located a needle-sized hole piercing the quill of the feather recovered from the crime scene in Blackie, proving it may have been part of some sort of body decoration or mask that the killer used.

Lines of waiting passengers snaked their way toward the security screening area and the boarding gates beyond. Prusik flashed her ID at the guard at the head of one line and passed through the metal detector without a wait—one of the few privileges of her job, though most of the time she didn't feel very privileged.

An overhead TV screen flashed 7:20 a.m.

"Christine?"

Thorne stood not ten feet away beneath a bank of arrival and departure monitors, inspecting his ticket. His brown briefcase perfectly matched his tortoiseshell frames.

"Why hello, Roger," Prusik said. She blushed, then reminded herself that she was over him.

His eyelids fluttered. "Was there something you wanted to tell me before I left?" He studied the shiny chronograph strapped to his wrist. "My plane for Washington's boarding promptly." He motioned forward with his head.

"Oh, you mean"—Prusik hoisted her heavy forensic case partway—"I guess we're both en route, sir."

Thorne's brow furrowed. "Funny, for a second I thought, how wonderful, Christine's trying to catch me at the airport to deliver some important last-minute news Washington would want to hear."

She restrained herself from blurting out an expletive and instead reported on the girl's body found in Crosshaven.

Thorne nodded. "Yes, I'm aware of it. Bruce called me from the mobile field unit. They're already on the road. He also told me they've turned up blood evidence. Why haven't I heard a thing from you about this Julie Heath who's gone missing for over a month?"

Prusik's cheeks warmed. "I'm on my way to the crime scene myself and will let you know ASAP what I find there." Why hadn't Howard told her about the blood?

"I was waiting till I knew a little more until I gave you a briefing. As I said, I'm on my way there now." It sounded lame even to her.

"All right, Christine. I know I shouldn't interfere." Thorne gave her a tight smile. "Actually, I had asked Bruce to call me since I hadn't heard of any solid leads directly from your team. I had hoped by now to have some names of potential suspects." He held her gaze for a moment and then looked away.

Christine nodded but didn't speak.

"Look, Christine, this isn't the time or place for interoffice squabbles, which, as I've said, I may have contributed to. For that I am sorry. You're right to be irritated." He cleared his throat. "However, you are not right to have waited to tell me about this Heath girl. You need to do a better job of keeping me apprised of the situation." He paused, studying her for a moment. "Keep in mind that the mobile unit *is* under Bruce's command and the lab team is under yours, technically speaking. Now, if you have nothing else to report on the case, please excuse me. I've got a plane to catch."

Christine watched him stride off, amazed at what sounded like an apology coming from her boss. "Will wonders never cease?" she murmured. Then she turned and made her way to her own gate, her mind already on the day ahead.

* * *

An hour and a half after takeoff the plane descended to the small airfield a few miles north of Crosshaven. Outside Prusik hailed the only taxi: a decrepit-looking hulk with DENNIS MURFREE'S CAR SERVICE stenciled on the cab door.

She slid over the backseat in her navy-blue suit. It had just enough polyester to make it travel well and, more important, flatten unnecessary bulges and flatter the good ones. She had picked it up at Marshall's off Lake Shore Drive, where the nouveau riche flocked to buy on the cheap but didn't like to admit it. It had stood the test all her clothes went through, proving itself capable of surviving a trek through the woods in all kinds of weather. She was sure she'd be scouring the woods.

"Howdy, ma'am." Murfree stayed slouched in the driver's seat. A cigarette bounced up and down between his lips. "Where to?" A coughing spasm cut him short and turned his face beet red.

"Dr. Walter Henegar's office, please," Prusik said. "Do you know where it is?"

Murfree grasped the steering wheel with both hands, his watery eyes staring blankly ahead.

Prusik futilely scanned the parking lot looking for a place to rent a car. "Would you like me to find you something to drink?"

Still unable to speak, he waved her off. The car reeked of tobacco even with all the windows open. Ceiling upholstery hung down, tattered and yellowed. Murfree recovered and jerked the car into gear. It chuffed once, then died. Prusik closed her eyes. A minute later they were bouncing down an access road on shot springs. Prusik clutched her bags tightly to keep her instruments from jarring loose.

Murfree drove through the middle of town past a diner. A neon sign in its window read FINE EATING HERE. Smoke funneled out a side chimney so thick and oily Prusik could smell it. Five minutes later Murfree pulled off the road beside an old two-story frame house. Nothing from its exterior gave the impression that inside a doctor ran a medical practice—no identifying name or professional sign, only a postal number crudely painted on a porch column. Prusik walked around the idling cab to Murfree's open window.

"You're sure this is the morgue?"

"Yessum, around back." Murfree's coughing returned big-time. "Go on through." He seemed to point toward the main door, though it was hard to tell due to what was becoming a nasty hacking fit. The cabbie's reddened face reminded Prusik of her own father's, though it hadn't been smoking that had made him so damn red. It was Yortza, Prusik's mercurial mother. She patted Murfree's narrow shoulder.

"Look, it's probably none of my business, but have you thought of getting a nicotine patch?"

His head bounced hard against the hub of the steering wheel as coughing shook his frame. "Yessum."

Prusik paid him and hoisted out her bags. The front door was ajar. "Dr. Henegar?"

Labrador retrievers came crashing around the corner, nails slipping and sliding on linoleum flooring. Seeing the eager animals, Prusik's spirits lifted. She put her bags down on the floor and petted them, talking sweetly. The dogs licked her cheeks.

"Don't let those brutes bully you. Dr. Prusik, am I right?"

Henegar hooked a finger under each dog's collar and shuttled them into what looked like a kitchen.

"It's Special Agent Prusik," she said. "I'm a forensic anthropologist, not an MD."

They shook hands. "Nice to meet you," she said while giving the place a cursory once-over. It was outfitted more like a rustic hunting camp than an up-to-code morgue. The hallway was stacked with cardboard boxes. A fishnet and a pole hung on the wall next to some rods and reels.

Henegar slapped his forehead. "Please excuse me for not making it to the airport. I thought someone at the sheriff's office would be arranging the pickup."

"It's quite all right, Doctor. Can we proceed to your path lab?" Prusik's brow lifted. "If it's OK with you, I'd like to get started." The forensic bag strap was gnawing at her shoulder.

"Yes, of course." The doctor pushed through the swing door and cleared a stack of *Field & Stream* magazines off a chair. "Let me make some elbow room so you can work."

"Where's the body?" she said, sounding alarmed.

He stopped midmotion with an armful of the glossy periodicals. "Oh, not to worry, we'll get her in a jiffy. She's safe and sound in the portable cooler out back."

Prusik's brow line stayed creased. Her mouth hung open a bit.

"It's under lock and key," Henegar said. "Safe from tampering—wildlife mostly, the odd raccoon that comes sniffing around. Not to worry. Billy and Josie woof them off."

Shaking her head, Prusik put down her bags. "Is this a board-certified facility, Doctor?"

Henegar dropped an empty coffee tin riddled with holes onto the counter next to the examining table. "Yes. The tabletop is clean and the body is as we found it in situ."

"Well, that's encouraging news." She caught sight of a trout creel in the corner. She removed her suit jacket and draped it over the back of a chair. "I hear your sincerity, Doctor, but state-of-the-art forensics requires something more than simply *wanting* to find a killer. It requires"—she let her gaze sweep the room—"something more than *this*."

"Agreed." Henegar nodded, his eyes closed. "Shall we bring her in?"

A small door led to a back porch where a blue tarp covered a steel-encased locker large enough to hold one body.

"What procedures did you use to decontaminate this?" Prusik asked.

"Strictly by the book, Special Agent. New bag liner every time. I changed the inner one, too. This body has on it whatever it had at the site and nothing else."

"But you've already done a preliminary exam of her, right, Doctor?" Her voice had a slight accusative quality.

"Yes, following forensic procedure, chapter and verse. Gowned and gloved all the way." He keyed open the lock and flipped the heavy-gauge latch. The retrievers began howling in the kitchen.

"I take it Billy and Josie didn't happen to wander in during your exam of the body?" she said.

He rolled out the tray that held the black Tyvek bag. "Absolutely not." Prusik held one end while Henegar hoisted the other. "Sorry, ma'am. I was expecting Sheriff McFaron to be here for this part." They lifted together.

Prusik eyed him suspiciously again. "So the sheriff helped you do the prelim? Removing the body from the crime scene?"

"He was at the crime scene, yes. A coon hunter found the body. Him and his dog." Henegar's cheeks and forehead flushed. "Methuselah was out of town—the bloodhound we use to track missing people."

"Did anyone touch the body without wearing sterile gloves, Doctor?"

"According to McFaron, the coon hunter was careful. Only marked the tree beside the corpse with some tape. The sheriff and I both gloved up extricating her, of course." Henegar walked backward into the examining room, holding the door open with his foot. They slid the tray onto the examining table.

Prusik got straight to work, pulling on a pair of powdered latex rubber gloves, being sure to draw the wrist ends over her lab coat sleeves. She studied the photos Henegar had sent to the lab, then unzipped the body bag. No flies zoomed into her face this time.

Julie Heath's unclothed body lay on the metal table under a bank of artificial lights. Her hair was a tangle of leaves and twigs. Heavy finger markings were distinctly visible around the girl's swollen throat. The neck was nastily broken, causing her head to lean unnaturally toward one shoulder. One of her forearms was streaked with coagulated blood where a branch or thornbush had scraped her.

"You found her buried?"

"Yes, under a pretty deep pile of leaves." Henegar's salt-and-pepper beard puffed out behind his face mask.

Which could explain the lack of flies, larvae, or any eggs having been deposited, Prusik noted, speaking softly into a handheld recorder. She also jotted details in a forensic examiner's loose-leaf book that was open on the counter behind her. She marked the placement of contusions on a diagrammatic sketch of a human form.

Prusik stepped to the stainless-steel table and then quickly jerked back her head, stricken by the strong odor of the decomposing flesh.

"You might want to smear some of that salve in the jar on the table under your nose," the doctor said.

Prusik fingered a wad of the goo over her upper lip. A numbing shot of peppermint shot up her nostrils. "Two cervical vertebrae are severely broken, partially crushed from the strength of the killer's grip," she said into the cassette recorder.

"The hands on this guy are pretty strong," the doctor said. "We're talking a man without question, right?"

Prusik nodded and continued with her initial assessment. With the doctor's help she gently rolled the dead girl's body over enough to reveal the grainy purple flesh where blood had saturated the surface skin—the same color as an encrusted gash along the side of her abdomen.

"See along both sides of her spine." The doctor pointed. "Lividity had already set in before he did the rest. See how the blood's coagulated along her back?"

The killer likely moved the body after strangling her. Possibly something interrupted him shortly after the strangulation, she thought. "Did you happen to notice any deposits, residues, or foreign bodies on the victim's clothing?"

"I did find some particles on her skirt," Henegar said. "Not a hair on her except her own. No obvious signs of semen, either. There was no sexual molestation that I could tell. Her fingernails are clean—she didn't scratch the assailant."

"What sort of particles?"

"Don't know for sure. A gritty substance—oil based, maybe," the doctor said. "Could be paint of some kind."

Prusik nodded briefly.

"Take a look at her left side, ma'am." The doctor pointed with a gloved finger. "Just below the rib cage."

Prusik carefully lifted the girl's left arm, exposing the torso to the fullest extent. At first all she could see under the bank of milky-white fluorescent tubes was greatly discolored skin, like an extended tattoo. Then she saw what she had hoped not to. This was the work of their man, all right. The girl's entire left side had been slit open.

Prusik's right hand was drawn like a magnet to the purple-black skin flap that extended from the victim's lower left rib distally to the pelvic girdle. She inserted her gloved hand into the slick abdominal cavity. A few beads of sweat crept down the crown of her head and raced across the top edge of her large, plastic-framed protective glasses. She reached past the peritoneum into the pericardium and pulmonary cavities—the chambers normally containing the heart and lungs—which were empty except for a few errant oak leaves.

"She's plum empty. Scoured cleaner than the funeral director down at Marsh's parlor does." Doc Henegar's face mask puffed in and out as he spoke.

"Thank you for that comparison, Doctor." She thrust her arm in all the way to the elbow. Her forefinger touched the base of the dead girl's shattered airway. Prusik breathed a little easier, relieved at not finding anything obstructing it.

She asked Dr. Henegar if he would mind wiping her forehead, then went back to the recorder, describing the crushed trachea from inside out. Threading her gloved index finger farther up into the tighter passageway of the esophagus, Prusik came into contact with something hard. With the top of her fingernail she pried, breaking it in two. The pieces tumbled into the pulmonary cavity.

She withdrew her gloved hand, which clutched the hard objects. Turning her back from the table and Dr. Henegar, she fingered the stone halves together. They joined perfectly.

"Will you excuse me, Doctor? I need some air."

She pushed open the back screen door and peeled the gloves off inside out, trapping the stones. She pocketed them in her gown, unbuttoned her shirt collar, and took in a slug of pine air. Another charm stone. Why was the murderer placing tribal charm stones, of all things, in his victims' throats? With her back turned to the door, she swallowed a new serotonin beta-blocker recently prescribed to her. Just then, from around the front of the house came the sound of a screen door slapping open and shut—Billy and Josie had broken free. They raced up the back porch steps and greeted Prusik, whining and pressing their noses against her legs. She dropped to her knees. Their wet licks felt good.

Henegar stood by the screen. "Give them the boot if they get too pushy."

Prusik shook her head. "They're great," she said, clearing her throat.

She returned to the exam room, stowing the crumpled glove containing the stone evidence in her forensic case. Dr. Henegar shooed the retrievers into the kitchen.

Donning a fresh gown and a new pair of latex gloves, Prusik resumed her examination of the body, praying for the medication to work its magic quickly.

She looked up as Dr. Henegar reappeared. "Anything else I should know?" she asked.

"I suspect you'll want to inspect where we found the body," he said. "Patrick State Forest is quite secluded."

"Yes, that would be good," she said.

"And there's something else that I haven't been able to make sense of."

She raised her eyebrows.

"In the blood evidence we found nearby, metabolites turned up, too."

"A blood dyscrasia?"

"No, an excretion from urine."

"What about the blood itself?"

"Well, it wasn't Julie's. And it was mixed with uric acid in too high a concentration to have come from the blood alone."

"Are you saying someone urinated on the same spot as the blood sample you collected?"

He nodded. "Must have. Joe phoned me right away after he found it, same day Julie disappeared. The blood drops looked only hours old. I didn't detect anything else unusual at the time."

"Here, let me see that report." Prusik ran her finger across the gas chromatograph peaks and valleys representing the chemical composition. Two sets of graphs ran in tandem for the urine and blood. "A trace amount of white blood cells was found in the urine."

"Indicating the presence of an infection?" Dr. Henegar said.

"Yes, possibly. More significant is whether DNA testing will reveal a match between the white cells and the blood found on the pavement."

"You're assuming the blood is the killer's," Henegar added. "Since it's not Julie Heath's type. That the perp peed on the sidewalk afterward?"

"Or lost control." *Or lost control.* She had nearly lost control only moments ago, rushing out the back door like that.

Prusik took a deep breath and let it out slowly. Control. She could maintain control. She had become a master of it over the years. "Well, Dr. Henegar. Shall we zip her up and go examine the crime scene?"

Christine followed Dr. Henegar to the front entrance. Scratching paws directed her attention to the kitchen door, where she observed both dogs' noses wedged between the jamb and a chair that the doctor had placed as a barricade. The pair shoved their way in, whining, in one last frontal love assault. Christine stooped down and let them lick her face.

"Unruly bunch," he mock scolded.

"They can be unruly all they want with me." After two hours spent examining the remains of a young girl's body so desecrated, the labs' kisses were a welcome relief.

CHAPTER FIFTEEN

The sky lowered. The air was clotty damp and did not taste good. David Claremont was agitated and exhausted. It was not good enough anymore just living at home in a room that he could not rest in. He needed to get away. He slid the pickup's column shifter into drive and pressed hard on the gas. Ten minutes later he turned into the farm bureau's dirt parking lot.

A car door slammed across the way from him. A petite young woman in tight-fitting blue jeans stepped lithely past a line of bright-red riding mowers. She wore her hair in a bouncy ponytail the way a younger girl does, and the ponytail bobbed as she walked. David followed her toward the main entrance of the ramshackle co-op building.

The young woman went down an aisle and disappeared out the back of the store where open-air bays were stacked with lumber, pipes, livestock fencing, and other farming supplies. A rumble overhead signaled rain, as did the fuzzy halo around the cloud-filtered disk of the sun.

David was forgetting himself, his reason for coming—to purchase four gallons of red barn stain—as he frantically poked his head between the bays looking for her. Something about her pulled him on, almost as if he had no choice in the matter. Halfway down a narrow corridor he spotted her tugging hard on a roll of wire. Relief flooded through him.

Rocking back on her heels, she looked up and smiled. "Say, mister, do you mind giving me a hand? This seems to be stuck." She had on a small pair of leather work gloves.

"Be delighted to," David said, reaching up.

The wire end had uncoiled and become entangled with the next roll. He focused on the task. As David worked the roll loose, her perfume—sweet honeysuckle—wafted up his nostrils. He swiftly gave the wire a jerk, and the roll came unstuck.

"Wow! Aren't you strong," she said, removing one glove and extending her hand. "Thanks. My name's Josephine."

David shook her warm hand. "I'd be happy to carry that out to your car, if you'd like? My name's...David."

"Thank you for offering, David. How can I refuse?"

Her voice was sweet and melodious, just like he'd known it would be; he felt calmer just hearing it. He lifted the roll to his shoulder and drafted in her shadow, mesmerized by her lovely gait, the steady stream of her perfume washing over him, her soft white hand shaking his. Mostly David basked in an unaccustomed sense of serenity.

They walked around the outside of the co-op building, a shorter way to reach her car.

David's visual field suddenly narrowed—like a buggy horse wearing blinders. A sensation of staring out of eye cutouts grew. At Halloween when he was ten he'd stared through holes like that in a brown paper bag on which he'd scribbled a crude resemblance of Frankenstein's monster.

His breathing became labored. The nice woman hadn't noticed that anything was wrong, but she was getting farther ahead.

Increasing uneasiness stopped him dead in his tracks. David sucked air through his open mouth, unable to get enough. His heart hammered, demanded more. He weaved unsteadily toward the car, urging himself, *Just get the roll into her trunk! Quickly!*

The woman was standing behind her car now, opening the trunk. "Let me help you with that," she said in a lovely disembodied voice.

The wire roll tumbled out of his hands. David wasn't seeing the woman where she should be standing. His field of vision had been devoured by a girl running through a deep wood, her elbows pendulums opposite to her stride in a mesmerizing pattern—the lovely white legs pumping in unison under a pleated skirt in a perfect motion.

"David, are you OK?" The woman's voice interrupted again, this time from David's side, punching a hole through a forest of oaks coming straight at him. He felt small hands touch his back—hers. He forced a smile. He liked her face; he would have followed her anywhere. But the trees wouldn't stop. He was seeing scattered oak trunks across a steep forest. They fused tighter together. Spiraling grids and swirls chopped his visual field. His heartbeats pulsed against his shirt—an impenetrable wall of confining oaks closed in, choking him. He was not at the farmer's co-op. At least some of him wasn't.

A scream etched the underside of his skull. David landed hard on his side.

"Get off of me!" The woman's panicked voice startled him. In and out of swirling dots of light David could see someone holding the lovely woman, pinning her by the shoulders, staring down at her from above.

"Let me go this instant!" Her sharper words stung him. A fingernail gouged his cheek. A knee slammed into his groin, and David recoiled, groaning on his side.

"Hey you, hold it right there!" A man's boot fell hard against David's hip, making him wince. The mechanics of a rifle bolt action clicked forward. The heavyset man with his boot pressed against David pointed the barrel of the gun at him.

"I...don't mean...harm...just...trying to help..." His ankle throbbed mercilessly.

The woman was speaking calmly now, coaxing the man to put down the gun, reassuring him that everything was OK. She was fine.

David closed his eyes hearing her words: she was fine. She was protecting him. He'd see her again. Feel her soft palm in his. There was reason for hope.

A few minutes later a smear of dust came funneling out behind a fast-moving truck. It turned into the parking lot. Its tires made a crunching sound, sliding to a stop. The driver's side door swung wide. David instantly recognized the white hair, silvery in places, and the reddened flesh accentuating where fine blood lines etched the diaphanous tissue of the old man's cheeks. His mouth was drawn tight, his lips made crumply from years of his pulling them tightly closed. His father was not inclined to a lot of loose talk.

"David! You there?" His father's voice sounded irritated. "What's with that tickle bug of a brain of yours, huh? You hear me?"

A second plume of dust ballooned in the parking lot behind a police cruiser that came to a screeching halt. Two cops jumped out and approached quickly.

On the ground, David's hip throbbed mercilessly. He squinted up at the sun, nearly directly overhead and shining through a break in the clouds. Besides the woman, it was the only good thing. He felt it was nearly blinding him, but he didn't care. It warmed him, soothed him. He waited for his punishment.

* * *

Henegar took a cell phone out of his coat pocket and punched in McFaron's number. "Joe, Doc here. Uh-huh. We're on the way over right now." He nodded. "I'll tell her."

Henegar beeped off the phone. "Amazing little gadgets. Sheriff's beat us to the crime scene."

"He's what?" Her sharp tone surprised Prusik as much as the doctor.

He took his foot off the gas. "Did I say something wrong?"

"Never mind, never mind." She waved the back of her hand. "I hope you don't find me too critical, Doctor. It's a frustrating business when all we have to go on are a precious few pieces of evidence."

"Sheriff and I did the best we could preserving the site," Henegar said warily. "It's hard this time of year with the leaves down, the rain and all. Oh—I nearly forgot to say—a Mr. Howard called Sheriff McFaron's office about an hour ago. Something about a flat tire north of Indianapolis."

A wry smirk parted Prusik's lips. "A flat tire? The poor thing."

"Is he one of yours?"

"Yup." Howard had her cell number yet had chosen to call the sheriff's office instead.

"You don't sound too fond of him."

"Just between you and me, Doctor, he's a subordinate with a real talent for getting under my skin." Prusik tried to suppress a smile as she visualized the ponderous forensic RV broken down on the side of the road, Howard stamping back and forth, waiting for a wrecker.

A forest appeared ahead. Henegar slowed the car and turned in. "The body was found about a quarter mile from the road. Down a ravine near a creek. These woods are pretty steep sided, with exposed limestone shelves in places. You don't notice the slope till you walk in a ways. Twisting an ankle is easy enough to do if you're not careful."

"Don't worry about me, Doctor. I wore my hiking shoes." Prusik slung her camera over one shoulder. "Now, shall we get to it?"

"Absolutely." Henegar joined her, insisting on taking her forensic case, and the two made their way into the woods.

* * *

Sheriff McFaron wore a pair of deerskin gloves. Sunlight bored through a stand of tall trees, projecting millions of particles in its luminous shafts. Wet leaves brushed his pant cuffs as he reconnoitered the area around the yellow police tape he'd previously yoked between two trees, marking the shallow grave of Julie Heath.

McFaron looked up at the sound of approaching footsteps. A striking woman with shining chestnut hair came toward him, holding Doc Henegar's hand for support.

"You must be Sheriff McFaron," she said, catching her breath. "Special Agent Christine Prusik, nice to meet you. Deerskin gloves from your hunting closet?"

McFaron immediately realized his error but didn't know what to do about it. "Beg pardon?"

"I'd appreciate it, Sheriff, if you'd remove yourself from inside the perimeter." Her eyebrows rose clear to her short-cut brown bangs. "And put on some latex gloves."

Doc Henegar held out a pair. "Here, Joe, I've got some extras. Better put them on."

McFaron lifted the police tape and stepped out. The three of them slipped on the gloves. Prusik carefully skirted the taped-off area, examining the depression in the leaves where the body had been found.

"Have you recovered anything, Sheriff?" she asked without looking up. "Gloved or otherwise?"

"Nothing," he said, irked by her unnecessarily holier-than-thou attitude. "Except for the blood we collected up by the road."

Without further conversation, Prusik examined the scene, carefully studying the nearby tree trunks with her notepad out. One oak stood larger than the rest at the head of the leafy grave site. She opened her attaché and took out the portable recorder.

She didn't ask him anything more, and he got the distinct impression that his presence was unwanted. "I can see that I won't be needed here any longer," he said curtly, then turned to leave.

Prusik looked up, startled. "Oh, Sheriff, please, I'm sorry. Forgive me for sounding so…"

McFaron waited. A line of sweat raced down his cheek.

"…abrupt," she said. "Just so we understand each other, you are not the only one here under the gun."

"I'm not questioning your authority to run the investigation." McFaron's hat fell inside the perimeter. He quickly squatted and retrieved it. It was awkward footing in the deep leaves covering the steeply angled wooded slope.

"Good. Then we'll get along just fine." She eyed McFaron, who silently stared back. "Look at it this way, Sheriff. At least you'll have someone to place the blame on besides yourself. The FBI does pretty well as a scapegoat, I've found."

"Well, I'm sure glad I introduced you two," the doctor blurted. "Now that we've covered the niceties, would anyone like to check the crime scene for anything else we might have missed?"

Prusik lowered her pad. "I'd prefer you stay, Sheriff. You're a long-standing member of this community and widely respected, from what the doctor tells me. I imagine I can use your help."

McFaron nodded. "So what would you like to know, Special Agent?"

She glanced down at the log leaning at an angle from the taped-off site. "I understand you and the doctor moved this log off the victim's body. Did you do it bare-handed?"

"I might have." McFaron became flustered again. "To get to the body. We pivoted the branch by one end so we wouldn't leave our fingerprints or smear any latent prints that might be lifted later," he added. "Then we both gloved up to remove the body. Followed police procedure to a T. Look, ma'am, this is my first murder investigation. I protected the scene as best I could as soon as it was reported. No one has tampered with it, I'm sure."

Prusik retrieved her Nikon digital camera and flashed a few shots of the burial site, listening to McFaron as she worked.

"For your information, Sheriff, this looks like the third victim of the same killer. We'll need to do more than follow police procedure to a T to catch him, I'm afraid," she said, snapping another picture. "Look," she said, softening, "I'm fully aware that you probably had to deliver the terrible news about this poor girl's death to parents you likely know well enough to call family. I'm not trying to be a jerk."

"You're right. I should have worn gloves from the get-go," McFaron relented, his voice less strained. "Law and order of this magnitude I've not had to deal with in my fifteen years as sheriff of Crosshaven, Agent."

"Christine, call me Christine." She held out her hand.

"The name's Joe." McFaron shook her hand. It felt warm. Sun highlighted reddish streaks in her hair. "I...I can't tell you how much this girl's death has kept me up all hours of the night. Anything I can do to help find the killer, count me in." McFaron removed his hat, wiping the sweat from his brow on his jacket sleeve.

"Let's see what we can discover here that might nail the bastard," she said. Her voice was steely, yet she was smiling at him.

The three of them searched the perimeter, careful not to unnecessarily stir the scene. Important clues could easily be hidden from view under the leafy forest floor.

McFaron pointed to something fuzzy snagged on the bough that had rested over the victim's body. Prusik retrieved thin forceps from a zippered pouch around her waist and carefully extracted the filament. She held it close to her face—a green linen fiber.

"See that whitish substance, like there's paint stuck to it?" She tapped the fiber into a clean vial. "Here, take a look." She handed the vial to McFaron. Dr. Henegar stepped closer to observe.

"The same color as the girl's skirt," the sheriff said.

"It sure looks like it to me," Henegar agreed.

"By the way," the sheriff added, "the victim's from the same school as Joey Templeton, who observed at the approximate time of the girl's disappearance a strange man, possibly the killer, stuffing something in the back of his truck."

Prusik imagined the panicked girl thrashing to escape, ripping her skirt. "I want to interview the boy who saw that stranger right away, Sheriff."

"I can set it up," McFaron said, pushing back the brim of his trooper hat. "He's the only eyewitness we have. I'm disappointed our police sketch hasn't yielded a suspect yet."

Prusik stooped; something else had caught her eye. Dangling from the underside of the same bough was a thicker strand, possibly canvas. She picked up her field case and handed one end to McFaron.

"Would you mind?" she asked.

"No, that'd be fine." He held the ends of the case while she fished around inside.

McFaron's awkwardness always bloomed around attractive women. It was an awkwardness that had turned the few dates he'd had in recent years into complete disasters. Worse was hearing the reverberations of each failed encounter throughout the town afterward, which kept his forays into companionship to a minimum. And yet he wasn't always awkward. Sometimes, he thought, he could be downright charming. Or so he hoped.

Prusik capped the vial containing the second thread and withdrew a tape measure from her zippered pouch. "Could you hold one end, Dr. Henegar?" She stretched out the tape.

"I'd be glad to."

The doctor held the end of the yellow metal tape, which was marked in both inches and centimeters, as Prusik proceeded to measure the length and width of the disturbed grave site.

She let the tape measure snap back into its holder. Her empty stomach tightened, reminding her that she hadn't eaten since wolfing down a measly croissant at the Chicago O'Hare food court before catching her flight. She had an urge to invite the sheriff to dinner, but hesitated.

A trickling sound drew Prusik's attention. Without a word, she left the crime scene, wandering down the wooded slope. All the victims' bodies had been found near running water. She followed along a track of disordered leaves that led down to some exposed flat rocks beside a small stream. Immediately her eyes locked on what appeared to be dried blood on one smooth stone.

Rifle fire sounded in the distance.

The sheriff stepped up behind her. "Could be from a deer carcass," McFaron said, noticing what had caught Prusik's attention. "Hunters are crawling all over these woods."

She pulled on another pair of forensic gloves. With forceps she flicked some of the blood into a vial and capped it.

"My field technicians will comb this area and inside the perimeter sometime tomorrow," Prusik said. "I'll plan on spending the night. Have any good recommendations for a place to stay?"

"There's only one really," McFaron said. "The motel by the interstate gas station. It has an all-night restaurant."

As Christine was nodding, a nearer blast of rifle fire caught her off guard. "Let's go see that eyewitness of yours before we all get shot."

* * *

A whistle blared shrilly. "OK, Sarah," Coach said. "You're in."

Sarah North's eyes brightened as she hustled to the right forward position, waving Olive Johnson, an eighth grader, off the field. The scrimmage resumed and the center quickly passed off to Sarah, who dribbled downfield.

"Good wheels, good wheels!" Coach's voice boomed. "Pass the ball, Sarah, out to the wing!"

Sarah instantly responded. Her pass to the girl at wing landed perfectly—two steps in front.

"That's it! Nicely done!" Coach barked through cupped hands.

The girl on wing beat the defender and centered the ball, dropping it midway between Sarah and the goalie. Sarah had to stretch, but she beat the goalie and kicked a low grounder inside the corner post. Nothing but net!

"Nice move, Sarah!" Coach said, marching out to midfield. "You just earned yourself a starting position in this Saturday's game, young lady."

Sarah had started the season second string on the Parker, Indiana, middle-school soccer team because she was a seventh grader. Sixth through eighth graders all played on the same squad, but seniority tipped the scales in favor of the older girls starting first string. Now she would be starting!

After practice, she headed home, kicking at the pinecones scattered along the roadside, replaying the goal she'd made. The team was beginning to click after practicing most of August, and Coach was openly boasting that they had a good chance to beat Carver, a school twice their size. Both schools were located in satellite communities of Crosshaven, the county seat, which was twenty-five miles away.

Sarah adjusted her pace for the two-mile jog home. She was just about to enter the shadows of a hemlock grove when a loud engine revved up behind her. She turned and was blinded by sunlight. A dilapidated truck was rolling straight at her, cutting her off. Sarah wedged her thumbs under her pack straps and sprinted over the curb. The driver ground the gears; one of the truck's tires had gotten hung up on a rock off the pavement.

She looked back from a few yards away. Why had the man driven off the road like that? Was he drunk? Suffering a heart attack? The driver was pounding the steering wheel. She thought she heard moaning through the closed window, making her more uneasy. She glanced in the direction of school. No one else was coming. When she looked back at him, the man's face was pressed hard against the driver's window, his face twisted in agony. She didn't recognize him from school or anywhere else. His cheeks were glistening. He was crying. It didn't make sense. It didn't look right, either.

The skin on Sarah's forearms tightened. A funny thought skittered through her mind—the missing Crosshaven girl she'd heard about. She started running, keeping to the center of the road, pumping her arms. Without slowing, she checked over her shoulder as she would on the practice field to receive a pass, only this time it felt like it was for keeps. The truck was still stuck, but she could hear the engine revving madly.

As she ran into the shadows of the hemlocks, cooler air flushed across her hot cheeks. She thought of dashing into the woods to a cave she knew, squeezing through its tight crevice entrance, a place the weirdo man couldn't get into. She looked behind her again. The truck was gone. It had disappeared.

She stopped, bent over and out of breath, not realizing how fast she'd been running. Perspiration trickled down her forehead. Sweat soaked through her clean shirt. The truck was nowhere in sight. She repositioned her backpack and ran on, and she didn't stop until she reached her own driveway.

CHAPTER SIXTEEN

Sheriff McFaron dropped Christine off at the Interstate Motel following the interview with Joey Templeton. Before they'd left the crime scene, she'd briefed him and the doctor on all the relevant details of the case—the museum theft, the charm stones in the second and third victims' throats, the profile she was creating of the killer. She'd declined the sheriff's offer of dinner, saying she had to hit the phone pretty hard. The digital clock radio on the small bed table read 6:55 p.m. Time to check in with Brian Eisen.

Prusik punched the AUTO DIAL button on her cell. "Let's hear what you got, Brian," she started right in, kneading her forehead with the butt of her hand.

Ten minutes later she grew restless listening to him rehash things. There was nothing new to report—Thorne's favorite refrain. She told Eisen she wouldn't be flying back tonight and ended the call, laid down her cell phone, and pulled off her jacket and pants, flinging them over the chair back.

Christine felt queasy, not having eaten a proper dinner. She should have accepted McFaron's offer. It was good business practice, and she knew it. Besides, he had a nice manner, he was considerate—not to mention his good looks. That she had good feelings toward him was undeniable, all of which made her cautious, fearful of screwing it up, whatever "it" meant. Men and feelings were hell on her nerves. Whatever else, she didn't need to add that complication into the mix right now. Prusik arched back her neck, longing for the lap pool, which was more effective than a drug and healthier for her, too.

Five months into the investigation and all the classic symptoms of her PTSD were surfacing at once. The tension had been close to intolerable today: Finding the charm stone in Julie Heath's trachea had almost sent her into a tailspin, putting her on edge for the rest of the day and making her overly argumentative with both the doctor and Sheriff McFaron. In the makeshift morgue, she'd had to grapple with panicky thoughts and do it without revealing that something more than the murders was bothering her; murders, after all, were something she routinely dealt with as part of her job. Prusik feared that Howard and Thorne would find her out and label her an incompetent, as her mother had been before being involuntarily hospitalized for intractable depression. Like mother like daughter—wasn't it that simple? Well, she wouldn't give in to her panic. She wouldn't.

She clicked open her attaché case and removed the rubber glove that was still bunched around the broken figurine. She freed the two stone pieces that fit together into a sterile collecting jar and screwed the lid tight. The carving was exquisite handwork; it had to be one of the stolen museum artifacts. The shortwave UV light Nona MacGowan had demonstrated would likely turn up the identifying micro etch.

She stripped and ducked into the small shower stall. "Don't sweat the small stuff, Christine," she mumbled to herself under the forceful spray. But there was nothing small about it. The gruesome murders were upsetting enough on their own, but once their uncanny resemblance to the ritualistic cannibalism of the Papua New Guinea highlanders became clear, the murders were beyond freaky.

"There's a perfectly logical explanation," she said, talking to herself loudly now, not considering whether this made her crazy like her mother. She turned the water down. "You've got a PhD in forensic anthropology, and you're working the lead on a serial murder case for the FBI. You've got plenty of backup. You're in America's heartland, for chrissakes. Not on some godforsaken island in the Pacific. You're in charge, Christine. In charge!"

She stepped out of the shower and toweled off. She liked motel rooms. Being able to rant about everything that had gone wrong in the day, carry out a diatribe while looking into a mirror, was especially gratifying in a neutral, impersonal space. She wasn't beyond throwing pillows at the bed, the floor, the walls. Prusik had learned tantrums young watching her mother's wild ones. At the end of a hard day back in Chicago, she often fantasized about finding a motel room nearby and giving it a piece of her mind. Now, she picked up a pillow with half a mind to hurl it at something. As she raised it above her head, however, the idea somehow lost its appeal, and instead she found herself sliding between the welcoming sheets.

* * *

A few hours later, Christine was awakened by the racing of her heart. There was little she could do to stop the uncomfortable metabolic sensation, a manifestation of her chronic anxiety. She slapped the bed table in the dark searching for her pills and swallowed two Xanax. She pulled off her nightshirt soaked in sweat. Trembling in the cold, dark room, she wrapped a blanket tightly around her shoulders, knelt between the twin beds, and rocked back and forth to steady her nerves. She checked her pulse—rapid—and scrubbed clammy fingers through her hair. She crept toward the bathroom in the dark, knocking over the chair piled with her clothes. She sat on the toilet seat, forcing herself to take deep breaths to slow her redlining heart.

Christine had a crazy thought to call Sheriff McFaron but knew that wouldn't be right. What would she say to him? Would you please come and hold my hand while I wait for my drugs to kick in? She located her phone under the clothes heap and dialed 411. A few minutes later the call went through to a twenty-four-hour hotline. A pleasant young woman's voice said her name was Amy. "Mine's Christine...I can't sleep...my heart's racing...I'm shivering...nearly passed out in the bathroom a moment ago. Look, I just need someone to talk to. Will you stay on the phone with me awhile?" She stood up and made her way to the outside door in search of fresh air, then slipped off the security chain and opened it.

"No, Amy, I'm not high on drugs. Only my prescription...in the prescribed amount. Please stop with the routine questions and just listen."

But Amy had her list to check off and kept asking anyway. "Yes, I took two antianxiety tablets a few minutes ago. No, this just happens. Yes, I've seen a doctor. Yes, my work is stressful."

Christine tuned out Amy's words and focused on her soothing voice. It *was* soothing in its calm, measured professionalism. A few moments later she realized that Amy was waiting for another answer.

"I'm sorry, I didn't hear your question."

"Are you having thoughts about hurting yourself?"

The idea was so funny Christine almost laughed. Instead, she rolled her eyes, which made her realize she was feeling a little better. The drug must be taking hold. "Actually, Amy, my thoughts are about other people who are inflicting damage. I'm not worried about myself in that way at all. But I do thank you for your concern." She reassured Amy that she felt better now and ended the call.

She paced the small room, waiting for the drug's full effect. An evanescence of moldy rot pervaded the space, matching her festering mood. She finished off a Snickers bar, supplying herself with much-needed glucose, which her overactive adrenals had depleted. To keep focused, she cataloged the day's events. The Heath girl crime scene had yielded some fresh though minor clues. Paint particles found on the corpse were similar to those found on the Blackie victim, and the thick canvas thread coated with more paint that she had discovered had possibly come from a workman's tarp. The dried blood on the rock by the creek didn't appear to be from a deer kill. The murderer hadn't been as careful this time.

She picked up the collecting vial containing the broken charm stone from the night table. What could a New Guinea artifact possibly mean to a killer rampaging in the Indiana forests, gutting bodies as deliberately as a Ga-Bong clansman would, depositing stones in them afterward? Had the Ga-Bong's spirit infused some escaped lunatic? Of course not.

Prusik tried to stay focused on what she knew. What she could verify. She had long studied cannibalism as a ritual among New Guinea tribes and the neighboring peoples of Melanesia and Micronesia. It had been practiced for hundreds if not thousands of years. Sipping the fluids of the dead was believed to bring male and female into balance and keep those on earth vitally connected to their past so that they might live again inside the next generation. It was worship of the highest order.

Could the same be said for the beast committing these horrendous acts? Prusik didn't think so. The victims were all haphazardly struck down, the only connection among the three being opportunity. Each had been alone, and that had played into the killer's hands. It was likely each had been taken without much of a struggle, lured in some cunning way, probably. There was one eyewitness who had not actually seen a victim—only what he thought was suspicious activity and possibly blood spatter on a frightening stranger's face and clothing. The killer had merely adopted the habit of implanting the charm stone, she surmised, because the museum exhibit appealed to him, was in some way related to his own twisted life. He had ritualized the stone into his own persona. Reinvented himself. The urine found mixed in with the blood scraped off the sidewalk on Old Shed Road, where Julie Heath presumably was abducted, spoke not of ancestor worship but of deep-seated feelings of persecution and humiliation.

She went back to the bed and flicked on the TV with the remote control; at last the drugs were working at full force. When the trill of her cell phone roused her, it was nearly midnight. Eisen was on the other end.

"Brian?" Hearing her own voice helped restore her alertness. "Why the late call?"

"I was going to wait till morning, Christine." There was excitement in his voice.

"I'm all ears."

"Using the Lucis program, I was able to enhance the coroner's black and whites of Betsy Ryan's head and mouth." Christine heard Eisen's pencil tapping his teeth and smiled.

"You made a positive identification?"

"Hold on. You will recall that there were distinct abrasions on Ryan's lips, inside her mouth, and down her throat—grit particles common to the locality. The same mineral grade and composition as gravel used in city lots. I've concluded the killer had tried to shove a coarse stone down her throat. Not carved chert, more like stone you'd find at a construction site."

A punch of old pain hammered up through her beleaguered brain. The museum thefts had been discovered during the third week of March. Betsy Ryan was last seen alive on March 30. If the killer had had the museum stones when he'd killed Betsy Ryan, why hadn't he used one of them?

"You there, boss?"

"I'm here, Brian. You're sure that the stone in Betsy Ryan's throat would have been coarse?"

"I can't be sure of anything, Christine. But, yes, that would be my conclusion."

Prusik closed her eyes and considered.

"You going to tell me what's spinning around in that brain of yours right now?"

"Good work, Brian. And, no, there's nothing to tell yet." But her own fear was signaling her loud and clear that there was.

CHAPTER SEVENTEEN

The early morning sun shone through the cab's rear window, projecting a shadow of the pickup on the road ahead. Things had been getting worse, his agitation increasing. Missing that girl two days ago had been a setback. He rolled down the window and stared out over the molting field of last year's yellowed cornstalks.

He tapped his fingers rapidly on the dash, leaning the undersides of his wrists over the top of the steering wheel. Sweat and dank midsummer air burned his eyes. The church bell ringing lifted his head. The Sunday sunrise service was finally letting out. Through the rearview mirror he watched people dressed in their best spill out the doors. They were chattering and milling about in the parking lot. Car doors were opening and closing as families dispersed. He deliberately turned his head toward the fallow field out his driver's side window as cars began filing past him, going home or out for Sunday breakfast. A few people walked back toward town, in the opposite direction.

He'd spotted the girl easy as pie. She was holding her navy flats in one hand, walking barefoot toward him—away from town and people—along the sandy edge beside the tarmac, her bonnet's blue ribbons matching her knee-length silky-smooth dress. She had well-developed breasts already. Her black waist belt tugged nicely down.

He wiped his brow with his sleeve. Processes inside him were already beginning. A growing sense of ease, like the release from that first beer after a long, hard day, was subduing things nicely. Undercurrents of the pitiful anguish that he'd experienced only a few moments before were nearly forgotten as she and her billowing blue dress took up more and more room in the rearview mirror.

She stopped to talk to a young woman holding the hands of two little blonde girls. The girls were wearing matching bonnets with matching yellow ribbons and bows tied exactly alike.

The blue-ribbon girl knelt in front of the two little ones and gave them each a hug. Even with his window closed, he could hear their laughter and giggling. It set his nerves on edge.

Soon enough, the little girls and their mother got in their car, and the older girl continued on her way. He watched her approach in the rearview mirror, then walk right by him and out in front of him. The way she sashayed, hips moving back and forth like that, was a definite invitation. She hadn't acknowledged him when she'd sauntered past him, or even glanced at his truck, but with a walk like that, he knew she'd seen him.

The silk ribbons that trailed out from her bonnet in the breeze were teasing him. Taunting him. He slowly shoved the truck in gear and followed down the same secluded lane the blue ribbons had taken.

The girl was only ten yards ahead of him. Forty or fifty yards beyond her was a sharp bend. A tall stand of trees hid the road beyond. Small towns in the southern part of the state ended abruptly and the forests began. It was perfect. He couldn't have planned it better.

He motored past the girl, snaking his head back for a second look. She hadn't looked up, hadn't acknowledged him. Right before reaching the bend, he turned off the motor and glided to a halt under the lower story of hemlock boughs. He leaned back his head against the front seat and waited. The sweet smell of soap wafted in through the open window, and he nearly cried out from the seat. Containing himself was more than he could stand. He glared into the rearview mirror, and like a magic pill, it worked. She saw the face of a madman and took off at a full run. The chase was on.

Sunlight suddenly flooded the forest, bathing wet bark in wine-colored light. Everything began to glow, a prismatic rainbow, as if the whole dell was dimly wired with his infernal juice. He got out of the truck and checked both ways, then sprinted around the bend that the ribbons had floated around moments earlier. He was desperate to put her back into view. In anticipation, his fingers fluttered and his chest did, too. He picked up speed and followed the sharp curve of the road, then stopped suddenly. The forest had come to an end. There was a great opening in the sky above him and huge expectant tracts of farmland seeded with new corn. His eyes narrowed, training on the girl, far ahead of him now and way out of range. She was still running and had almost reached a farmhouse.

How had he misjudged things? How had he not seen it coming? He staggered back to the truck, not taking in the great repeating lines of dark tilled soil drawn right up to the edges on both sides of the road. A terrible confusion beset him. He hadn't expected to lose her so cruelly. He hadn't prepared himself at all for that.

* * *

Deputy Richard Owens of the Weaversville Police Department chewed his Doublemint gum very slowly, concentrating on the figure stooped halfway down the steep-sided ravine. It was a heavily eroded area, where reams of stones had washed out from the culvert that ran under the road.

"What's he doing down there?" said his partner, Deputy Jim Boles, who sat behind the steering wheel of the cruiser, sweating in the midmorning sun. "I say we go bring him up now. Sure looked like he was driving drunk to me, swerving like that."

Owens stopped chewing and told Boles to shut up, then went back to gazing through the police-issue Swift 10 x 40 wide-angle lenses. He watched the man lever up a large rock with a stick, then drop to his hands and knees, partially out of sight.

"He's hunting for something, that's for sure." Deputy Owens's tone of voice escalated. "Go check the license tag to that truck, Jim. Run a check on the guy. See who we're dealing with here."

Five minutes later Boles climbed in behind the wheel of the cruiser, having heard back the tag information over the police radio.

"It's registered to a David Claremont," Boles said. The field glasses were still glued to his partner's face. "What's going on? You seeing something?"

Owens exited the passenger side, hunched low, signaling his partner to do the same. They approached the pickup quietly.

Claremont reached the pickup truck a few minutes later, out of breath, clay caked to his boots. Holding on to the vehicle's bed for support, he knocked off the clods, then spotted the two deputies. They both wore Ray-Bans and stood by the driver's side of his truck, hands resting on their gun belts.

"Hello, Officers."

"Your name is David Claremont, right?" The officer noticed the legs of the man's jeans were spattered with reddish-brown paint. So were his long-sleeved shirt and the tops of both his hands.

Claremont nodded, squinting in the sun.

"You've been painting recently?" Deputy Boles said.

"Well, staining, actually. The barn on a neighbor's farm."

"May I ask what you were doing down there, Mr. Claremont?" Owens said.

"Nothing, I guess," he said, hunching his shoulders as he spoke.

"Nothing, huh? Forty-five minutes is a lot of nothing." Owens noticed Claremont fingering something in his front jeans pocket. "What you got there in your pocket?"

Claremont removed his fist and opened his palm. "Just a few stones I picked up." To him the jasper mineral was a perfect shape, and the pale-red translucence made it ideal for carving.

Deputy Boles muttered something into his partner's ear, handing the deputy a folded paper from his jacket. Owens eyed the police sketch, then Claremont. The drawing had the eyebrows right, the sunken hollows of the man's eyes, too, and the mouth. It wasn't an exact likeness, but it was pretty darn close.

"Let me see your license, Mr. Claremont."

Claremont took his wallet out of his back pocket. A ticket stub fell out. Deputy Boles stooped and collected it, read aloud, "Chicago Museum of Natural History. You been there lately, Mr. Claremont?"

"No."

"No? It's date-stamped here Tuesday, August twenty-first. I'd say two weeks ago counts as lately. What were you doing way up there?"

"It's open to the public. Nothing's wrong with that." Claremont handed the deputy his license but wouldn't meet his eye.

The police officer flicked it a few times on his palm and then handed it back. "Mr. Claremont, I'm going to ask you to follow us back to the station to answer a few questions, if you don't mind." It wasn't a question.

"Well, I do mind. Am I under arrest? I haven't done anything wrong."

"No, sir, I didn't say you have," Owens said. "Just some routine questions. We'd appreciate it if you'd come voluntarily."

Claremont frowned, then nodded. "I guess I'll follow you." He looked over toward his truck.

Owens judged the man's demeanor. He appeared calm. Not a flight risk. "All right then."

Claremont pocketed the keepers and got into his truck, grimacing.

The cruiser led the way. Deputy Owens notified the dispatcher to contact the state police special crimes unit to say they were bringing in a possible suspect for questioning regarding the murder of Julie Heath.

"All I'm saying is," Deputy Boles said, checking the rearview mirror, "we should have taken him in the cruiser on account of reckless driving, not to even mention the fact that he could be a goddamn killer."

Owens leaned his arm over the seat back and looked over his shoulder at Claremont following them in his truck. "First off, he ain't drunk. His breath didn't smell of alcohol. And where's he going to go?" The deputy flicked the arm of his partner with the back of his hand. "If we got the killer dead to rights, he ain't going nowheres." He patted his holstered sidearm. "Believe you me. Nowheres."

CHAPTER EIGHTEEN

The sheriff pulled off the road above the crime scene, eyeing his rearview mirror as the traveling lab crept around a bend and then rocked unsteadily over the ruts to a halt. Static interference on the two-way radio signaled an incoming call from his office. Mary had Rodney Cox, a retired trooper from the state police post, on the line. Cox lived in Parker, a twenty-minute drive from Crosshaven.

A federal agent in aviator-style dark glasses hopped out of the RV's front passenger side and slowly approached the Bronco. A photo ID hung from a lanyard around his neck.

"Patch him through, Mary," McFaron said into the mike, eyeing the agent in the side mirror. The man's hands drifted to his hips in a deliberately nonchalant gesture, waiting for McFaron to get out. The sheriff grinned. No wonder Christine didn't like Howard, assuming this was Howard. McFaron didn't like him, either, and he hadn't even met him yet.

"Rodney, what's going on there?"

"Ezra North and his girl Sarah are sitting here in my living room, Sheriff. They got something to talk to you about."

Outside, the muffled voices of technicians climbing out of the RV intruded. They gathered beside the forest, busy with equipment. One tested a luminous light instrument against the bark of a white pine.

"I'm kind of occupied at the moment, Rodney. Can I get back to you? Over."

"It's that man in your sketch she saw," Cox said point blank.

McFaron straightened up. "Say what?"

Mr. Cool was now standing beside the sheriff's door. McFaron rolled down his window.

"Give us a minute." The sheriff tipped his hat and closed the window.

Without a word, the FBI agent sauntered back to his crew.

"Is the girl hurt?" McFaron said anxiously.

"Not a hair on her head has been mussed. Had the daylights scared out of her, though. According to Sarah, this guy just about ran her down after soccer practice on Friday. She didn't tell her parents till this morning. Too scared."

McFaron's cheeks burned. "Damn! She's sure about the ID?" He ripped open a new roll of Tums, chewed three at once.

"Says the picture's the spitting image."

Outside, apparently preparing for a siege, federal agents were setting up sensing devices and wielding scanning pods on the ends of long metal poles. A female agent, her blonde hair in a ponytail, positioned a headset over her ears and clipped a pod to a vest harness. She began waving the sensor over leaves at the edge of the forest.

"Called you as soon as I could, Sheriff. I knew you'd want to know about this."

"Listen, Rodney, hold the girl there. We'll need to get her statement. You'll hear from me within the hour."

McFaron hung up. Parker was practically on his doorstep. This was one bold bastard on the prowl. Christine Prusik would be damn pleased to hear about this development.

Mr. Cool started wandering back over. McFaron exited the Bronco and found that his initial annoyance with the FBI team's arrival had receded.

"Sheriff McFaron, Crosshaven County." He extended his hand. "Nice to meet you."

"Special Agent Bruce Howard." They shook hands, and the agent gave McFaron a business card.

"Afraid I'm all out of cards," McFaron said with a straight face. He gave Howard his cell and office phone numbers and watched the agent key the numbers into a BlackBerry.

"We'll follow you down, Sheriff," Howard said, his voice neutral. Despite an overcast sky, he kept his shades on.

His perfunctory response was fine with McFaron. Better to keep things businesslike.

Agents wearing khakis and lightweight navy Windbreakers with the large yellow FBI logo stenciled across their backs spread out across the forested slope. Stepping down the steep embankment, McFaron followed the trail through the disturbed leaves. Halfway down, he said, "That large log to one side was positioned over the body." He pointed. "The one curving downhill slightly."

"Got it. Thank you, Sheriff. We'll take it from here." Howard motioned left then right to his technicians, who descended on either side, carrying electronic equipment.

A technician in goggles flicked on a fluorescent light attached to the end of a long-handled pole. McFaron knew he was looking for trace evidence that would glow under the special ultraviolet lamp.

The sheriff backtracked to his truck, yelling over his shoulder, "Give a holler if you need anything."

Howard gave a mock salute. The smug prick, thought McFaron. At the same time, he prayed they'd find something significant. Wrap this thing up before another girl wasn't as lucky as Sarah North.

He slammed the truck door and sat behind the wheel. A tingling sensation started up in his chest. Too much stress on his heart? His dad had died suddenly at forty, barely middle-aged. His doctor had blamed years of smoking for leaving him slumped over a log at the mill yard, ending life with a burn mark between two fingers from a last cigarette. "So long, son" had been his last words to McFaron earlier that morning, the same words he'd always said as he passed his son's bedroom door on his way off into the predawn air. And then he was gone, just like that.

How many more years did he have, McFaron wondered. And how would he spend them? In a certain way, his world hadn't changed much since his father's death, when a kind of emotional numbness had set in. By the time of his mother's death, McFaron had felt nothing. And when he did recognize feeling something more than the irritations of the workday, it was emptiness, like the barely visible face of the moon against a pale-blue sky, a great silent presence. With the coming of night, when the moon loomed brightly, turning the backyard into stark shapes and shadows, McFaron's struggle would begin anew, and the void within him would blacken. Swigs of Kentucky bourbon did little more than lighten its edges. Sooner or later he feared the pain would win.

McFaron retrieved Christine Prusik's business card from his wallet. If he was lucky she might not have eaten lunch yet. He called her cell phone number and accelerated without looking back.

* * *

The phone beeped over the racket of idling diesels outside her window. The Interstate Motel shared a parking lot with a large truck stop plaza. Prusik found the receiver on the fourth ring.

"Special Agent Prusik."

"Can I take you out for a sandwich, Christine?"

She yawned aloud. She'd gotten up early, unable to sleep, and had been on the phone with her team and working on an update for Thorne all morning. Her stomach gurgled loudly. "Now that you mention it, I never had breakfast. A sandwich sounds good. Anything sounds good as long as it comes with lots of coffee."

"I can arrange that," McFaron said. "Your man Howard and his team are going over the crime scene as we speak. They have all their hardware out."

"What do you mean?"

"Well…I mean they're going over the crime scene," McFaron said slowly. "I led them out to the site a little while ago."

"Right," Christine said after a moment.

"Shoot, Christine," the sheriff said. "I just assumed he'd called you."

"You assumed wrong, Sheriff." She winced. McFaron didn't deserve her sharp tone.

"If you don't mind my saying, he seems a bit full of himself."

"I don't mind your saying," she said, leaving it at that. She reminded herself to put in a call to Howard right after getting off the phone. She would afford him that civility even if he hadn't bothered to call her on arrival, as all professional courtesy would demand.

"One more thing," McFaron said. "Actually, the most important thing."

"Yes?"

He filled her in on Sarah North's sighting.

She felt her adrenaline start to pump. "Jesus Christ, he's getting bold." She took a breath. "This is great. We can go right over and interview her."

"After lunch. A few extra minutes won't cost us anything, Christine. Didn't your mother ever tell you about the importance of three meals a day?"

"She wasn't that kind of mother."

Joe smiled wryly. "Mine neither. I'll pick you up in thirty minutes. I need to make a couple of phone calls."

Prusik nearly hit END but hesitated. "Uh, Joe?"

"Yeah?"

"You didn't mention any of this to Howard, did you?"

"Didn't think there was a need to."

"OK. See you in a few."

So Prusik wouldn't be flying back to Chicago right away. McFaron would pick her up and they'd grab some food to go before driving to Parker to interview the North girl.

Prusik toggled through the address list on her PDA's screen and steeled herself. "Bruce," she said in her most congenial voice,

"I understand that Sheriff McFaron led you and the field team to the crime scene? Any findings to report?"

"Nothing yet. I've got Goodyear and Morrison checking several hundred yards out from the perimeter doing concentric rings."

"Good, good. I'm gathering my notes together from the postmortem and my interview yesterday afternoon with a witness." She left out McFaron's most recent revelation of a possible second witness. It was premature, she decided. And besides, she had no direct information yet. "I'm about to meet McFaron to discuss the other people he's interviewed. Get a lay of the land. Shall we check in a couple of hours?"

"Sounds like a plan," Howard said.

"Great." She clicked off the phone and sighed. Howard had said all the right things and so had she, but it was clear that neither one of them trusted the other. It would be nice to work with a real *partner*, someone who believed in teamwork and wasn't always jockeying for position, someone who wanted to solve the crime because he wanted to *help*, not because he wanted more power. Someone like…Joe.

Slouching her shoulders forward, she examined herself in the mirror that hung over a small writing desk. Her face appeared smooth in the murky light, which hid the furrowed brow line no wrinkle cream could conceal. Not so bad for thirty-five, she thought. Thirty-five. Was that considered middle age?

She whisked into the bathroom. McFaron would be arriving soon. She felt a bit of a wreck from the previous night's terrors, but there was a tingle inside, too. There were two new developments to pursue, and if she were honest with herself, the prospect of pursuing them with Joe, at least for the morning, was exciting. Her response to him was bewildering but unmistakable. The sheriff had strong-looking hands and a handsome face. The day before when he'd driven her to the motel after she'd interviewed Joey Templeton, she'd found herself staring at the dark hair on his fingers.

She took a quick shower and toweled off briskly, groaning at the prospect of putting on her dirty, wrinkled clothes. But it was that or pick out some cute cowgirl outfit at the farmer's co-op she'd seen. Luckily the pantsuit had held up. Thank goodness for polyester.

The rumble of a truck motor shot straight through the bottom of her black leather Rockport all-weather shoes, filling her with a tangle of emotions—dread, self-doubt, and resolve. She looked in the mirror again and gave herself an encouraging smile, then started to the door. The room was too depressing. She'd wait for McFaron outside.

When her hand was on the doorknob, she stopped and made her way back to the mirror. Reaching into her handbag, she rummaged around until she found an old tube of lipstick, then slowly, carefully, she applied it to her lips.

CHAPTER NINETEEN

Joe held the bag with their sandwiches in one hand and opened the door of the truck stop café with the other. "After you, Special Agent."

She smiled and led the way outside, a large cup of coffee in each hand, one for her, one for Joe. "Thanks, Sheriff." After one cup of coffee quickly consumed while they were waiting for their takeout orders, she already felt much more human. After a second cup, along with a roast turkey sandwich, she thought she might feel downright civil.

She started toward the sheriff's Bronco, then stopped abruptly when she saw the FBI van pulled in next to the sheriff's vehicle. Howard hopped out and motioned her over.

She crossed the parking lot quickly. "Has something happened?" she said to her reflection in his mirrored lenses.

Howard nodded toward McFaron. "Sheriff's dispatcher said he'd probably bring you here for something to eat. I hope it was good."

"We're just grabbing takeout before heading back to work, Bruce. What's up?"

He pulled the aviators down far enough to make eye contact over the frames. "Managing director's on the line. Asked to speak with you." He handed her his cell phone.

"Christine?" Thorne's voice sounded tentative. "Listen, has Howard told you?"

"Told me what?" Prusik ducked behind the Bronco, pressing her free hand against her other ear to block out the clattering engine noise of the truck lot.

"Howard's connected the police sketch with a farmhand who lives in Weaversville, Indiana. A police photo of David Claremont was a ten-point match. He recently attacked a woman in a local parking lot, and police were called to the scene."

"What? What kind of attack? What happened to the woman?"

"Oh, she's fine. Didn't press charges. She could have, though. There were plenty of witnesses in the parking lot. I don't know any more than that right now. Anyway, according to the local police in Weaversville, this Claremont has got an old pickup truck, too. Howard said you've got a witness in Crosshaven who saw an old truck. Is that right?"

Prusik bit her lip. She'd just spoken to Howard no more than forty-five minutes ago. Had all of this new information really just come to light since then? Unlikely.

"Still there? Christine?"

"Yes, I'm still here, Roger," she replied, her voice muted. "I'll check it out right away."

"I needn't tell you how delighted Washington is with the turn of events," Thorne said happily.

You just did, she thought glumly. "I'm sure they are, sir."

"In fact, delighted doesn't quite say it, from Washington's perspective. They've appointed Howard logistical lead. Just from the case-management perspective, of course. You're still lead forensic investigator on these cases. I need you, Christine. You're vital to the success of the team, to producing a successful outcome."

Prusik could feel Howard's eyes burning holes through her back. Surely he was picking up from her body language what she was being told. She stood up straighter.

"You'll remain in charge of your forensic lab team." Thorne was repeating himself, filling the void. "And Washington has even nixed sending in an auxiliary unit now that a bona fide suspect's surfaced. I trust I can expect your full cooperation in reporting to Bruce?"

"Somehow that doesn't sound like a question, Roger."

"Cut the attitude," he said sternly. "Face it, Christine, you're a day late and a dollar short. Five months without a suspect—look at it from headquarters' perspective. You haven't delivered the goods." Relenting, he added, "You know I need you working with the lab team. It's your forte, Christine. You're still the best. It's all for the best. We're moving forward as a team."

Prusik crouched behind the Bronco, thoroughly humiliated. Giving her the news in this manner—in such a public setting, with the sheriff and Howard and his crew all nearby—was beyond demoralizing. And Thorne hadn't even bothered to call her on her own cell phone. She swallowed hard.

"Make no mistake, you're still in charge of the forensic—"

"Reporting to Howard, yes, yes." A bitter aftertaste filled her mouth. "I heard you the first time, sir. Anything else?"

"OK then." Thorne's voice moderated. He'd said his piece. "Good luck at the lineup. It's scheduled for later today. Talk to Howard about it."

The sound of Howard yukking it up with his men by the RV snapped her out of it. She walked the phone over to him and returned it. "Congratulations to you, Bruce. Shall I meet up with you in Weaversville at the lineup?"

Howard grinned at her, his sunglasses firmly in place. Her reflection in the mirrored lenses stared back at her.

"Absolutely. And, say, your sheriff can come along, too, if he likes," Howard said, lifting his chin toward McFaron, who was standing behind Prusik, his hands on his hips. "Scheduled for four o'clock."

She bit her lip and climbed aboard the Bronco, hastily slamming the door, then glanced McFaron's way. "Well? Shall we get started?"

The sheriff didn't have to ask if there had been a transfer of power.

"How far did you say Parker is?"

"About a twenty-minute drive," McFaron said, accelerating out of Crosshaven. "The North girl's spotting him like that is pretty damn lucky, don't you think?"

"We'll see." It *was* a good break. And it was something she needed to tell Howard about. She should have said something back there in the parking lot, but she'd still been reeling. And *your* sheriff? Come on, Howard. How juvenile. Prusik shook her head. OK, she'd been juvenile, too.

She gritted her teeth and speed-dialed Howard. "Bruce, we've just heard about a possible sighting of the suspect yesterday in a little town called Parker, about twenty minutes from here. I'd like to follow up on that."

"Sure, Christine. I'll take care of the flesh-and-blood suspect. You go on over to Parker with the sheriff." Howard disconnected without waiting for her response.

Prusik closed her eyes and forced her attention to the matter at hand.

Giving in to irresistible impulses was one of the killer's weaknesses. If the North girl's sighting was legitimate, it meant that he'd attempted an attack in very close proximity to the Julie Heath crime scene after three previous attacks more widely spread out. Perhaps, rather than planning an attack and lying in wait for a victim, he'd seen an opportunity and tried to grab it. She shook her head, trying to make sense of the emerging inconsistencies. He seemed to prefer desolate places in which to select his victims, so why would he attack someone in a parking lot? And what about Missy Hooper? He had been careful enough that nobody remembered him, but picking up Missy with so many other people around was bold. His Friday encounter with Sarah North—if he was the one who had terrified the young soccer player as she jogged home—was even bolder. Perhaps he was beginning to make mistakes.

"If you don't mind my saying, you seem distracted," the sheriff said.

"Sorry. I just was thinking about Sarah North, about the victims." She forced a smile. "Kind of hard to shake the image of one of his victims once you've seen what he does to them."

Another pause lengthened into the space between them. Finally the sheriff cleared his throat. "You sure made Arlene Greenwald's day back there at the truck stop, agreeing to come back and address that Brownie troop of hers sometime. You do that kind of thing often, speak to groups of people?"

"Often enough. When I'm speaking to children, it's usually a pleasure. It makes me happy to show young girls they can be successful in a job usually reserved for men." She blushed. "If that doesn't sound too ridiculously self-important."

"Not at all. That's why Arlene said she invited you. It makes a lot of sense."

"When I speak in front of adults, it's not always as pleasant." She thought back to the museum opening on April 1. April Fool's Day, indeed. She had certainly made a fool of herself.

The land grew brighter and then darker as the sun poked in and out of clouds. It was fickle weather and more humid heat was forecast. They passed fields of tall corn tasseled out. Out Christine's window it looked as if they had just crossed into a third-world country: metal-roofed shacks and mobile homes were set back in the middle of dug-up brown yards scattered with trucks and trash. They passed a small, square white sign for a town called Utopia. Several bullet holes pierced through the u.

"Friendly," Prusik said, unsmiling.

"Down here signs make good target practice. Doesn't mean a thing."

"Right. They do that in Chicago, too. It means something." She wished she had her ankle piece—a snub-nosed .38—buckled on now.

"Country boys aren't like that," he said. "They don't mean anything by it. Really."

They drove in silence for a minute. "It's pretty here," she said finally. "I don't dislike the country. It's just...the unknown quantities."

Christine sighed. "Something's not adding up, Joe. Weaversville is—what?—a hundred miles south of here? And three hundred miles from Chicago, where the first victim was murdered?"

"That's about right, yes."

"The first victim that we know of, her body was snagged on a boat's anchor in Lake Michigan, near Chicago. With the second and third killings, and now this North girl sighting—assuming it bears out—we have strong indications that the killer is expanding his range southward. But a farmhand from southern Indiana who attacked a woman in a public parking lot in plain view of witnesses?" She shook her head. "Without knowing anything about the attack, I can say that it's not consistent with his normal pattern. And a ten-point match on a hand-drawn sketch, with detail supplied by a boy riding by on his bicycle—it just doesn't add up. Not in my book, not one bit."

Christine reflected. Was it her anger and frustration speaking? Her annoyance at Thorne's giving such credence to a preliminary lead supplied by Bruce Howard? Or her shame at being sent back to the lab to do backup technical support?

The sheriff pondered her points. "You have to admit, Christine, it does sound kind of promising. Claremont could have driven north to start. We can check that out. And the picture matching up is something more than coincidence. Parker is not that far a drive from Weaversville."

"What I'm trying to say is that my profile of this killer doesn't mesh with a man who attacks grown women in public places. Don't be bowled over by this development."

She looked over at McFaron to gauge his reaction and realized this would probably be the last time she'd be seeing him. There would be no need for both her *and* Howard to conduct inquiries on the ground here unless things got really out of hand.

"It would mean a lot to me if you could keep an open mind about this," she said. "I've appreciated working with you. Really I have." Prusik flushed with embarrassment. She felt like she'd bared her soul to him, even though objectively she knew she'd done no such thing.

"Well, as a matter of fact, I'm in agreement with you," McFaron said. "It doesn't sound to me like it's a sure thing at all, which is why I'm interested to know what Claremont has to do with these cases—if anything."

Immediately Christine felt lighter, but she could think of nothing more to say than "Good."

"Christine?" McFaron said after a moment.

"Yes?"

"You were waiting to hear some information about the first victim?"

Christine cleared her throat. "It looks like she had a stone jammed into her esophagus, too. But it was most likely a coarse one, not a museum piece like the others. Even though the theft had already taken place."

He frowned. "Odd."

She nodded slowly. "Odd."

They drove in silence for the next few minutes, each mentally arranging and rearranging the puzzle pieces of the case. As they passed a flock of sheep huddled along the edge of a field, Christine stared. She pointed to a massive coil of a plant that stretched out of sight over the top of a hill.

"What are those large hedges the sheep are grazing next to?"

"Thornbushes. Don't get near them. They'll hang you up fierce. I knew a guy who got too close to them while he was riding a tractor. Vicious thorns pulled him clear off. The tractor kept on going, disappeared without him. Had cuts on his arms as deep as a dog bite. His wife found him there, stuck. It took a chain saw to cut him loose. If those sheep stray into it, they'll get caught up and die unless the farmer comes in time to cut them free."

Something clicked in Prusik's brain. "Is that the same thing as *multiflora*?"

"I believe that's it. Wicked stuff," he said, glancing over at her in the passenger seat. "It's kind of prevalent around here."

Prusik flipped through the pages of her notebook. "Last week, an expert botanist identified the different seeds we found on Missy Hooper's clothing. Several came from a *multiflora* thornbush."

"What other kinds did she find?" the sheriff asked. "You said different seeds?"

"Mallow, a common weed found near barns and farmhouses. The killer may live on a farm."

"Right," McFaron agreed. He slowed the truck as they approached a collection of buildings that scattered over a few blocks. PARKER, POPULATION 2,037, a peeling signpost read. "We're here. Now let's go see what Sarah North has to say."

* * *

Under the glare of spotlights a deputy escorted seven men into the room. Each held a number card chest-high and was instructed to stand on a corresponding number painted on the dingy linoleum floor. The lineup faced a mirrored panel of one-way glass, the white wall behind them marked off with lines indicating feet and inches.

I can see them, but they can't see me. I can see them but they can't see me. Joey repeated the words to himself like a mantra, squeezing his clammy fists as he gazed at the group. He was approximately the same distance away as he'd been when he'd ridden by the stranger over a month ago. He knelt, moving his hand over the glass, as an officer instructed each man to step forward, then back. The officer had to ask number four twice to step forward. Grudgingly he did.

A spotlight shadowed the hollows of the man's eyes. Joey's uneasiness escalated. He kept looking over his shoulder at his grandfather, who sat on a bench at the rear of the viewing room, then back at those sunken eyes. Something wasn't quite right with the man's mouth. Or maybe it was his chin, he couldn't tell. Joey looked at his grandfather again, still not positive, and glimpsed a sudden movement above the old man's white hair. Against the rear wall of the viewing room there was a large one-way glass, which adjoined a now-darkened interview room. In the glass the boy saw a reflection of number four wiping his nose.

Joey froze. His heart felt like it was about to explode in his chest. He spun around, facing the lineup again, then swallowed hard to clear his throat. In his mind there was nothing between him and number four, nothing stopping the man from reaching in and grabbing him, then stuffing him in the back of that rusty old pickup like he had Julie.

He spun back toward Elmer. "Oh my gosh! It's him! It's the man, Gran!" Joey cried, pointing at the reflection in the window behind his grandfather. "That's the man I saw."

Elmer was at the boy's side in three quick strides. "It's OK, boy. The man can't see you." He held his grandson close. "You did real well."

* * *

The arrest of David Claremont for the malicious and wanton killing of Julie Heath seemed almost anticlimactic to most of those who had watched the boy. He had made a clear identification of Claremont. Joey Templeton was the man of the hour.

Shackled and surrounded by police, Claremont said nothing when read his rights. Hilda Claremont's uncontrollable sobbing was the only sign of emotion in the crowded police station. Claremont's father had his arm around wife, bracing her shoulder.

Claremont refused counsel, claiming he was innocent and didn't need a lawyer.

Within minutes the news media descended. Vans with generators cranking power to cameras and portable satellite feeds soon filled the Weaversville Police Station parking lot. Scattered in clusters were cameraman–news reporter teams delivering updates. Grunts toweled off the sweat that poured down reporters' faces in the muggy heat. Anyone exiting the station was accosted for information about David Claremont. One precocious up-and-comer from a CNN affiliate cajoled a day-shift janitor on a cigarette break, wagging a fifty at the man. The janitor took the money and said into the camera, "He's a real nutcake, all right. Everyone thought he might flip his lid some day."

Christine sat quietly with McFaron in a small interrogation room while the commotion continued unabated in the police station and the parking lot outside. She was playing and replaying Joey Templeton's ID of Claremont in her head. She couldn't dismiss the agitated certainty of it, but something about it wasn't right. It didn't add up—but what was it that didn't add up?

CHAPTER TWENTY

His interest in the insides had started young. When he was seven a cat had made a mad dash in front of traffic and been run over. One eye had burst out several inches from its crushed skull, and the seeing part—a dark, perfect disk—had glistened in a way that intrigued him. He had thought about that cat, and that black shiny orb, for weeks, maybe months, and that was when he'd realized he was different. Special. He could see and appreciate things that ordinary people just didn't notice or understand.

He got out to fill the gas tank. He ached from losing touch with these latest ones. They'd been fast—worthy prey—and luck hadn't been with him. He figured they'd have tattled to someone at home by now, and he berated himself for his failures. Slowly, purposefully, he jabbed the tip of the well-honed number-six paring knife through his pants pocket and into his thigh.

The man gave the gas station attendant a rumpled twenty. Across the street a red, white, and blue banner hung above a hardware store, advertising that a weeklong Labor Day sale was still going on. He remembered that he was running low on supplies. He cruised the narrow aisles, past bins of number ten nails and quarter-inch, half-inch, and inch-long stainless screws to where the nylon and more expensive boar-bristle paintbrushes hung on hooks. He collected a half dozen of the nylon ones with broad heads good for staining barn siding and selected a three-pack of putty spatulas that would come in handy for edge work and trim.

"Help you with anything, sir?" A friendly store clerk approached him from behind.

He handed the brushes and putty knives to the clerk and gave the man an affable smile. "Need two cases of the extra-large canning jars, twenty-eight ounce, if you have any," he said, adding, "Mom's doing a big job today."

The clerk returned from the storage room and placed two cartons beside the cash register.

"Will that be it then?"

"That'll be it."

He left in a hurry with the painting equipment and jars. It took him three more hours' steady driving, staying off the major highways and interstates, to reach the industrial squalor where he had grown up among the smokestacks and pipelines.

Delphos was cloaked in the afternoon haze of an early fall heat wave. He passed the rusted-out hulk of the old battery plant where his mother had been laid off four years earlier. He drove by the facades of abandoned businesses and turned onto Second Avenue. There was no traffic here, only smashed-out storefronts, establishments ravaged when the economic tide had shifted overseas to Asia a decade ago.

At the corner stood a large billboard featuring an architectural rendering. The old neighborhood would soon be razed to make way for a mammoth inner-city multilevel mall complete with a waterfall and pond with real ducks and full-size trees growing inside a large atrium. All that money—a contractor's wet dream of pouring fresh concrete by the hundred yard, drawing South Shore spenders to stroll and shop in his old stomping ground. Imagine that. No-man's-land on the outskirts of Chicago was about to get a makeover.

Abandoned and in shambles though it was, the familiarity of the old neighborhood block brought him comfort. He closed his eyes for a beat. Felt himself as a boy kicking rocks into storm drains, running an errand at Wallacker's Meat Market for his mother. In the months since his encounter with the young hitchhiker by the Little Calumet he'd begun returning to the condemned walk-up. A gas stove in an upstairs apartment had been left connected, allowing him to properly boil and can as his mother had done. Stock a good supply for the harder times when luck was against him and the anguish grew too enormous to cope with.

The choppy surface of the creek came in and out of view between the boarded-up buildings. It passed under the street and dumped into the Little Calumet River. He pulled over near a burned-out storefront and idled the truck. He squeezed the charm stone around his neck, but it wasn't enough to quell the losing feeling—an ache deep inside that stretched to infinity, shrinking him down to the size of a dust particle.

He shifted the truck into first gear and pulled away from the curb. His mind raced. Each rotation of the truck's wheels brought him closer to home, closer to the sting of his mother's heavily accented voice, closer to the ridicule that had once kept him sitting up all night in the wooden chair in his room, waking to the sound of his own dripping. But at least not another wet bed. As a boy, he used to ride city buses with his mother. Once, in broad daylight, he had soaked himself and her dress in a tepid puddle. She'd cursed him right then and there in front of the other passengers. Exclaimed out loud that he'd soiled himself deliberately, then squeezed his hand too tight in hers and tugged him off the noisy public transport two stops early. He'd left a trail of drips along the center aisle of the bus.

When they'd gotten home and she'd said, "Take your penance," he'd obeyed her and opened his mouth, as he always did. As solemn as a Catholic receiving Communion, he'd received his stone, swallowing hard to get down the lumpy piece of gravel she'd collected from the back lot. There was an endless supply of the painful stones to match his endless accidents.

Without signaling, he cut down an alley and parked the pickup in the back gravel lot of the boarded-up tenement. Quickly he entered the old building. Upstairs, he shoved open the small half door inside the kitchen and climbed the steep, narrow flight that led to the rooftop of the condemned building. In pitch darkness he brushed aside the loose chains he'd cut months before and swung open the fire door, wincing from the dazzle of the bright sunlight. Old roofing tar bubbled in the superheated air. The heat was bracing.

A moment later he retreated inside the stuffy top story, blinking until his eyes adjusted and he could make out the murky shapes in the small, dingy room that had been his since he was a boy. Entering, he inhaled the familiar dank odors. For a moment everything lay still in his head. He hunkered on the edge of the old stained mattress, gently bobbed up and down to comfort himself, and then donned the feather mask that was tucked inside his shirt.

A free ticket his mother had given him to the Museum of Natural History just before her death had changed things forever. Given new meaning to his fascination with the insides of living things. On the second floor of the vast cool building, an outrigger canoe hung suspended above a darkened passageway, heralding the Oceania exhibit room. In a large display case decorated with a jungle leaf motif, a row of carved stone figurines gleamed under the spotlights. The lights cast upon one of the stones produced a magnificent apple-green glow—as if the precious relic were endowed with a powerful light source of its own. Beneath the jewellike objects he read the words: *After eating the internal organs of the killed, the fierce New Guinea Highland clan would deposit charm stones into their victims' bodies.*

Sounding out the words had raised the hairs on the nape of his neck. Never mind where his mother had learned to feed him stones from. Those hard lumps of back lot gravel she'd made him scrape down his own throat finally made sense standing in front of the museum exhibit: stones were meant to be placed inside people after killing them.

The write-up next to the exhibit was full of anthropological observations and theories about religion and ritual symbolism that did not inspire. Whatever the particular significance to Papuan highlanders of placing carved stones inside the dead in honor of ancestral spirits was lost on him. Only the first words he'd read held true magic—this charm stone collection had sailed across the Pacific Ocean for him to see. Feather-masked human-eaters of the Papuan rain forests had given him his instructions. He had thought it was time to get the stones back inside where they belonged.

Yesterday, while paying a clerk for gas, an overhead TV broadcasting a report caught his attention. It had showed that pretty female agent's face as the reporter described a forested location where the body of the amusement-park girl had been found. It was the same lady agent who'd fumbled so badly at the museum opening he'd made his way into—the one who'd been unable to speak and had rushed out of the exhibit room ceremony. He knew why. It had been the same for him the first time he'd seen the stone. Its power had silenced him, too. The thought of the secret they shared made him feel warm inside.

On the news report, the agent had described finding the body of Julie Heath, the turtle girl, similarly situated at the bottom of a ravine. This woman agent was good—what she'd said about him being a loner, traveling in an old truck, odd-jobbing, and maybe even living out of his truck. A regular smarty-pants she was, except she hadn't said anything about the charm stones he'd stolen from the museum. That still had her stumped, he bet. And not a word about his truck stop girl last spring. What a sweet experience that had been. Gazing blankly through the mask's eyeholes, he replayed in his head the young hitchhiker he'd encountered. She'd climbed down from the semi at the large lakeshore gas terminal and waved good-bye to the driver before slinging her duffel over her shoulder and sauntering off toward the dunes. Walking into the distance, she had been framed by the vibrant twilit sky.

A real museum piece. He grinned to himself. How wrong Mother had been to say no girl would have him if he wet the bed. What a beautiful evening it had been.

He lifted a small family portrait from a bookshelf. It was a five-by-seven snapshot in a cheap brass frame showing his then-young mother leaning against a railing with a woman friend. Each was holding a baby on a knee, mugging for the camera. He smudged his forefinger back and forth over the picture glass between the two infants and wondered vaguely what it would have been like to have had a brother, someone who could have stood up for him or taken the blame when necessary. Someone like him. Someone who appreciated the same things. Who could understand without him always having to explain.

He placed the portrait back on the shelf. A sluggish contentment leaned him back against the bed. For a moment the comfort of the familiar took hold of him as he inhaled a long, lazy lungful of the pungent air and closed his eyes. Sleep would come easily. It always did when he was happy.

* * *

Three hours after the positive identification of David Claremont, Jasper got in his pickup and headed south again. When he heard the special news report about the arrest, he pulled over to the side of the road and laughed out loud, pounding the steering wheel in pure pleasure. It was just too damn perfect. An innocent dumb-shit arrested for what he'd done. Maybe that lady agent wasn't so smart after all.

He decided to turn around and find a place where he could watch the events unfold, a store or any such place where they'd have a television babbling in the background. Five minutes later he pulled into a 7-Eleven, and sure enough, the clerk was watching the news. He didn't have to wait long before his story was on the air.

And then Jasper felt sick to his stomach. Rage started to bubble up inside him, and it was all he could do to back out of the store without drawing attention to himself. The clerk never even glanced up.

The resemblance had shaken him to his core. The baseball cap and sunglasses he'd fished out of the back of the truck and immediately put on couldn't change the fact that for the first time in his adult life, he felt vulnerable. Through no fault of his own he was in danger of being found out, and he was damn angry about it. It racked him, too, that the television picture would be as close as he would ever get to see the face that had taken the fall. Then a synaptic shock wave coursed through him. This David Claremont might somehow rat on him—unless he took matters into his own hands first.

* * *

Prusik was famished. McFaron had hoped that there'd be no annoying reporters with their poking mikes joining them at the Weaversville Chimney, and he was right. He chose a corner booth, and they ordered two glasses of Chianti and the spaghetti special. Walking to their table, Christine eyed a patron—a heavyset middle-aged man with steel-rim glasses—who was staring at her chest in an obvious way. The man winked at her as she passed by.

"Do men always see a woman sexually first?" she asked, instantly regretting the question.

"I guess." A distinct flush suffused McFaron's face. "I mean if you're attracted to someone, yes, it can be physical, at least at first. Why else would you care to go further?"

Prusik stifled a cry of exasperation. "Have you ever thought just maybe you might get to know someone first in the process of working together? Without the least intention of having an affair?"

"You asked me what a man sees first," he corrected, "not about working with a woman and developing feelings later. That happens every day. Friends of mine got married after meeting on the job and working together for a couple of years. It may sound crass, but a fine figure is pleasing, and I'm not ashamed to say it." McFaron took a swallow of his wine, his eyes briefly catching hers before he glanced down.

"Then why the blush?"

"I guess you kind of took me by surprise," McFaron said. "My mother always said I turned color easy. I guess she was right." He looked her in the eye and smiled.

"Must have something to hide, huh?" Prusik took a sip of the Chianti. It had bite.

"Must have." The back of McFaron's hand brushed against Christine's as they both reached for the garlic bread at the same time. A jolt of warmth suffused her body, and she looked away shyly.

"Honestly," he said, "I spend so much time running around by myself taking care of other people's problems that I hardly give my own a second thought." A hot streak shot up the sheriff's back. He hadn't said it right. "To tell the truth, Christine, this case has me pushing pretty hard. Everyone wanting to know whether we're zeroing in on the killer."

"Oh, really?" she grunted. "Well, I can't tell you how pleased I am with the way things are going." She took another sip of the wine, and several uncomfortable moments ticked by.

"Let's drop the shoptalk, shall we?" she said finally in a softer tone, resting her chin on folded hands.

"I like that idea."

They sat in silence while the waitress replenished their bread basket, and then Christine leaned forward. "I'll tell you something not many people know about me. Before I joined the bureau, Joe, I did something really fun. I had this summer job during college working at a children's zoo."

"A zoo?"

"An honest-to-goodness zoo. I operated this zoomobile: a great big van painted with black-and-white zebra stripes, specially outfitted with portable cages for carrying exotic animals. Two trainers assisted me in going around to schools and camps, letting kids pet the animals. The idea was to make the plight of endangered species more immediate and meaningful to the communities we visited." She grinned. "It was a blast."

"I never would have guessed you were an animal lover," McFaron said. "Thought all you city slickers were too sophisticated to handle livestock."

"No way. I loved it. In fact, it had direct implications for my current job."

McFaron's eyebrows rose. "Oh, this I've got to hear."

"You know that rolling road show of forensic science that Special Agent Howard is in charge of? My idea. Directly inspired by the zoomobile." She shrugged. "The only real difference between it and the mobile zoo is that the workings of the forensic RV aren't on display to the public."

"You amaze me, Christine."

Christine grinned again. "There was this spider monkey named Squeakums who used to hold on to me with his hands and feet and a prehensile tail curled around my upper arm. Anyway, Squeakums would purse his lips and let out this high-pitched howl, clinging to me so tightly I wouldn't have to hold on to him at all."

"I'd like to have seen that. Christine and her little Squeakums."

Christine threw her napkin at him. "It was hard, dirty work. But you know what? Even with all that sweat, I loved it. Seeing the children's excitement, hearing them giggle when Squeakums began his rutting call, clutching me."

Her cheeks felt warmed by the wine. "Sometimes I wonder why I even bother." She shook her head, frowning. "The real-world grind all seems a mistake when I listen to myself go on about that summer. At this moment I can honestly say I have never relished anything so much as those three months spent with the animals and children."

"You impress me with your talents, Christine," McFaron said softly.

"Do you know what I mean, though? All the dead things we do every day, Joe?"

"I hear what you're saying." He smiled wryly. "I started out at twenty-one, the youngest sheriff Crosshaven has ever known. But I haven't had a single regret since."

"Twenty-one?" Prusik said. "What about fun?"

"I take the fun with the not-so-fun right on the job, I guess. Mostly, staying busy keeps my head on straight. Too much time away from work and I get lost." The words had just slipped out.

Christine raised her eyebrows.

"In a manner of speaking," McFaron said.

"But you don't seem lost to me. What do you mean?"

"Alone, lost," the sheriff said, "what's the difference really?"

"To me it means more. To be lost you must know what it is to be found again," Prusik said with conviction.

He smiled. "Christine, foster mother of Squeakums *and* a great philosopher. What else are you? OK, let's try out 'lost.' I am found at work, and I feel lost without it if I'm idle for too long. I guess that suits me right."

"You guess that suits you right? Men!" She folded her arms against her chest. "Why can't you be a little less than totally opaque?"

"What, and have you women see right through us? No way."

They ate their food slowly and with pleasure. Finishing her second glass of wine, Christine gave Joe a long, slow smile, which ended in an even longer, slower yawn.

Joe smiled back at her. "Tomorrow's a big day," he said. "You'll need your rest for the Claremont interview."

She nodded. He looked away to signal the waitress for the bill, and when he looked back, she was waiting, already greeting him with her hazel eyes set on his.

"I really enjoyed our conversation," he said in a soft voice. "Getting to know about your love of animals, Christine, is… well…thank you for telling me about that."

After paying the bill, McFaron drove Prusik back to the rooming house she'd relocated to earlier, near the Weaversville Police Station. He walked her to the door. The street was quiet.

"Meet you in the morning?" he said. "A little before eight?"

Prusik nodded, then hesitated. "Joe? Thanks for the dinner," she said, "and for listening." Prusik put down her forensic case. "I mean, I really did enjoy myself, even if I was doing most of the talking. Truthfully, I can't remember the last time I shared a meal with someone without endlessly talking shop. Maybe we could do it again?"

"I'd like that very much, Christine. I enjoyed every minute of tonight. And we covered some good ground on the case today."

McFaron thought about the Sarah North interview in Parker that morning. How caring and supportive Christine had been, sitting in a chair beside the girl, leaning her head close. She had made it easy for the young witness to confide in her; the sheriff had seen that clearly. The sheriff also recalled his concentrating attention on Prusik's back. Under her beige high-collared shirt he could see the distinct outlines of her undergarment straps, her square shoulders, the smooth tiers of muscle that fanned down her sides. On the ride over from Crosshaven she'd told him how she would often work off tension from work swimming backstroke into the wee hours at a downtown Chicago health club. Most fit women McFaron knew were tiny in comparison, almost a subspecies compared to Christine's muscular form.

He removed his hat, rolled the brim between his fingers. He looked at her. "You're quite a person, Christine."

It contented her, hearing his awkward acknowledgment. His restrained manner reminded her of her father, and so had his willingness to help at the crime scene in Crosshaven. She placed a palm on his chest and stood on the balls of her feet. They kissed.

McFaron looked into her eyes from a few inches away, then kissed her again, pulling her close to him.

"What I said tonight, you know, about men and women." Prusik broke apart, suddenly self-conscious. She smiled unabashedly at the sheriff, seeing that he was in no rush to leave. "Well, anyway, don't pay attention to everything I say. That's all." She patted him on the chest affectionately, then picked up her case.

"See you at eight, Joe."

He replaced his hat and tipped his head her way. "I'll fetch you right here, Christine."

The residue of warm feeling lingered as she watched him slowly drive away in the Bronco, knowing he'd be waking very early tomorrow to make it on time to Weaversville from Crosshaven, a good seventy-five-mile drive. Why hadn't she invited him to stay with her? Because she was a professional, that's why, and she was working on a case.

And maybe she was just a little scared.

She walked up the stairs to the rooming house and hesitated at the front door, savoring the evening and the glow Joe seemed to light inside her. The sky was fading from a deep lapis, with just a few bright stars poking through. And then without warning the heavens blossomed out black and glinting, filled to their edges with a multitude of bright specks as though the sun itself had burst.

* * *

At midnight, the express bus from Chicago pulled up to the Greyhound terminal in downtown Indianapolis. Henrietta Curry descended its steps gratefully, exhausted at the late hour and relieved to be able to stretch her stiff legs at last. Muggy air laced with diesel fumes wafted into the waiting room as she entered through the automatic doors, carrying her suitcase and a cookie tin wedged beneath her arm. She'd missed the five o'clock bus and had had to take the nine o'clock one instead, getting her into Indianapolis at a time she was normally asleep in bed. But she'd promised her daughter that she'd be available for three days of babysitting starting first thing in the morning, and she didn't want to let her down. Being a working single mother was hard enough without having to worry about child care at the last minute.

An accidental bump into someone staring up at a large television monitor in the cavernous room caused Mrs. Curry to look up, too, just in time to see a report on the arrest of Claremont earlier that day for the murder of an Indiana schoolgirl. The old woman's suitcase thudded to the floor. The face of the arrested man on the screen was unmistakable. That very man had sat next to her on the bus from Chicago.

He's escaped!

Mrs. Curry hurried forward to see if she could spot the man who had turned down her homemade cookies without even a polite word. Her best recipe, too. She peered through the tops of her trifocals, trying to connect the face on the news with the man who'd brushed ahead of the women and children getting off the bus. It was him. She was absolutely certain. She pressed her way through a crowd of arriving passengers, completely forgetting her suitcase in the process. But there was no sign of the stranger in the baseball cap and brown farm coat.

"Hey, lady." A redcap tapped Mrs. Curry's shoulder, making her jump. "This your bag?" The uniformed black man had silvery sideburns and wore a red captain's hat. He held the suitcase forward.

"Why, yes." She closed her eyes for a second. "I must be losing my head." She felt in her purse and handed him a dollar bill. "Thank you."

"Thank you, ma'am." The redcap tipped the glossy brim of his hat. As he turned to leave, Mrs. Curry tugged at his sleeve.

"Listen." She stepped closer. "I think that man wanted for killing all those girls has escaped. He was riding next to me on the bus from Chicago." She pointed through the waiting-room window at the TV screen, which still displayed Claremont's face.

Mrs. Curry pulled a crisp twenty out of her purse and pinched it between her fingers. "He got off the bus not five minutes ago. He couldn't have gone far. Help me find him. Check the street. Come back when you spot him. I'll keep my eyes open in here." She flashed the money. "Spot him and this is yours."

The redcap smiled, looking confused. He squinted at the monitor to get a clearer view just as Claremont's face faded and a young punk squirting cola down his throat appeared. The redcap glanced back at the twenty still clutched in the woman's hand, then bolted outdoors and went to work, shading one hand over his eyes, scanning up and down the street. Ten minutes later he found Mrs. Curry in the waiting room and reported that unfortunately the man seemed to have disappeared.

Mrs. Curry thanked him and handed him the cookie tin. "Here, take this for your trouble. It's my best recipe. I'm going to call the police. I know what I saw."

She lugged her suitcase over to a row of phone booths against one wall and called her daughter. It was nearly twelve thirty when she finally got through to Indianapolis Police Headquarters. Obstinacy with a dash of well-placed kindness eventually got her patched through to a local FBI representative. Mrs. Curry's description of her seatmate's features was detailed and thorough, as was her account of how he had refused her cookies so rudely. She was certain he was the same person she'd seen on TV.

She gave the agent her name and her daughter's home telephone number. And she didn't leave out the detail about the sweet girl sitting across the aisle and one row back. At one point Mrs.

Curry had looked up in time to catch the man next to her turned around in his seat, eyes locked on the child. One mean stare—ten seconds' worth of pernicious concentration—had made that poor young thing gag.

CHAPTER TWENTY-ONE

Christine shifted in her seat. The air-conditioning in the small interview room was barely functioning, and she was sweating before they'd even started. She had discussed with Bruce Howard the merits of her conducting the interview rather than Bruce. They had learned from talking with the suspect's parents that he had a more difficult relationship with his mother. Christine thought there may be an opportunity to possibly provoke a confession out of Claremont if she interviewed the man. Howard agreed.

Claremont's eyes were deep set, as Joey Templeton had reported. She noted the zygomatic arch—the bone running from the lower eye socket and cheek prominence back to the temple—was more pronounced than normal. His browridge overhung the apex of the oculus, making it difficult to see the man's eye movements and producing an uncomfortable sensation in Prusik.

She met Claremont's gaze and gave him a brief nod. No time like the present. "I'm a physical anthropologist by training. Do you know what that is, David?"

"You study bones, right?"

"Very good. The two hundred and six bones that compose the human anatomy, to be precise."

Claremont nodded.

"As a forensic anthropologist I examine victims of violent crimes. You say you're innocent. Would you consent to a blood test?"

"What's my blood got to do with it?" He looked her straight in the eye without flinching. "I told you already. I've done nothing." Said believably enough, but a calculating mind would practice until perfecting the look of innocence. A psychopath, on the other hand, could lie convincingly the very first try without as much as a flinch.

"Then you've got nothing to hide, have you? A DNA test would clear you of all suspicion." Assuming they were lucky enough to find some of the killer's DNA on a victim or at a crime scene to cross-match against, she thought. "Isn't that what you want? To be exonerated? With a clean blood test you'd be free to go." She searched his face. "Wouldn't you like to go home, David? Clear your name? Put all this behind you?"

"How do I know you're telling the truth?" He wrung his hands under the table.

"Fair question. We're after the killer. If your DNA clears you, it means the real killer is still out there and will go on killing." Prusik looked for any sign of hostile movement, observing nothing more than the expected wariness. "We're not looking to pin something on you that you didn't do."

Claremont lowered his right hand to the tabletop. She removed a small puncture blade from its antiseptic seal and extended her hand toward his.

"A skin prick and two drops of blood on this special cardboard and we'll be all set."

Prusik firmly gripped the suspect's index finger, harpooned the tip, and touched the deep-red bubble twice to the rectangular test pad. Claremont withdrew his hand.

"Would you like a Band-Aid?"

He shook his head. The man's face muscles tightened around the bony protrusions of his browridges. If sculpted from stone, Claremont's visage would have represented midstage in the carving, needing many more refining rubs to smooth out its exaggerated appearance.

Prusik noticed some adhesive tape covering the outside of his left palm. "Hurt yourself?" She nodded toward his hand.

Claremont slipped it beneath the table and shot her a steely look. "Not what you're thinking." The tendons in his forearms tensed, pressing against the table's edge.

"What am I supposed to be thinking?"

"I've done nothing wrong!" he said. "This is all a mistake."

Prusik nodded. "That's what we're hoping the DNA will show. Now show me your hand, David."

He slowly pulled back the tape, wincing, and revealed a nasty human bite mark—unmistakable and recent. Prusik swallowed hard. Her rational mind could frame the question, but deep inside, a voice was shouting for her to get out of the room.

"How'd that happen?"

"I...I don't know exactly." Claremont's voice faltered. His agitation seemed genuine enough.

"I would like your permission to take a bite impression of your teeth."

He obliged her without having to be asked a second time. She unzipped the forensic pouch around her waist and removed stainless-steel calipers, thinking how Brian Eisen would compare Claremont's uppers and lowers with the digital postmortem photographs of the teeth marks on Betsy Ryan's shoulder, close-ups he'd enhanced using the Lucis software.

Prusik went to Claremont's side of the table and asked him to display his teeth. His hot exhalations against the back of her hand triggered another uncomfortable wave of anxiety. She couldn't stop the pulsation emanating from deep within her amygdala—the primitive seed in her brain, the animal part she couldn't control, and the problem area researchers had successfully isolated as the main source of debilitating fear and panic reactions. She rested her hand on the table edge and waited for the moment to pass.

"Sorry," she said. Regaining her composure, she said, "Let's try that again. Open wide, like you do when the dentist cleans your teeth." She measured the gap between his eyeteeth on the upper jaw, then applied the calipers between the lower canines. She then measured the clear eyetooth punctures on his hand—it was a perfect match, meaning the wound had been self-inflicted.

Prusik removed some blue molding adhesive from its airtight package and pressed it firmly against his uppers, carefully repeating the procedure for the lower dentition. She would compare the impression with the Ryan victim bite mark.

"Why'd you bite yourself?"

"I...I can't remember."

Prusik didn't press the point. She removed a yellow legal pad from her briefcase. "Let's talk about your daily routines, shall we?" Abruptly changing gears was a questioning strategy she preferred, believing it prevented a suspect from having time enough to fabricate answers. "Give me a sense of your workweek, how you spend the hours of each day. How much time do you spend on the farm?"

"Most days, I guess." He shrugged. "On and around the property."

"Dawn-to-dusk hard work?"

"Here and there, running errands mostly." He studied the top of the table.

"According to your father, the bottomland is leased out to a neighbor who works it. He says you hardly do any chores at all on the place other than hang out in the barn a lot."

David's upper lip was beginning to shine. "Not true. I stained the neighbor's barn. I did the whole thing myself."

Christine flashed on the paint fragment evidence. "What sort of errands do you run?"

"In town, up to the farmers' co-op, getting more stain, groceries, things like that."

"The farmers' co-op. I heard about some trouble you had there recently, attacking some woman in the parking lot?"

"No! I didn't attack her. I carried a roll of wire out to her car for her. It was heavy, and I...I..."

"You thought she owed you something for your trouble?"

"No! I was helping her. She...she didn't press charges. She knew I didn't mean her any harm. She knew. I don't even remember exactly what happened," he concluded softly, defeated somehow.

Prusik nodded and switched directions again abruptly. "Your mother said this spring and summer you took a bus to Chicago twice without saying a word about where you were going." She took out a large gray file from her forensic case. Dr. Irwin Walstein had dropped it off at the police station at her request.

Claremont's leg began to wiggle.

"That's a pretty strange thing to do. Chicago's a long way off. What were you doing there? Did you meet anyone?"

"Getting hobby supplies mostly."

"What sort of hobby is that?"

"Carving. I like to carve things."

Christine swallowed hard and looked down, pretending to consult her notes. She let a moment pass, then looked up again. "How come you didn't tell your parents you were going? Your mother was very upset about it, David."

"Don't know. I just didn't."

"So when did you take the bus to Chicago?"

"I'm not sure. I think it was in March."

"And the second time, when was that?"

He shrugged, looked down at his lap. "Might have been two weeks or so ago, I'm not sure." The dull slapping thud of his knees increased.

Perhaps he had stashed a vehicle in the Chicago area; keeping it away from home would have been smart planning. But not telling his parents and being gone for nearly twelve hours on each occasion was plain stupid. Surely they'd worry. They might even have called the police, searching for him. Unless, of course, they hadn't, to cover for him, to protect him, assuming they knew something far worse. Yet when Prusik had briefly met with Claremont's parents before the interview, neither had impressed her as being capable of the kind of behavior necessary to protect a lawbreaking son, nor did they seem like the kind of people who would be able and willing to conceal evidence of horrifying crimes.

Prusik had confirmed with the Weaversville police what both David's parents had said—he did spend most days, including weekends, around the farm, keeping to himself. He was kind of a homebody. And he didn't usually venture by himself much farther than the farmers' co-op. Except for these secret adventures to Chicago.

One thing that surprised Prusik was the quality of Claremont's responses. His short denials belied the impression she'd gotten from Dr. Walstein—that David behaved fearfully. The doctor's file notes disclosed that he frequently displayed a helpless attitude toward his disabling visionary attacks—hardly befitting the profile of a confident and efficient killer.

"Tell me what you like to carve, David."

"Animals, figures, anything that comes to mind." He rubbed a hand over his short-cropped hair. "They're at home. You'll see them, if you haven't already."

"By any chance, did you visit our fine natural history museum while you were on one of your jaunts to Chicago? The Museum of Natural History?"

Prusik felt the table shake from David's vibrating leg. But he wouldn't answer the question.

"Ever experience blackouts before, David? Hear voices in your head? Have an upsetting vision that seems real as life? A person screaming, a bad dream?"

Prusik presented the facts that had been written down in the psychiatrist's file as questions, piling them up, pushing him toward the edge of toleration, which wasn't nearly so invisible now as it had been earlier.

His brow furrowed. "You're working with Dr. Walstein?" He lifted his head, focused on the documents open in front of the forensic anthropologist. "That's whose file that is?"

"Yes, I've read your medical files. We subpoenaed them. It's my job as a forensic investigator to be thorough, David. Tell me about these visions of screaming girls. According to your file, they started last March?"

"Then you already know everything." He scowled. "What's the point in asking?"

Prusik steeled herself—the time bomb inside David Claremont was fused to go off at any moment. She knew all too well that world of out-of-control, pile-driving fear. Easing, she changed her tack.

"You don't know what's happening to you when a vision strikes?"

"There's a difference, you know, between seeing things and doing them," he said forcefully. "They're not the same thing at all."

Prusik nodded, sympathizing. "You're right. There is a big difference."

She slid a blank piece of paper and a pencil across the table. "Do me a favor, David. Write down your name."

He picked up the pencil with his hurt left hand and printed out each letter.

"This time I'd like you to try writing cursive, in long hand," she urged. "Using your right hand."

Claremont put down the pencil. "Can't write that way."

"Some people are naturally ambidextrous," Prusik said. "Maybe you're one."

The pencil clumsily popped out of his right hand twice. Breaking off the pencil point, he scratched a hole in the paper. The muscles tightened around his jaw. He cast a despondent gaze down at his lap.

Claremont was most definitely a lefty. From the forensic evidence the killer was clearly right-handed. And the implication was just as clear to Prusik. Claremont was not the man responsible. But she could not dismiss the possibility that he was somehow involved, either.

"Ever give someone a ride in your truck, David? While out running errands?"

"Might have once or twice."

"A girl, for instance? Ever offer a ride to a girl walking home?"

He bowed his head. "I…I don't really know any girls."

He sat stiffly. The sound of knuckles cracking under the table confused Prusik. So many of Claremont's nuances and behaviors ran counter to his seeming helplessness, as if the man was a battleground for good and evil and the winner hadn't yet been declared.

"You'd remember taking a girl somewhere, wouldn't you?"

He looked her straight in the eye, desperate. "You want me to say it, don't you? That I'm the one you're after?" He tapped his temple with a sardonic grin. "A damn killer's trapped in my mind is what." His face became somber. "You think asking questions is going to help any? It's not going to change one thing, no matter what I say. The way people always look at me twice. Their eyes say it, their frowns. They see something's not right. Like I should have been the one born dead."

Prusik wrinkled her brow. "Why would you say that?"

Claremont continued staring somewhere past the far corner of the room. "Could I have been born dead? That would explain it, all the things I see. Coming back from the dead, they say you remember seeing things."

Concerned, Prusik reached out her hand, touching the top of his. It felt clammy and tense.

"I read about it once," he continued, in a more animated frame of mind, "the way people can come back from awful experiences, from drowning, car accidents. When their hearts stop." His face eased noticeably. "Seeing themselves all torn up from far above their bodies, like they're in two places at once."

"Is that what you feel, David, in two places at once?"

"Seeing them lying there on the ground…all cut up." He hung his head, defeated again.

"Covered in your blood, David, or someone else's?"

He flicked his hand away from hers, as if electrically charged. He scrubbed his fingers across his crew cut again, his biceps bulging noticeably under his shirt.

"Car-accident scenes are different, aren't they?" Prusik said, playing along with his idea. "You look down. You see yourself, maybe another passenger who was with you in the crash. But the action's stopped, hasn't it? It's over, except for seeing the mangled body down there, and you looking down from above…"

She needn't have repeated his words; he was already there.

"Right, right! So does that make me a killer? Seeing it? Hearing it?" He crossed his arms and gripped his biceps, his fingers white with tension.

"Your visions are pretty upsetting," Prusik said sympathetically.

What Claremont had said a moment ago—that he should have been the one born dead—intrigued her. As had his reference to being in two places at once. Both were said reflexively and sounded truthful. Prusik returned to Dr. Walstein's file, reviewing one paragraph she'd earlier marked off in which the psychiatrist had summarized his comments: "The patient shows remarkable recall for certain events that take place during his blackout periods in the wakeful moments afterward. Descriptions include that of a girl's face, identifying clothing, seeing her running and screaming and falling down in the woods, then being butchered."

"I understand you've put a name to it?"

His gaze narrowed on the file lying open in front of her. "So what if I have?"

"That you call this man in your visions a two-face?"

"Is that a crime?"

"Anyone you know ever double-cross you before?"

"Not really."

"Oh come on, David. No one's life is that perfect. Maybe someone you knew in high school? Someone you ran into while you were out running an errand? Or when you went up to Chicago?" she needled. "Someone you don't like very much and would rather not speak openly about? People who hurt us, David, we don't usually like to talk about."

His eyes widened, and something stirred behind his lids. "I don't know. I suppose it's a common enough thing not being able to trust people."

Prusik sensed he was hedging. "Could this two-face be a relative?" she continued. "Someone who might have dropped by the farm infrequently, someone you might not have seen since you were much younger? A distant cousin even?"

Claremont gazed blankly at the table. "Can't say exactly where he comes from. But he's there all right." He swallowed hard and tapped his sternum when he did. "Right there inside."

"So you do know him."

"I…I can't"—he massaged his throat—"stop him."

Prusik thought she detected the dilation of his pupils, but wasn't sure.

"Look, David, things will only get worse from here on out. A search warrant has already been issued. The field unit will tear up every board in that barn if they have to. They'll take apart the seats and bed of your truck, and your parents' truck, too. They'll go through your room and the rest of the house with a fine-tooth comb. As soon as they find evidence—and a single strand of hair is all it will take—linking you to Julie Heath or any of the other victims, your case will be transferred to the US attorney's office in Chicago for federal prosecution. Cooperate with me, talk to me, and I'll see what I can do to help you."

"I told you. I've done nothing wrong," David said, his face agonized. "There is no evidence. There can't be. Except for my blanking out, seeing things…"

"And I *do* believe you." It surprised Prusik, hearing her own conviction. "But an eyewitness puts you at the scene of Julie Heath's abduction in Crosshaven."

Prusik tapped the tip of her forefinger on the center of the tabletop. "Another witness from Parker claims two days ago you followed her in your truck after her soccer practice. She described the gray fender paint, said you scared the living daylights out of her. I want to help you, David. But to do it, I'll need your complete cooperation."

She played the hunch she'd been considering since Claremont's puzzling revelation about feeling that he was in two places at once. "If you're innocent—and I believe you are—it means someone else out there who looks like you is committing these crimes. Someone who's probably laughing right now seeing it all pinned on some fool named David."

He blinked. "Nobody could have seen me in Crosshaven, because I wasn't there. I wasn't in Parker, either, unless I was passing through with my parents. It couldn't be my truck they saw. It's a mistake, I tell you." Claremont's eyes implored her. "What you were saying before…"

"About your visions?" she said. "Seeing him, this two-face of a man?" She sensed the depth of the man's despair, felt she could almost follow the neuronal pathway to the very source of his pain.

"Things have been getting worse." Claremont rotated his hurt hand in front of his face, staring at it as if it weren't his own flesh. A bead of sweat raced down his cheek.

"Tell me." Prusik's voice was calm, soothing. "What other bad things does he do to you?"

"It's not a dream, is it? It's too real to be. Oh God," Claremont moaned.

Prusik shoved another notepad across the table. "Write it all down for me, David. Everything you can recall about him, about the visions, what he does to the girls, when he does it. Locations, ones that may be familiar to you—it's crucial that I know every detail if I am to help you."

Claremont flattened his palms on the tabletop, surrendering. "Do you think I'm crazy?" On his weary face was the look of a man who very much cared.

"Sometimes we're our own worst enemy, David. But my opinion won't save you now. Give me something to go on, and then we'll see." Prusik pointed to the pad. "Try to remember every detail. Even ones that don't seem important could be key."

Prusik checked herself, wondering if Claremont's visions could be explained by a psyche trying to exonerate itself, externalizing the horror, placing blame on a construct, some fantasized other, this "two-face" manifestation. She'd discuss it further back at headquarters with Dr. Katz in behavioral sciences.

"Let's end here, David," she said. "You write everything down for me, just like I've asked, and we'll talk again soon."

CHAPTER TWENTY-TWO

She slipped out the door and crossed into the ten-degrees-cooler hallway, then took her time making her way to the front of the police station and the parking lot beyond. The muggy southern Indiana air seemed to seep through her clothing right into her skin. Two news trucks with satellite dishes had already staked out claims along the chain-link fencing; technicians were setting up cameras for their respective news teams.

The FBI's RV was idling inside the station lot, Howard's men milling beside it. Howard himself stood among a gathering of state troopers, looking ready for the television cameras in his navy-blue Windbreaker and trim khaki twills. He was yukking it up with some of the troopers, enjoying himself immensely. Jocular laughter erupted from the group—in response to some male chauvinist remark by Howard no doubt, Prusik thought sourly. The man's cells didn't contain enough DNA to respect a woman, much less a woman who happened to be a scientist.

She leaned one hand on her hip, assessing things from the top of the steps. She could imagine Thorne cooling the champagne, Howard getting ready to pull the cork after she'd just finished serving up Claremont on a platter, delivering everything but a complete confession. Judging from Howard's cockiness, the lack of a confession hardly seemed to matter. But the niggling thought that wouldn't leave her—that Claremont was just another victim who somehow held the key to the killer's identity—was getting stronger and stronger.

The killer was right-handed, she was sure. The strangulation had been performed face-to-face in each case. The killer's right hand was far stronger than his left and had crushed the hyoid bone under the larynx in all three murders. Claremont was a natural lefty. The ease with which he'd signed his name with his left hand proved it—physical evidence that further buttressed her growing suspicions that the killer was somehow exploiting David Claremont, tormenting the man. As fantastic as it sounded, no other explanation fit, in her estimation. If she shared her suspicions with either Howard or Thorne it would finish her as far as this investigation was concerned. She needed time to corroborate, but investigating potential leads would take her away from the lab, and she'd have to be careful or she'd risk infuriating her two direct supervisors, who'd see her actions as hostile insubordination or worse.

"Christine?" Howard pulled his sunglasses partway down the bridge of his nose and motioned for her to approach. "Have you got a moment?" The troopers dispersed.

Prusik walked toward Howard, stopped halfway, and put down her case. She tried to keep her expression neutral.

Howard sauntered over. "Finish up with Claremont then?" he said, repositioning his aviator glasses higher up on his nose. "Your assessment was correct. You certainly were the right person for the job."

"Who said anything about finishing up?" she said levelly. "I'm heading home to Chicago, assuming you still want me to chase down forensics on the suspect we're questioning."

"Suspect? Come on, wasn't that a full confession? Pretty clearly he had no rational response to half your questions."

She picked up her bag. If Howard thought that was a full confession, he was more of a dimwit than she thought. "Yes, his answers were puzzling, I'll grant you. But be that as it may, he doesn't fit at all the profile we've developed of our killer. And he's left-handed, while our killer is clearly right-handed."

"Well, be that as it may, profiling has its limits. As for handed-ness, there are ways for a clever killer to disguise that. We're damn better off having Claremont on ice while we sort out the evidence," Howard said. "See that you report any findings—incriminating or exculpatory—to me when you're done." The corners of his mouth turned up just slightly and he gave her shoulder a little pat. "Nice work, Christine."

She brushed past him, banging the forensic case against his right leg, and headed straight toward the Bronco.

Waiting for McFaron in the truck, she reviewed her notes of the interview. The cell phone trilled in her jacket pocket. "Special Agent Prusik."

"Congratulations, Christine!" Thorne sounded thrilled. "I understand from Howard that the Claremont arrest is a clean wrap."

"Not quite, sir. Yes, he's been arrested, and he's in police cus-tody. I've conducted a preliminary interview. Mr. Howard's men are in the process of searching the farmstead for incriminating evidence. I don't really think it's a done deal."

"You're too modest, Christine. Congratulations *are* in order. In fact, I've already notified Washington of the killer's arrest."

"Isn't that a little premature, sir? I'm certain that the killer is right-handed, and David Claremont is a natural lefty. That's one thing, and another thing is that—"

"I'm confident Howard will gather whatever we need to make it stick," Thorne said, cutting her off. "Good going to you. And you see?" Thorne continued without pausing for breath. "It's all worked out fine. Looking forward to seeing you tomorrow and reading your full report or a synopsis at least." He clicked off.

Prusik eyed Howard through the windshield of the Bronco. He was facing her, but she couldn't tell if he was watching her or not, thanks to the aviator glasses.

McFaron opened the driver's side door, startling her.

"Where have you been?" she snapped.

He looked at her, puzzled. "I had a call to make. What's eating you?"

"I'm sorry." She closed her eyes and groaned, massaging her temples. "Please excuse me. Can we just leave?"

McFaron scanned the parking lot, saw Howard laughing with the troopers, and guessed what was bugging her. He pulled out of the lot without another word.

A few blocks from the police station she breathed easier. She studied Joe as he drove in silence and was taken by surprise at the depth of gratitude and appreciation she felt welling up inside her.

"I'm sorry, Joe. It's not your fault."

McFaron was silent as they passed an old stand of oak trees lining the road; the tops of their roots broke through the edges of the asphalt surface.

"I need to go to the airport. But I hate leaving before things feel right with this case."

He grunted.

Christine squeezed his shoulder. "And before things feel right with us, too. Now I've gone and offended you, and all you've done is help me. Really, I'm truly sorry, Joe, for lashing out like that. I didn't mean it." Prusik nudged him with an elbow. "Hey, don't go all quiet on me." She leaned over and kissed his cheek, then drew herself closer to the sheriff and rested her head on his shoulder.

McFaron pulled over and cut the engine. He kissed the top of her head and then her forehead and finally her lips. Like magic, he broke into a wonderful grin. "See, I'm not going quiet on you. I was just thinking. What do you make of Claremont's accusation?"

"Well, aren't you the romantic one?" She couldn't help but grin back. "But what accusation are you talking about?"

"Claremont's blaming it all on this other guy in his head. I don't buy it one bit."

Christine sat up straight in her seat. "The mind is a hard thing to judge, Sheriff, especially when it's under extraordinary pressure."

"So he's got a guilty conscience, right?"

"Of course, that could be true. That might explain it. It's why I hammered away at him so much." She gazed out her side window. "To be honest, I'm not at all sure what's happening with Claremont. If this were the first time he had mentioned this alter-ego maniac I might agree with what you say. But it isn't. Dr. Walstein's file is filled with disabling visions and incidents Claremont has experienced and reported on in great detail. There are at least three separate entries, distinguishing events, and we've found three bodies."

"Couldn't that be just as easily explained as a sick mind's way of crying out for help? A way of confessing?"

"It could be. But I think it's a little more intricate than that. And this business about going to Chicago—it's truly remarkable timing, bewildering really, when you consider he's a virtual recluse, rarely setting foot off his parents' property. OK, yes, he did say he painted his neighbor's barn. And we confirmed that he did. These mysterious jaunts to Chicago aside, he usually tells them where and when he's going and returns when he says he will."

She maneuvered one of the air-conditioner vents to blow coolness directly into her face. It felt good against her hot skin.

"Howard's men should be able to help clear the air." He glanced over at her. "No offense. And I don't mean to suggest that what you're saying isn't—"

"None taken. Believe me, I'm resigned to the fact that I was never cut out for management. Thorne was right to take the lead away from me."

"I disagree."

Christine mustered a smile for him. Right or wrong, Thorne's decision hurt. And his praise now was ill founded and disorienting. And just when she was getting to like the sheriff, she was having to go back to Chicago, which depressed her. He was a good man, McFaron. Solid. Trustworthy. He wasn't full of himself, like so many of her FBI colleagues were. She often wondered if that was a job prerequisite for male FBI agents—being full of themselves.

She sighed. She wanted to stay, to get to know this lanky, unprepossessing law enforcement officer a little better, but right now her responsibilities lay in Chicago.

* * *

At the small commuter terminal Christine climbed out of the Bronco with her gear, shuffled around to the sheriff's side window, and leaned through, the sun cooking her shoulders from high overhead.

"Look," she said, "it's been a whirlwind few days."

Before she could get another word in, he kissed her, cradling the back of her head in his left hand. She let her bags drop on the sidewalk and kissed him back.

"I don't really want to leave, Joe. I confess it." She studied his brown eyes with her own hazel ones. "I can't tell you how much I've valued exchanging ideas with you. And I had such a great time at dinner last night."

A cab pulled in front of the Bronco. People got out, talking loudly.

"The pleasure was mine, Christine." The edges of his top teeth showed in a broadening smile. "I think you know that. And I don't want you to leave, either. I would like to stay in touch, and not just about the case."

Her heart quickened, hearing him say that. She leaned her head farther inside his window to escape the sidewalk chatter. Feeling more confident, she said, "You know, Sheriff, I'm not always the bitch you may think I am."

"Never felt you were really, Special Agent." He cleared his throat awkwardly. Even in broad sunlight she could see the growing flush descend from his cheeks down his throat. "I mean Christine."

"Well, anyway, I was wondering about my invitation."

"Invitation?" He looked at her, puzzled. "Oh, you mean having dinner together again?"

"Never mind. I just thought if you were ever coming to Chicago…it's no big deal." She moved to pick up her forensic case.

Gently he tugged on her forearm, still resting on the windowsill. "I meant what I said—I'd like that a lot." He didn't blink when he spoke but looked straight into her eyes. "Just tell me when, and I'll be there."

"You'll really fly up?"

"You mean now?" His voice went up an octave.

She laughed and bumped her forehead against the top of the window frame.

"Well, maybe not *right* now." She shook her hair out of her face, feeling a blush coming on. "Maybe soon?"

"Now look who's turning color." He laughed. "Aside from spending all my waking hours on this case, my calendar's pretty much clear to go."

"Ever try Ethiopian cuisine?" she said, her mind humming.

"Shermie Dutcher always serves up Ethiopian on Thursdays, didn't I tell you?"

"I'll reserve a table at Ashanti's," she said, laughing. "Just let me know for when." The warmth of his hand, which still rested on her sleeve, radiated up her forearm. She made no effort to leave; she allowed herself to bask in the pleasurable sensations that were suffusing her body.

"I'll pick up the tab. Even show you a little of the town, Joe." She thought of the chaotic piles in her small apartment. She'd have to neaten it up, make it inviting. When would she have time to? She'd make time.

"Sounds like too good a deal to pass up. I'd like that very much, Christine."

She shifted her stance, not wanting the moment to end, not knowing what else to say. The awkward small talk between them was inconsequential; her heart knew otherwise. So did her kisses. And his. She would have said yes had he offered to drive her back to Chicago. Privately she wished he would, knowing full well his duties as sheriff would prevent it.

"Consider it a done deal then," he said, his face only inches from hers, drifting closer. "I'll give you a call," he said, softly as a whisper.

"OK then." They kissed one last time. Christine leaned down and picked up her cases.

"Have a safe flight," McFaron shouted after her before she disappeared through the terminal's automatic glass doors. She turned and waved back at him. He didn't drive away until she was past the security gate and out of his sight.

* * *

Later that same afternoon, Prusik topped off the gas. She'd driven the maroon sedan from the West Street garage that served her office building an hour east to the Portage, Indiana, truck stop where Betsy Ryan had last been seen alive. A cold wind whisked off the lake, tumbling loose trash across the broken pavement into a hedge across from the all-night restaurant. Accumulated refuse hung up in the bushes. Her gaze rested on the blinking emergency lights of a semi pulled onto the shoulder near the highway on-ramp. Weedy undergrowth next to the parked semi swayed violently in traffic-made wind. What a desolate place to end a life, she thought.

Prusik lingered beside gas pump number two under the blazing lights of the truck plaza, where the truck driver who had given the young runaway a lift said he'd waved good-bye to her and then watched as she'd hoofed it in the direction of the dunes. In the distance, over the drone of interstate highway traffic, Prusik detected the rhythmic lapping of waves against the shore. She wondered if the peaceful sound of the tide had lured the girl to her death.

Prusik had driven here to immerse herself in the atmosphere of a place where the killer did his hunting. She'd been here before, of course, back when Betsy Ryan's body had been discovered, and it had been determined that the truck driver was the last person to see her alive. But she'd felt a need to visit again, to see how David Claremont might fit into the picture. To see what else the asphalt and the gas pumps and the water and the sky might tell her.

The Ryan girl had been dropped off at around this time, dusk. The plaza was well lit, in contrast to the surrounding vegetation—mostly thickets of scraggly brush and long-blade grasses that stretched all the way to the national lakeshore boundary. The victim had probably planned to sleep out among the dunes where no one would be likely to see her. Normally, Christine guessed, it would be a safe enough bet. But the bright-lit recesses of the truck plaza had also made her an easy mark from a parked pickup. No one would take notice of a man sitting in a truck at a truck plaza. He must have waited until only her silhouette was visible moving over the sandy soil through the low-lying brush. And then he'd made his move. He'd submerged the victim's remains afterward, and they'd been flushed by underwater currents until they snagged on an anchor chain like so much flotsam.

Prusik stood silently next to the car, carefully observing the comings and goings of the drivers and their vehicles. Yes, she concluded, that's how the killer would have done it. And it would have taken time. If Claremont were the killer, he would have had to make the four-hour drive to Portage, wait for the right opportunity, do the deed, clean up, and then drive back to Weaversville. But it was well established that he was a homebody, and that his parents always knew his whereabouts—with the exception of those two trips to Chicago.

Prusik started to walk parallel to the exit ramp, looking for a break in the thickset shrubbery that buffered the dunes from the roadway. She could smell the water that she couldn't yet see. Being next to an interstate highway, there was no public ingress. She walked a quarter of a mile farther and was about to turn back when a loosely draped cable cordon appeared in the scattering headlight beams of a turning tractor trailer. It was much darker here, far from the lights of the truck plaza. She flashed her Maglite on the ground next to the cable and saw that this was apparently a popular way in; a jumble of footprints led over the sand and disappeared across the humpy terrain of a large sand dune. Christine glanced over her shoulder, carefully stepped over the cable, and made her way through roadside rubble. Past the shadowy bushes, the vista opened up: sand dunes and beaches extended as far as she could see in either direction under the dimming sky. Out farther still, the deep waters of Lake Michigan mirrored the dark night sky. For a moment, the place almost seemed peaceful.

She knew she couldn't be far from the crime scene. She walked slowly toward the water, taking her time, letting her mind wander. Far behind her, a truck door slammed. Sound would carry far here near the water, and if there had been a breeze from the lake, which was likely, surely the young girl's screams would have been heard. She must have been murdered in the hours after midnight and before dawn, when any truckers at the stop would have been asleep in their cabs.

Christine rubbed the back of her neck, suddenly uneasy. The thought of the terrified teenager screaming into the void made her shiver involuntarily. She sucked in a tense breath and headed back toward the truck plaza, her footsteps sinking in the deep sands as she trudged. As she stepped back over the cable, the ankle holster on her trailing foot caught, and she stumbled to the ground. *Very graceful, Prusik.* She brushed off the sand and grit that clung to her pants and hands and started to stand.

The bushes in front of her rustled, and a shadowy figure exploded out at her before Prusik had time to get to her feet. From her knee, she withdrew her weapon.

"Stop! Raise your hands above your head! FBI!" She flashed her Maglite at his face, her gun pointed at the man's midsection.

He obeyed instantly. "I ain't done nuthin'." His voice was high and scared, and his hair hung long and greasy from under a hooded plastic poncho that was badly torn, probably pulled out of the trash up by the public restrooms. His beard was untrimmed. After a moment his right hand dropped toward his waist.

"Keep your hands up!"

"I ain't done nuthin'," the man whined.

Prusik took a breath. She realized this homeless man couldn't possibly be the killer she sought, but her heart was racing all the same. "Right. You were just rushing to help me to my feet."

"I was just...looking for something to eat. Or some money or something."

Prusik rose to her feet. "You know there are laws against vagrancy."

"I know, I know. I'm sorry. But I didn't do nuthin'."

"You came at me pretty quick. That's something." The words sounded weak even to her.

He squinted at her, his sheepish smile revealing a number of missing teeth. "Gee, I didn't mean to scare you, ma'am. I'm sorry."

Prusik stifled an urge to groan. Her fear was so obvious that a homeless man was taking pity on her. "OK then," she said shortly. "I'll let it go this time." She dug into her pocket and threw him a package of peanuts she'd gotten on the airplane, then turned and strode toward the lighted parking area and her car.

"Thanks, lady. I appreciate it. You have a nice night," the man called after her.

Christine's forehead felt hot in the cool night air. Inside the car, she locked the doors and tried to slow her breathing. After a few minutes, she gave up on natural relaxation and swallowed two Xanax tabs on a dry throat. Then she turned the key in the ignition and accelerated out of the truck plaza fast, hoping to leave behind the specter of death.

* * *

Parked nearer to the interstate, the Sweet Lick Resort's borrowed truck faced out toward the dunes and open water farther in the distance. The sky turned suddenly blacker and the lake, too, in spite of the dull fluorescence emanating from the truck plaza terminal bays. He fingered the key fob's medallion with the gold intersecting initials—SL—of the resort. He'd taken the bus from Chicago down to Weaversville last night as a precaution. Besides, his own truck still needed parts and was safely hidden behind an abandoned building in Delphos three blocks over from his own old place. When the lady agent flew out of Weaversville earlier in the day, he'd followed his instincts, borrowed a truck, and driven straight back to Chicago. It had been easy to locate the downtown FBI office in the large federal building, park on the street opposite the garage, and wait. He quickly had deciphered the government-issue plates designating the bureau's vehicles coming and going, and he caught a lucky break seeing her drive out in the large maroon sedan—all by herself.

His right leg caught in a high-speed jiggle. His mind spun wildly. He was paying the price. He'd restrained himself as he'd watched her linger by the sedan and then hurry into the shadows. It had taken mountains of self-control, but he'd done it. When she'd emerged from the brush back into the bright lights of the truck stop, he'd almost sobbed with relief. Five more minutes and he'd have followed her into the blackness, and he knew that wasn't a good idea. Not yet.

He blinked away the old tears that sometimes found him in moments like these, moments when what he wanted most was suddenly terribly gone. Following the FBI woman back here had been more than curiosity. He would have come anyway, eventually, to rest on the beach, watch the sky go dim and die, and remember the young loner warm and wet there with him.

In the confines of the parked truck, he twisted both hands around the steering wheel, riding out wave after wave of desperate longing, wave after wave of an endless sorrow that took him right back to that raw boy all cold and wet in the dark of his room. Cold and wet and so terribly alone.

CHAPTER TWENTY-THREE

After meeting with her team the following morning, Prusik took the inner stairwell one floor down to Dr. Emil Katz's office. Katz had turned out to be a damn good forensic shrink, well read on the workings of sick minds. He had teamed up with her on the Roman Mantowski case, the one that had been cause for Christine's promotion to senior forensic scientist, a title she never used with introductions, choosing to simply refer to herself as a special agent. Prusik deeply respected him for the tact and careful manner he had shown her while working at the bureau.

Stepping down the flight of stairs, Christine shrugged to herself. The workings of sick minds. She knew that her personnel file with the FBI contained her full health history, including the hospitalization for injuries suffered in New Guinea. Years of on-again, off-again therapy sessions were, no doubt, in her record, too. But she had never once intimated the reason for it with anyone at the bureau.

"Christine, come in, come in." The roly-poly man with the graying sideburns held a well-chewed ballpoint pen. Unlike many private practitioners whose offices included an acre slab of some exotic wood uncluttered by papers, Katz's battleship-gray Steelcase was piled high.

The doctor shuffled around to the front of his desk and took Prusik's free hand in both of his. "How good of you to come see me."

"Sorry I'm late," she said, eyeing a wall of swinging pendulums. Prusik couldn't fathom or abide Katz's obsession with clocks. The room was deafening with ticktocks.

"Shall we go across the hall to the conference room?" Katz asked graciously. "Where it's quieter?"

Prusik sat down and went straight to the point, giving Katz a synopsis of the murders and describing the gutting technique and removal of vital organs from the crime scenes. "In the last few months the suspect recounted to his psychiatrist the grim details of what could only be explained as facts relating to the killings. Notably, his therapy appointments were consistently held shortly after each killing." She crossed a leg over her knee.

"Well, then, you do have something." The doctor threaded his fingers together and leaned back in his chair, attentive.

Prusik described her interview with Claremont, his idiosyncrasies, his appearing to struggle with himself, the conflicting physical attributes—such as his left-handedness—that were at odds with her profile of the killer.

"These visions"—Katz twirled the end of the ragged pen between his teeth—"delusional tendencies or do you mean something quite different?"

"Different, but I'm not quite sure why."

"This is a bold one." Katz nodded. "Very bold indeed."

"Oddly, Claremont has no previous police record for violence, except a recent incident where he appeared to be functioning in blackout for a minute or less. He more or less fell on a woman in a parking lot after carrying something to her car for her, but he didn't let her up right away. She didn't press charges. There are two other reports of his blacking out in public. Once at a farm show this spring and then more recently while having dinner at a local restaurant with his parents. He rarely leaves the farm. The police down there have confirmed as much."

"Mmmmm."

"Which brings me to this." Prusik looked straight into the doctor's eyes.

"Ah yes, your reason for coming."

"The eyewitness identification was by Joey Templeton, a local boy, eleven years old. He knew Julie Heath, the latest victim we're aware of. This boy claims he biked past Claremont on the same day the victim went missing. Claimed Claremont was stuffing something in the bed of his truck, which was parked along the same road where the victim had earlier visited the home of a friend.

"Thing is"—Prusik stared down at the swirling pattern on the vinyl floor tiles, remembering the moment in the lineup viewing room—"something's not quite right about the identification. It won't stop bothering me."

Katz raised his eyebrows. "I'm listening, Christine. What is it?"

"Seven men were in the lineup. I stood directly behind the witness. He was clearly frightened but concentrating hard. No one seemed to jump out at him. Every once in a while he looked back over his shoulder at his grandfather for reassurance. Then number four stepped forward. The boy gave the man a good look straight on from not ten feet away through the glass. The kid paused, frowned a little, seemed puzzled, but had no other reaction. I tell you, if Claremont *had* lawyered up, there's a very good chance the lineup would have been ended right then."

"Coercive circumstances?"

"Well, yeah, a lawyer would have said so. Throughout the session, the boy kept turning around, checking with his grandfather, it could be argued, as if they had some kind of identification code."

Katz nodded, tugging off bits of ballpoint with his teeth, listening intently.

"After the kid studied number four for a minute, he turned one last time toward his grandfather. It was then that it happened. The boy froze, staring toward his grandfather, who was sitting in the back of the room. Except Joey wasn't really looking at his grandfather at all." Prusik paused. "He was looking *above* where his grandfather sat, at a reflection in an interior window of a darkened office."

Katz nodded again and spit out some of the ballpoint pen.

"In that interior window there was a clear reflection of the man who had stepped forward. The witness practically fell against the one-way glass of the lineup room, horror-stricken. All eyes in the room were riveted on the boy's obvious reaction. After catching his breath, the kid practically collapsed, scared shitless."

"So there was no positive identification until the witness spotted your suspect's reflection?"

"Yes, not until then. Now somehow I feel sure of it. The reflection is what did it."

The door rattled before springing open. "Oh shit! Sorry, sorry, Christine, for not knocking before entering. But I knew you'd want to hear this right away. Hi, Doctor." Brian Eisen nodded briefly at the doctor and handed Prusik several fingerprint program printouts.

"Something kept jamming on the new Automated Fingerprint Identification Systems technology. Or that's what I initially thought." He held his free hand up by his head, as if assembling his thoughts.

"Yes? We're listening, Brian."

He nodded his head rapidly. "OK, the thing is that the partial palm print we lifted from one of Missy Hooper's running shoes, while not identical to the suspect's, does have a meaningful correlation, very significant, in fact." He spread the pages on the conference table. "See here, the whorls on each palm? They're nearly identical to David Claremont's, only they swirl in opposing directions. It's as if you're looking through a mirror. They're exactly opposite but the same in every other respect." A broad grin spread across the technician's face.

"Mirror twins," Katz said softly.

"According to the data, I'd say absolutely one hundred percent," Eisen agreed. "And—you're going to love this, Christine—we confirmed from a bite mark on the shoulder of one victim that the killer without a doubt has a chipped right eyetooth."

"While Claremont's is very much intact," she said. "I took the suspect's dental impressions myself. Incredible. And Howard's men have scoured the Claremont farm," she added, "and have not turned up a hair, fiber, or any bloodstains that tie Claremont to any of these killings."

"Of course not," Eisen said. "He's not the murderer."

Prusik shook her head slowly. "No. No, he's not. Thank you, Brian, for bringing this to me immediately." Silently, she added a thank-you for not filtering it through Bruce Howard first. "Great work."

"It's moments like these that I love my job," Eisen said with a boyish grin, and he left the conference room.

"This mirror-imaging business…" Katz bridged his fingertips, flexing them in and out. "I could tell you a diabolical twin is actually committing these crimes. There are some documented cases of transposition phenomenon, which may be at work here. A Minnesota twin study has reported such occurrences."

"Translation please, Doctor?"

"It's one researcher's description of a psychological state experienced among close family members, not only twin siblings, especially in the context of an emotional crisis." Katz paused, tapping his fingertips together. "Let's say someone is involved in a serious car accident. All of a sudden, out of the blue, a sibling or parent in the next town over, or even across the country, has the fear something terrible has transpired. They may even proclaim their fear to someone they're with, that a family member has been badly hurt in an accident. A call is made that verifies the accident has resulted in serious injuries, even death. Somehow the relative knew this." The doctor shrugged. "I'll admit it's far-fetched, but your David Claremont's visions may be transposed images."

"How so?" asked Prusik. "And it wouldn't be Claremont's family in trouble, because David is an only child."

"Assuming Claremont's visions are not a manifestation of some psychotic episode unique to him, then, hypothetically at least, he could be experiencing an exciting event of this other person—a family member he may not even know exists. In the case of Claremont, it would have to be a twin, a mirror image of himself. Hence"—Katz was nodding to himself—"your young witness's recognition of Claremont in the *mirror*."

Christine's heart pumped faster. "There was precious little about Claremont's childhood in his file. Might he have had a brother who was given up for adoption?"

"Or might he himself have been adopted?" Katz asked.

"Jesus. If that's so, how could any reputable psychiatrist neglect to find that out and note it in his file?" She took a deep breath. "Never mind. I'll have Eisen contact the parents immediately." She pulled out her cell phone and gave Eisen instructions.

She turned her attention back to Katz. "Could this transposition phenomenon explain Claremont knowing this other man through his visions? He says this 'other,' a 'two-face,' he calls him, lives inside of him."

Katz mulled over the question for a minute. "If mirror-image twins are involved, it's not purely through visions that your suspect has come to know this man he claims is inside him." Katz tapped his temple with his forefinger. "There is a physical history between them, albeit truncated, leading ultimately to their separation. Whether or not the twin's the true killer—if there is a twin—well"—Katz shrugged again—"that I cannot know."

"In your best judgment, realistically speaking, if there is indeed a twin, is this mirror-image twin theory plausible enough for me to go on? Or will Thorne have my badge for it?"

"I can't advise you as to your next course of action, Christine. I can only say that in my best judgment it is in the realm of possibilities, especially with the fingerprint information from your Brian Eisen. In matters of telepathy the finely tuned psyche is a cosmos we are only now beginning to fathom, scientifically speaking. Frankly, these areas of consciousness are profound and not at all well understood." Katz leaned his elbow on the table. "And another thing—transposition phenomenon is reportedly highest among mirror-image identical twins. There is a long-term study on identical twins that has documented this. Oddly, it seems to occur most frequently among identicals separated soon after birth. Something to do with the twinning bond that forms at a very early age, some believe in the womb itself. The need to maintain the connection with a lost part of oneself, if you will, cannot be overestimated."

Prusik thought about the lineup. It wasn't a code that Joey Templeton had had going with his grandfather. The boy's initial wavering as he stared through the one-way glass at number four had shifted like day into night, into unspeakable terror. When he spotted Claremont's mirror-image reflection, Joey recognized the real killer, she was certain.

"Mirror image—would that include other opposing physical attributes?" she said. "Such as being left-handed or right-handed? Claremont is a lefty, but the killer without a doubt strangles and cuts with his right."

"Yes," said Katz, "it can describe opposing physical attributes and even disparate temperaments. One could be active, the other passive. One an extrovert, the other quiet as a mouse. Reversals of hair whorls and cowlicks on their heads and physical abnormalities such as the reversed placement of internal organs. Particularly notable is the configuration of facial biometrics—they could be exact opposites down to the placement of dimples on different cheeks."

"One good, the other evil," Prusik said.

"Quite provocative. And not entirely out of the question." Katz cocked his head. "Psychopathology among monozygotic twins—genetically identical and formed by a single divided egg—is quite significant. But even among siblings who share the same exact genes, one may suffer from, let's say, schizophrenia, and the other may not."

"So, the killer could be deranged and his identical twin normal?" Prusik said.

Katz danced his head right and left. "Quite possibly. You should also be aware of another very remarkable trait that could be at work here. This twinning bond has another equally compelling feature that frequently causes separated twins to search out each other's existence. The mind picks up signals. Signals from a twin may be the strongest link of them all."

Prusik removed a vial from her lab coat and placed it on the table.

"The killer deliberately places carved stones inside his victims. It's his marker. He's saying, 'She's mine.' I found this stone in the esophagus of one of his victims, Missy Hooper. I retrieved a nearly identical one from the body of another victim, Julie Heath."

Katz twirled the vial above his face. "Looks something like a chess piece." He held it closer to his eye, as if under a microscope.

Prusik took another vial from her pocket, this one containing a cruder stone figurine similar in height and size to the first.

"This other one is made of a local mineral called chert. I understand that it is commonly found in limestone formations, which form the bedrock of southern Indiana. It's David Claremont's handiwork—a pretty amazing parallel to the genuine article, don't you think?"

"A very close match, indeed," the doctor concurred.

"What's more, last March five museum artifacts including this one and the one from Julie Heath were stolen from the Chicago Museum of Natural History. Oddly, around this same time period, David Claremont took a bus to Chicago without telling his parents, a very uncharacteristic act. Claims it was to get hobby supplies for stone carving."

"You're the anthropologist—what do you make of it?" Katz said.

"Ultraviolet light identification establishes that this stone is, in fact, one of those stolen from the museum. An encoded number is etched on its base, invisible to the human eye under normal light. It's a highland New Guinea charm stone, which had been on display at the museum's Oceania exhibit when the thefts occurred."

Her pulse quickened. She combed her fingers through her hair. "No question some kind of advanced ritualistic behavior is at work, Doctor. I don't believe the killer is the least bit interested in his victims' souls, though." She cleared her throat.

The bank of overhead lights suddenly glared harshly. Prusik felt the heat. Her ears filled with the sound of mud sucking at her back. She pressed two fingers to the inside of her wrist, checking her pulse: shallow and rapid. She couldn't slow the beats.

"What seems to be the matter, Christine?" Katz asked, concerned.

"Nothing, I'm just a little tired."

Katz stood. "Come, come, I'm not so stupid as to not recognize an anxiety reaction when I see one." He rested his warm palm gently on her forearm. "Please, lie down on the sofa. I often take naps here when the world won't leave me alone."

Prusik didn't resist. Katz's fatherly concern helped ease her mind. She laid her head back against the leather armrest. The doctor draped a mohair shawl over her shoulders and dimmed the overhead lights.

"One of the virtues of our both being government employees is that we're well acquainted with the stresses of working on nightmarish cases that won't go away."

Prusik held out a hand. "Dr. Katz?" He pulled a chair beside the couch and gently squeezed her hand.

"Whatever is on your mind I assure you won't go any further than these walls. But then you already know that."

She glanced back at the vial, at the charm stone that had been gripped in the killer's hand, then shoved inside a still-warm throat.

"Highland New Guinea tribes carve stone figurines. They believe placing a stone image inside the dead is respectful of the ancestral spirits that live for an eternity."

Prusik's eyes remained fixed on the tiny bottle, her mind drifting back to the unending New Guinea heat. "But this charm stone is nothing but an object of death," she said, her mind exploding with images of thick jungle greenery, brown waters, and the choking Papuan mud. "It's meat he's after, plain and simple."

"I can tell you this much." He shook his forefinger in a paternalistic scolding fashion. "Two things are distinctly at work. One is this peculiar case of yours. The other is your stress disorder."

"Come on, Doctor." Prusik shrugged. "I know the difference between the heebie-jeebies and the normal stresses of work."

"For sure, you are strong, Christine. You are a forensic investigator, a professional scientist pursuing this killer with the same cunning and zeal with which he enjoys dispatching young women."

Christine sat up, stung by the doctor's brutal comparison. "I can't...I can't believe you said that."

"Ah." Katz smiled. "You don't see yourself as possessing cunning and zeal? I'm sorry if my comparison upsets you, my dear. Let me just say that I know you are the perfect person to track down this killer."

Slowly Christine rose to her feet. The doctor followed her out into the hallway. "If it means anything, I would be more than glad to attest to your thoroughness and the logic of your reasoning should it come down to Thorne's questioning your judgment." He clasped both her hands in his and squeezed. "And you *are* the perfect person to track down this killer. Both of us know that. But please"—he squeezed her hands again—"please be careful, Christine."

Prusik thanked the doctor and returned to her office, once again taking the stairs rather than the elevator; no need to run into Thorne or anyone else she didn't want to make small talk with. She needed time to think, time that she didn't have. She was unable to shake the idea that Claremont had a twin: a lurker whose soul was in no way identical to his tormented brother's. Their paths had very much divided, and puzzling as it truly was, the killer's grisly actions were dismantling the life of his innocent twin brother.

CHAPTER TWENTY-FOUR

Tears caused by the wind streaked down Prusik's cheeks. She pressed the remote key fob, and the dark government sedan whistled back to indicate that it was locked.

Her appointment was at nine o'clock sharp, in fifteen minutes. Brian Eisen and Paul Higgins had done good work. Hilda Claremont had confirmed that she and her husband had adopted David in Chicago when he was eleven months old. Typing David Claremont's name into an "All State Court" index file search of birth records had turned up the Chicago adoption agency that had the complete files.

A sharp gust of wind mussed her hair as she crossed the street toward a building with the bronze entry of an art deco design bordered by a bold geometric pattern that repeated along the molding inside the front hallway. She fingered her hair back into place. James Branson, the president of the Loving Home Agency, was too booked to see her on such short notice. He'd passed her along to a Joan Peters, his custodian of records.

Pushing open the outer door released a great suction of air, ruffling her hair again. "Damn it," she muttered.

"Blustery day, ain't it?" The security guard chuckled. HANSEN SECURITY was stitched above his breast pocket.

Prusik scanned the wall directory behind the guard's desk. "The Loving Home Agency still on the fourteenth floor?"

The guard leaned over the counter, "Yes, ma'am. Right through there," he said, pointing to a bank of elevators.

She was in a good mood. Thorne's keeping her in charge of forensics meant she had time to pursue this information on Claremont's past. When the elevator doors opened on fourteen, the custodian of records of the Loving Home Agency was waiting there for her.

"Ms. Prusik? I'm Joan Peters. Mr. Branson wanted to make sure you didn't have to wait." She walked briskly down the corridor ahead of Prusik. "He's so particular about his clients." She dropped her voice. "He didn't want anyone to think—well, you know, being you're a policewoman—how it might look. You understand." She crinkled her nose, gave Prusik a well-practiced smile.

"No, I don't understand." Prusik returned the smile. "Unless Mr. Branson has something to hide?"

"Oh, nothing like that, I assure you. It's just that with all the stresses adoption brings, we try to relax our clients as much as possible."

"And police trouble isn't part of the equation," Prusik said bluntly.

"Well, no. It isn't."

Peters led her past a posh office, its door ajar. A young couple seated on a crimson couch gazed expectantly at a large catalogue of babies. A leaded crystal chandelier hung low in the center of the room. The Liberace effect rubbed Prusik wrong. So did the baby catalogue.

The custodian inserted a key and pushed her shoulder against a door marked PRIVATE. "It's so musty in here. I apologize."

"How are they organized?" Prusik stepped past Peters and began to walk down a narrow canyon of stacked bankers boxes.

"Crowder Agency records I can't help you much with. My employer purchased the business before I started. I'm afraid most of the files were simply dumped in here as is."

"I don't see any dates on these covers," Prusik said. She pulled out a box.

"What's here is here, Ms. Prusik. I've come in here maybe once or twice in the last year. An older child looking for a natural parent, something like that. If you ask me, adoptees make too big a fuss trying to find their biologicals."

"Cut the crap, Ms. Peters," Prusik said coolly from years of practice. "Unless I can enlist your help right now, I will bring my team in to move all these boxes back to my office. What would your clients think about that?"

The woman's brow sharply creased. "You can't do that. They're confidential, protected by—"

"Ms. Peters, I don't care what they're protected by, and I'm not sure I care for your adoption agency, either. It looks to me like you've got people shopping by catalogue for babies out there, and that really pisses me off. Find me David Claremont's file, or I'll be back in twenty minutes with a warrant. My team will tear apart every single office, including Mr. Branson's."

The woman's mouth formed a perfect circle. "You can't do that!"

"Try me," Prusik said, hoping her bluff wasn't showing. Christine really did need Ms. Peters's cooperation. "Look, this information is very important to an investigation we are conducting. I'm sorry if I gave you any misimpression that the FBI is the least bit interested in learning how you conduct business here in your agency."

"Well, you don't have to threaten me like that!" Peters knelt at Prusik's feet and obediently pulled out a carton. "Everything we do here is one hundred percent legal."

Prusik flipped open the top of the box and read Dennison, Driver, and Duke across the tabs. She pulled out the next box, landing it hard on the floor.

"Here are the Cs," Prusik said.

Peters joined her. "Here, let me help you with that."

"Thank you," Prusik said, pleased by the woman's newfound cooperative spirit.

Peters rapidly fingered through the files. A minute later she held out a yellowed folder.

"Lawrence and Hilda Claremont, did you say?"

"That's the one."

The application was written in a difficult-to-read script. Prusik scanned through it. "Is this the birth mother's name, Bruna Holmquist?"

Peters stood shoulder to shoulder with Prusik, peering down at the form. "It seems so. Yes."

"The space for the mother's social security or identity number is blank," Prusik said. "No address is given, either. How can an official record be filed like this?"

Peters raised her palms in conciliation, nodding. "I know, I know. Some adoption agencies have lax record-keeping habits. As I recall, lots of partials came from Crowder. Keep in mind, Crowder's mothers were often in desperate straits."

Prusik studied another official document. "The affidavit filed with the county court is stamped with the name of a Crowder Agency representative. The mother didn't sign off on her child? How could that be?"

"I believe it was common practice for some agencies to petition on behalf of the natural mother. Foreign immigrants frequented the Crowder Agency. The mothers may not have known English that well, if at all." Peters eyed Prusik nervously.

The remaining documents in Claremont's file gave information about the prospective parents' suitability, livelihood, income, and standing in the community. Prusik needed answers about Bruna Holmquist, and there was nothing here.

She brushed past Peters, heading straight for the office with the luxurious couch. The door was closed now. She knocked once, then entered without waiting and held out her badge to a man wearing a three-piece brown suit. He was seated beside the same couple she'd seen earlier. The suit had to be Branson. His glazed-over hairdo looked pressed into place.

"May I help you, miss?" Branson's eyebrows rose, and his face went pinkish.

"Mr. Branson, Special Agent Christine Prusik with the FBI. I need to speak with you alone." She paced her words no differently than if she were making an arrest. "Right now if you can, sir."

His face flushed red. "Please excuse me?" he said to the couple, motioning them back to the waiting area outside his office.

"What's the meaning of barging into my office like this, scaring the hell out of those dear people?" he said angrily, and then he lowered his voice. "Do you realize what they've been through? No, of course not."

"Finished?" Prusik said. "When I spoke to you on the phone earlier, Mr. Branson, you assured me that you'd give this matter your personal attention. Perhaps you haven't been following the news lately? Three girls in Indiana have been viciously murdered. There may be others. The murders have led me straight to your agency."

Branson blanched.

Prusik eased her tone. "Now, look, I'm sorry I barged in on your private meeting. But I do need your assistance to locate information on a suspect. Do we understand each other?"

"Yes, yes we do, Ms. Prusik," Branson said, flustered. "I had scheduled previous engagements, it's true, but I don't want any trouble. I don't see what possible connection this agency could have with any *murders*." He shook his head.

"Well, there is a connection. I have a suspect with a name, and he was adopted through your agency. You have records with missing names and missing information," Prusik said. "What do you know about the Crowder Agency?"

"Owen Crowder and I didn't know each other very well. He was much older, kept meticulous records on three-by-five cards. Before computers, you know." Branson removed a drawer of a large oak cabinet that stood against the wall behind him and placed the rack of cards on his desk. "Two separate file systems—one with clients seeking adoption, the other the mums giving up children, of course," he said, fingering through the tops of the cards, reading the names as he went.

"David Claremont's DOB is on or about December tenth, nineteen eighty-seven," Prusik added, leaning over Branson's desk, watching the man carefully as he handled the cards, not trusting him. "The files Ms. Peters showed me were incomplete," she said. "No social security numbers. No address of the mother or identity of the father or mention of there being any siblings."

He shook his head. "As good as Crowder was at keeping track of things on these cards, he couldn't always get cooperation from the mothers. He did a fair amount of business with immigrants, often a desperate bunch."

"So he bought babies from illegals—is that what you're saying, Mr. Branson?" Prusik stared him down.

He smiled nervously, backpedaling. "You mean the missing social security numbers? Look. It's not good practice, but Crowder would have never knowingly harbored illegal aliens. In this business, a woman out of wedlock who gets in trouble is very likely to use an alias, especially if new to this country. Not in my agency, mind you, but foreign mothers frequently don't give out their alien identity card information for fear it will get them deported."

Branson removed another card tray that contained information on the adoptive parents. He came around to Prusik's side of the desk and flicked through the yellowed cards. "Unfortunately, I haven't the staff to computerize all these. I really should. So many people are looking for their biological parents these days." He stopped and pulled out a card. "Here, at the bottom, it says B. Holmquist is the birth mother." He handed it to Prusik. "Not very much, I'm afraid."

Prusik scanned the card. "There's also a reference here to the birth mother's own *card*, Mr. Branson. Right here." She pointed.

Branson donned a pair of reading glasses. "Ah, so there is." He shuffled through more oak drawers. The heavy wooden filing cabinet looked ancient; Prusik wondered if he'd inherited it, file cards and all, from Crowder. "Here are the *H* mums. Holmquist comma Bruna. You are so right—another card for the birth mother."

Prusik studied the neat blue ink. Bruna Holmquist, age thirty-eight, white, from Oslo, Norway. Under the heading PREVIOUS CHILDREN BORN there was a smudge mark, an erasure. Something definitely had been scratched out. Again, no address was listed.

"What's with this entry, Mr. Branson?" Prusik said, handing him the card.

The agency director stood silent, blinking down at the card.

"Have you any more cards you aren't telling me about, Mr. Branson?"

Branson cleared his throat. "Let me check. I really had no idea about these particular cards."

"The line before PREVIOUS CHILDREN is smudged," Prusik pointed out. "Couldn't it be referring to the fact that there was another child born, unreported? One with another Crowder three-by-five card somewhere else?"

"It's possible, yes." Agitated, he went back to the heavy oak file drawer and removed the cards immediately following Bruna Holmquist's. Two of them were stuck together, and as he fingered them apart, one fell on the floor.

"What's that?" Prusik pointed. "Something's stapled to it?"

Branson picked it up. A lined note bearing the logo of St. Mary's Hospital was stapled to a three-by-five card with "Holmquist, Bruna, card two of two" printed neatly across the top. The name and address of the now-defunct Crowder Agency and the words "8:00 p.m. sharp" were all that was written on the notepaper.

"St. Mary's was torn down ten years ago," Branson said. "But the hospital records must be stored somewhere."

"Something's written on the back of the index card." Prusik drew closer.

He handed it to her. The name Donald was deliberately crossed out and the name David written in its place. *Donald.* Below that was something else.

"*Sons'* father?" Prusik placed it in front of Branson. "In your lifetime of experience in the baby-dealing business, what do you think it means, Mr. Branson, when an *s* trails a noun?"

"More than one son?" He gazed at her with a furrowed brow.

"*Very* good. And wouldn't the fact that the name Donald is crossed out and the name David written in its place bear that out? Wouldn't Mr. Crowder have been indicating that the mother had two sons? It is Mr. Crowder's writing, isn't it?"

"I see your point, yes. Perhaps it was the mother's decision not to give up the other son?"

"Thank you, Mr. Branson." Prusik tucked the cards and the note into her overcoat pocket, showing herself out.

"Ms. Prusik." Branson followed her out into the hallway, clasping his hands in a praying gesture. "You won't be needing to come back again, will you?"

She gave a sweet smile. "Let's just see how things go, shall we?"

* * *

Prusik sat in the idling car with the air on maximum cool, studying the yellowed Crowder Agency cards. She pondered the significance of the erasure. Had Bruna Holmquist had a change of heart about which baby to give up for adoption? Had she planned to give up both, then decided to keep Donald? Bruna Holmquist had no doubt been poor, vulnerable, and new to this country. With spotty English and twin babies, her road would have been a hard one. So she'd tried to do her best for them by giving up one of them, who'd become David Claremont, a troubled loser. The other son, whom she kept, became Donald Holmquist, a bona fide serial killer. She'd get Eisen on it immediately. Have him reverse the image of the photo of Claremont and circulate it, with information that he might have been a painter on the museum project last March who could have gone by the name Donald Holmquist.

Prusik's hands were trembling as she reached for her cell phone. And her pinkie throbbed mercilessly.

She took her time driving back into the city. When she finally got downtown, she accelerated past the underground parking garage entrance to her office building, needing to think in peace. Fifteen minutes later she was in her Speedo, muscling down a smooth lane of water between the float lines. She'd already come up with a plan, and she was praying to God that her next move wouldn't cost more lives than it would save.

CHAPTER TWENTY-FIVE

Prusik eased the sedan into the government-only spot at O'Hare Airport and levered the shifter into park. Thick gray clouds drifted in from the west, cutting the muggy midafternoon heat by a few degrees. Sheriff McFaron had accepted her proposal and would be arriving shortly.

In the past four hours, Paul Higgins had found out that Donald Holmquist had only made it through his junior year at Southside High. The school's guidance office had his last known address listed as 1371 Hawthorne Boulevard, apartment 3C, Delphos, Illinois, which was a tenement building among a raft of condemned blocks that were scheduled to be torn down next spring. A scan of police records in the greater Chicago area had yielded another hit, which had led to a meaningful conversation with a Sergeant Gatto, who seemed more than pleased that someone was looking for Donald Holmquist five years after five-year-old Benjamin Moseley, who had lived in the same building, had disappeared. Holmquist had been the last to see the young child. Gatto had suspected him of foul play but had been unable to prove it.

Bruce Howard and the field unit remained in Weaversville, assiduously searching the Claremont property, ferrying plane-loads of bagged items back to Chicago for Prusik's team to examine. Thorne's last voice message had demanded that she hand in an overdue summary report of evidence findings to substantiate the case against Claremont, as if the case was all but sewn up. But there were no findings to substantiate the case.

Her BlackBerry beeped. Brian Eisen's name flashed across its screen. "What you got, Brian?"

"What I got is a copy of Bruna Holmquist's St. Mary's Hospital admission. You're not going to believe this. Three years ago she was admitted, having suffered a stroke and been rendered aphasic. Unable to do more than blink, according to the nurse's station notes."

"Yes?" Prusik scanned the entrance doors looking for the sheriff.

"She died the same night she was admitted. An autopsy yielded one significant contributing factor. Her throat was partially blocked by a coarse granite stone that had been wedged there. Her esophagus tissue was heavily abraded. Mystifyingly, there is no follow-up report. No notice to the prosecuting attorney's office. I guess public hospital patients don't count for much."

Prusik said nothing but wondered what this mother had done to her son to deserve that. "As always, excellent follow-up work, Brian."

McFaron's tan trooper hat appeared through the automatic sliding doors. Christine got out of the car and waved him over. "I've got to go. Keep me posted."

Quickly she scanned the street to be sure that no one from the bureau who might recognize her was in the area. She gave Joe a kiss, slipped her hand inside his arm, and coaxed him toward the waiting vehicle. His clear brown eyes sent a surge of warmth coursing through her, which made what she had to do even harder.

"I have a confession to make, Joe," she said as soon as they were both in the car. Her head slumped forward, her short hair momentarily concealing her eyes.

McFaron rested his trooper hat on the large sedan's dashboard and looked at her, puzzled. "I'm listening."

"I really wanted to see you, and that's why I asked you up. But not just for dinner." Christine felt embarrassment and shame. Had she taken unfair advantage? Probably.

Joe remained silent.

She peered out the window, searching for the right words. A huge jetliner, its flaps and landing gear fully down, descended straight at them. Christine blinked as its shadow and thunderous engines passed not more than a few hundred feet over them. McFaron sat expectantly, waiting for her to speak.

"I haven't exactly been truthful." She looked him squarely in the eyes. "Whatever you might think of me, please remember that I really wanted to see you. But it's not the main reason I've asked you here."

McFaron gazed at her levelly. "OK. Spill the beans already."

She took another deep breath. "Unbeknownst to Thorne or Howard, I've been investigating a different line of information that my team has developed."

"Sure that's the right thing to be doing?"

"Obviously not, and it's why I feel troubled about involving you directly in it without warning you, either."

"So what are you saying, Christine?" McFaron's expression was hard to read. "Are you telling me now to see whether I'll cut and run, or are you asking me to stay? Is this some sort of test to see if I'm worthy? Wait and see if Joe flies up, spring it on him, and then see if he leaves or stays?"

She told him what she'd learned from Dr. Katz about mirror imaging and the twinning bond and about delving into David Claremont's past at the adoption agency.

"So will you stay?" she pleaded, searching his face for signs. It was McFaron's turn to study an incoming plane, its landing gear in the ready position.

The sheriff waited for the flickering shadow overhead and the loud engine noise to subside before answering her. "You don't make it easy, Special Agent Prusik." A small smile turned up the corners of his mouth. "But I'll stay. You got that good place to eat picked out yet?"

Christine let out a sigh of relief. "You'll have to earn your keep first, cowboy." She drew closer, still a little cautious, and kissed his cheek. "Thank you," she whispered.

From O'Hare Prusik gunned the sedan down the inter-state connector south under a thin veil of building clouds. She filled McFaron in on the details: information she'd picked up at the adoption agency and the fact that Claremont not only had a brother named Donald Holmquist, but that Donald had grown up in Delphos, just down the road. And that his mother had died of a stroke three years earlier—with a stone lodged in her throat.

"Holy Jesus," the sheriff said, shaking his head. "From what I hear, Claremont has not been very cooperative. He still main-tains his innocence, and nothing has come my way to corrobo-rate his being seen in either Parker or Crosshaven, aside from Joey Templeton's lineup ID."

"In my last call with Bruce, he didn't sound too pleased with the recovery effort at the Claremont place," she said.

"Does Thorne still feel it's a wrap?"

She glanced at the sheriff and then quickly turned to watch the traffic. "He hasn't said anything yet to suggest otherwise. These new developments and whatever you and I turn up will change his mind."

Less than an hour later, she signaled right, turning onto Second Avenue in downtown Delphos. They passed block after block of boarded-up tenements. A hangar-size battery plant at one end of the avenue stood like a great rusted mausoleum, a tribute to better days gone by. Prusik wondered whether Donald's mother had worked in the battery factory, maybe even met his father there. She took a left onto Hawthorne.

"Kind of bleak, ain't it?" McFaron said, craning his neck. "Can you read any street numbers?"

"The number four twelve is above that entry," Prusik pointed out, "meaning thirteen seventy-one Hawthorne should be on the right."

The residences were brick-built units constructed in the late thirties as the country had begun to creep out of the Great Depression. Many had the same sturdy architectural style as the public works projects from that era. Ten blocks farther on, concrete steps led up to unadorned entrances, less desirable places to live for people with even less money than battery-making paid.

"Thirteen seventy-one," McFaron said. "Goddamn, it looks like a war zone." McFaron observed a creek to the right that passed through a culvert under the roadway and spilled out the other side into the Little Calumet.

She pulled up to the curb.

The plywood sealing the main entrance looked intact. "What about trying the back," the sheriff suggested. "Through that alley? It may have an easier access."

"OK then."

The car rocked over loose rubble in the alley between buildings. They got out into an empty gravel lot covered with weeds. The hush of the abandoned buildings surrounding them muffled the distant hum of traffic on the interstate. The only sound came from the trickle of the creek that ran parallel to the parking lot. No pigeons flew overhead. The sky was fuzzy slate. Life had forgotten this part of Delphos.

McFaron walked toward a sheet of plywood loosely propped against the back door. He pushed it aside. "That was easy."

"Someone's obviously been here. Better put on these." Prusik handed him a pair of latex gloves. "To preserve any prints that might be on that knob."

"Here goes nothing." McFaron flashed his Maglite up and down the gloomy hallway and entered the building.

"It better be something," she said. "I'm counting on it."

The sheriff tested the first-floor apartment door, but it was locked. He wedged a screwdriver into the jamb, dismantling the flimsy hinge. The door collapsed inward.

"Why are you doing that?"

"What if this creep has taken up residence downstairs?" He grunted, shoving an old stuffed chair out of his way and inadvertently knocking over a standing lamp, breaking the bulb. Slowly, methodically, McFaron flashed the light through dust billowing in the interior. More of it lay undisturbed on the floor. "Looks like our boy didn't take up roosting in here."

Watching him working in the shadows of the squalid apartment, Christine was grateful for the sheriff's presence on more than one level.

"The Holmquists lived on the third floor," she said. "My money says we start at the top and work our way down if we have to."

"Whatever you say, boss." He grinned, shooing away a cobweb from his Stetson. "Say, how far is that restaurant from here?"

"Quit the chitchat and get going," Prusik whispered, stepping over an old pile of newspapers. Her feet crunched on bits of debris.

"Why are you whispering?" he whispered back.

"I guess I don't want to disturb the ghosts." She was sort of joking and sort of not. "Let's go."

On the way down the hall to the staircase, they passed an old bureau with missing drawers angled precariously on three legs, a stuffed chair with its pillowy contents blackened from a small fire, one squashed shoe without a lace. The smells were musty and dank, devoid of anything resembling life.

"Third floor," the sheriff said. "Ready or not." They climbed the steps slowly, McFaron shining the light near Prusik's feet.

The door to apartment 3C swung open at his touch. He scattered the beam of light around the kitchen. Footprints smudged the floor everywhere. "Got that camera ready? Someone's definitely been in here. Recently, too."

From the hallway Prusik flashed several long shots with her camera, and then she knelt inside the threshold for a close-up of one clear boot print. As their eyes adjusted to the dimness, Prusik and McFaron inspected the living room. Daylight filtered through lathe strips that covered the windows. McFaron shone the light past the living room. In the bedroom next to the apartment's front door Prusik discovered a mattress mounded several feet high with women's clothes. In one corner a fine layer of dust had collected on an old TV set. It looked untouched. The bathroom window contained the only intact pane of glass, frosted for privacy.

Prusik poked around the pile of old clothing on the bed. She detected a sharp ammonia-like odor—bed-wetting was a common behavioral antecedent of psychopaths. And also drunks and drug addicts, she reminded herself.

McFaron returned to the kitchen. A Formica-topped table looked as solid as new with two stools neatly tucked under it, as if the last occupant hadn't intended to abandon the premises. He worked loose a window board, letting in more daylight, and pried off the sheathing from another window. A bottle cap blew off the sill.

They had been working for nearly an hour in the stuffy walk-up—kneeling, poking in corners, finding and bagging as evidence for later examination a moldy, empty woman's purse with a torn strap, a pair of old pantyhose that were ripped nearly in two at the crotch, and a stack of mildew-stained weekly advertisers. But no sign of stale food—not a crumb, empty cans, or any recent-looking garbage indicating anyone had been holing up, which puzzled McFaron, given the myriad shoe prints covering the kitchen floor. Hunger was past gnawing at his stomach. Christine's last-minute invitation had wreaked havoc with his schedule. Tired, he leaned his shoulder against a narrow door in the corner of the kitchen. The door suddenly gave way, unbalancing him.

"Jesus." McFaron rubbed his arm and aimed the Maglite up a steep passageway. It appeared to access the roof. The sheriff grazed both sides of the passage climbing the flight. Halfway up, a sharp, rotting odor stopped him. Reflexively, he drew his gun and continued slowly, the weapon aimed forward, breathing through the top of his jacket collar. In the line of the flashlight beam, he saw brownish-red stains around a smudgy doorknob of a small room on the way to the roof.

Fingerprints.

He eyed them briefly. With the lens end of the flashlight he shoved open the grungy door and quickly shone the light around, aiming his gun chest-high. The light sent shadows dancing against a cracked plaster wall.

He blinked, his eyes still adjusting to the dimness. Slowly he holstered his gun, finally convinced that he was alone and feeling a bit foolish. When he turned to leave, McFaron caught sight of someone standing still in the corner of the room. Instinctively, the sheriff ducked and withdrew his gun. "Hands up!" No movement. He squinted at the figure—a mannequin. It was propped against the back wall; a tattered headdress of some kind rested over its plaster head. "What the..."

"Joe?" Prusik called up the stairwell.

Around the mannequin's neck hung a small green stone that gleamed in the beam of his flashlight. On the floor next to it lay a yellow-stained mattress, splattered with dark lumps. A Styrofoam cooler sat beside it, finger markings darkening its lid. It looked recently handled. Nearby stood six filled canning jars, still sealed.

"What the hell?" He knelt beside the mattress and jars. It took him a few moments to comprehend what he was seeing.

"You OK up there?" Prusik called again. He could hear her footsteps on the staircase.

The sheriff stood shakily. He stepped cautiously out of the foul-smelling room and returned to the top of the landing, his revulsion making him queasy. "I need a forensic anthropologist up here, Christine. Quick." He swallowed, with difficulty. "You'd better brace yourself."

* * *

The skies were lightening as Prusik and McFaron made calls from the car late that afternoon. Prusik immediately called Managing Director Thorne's office.

"Hi, Roger, it's Christine. I'm at a derelict tenement building in Delphos, sir, which we believe to be a place of significance to our killer—David Claremont's identical twin. Well, genetically identical, at least."

"You're where? Do you realize Bruce Howard has left at least six phone messages inquiring about the status of your examination of the Claremont farm material?"

"May I explain, sir? We have uncovered significant—"

"Christine, consider this a friendly warning. Get back to the lab ASAP. Stop putting your job on the line like this."

"But, sir, there is physical evidence here that…"

"You have *mountains* of physical evidence waiting for you back at the lab. Get back there and do your job."

Thorne ended the call.

She phoned her lab.

"I need you and Hughes over here ASAP for some discreet fieldwork," she told Eisen. She described to him the location of the small room near the roof exit, architecturally designed for holding roofing equipment for the tenement buildings of the day, and told him about the soiled mattress and canning jars.

"Make sure Hughes brings his fingerprint and stain-retrieval kit. And the tissue collector, too. And bring plenty of dry ice."

"Howard's riding us pretty hard." There was a discernible edge to Eisen's voice. "We've got nearly two hundred evidence bags from Weaversville to screen. He's asked several times to speak with you, Christine. He wants to know why you're not here checking for evidence."

"Listen, Brian, now's not the time to quibble. Just get down here right away. It's the murderer's fucking lair, for Christ's sake."

"OK, OK. By the way, I picked up this weird tip from a friend who works the police beat at the *Indianapolis Star* newspaper."

Prusik sat up attentively. "And?"

"Evidently, a woman riled enough to call our Indy field office after midnight Sunday night said that the suspect shown on TV was seated next to her on a Greyhound bus bound from Chicago to Indianapolis. The spitting image of the suspect, she was quoted as saying. It was the day Claremont was charged with the murders."

"See!" Prusik smiled at McFaron, who looked back, curious. "Does Howard know yet? This business about Indianapolis?"

"Not to my knowledge."

With the usual plethora of erroneous call-ins and claimed sightings, Prusik doubted he would have given it much attention even if he had heard.

"Keep it on ice, Brian. I need more time without Thorne interceding and shutting down this line of investigation. You and Hughes get down here as fast as you can." She clicked off her phone.

"Son of a gun."

"Well?" McFaron said. "Are you going to tell me?"

"It's possible our Donald Holmquist chose public transportation and is deliberately avoiding his own vehicle." Prusik wanted to believe the information Brian had passed on, but rationally she knew it was a long shot. Still, her intuition was working on overdrive. She turned sideways, facing the sheriff. "He's being careful, very careful."

Christine opened her forensic case and withdrew the small brass-framed picture she'd recovered from the room in the apartment. It was sealed in a clear plastic evidence sleeve, and she held the old black-and-white photograph close to inspect it. She could hardly contain her excitement. She nudged Joe, who was looking over her shoulder at the picture of two mothers, each holding a baby.

"Do you see it?" she said. "Look closely at each child." Christine handed the framed picture to him.

She noticed the sheriff squinting. "You can't see it?" she said, unable to contain her excitement.

"I'm not sure what it is I'm supposed to be looking at," he said. "Why don't you just tell me?"

"I'll admit that it's subtle. And you haven't had the benefit of speaking directly to Dr. Emil Katz, our staff forensic psychiatrist." Although it was only a five-by-seven photograph, the camera that took the picture had an excellent lens, because the details captured were sharp, unmistakable.

"Notice the babies' hair." She pointed to each child's head. "Opposing whorls—their cowlicks go in opposite directions. One infant is raising his left hand, see, and the other, his right."

McFaron blew air out his lips in an expression of consternation. "For starters, Christine, how can you be so sure they're both boys, even?"

"From this picture, I can't. But it's the only thing that makes sense. David Claremont as the killer certainly doesn't make sense.

"Imagine being separated at an early age from your twin brother. You grow up and don't hear or see or perhaps even remember much of anything about this other you've been taken from. Then, all of a sudden, voilà, his face—your face, or nearly so—appears on every TV set in America, every newspaper. There it is. Your face is his. And your crime is also his now. Still, it's a face you're seeing for the first time in years. Someone who looks like you, a presence that you've had more than an inkling of at different times."

Prusik's heart was racing. "He can't stay away, Joe. He traveled on public transit to Indianapolis because he can't stay away."

"The state capital, the transportation hub," McFaron pointed out, "where he would need to go to catch another bus to Weaversville." The sheriff still wasn't fully on board with Christine's assumptions, but the infants in the photograph did show a distinct familial resemblance, and the adoption records definitely confirmed there were brothers, if not twins.

Prusik squeezed the sheriff's forearm with both hands. "He's going to meet his brother." She banged the door panel hard. "Yes! It fits."

"Take it easy with that door," McFaron said. "Taxpayers' property."

She weighed her choices. It couldn't wait. Things were happening too fast. Joe and she had struck the mother lode and were hot on the killer's trail. There was no time to convince and redirect Thorne's and Howard's attention before the trail would run cold, or worse, Holmquist would kill again. On that last thought, Christine nervously scrolled through her cell phone's directory of courts and prosecuting attorneys for the southern Indiana district. She hesitated. What she was doing could mean her job. Prison even. Did she really have no other options? Her pinkie began throbbing—she hadn't even realized she was clenching her fist. Slow down, Christine, think it all the way through, she counseled herself. Not only was she contemplating doing something her superiors would never condone, but it would surely bring down the wrath of the whole bureau on her. She'd be breaking the law. No question. Like he'd be, snuffing the last breath out of another innocent girl. What other viable alternative did she have that could stop that from happening?

Without further discussion, Prusik got out of the car, tapped in the number to the Weaversville, Indiana, prosecutor's office, and slowly walked down the sidewalk, not wanting McFaron to hear. "Prosecuting Attorney Gray, please."

"Preston Gray here."

Prusik filled him in on the developments: since Claremont's arrest three days earlier, not a particle of concrete evidence had been retrieved that tied him to any of the killings—no foreign blood, no semen, no identifiable DNA in scrapings taken from under any of the victims' fingernails or Claremont's. She assured Gray there wouldn't be any. The case wouldn't stick.

"It was my impression Bruce Howard and his team were still collecting evidence at the Claremont farmhouse and outbuildings, Special Agent Prusik."

"Mostly they're circling back over evidence we've already tested," she said, her mind humming. The information that Holmquist was in transit meant that things were moving fast. Timing was everything, and she needed to motivate Gray to help set the trap.

"We've uncovered proof that Claremont has a brother, an identical twin," she disclosed with an increasing sense of vindication. "We've verified it with fingerprints and obtained blood-typing matches identical to Claremont's own blood group. More detailed DNA profiling analysis is under way. The point is, we have a window of opportunity here, sir, and I am authorized to convey to you our support of a petition for bail." Her heart raced. As much as she disliked going out on a limb, lying to a public official, she feared more the clock ticking and the increasing chance of another young girl crossing paths with Donald Holmquist.

"Surely you're kidding?" Gray sounded incredulous. "You have any idea what you're saying? The media will have a field day."

"I'm not talking about letting him go completely free, Counselor, far from it. I'm talking around-the-clock surveillance. I'm talking about catching the real killer." She swallowed hard, turned, and faced McFaron sitting in the car, watching her. She looked down at her feet. "I have authorization for this request. You have the full backing of the bureau on this."

"You're saying the FBI will accept full responsibility?" Gray said slowly.

"I'll have my office fax it to you tonight."

"You say Claremont has an identical brother? A look-alike who's responsible for these killings?"

"Yes, sir. Our evidence backs it up without a doubt."

"How can you be sure it wasn't Claremont, rather than his twin, who committed these crimes?"

Christine could practically hear Gray shaking his head back and forth, trying to process the information and assess the effects of her request on his office. "Look, I understand your concerns primarily lie with your community. How it would look to release Claremont on bail? We've formulated a plan that our experts believe will break the case and give you what you need for a successful conviction." She covered the receiver while taking in another deep breath.

Silence on the other end. Prusik could tell Gray needed more. He wouldn't be able to go to the media or answer the phones that would surely ring off the hook, explaining that a twin had committed the crimes, a brother who hadn't yet been apprehended. That would strain his office to the limit.

"There is a phenomenon at work here, Mr. Gray, a form of twin bonding that is difficult for me to explain over the phone. Suffice it to say that the best minds at the bureau support this view. Claremont's interview confirmed it. Subsequently we've uncovered proof that he has a twin. Lawrence and Hilda Claremont adopted David before his first birthday. I don't believe Claremont knows for sure he has a brother. We're very close to bringing this man in. The brother. The killer, sir."

"Close? I'm sorry, Special Agent. Close won't cut it. Not down where I live, it won't." She headed down the block, farther away from the car.

Prusik had expected that convincing Gray would be a long shot, and losing her cool now would do no good. "Admittedly, sir, it's not what the bureau would prefer, either. *If* we had a choice. It's the public we all want to protect." Her tone grew more urgent. "That's precisely the reason for the bureau's request now. In order to catch the brother before he commits another heinous murder we must all take a chance, Mr. Gray. Claremont won't ever be out of our sight. Count on it. But in order to bring his brother to bay there must be publicity. It's the bait—announcing on every radio station and TV channel that David Claremont has been released into his parents' custody on the Claremont farmstead in Weaversville. We're counting on the media to do its part, sir. In our bureau chief's best judgment, it will lead to the murderer's arrest. Time, however, is of the essence." She stopped before asking him whether he wanted to have the next gutted girl on his conscience.

More interminable silence on the other end—Gray was apparently mulling things over. He emitted an extended sigh, then said, "Send that directive. I'll examine it. If it says what you say, I'll agree to house arrest, meaning Claremont stays in his parents' house twenty-four seven under police surveillance and monitoring. My office will stipulate as to bail. I'll start the paperwork tomorrow first thing."

"Good."

Prusik had been successful. If the transposition phenomenon was at work, freeing Claremont should serve up the killer. Still, it was a daring move, which Thorne would never have approved—or thought of. He hadn't a clue of the dimensions of this case. He *would* have her head for it, unless she delivered.

She made one more call to her secretary, Margaret, and then got back in the car. She looked at Joe, then stared into her lap, unsure how to broach what she had just set in motion.

"So are you going to tell me what that call was all about?" McFaron said.

Christine met his eyes and smiled faintly, knowing it might be their last conversation for a while. She took a breath and explained.

McFaron didn't respond right away. Finally, he cleared his throat and spoke. "Christine, I have to say that's kind of…a gutsy thing to do without passing it by Thorne first, don't you think?"

Christine agreed with him completely, but she couldn't bring herself to admit it. She gave him a stony look.

"I'm just thinking of what's best for you," he continued. "I don't want to see you in a fix. Lose your job or anything."

"Try telling that to Holmquist's next victim, why don't you? Or her parents."

"But sending an agency directive?" he said. "There's got to be a better way. It could end your career."

"Don't you think I know? But you know as well as I do, when the importance of filling out routine forms or summary reports redirects our focus, it's the people who fall between the cracks. And lives are lost. Don't you see? With any luck, Holmquist will surface in Weaversville very soon. There's no time for politics, Joe. Not now."

"I'm not going to tell you how to do your job." He paused, gave her a serious look. "And I won't argue with you if you're in actual pursuit of someone, apprehending a suspect. But this? If you want the truth, Christine, what I'm hearing is justification at any cost, the means to an end."

She opened her mouth to respond, but McFaron held up a hand. "Police procedure and bureaucracy *are* important. It's what makes arrests stick, criminal convictions hold. I've got to deal with the state police, other counties' sheriffs, prosecutors, the FBI, state crime lab, state bureau agents. My point is, all this rigmarole that you speak of—and I do often see it as that, too—doesn't give me the right to cut to the chase, ignore probable cause, trample down someone's door, and especially not lie to a prosecuting attorney."

He looked at her resignedly. "So if things don't pan out the way you hope, what will you do?"

Prusik looked grim. "Assuming I'm not wearing an orange jumpsuit and asking permission from a prison guard to make a phone call to my lawyer?"

"Well, golly, Christine, did you think for even a moment about discussing this scheme with me?" McFaron rubbed his finger over his lip.

"Of course I did." She closed her eyes. "And I knew what you'd say."

"But, come on, Christine, we have the goods, the apartment evidence. Is it really worth potentially throwing away the case like this?"

"It's really very simple, Joe," she said matter-of-factly. "The killer is on the move. I made the call to catch him. And if I'm dead wrong, or get fired or worse, so be it."

McFaron got out of the car. Prusik followed. A half-moon peeked above a row of tenements.

"Pretty, isn't it?" she said, referring to the moon, hoping to save the tense moment from becoming any tenser.

"Yes, it is, Christine," McFaron said with obvious resignation. "Look, under the circumstances…" He shrugged. He couldn't let it go. "Christine, did you even stop and think that my job may be on the line, too? Did you ever consider that?"

"If you want to back out, I'll entirely understand. I stepped out of the car before making the call, Joe, to keep you from being a witness so that your job *wouldn't* be on the line. In fact, no one from my office even knows you're here in Chicago. You can walk away into the night," she said flatly, "and I won't hold it against you one bit. You've done me a huge favor helping out in Delphos. I couldn't have done that alone."

McFaron studied her face. "No turning back with the directive, I suppose. It's a done deal?"

"It's probably in the prosecuting attorney's hands as we speak, or it will be shortly." Prusik had called her secretary and listened as Margaret keyed in word for word the directive to send to Prosecuting Attorney Gray, and then printed it out on the bureau's embossed stationery. The older woman had shrugged off Christine's promises to take the blame for any fallout, saying that if it came to it, she really wouldn't mind taking an early retirement. After reading the copy back, she had faked Prusik's signature and messengered the document over to Gray's office.

"Look, I'll admit it's a risky move, and I understand your disapproval." She looked Joe in the eye. "I'm prepared to take the heat if it backfires. If you need to be reminded, we're talking about preventing the next murder, Joe. And evisceration."

McFaron nodded somberly. "Under the circumstances, I think it's best that I return tonight, see what's what." In a soft voice, he continued, "You and I both know that I'm not going to be of much help to you at this point. Convincing your people. If anything, they'll misconstrue my presence, making things worse for you. And I certainly won't be any help to my own office, the people of my county. You agree?"

The look of dejection on the sheriff's face pained her. Dinner in a nice, cozy restaurant wasn't to be. She had made her choice—made her bed as it were—although she believed in her heart that the decision had been made for her by circumstances at work that were beyond her control. She had no choice. She wished the sheriff would stay but knew that he couldn't.

Christine took a deep lungful of breath. "OK then. Shall I drive you to the airport?"

The twenty minutes to O'Hare were passed in silence. As much as she wanted to, Christine restrained herself from explaining, again, her rationale for her actions; she realized that any hope of salvaging things with Joe would have to wait for another day. She glanced at him and was aware of his tight jaw, the muscles twitching by his eye. Whatever he wasn't saying was costing him, too.

The car idled at the curb in front of the United Express entry doors. "I appreciate your flying up on such short notice, Joe," she said. "I couldn't have gone into that awful place without you. No way."

McFaron pursed his lips in curt acknowledgment of her words. "OK then." He opened the car door and placed one foot on the sidewalk. "I'll call you later tonight. See how things are going."

She couldn't bring herself to make eye contact with him, fearing she'd lost more than just a good friend. A moment later Christine looked up as he was passing through the security kiosk near the entrance. He waved politely, his face restrained now, not like when he had first arrived and given her a beaming smile. Tears filled her eyes in the privacy of the car, and feelings of being at the end rather than the beginning of the relationship consumed her.

A clap of thunder startled her, and heavy raindrops started to splash against the windshield. Christine pulled away from the passenger unloading area and flipped on the wipers. Then she slammed the brakes and jerked the car back to the curb, staring at the wiper blade now stopped in its upright position. A thin line of red trickled down the windshield, then was gone under a hard rain that couldn't wash away the fact it was real, as real as the evidence they'd uncovered this afternoon. She grabbed her purse on the passenger seat and fished out her pills, then removed a new evidence bag from her forensic case in the backseat and stepped out of the car, oblivious to the torrent. Warily, she scanned both directions of the access way leading to the airport, blinking away raindrops. Then she carefully lifted the wiper blade and with her other rubber-gloved hand gently removed the small blue-green feather caught underneath it and slipped it into a protective sleeve.

CHAPTER TWENTY-SIX

The next morning, two hundred and eighty-five miles away in Weaversville, Claremont's parents posted a $500,000 property bond after a bail hearing, literally betting the farm on their son's innocence. Afterward, Hilda stood beside her living room window, staring out into a late-morning haze, waiting for Dr. Walstein to arrive. Her husband hadn't wanted any breakfast and was troubled by a new rattle that had developed in his Chevy truck right after the FBI had removed the seats, looking for evidence they didn't find.

The Claremonts' son remained the only suspect in the sensational case. Under the court order, he wasn't allowed off the farm. Two deputies were to be posted there around the clock, and Deputy Richard Owens and his partner, Jim Boles, of the Weaversville Police Station were standing the first watch at the end of the Claremont driveway after accompanying the suspect and his parents home. Hearing air brakes, the police officers looked up. A local bus came to a stop at an intersection near the Claremonts' cornfield. Alerted, the deputies watched for anyone getting off—a clever news reporter or photographer hankering for a camera shot of the suspect, but neither deputy could see as the doors opened on the other side. A moment later the bus started up, passing Owens and Boles in a flourish of diesel exhaust. Owens studied the spot in front of the cornfield from which the bus pulled away. No one was there. Maybe some kid on board had gotten woozy and had to puke and then gotten back on board, he thought, and put it out of his mind.

A few minutes later, a jet-black Chrysler Concorde LXi pulled up to the deputies. Dr. Walstein tipped his Irish tweed rain hat and handed Owens his driver's license. Owens checked his clipboard and then motioned Walstein to proceed down the drive.

The bail release terms required Claremont to submit to a psychological evaluation twice weekly. It also required the Claremonts to pay the doctor's fees for each visit. Hilda hurried down the front porch steps as Walstein's car crept down the drive. She handed him a check through the window so he wouldn't have to get out.

"David's down at the barn doing his chores, Doctor."

Walstein followed the well-worn tractor traces around to the back of the barn. A muffled police broadcast sounded off in the cabin of the car. Walstein flipped open the glove box. The scanner's diodes were flashing. "Jenkins reported that it's for real—not a ten-fifteen. Claremont's out on bail." Walstein knew what the police code meant, confirming that David was no longer in police custody. He slammed the glove box shut, feeling nervous. David had been set free on a technicality, something about a lack of corroborative evidence. Was it more than just troubling visions? Had he missed something in the diagnosis? He drew his coat sleeve across his forehead to blot up the building perspiration.

A wooden ramp led up to a large set of doors that hung wide open. Walstein cut the motor, letting the car glide in neutral the rest of the way. He tapped the brakes, straining to see inside the cavernous barn before slipping out the driver's side. He checked his jacket pockets. The syringe was in its baggie. He inserted his other hand cautiously in his other jacket pocket, careful not to touch the switch as he ran his fingers over the high-voltage Taser. He had no intention of using the sedative or the stun gun, but he'd promised his wife that he would bring them in order to allay her fears.

Walstein checked behind him one last time. He could see the police car at the top of the drive, just where it was supposed to be. The doctor let out a breath.

A shadow flickered past the ramp through the double doors, catching the doctor's attention. Adrenaline pumped the doctor up the ramp. He hesitated by the open doorway, sniffing the fusty odors within. Bits of straw that had fallen from the high loft lay strewn about the heavily grooved floorboards.

"David?"

There was no answer.

Walstein ventured into the shadows, his shoes making hollow thuds, though he tried to keep his steps light. At the end of a long row of metal stanchions where cows had once stood to be milked, he saw light coming from behind a door cracked slightly open. An old rock tune was playing on a radio somewhere in the back.

"David?" Instinctively Walstein's fingers entered the flaps of his jacket pockets. He walked past the stanchions, called out David's name again.

Still there was no answer.

Something behind him bumped. Walstein spun on his heels, his hands in the ready position. He strained, blinking at the dark recesses, but saw no one there. A breeze caught one of the outer doors, slapped it back and forth. Overhead, there was a hay chute. A few wads of straw hung from its edges. A draft of cooler air found Walstein's brow. He relaxed his grip a little in his pockets.

"David, this is Dr. Walstein. I've come for the required check-in, remember?" The doctor walked slowly forward. The doorway to the lit room was not twenty feet away. "If you're busy, I can wait outside the barn in the car."

Both barn doors crashed shut at once, consuming the doctor in sudden darkness. He aimed the Taser gun in the direction of the closed doors. The distinct tip-tap of rapid footsteps whirled him to his left. He thumbed the power button on. Six green lights glowed, registering full-strength voltage.

"Why, David." Walstein sucked in a breath. "I...I didn't hear you coming."

The doctor took a step backward and tripped over a roll of baling wire, landing hard on the floor. Gasping, he struggled to pull his left hand out of his pocket. Rolling onto his side, he managed to free it. The hypodermic syringe hung from the doctor's palm. Holding it closer, he focused on the measuring lines along the cylinder. The stopper was flush with the end of the cylinder, but somehow it didn't disturb him that he'd injected himself with what was for him an overdose of sedative, given his slighter build than David's.

A spear of sunlight cut through a loose barn board, highlighting the endless passage of dust particles. It wasn't at all bad lying in the dark, only a little harder to breathe. Lethargically, Walstein blinked a few times, fumbled at the needle with fingers growing too numb to extract it from deep in his left palm. His arms went limp as a marionette's, and he stared unfocused into space. The dimness above him shifted. Two eyes were gleaming down from the dusty vacuum of the barn—David Claremont's face.

Or not.

Walstein couldn't process the thought. A minute later he couldn't even recall he'd had a thought. Suddenly he was rising with the dust onto his feet. How nice it was to be carried.

"David...you...shouldn't..."

Walstein's words came out not sounding like his, but that was because his mouth was squashed against the man's shoulder. The doctor relaxed his chin into the well-worn cloth of the man's jacket, like a baby does as it falls asleep. The lights went out.

* * *

Thirty minutes after Dr. Walstein had been cleared to enter the Claremonts' residence Deputy Owens waved the sedan back out the driveway, recognizing the doctor's Irish tweed hat, which was pulled down low over the driver's brow. The other deputy, Boles, glanced inside the car as it passed by him and turned onto the blacktop: no passengers. Owens checked off the doctor's name on his clipboard and watched as the automobile slowly accelerated down the county road.

Neither deputy noticed the small swatch of fabric from Dr. Walstein's jacket that had been caught in the trunk lid as it had slammed closed. And although the window glass was tinted, the appearance of a rumpled blanket across the backseat registered something in Deputy Boles's mind. Whatever it was that registered, though, was lost when his cell phone chirped. He saw his new girlfriend's number flash on the display, flipped open the phone, and gave her his full attention.

* * *

Shortly after the lunch hour Prusik got the call from the lab that she'd been waiting for. She now had the goods on the killer: the canning jars recovered from the Delphos tenement clearly contained human viscera. She had hoped preliminary DNA testing would be completed, matching the remains to one of the victims before giving Thorne the full details, but that would take another seventy-two hours, and she didn't think she should wait.

Entering the managing director's office, Prusik was surprised to hear Howard's voice on the speakerphone. Beside Thorne's desk stood a security guard.

"What in God's name is the meaning of this!" Thorne slammed his best inkwell pen—the Montblanc—on the desk so hard it bounced. Veins bulged on either side of his shirt collar.

Thorne sailed a fax over his desktop. Prusik scooped it off the floor: the signed directive.

"What were you thinking, Christine? That you'd wait until Howard was out of the office before springing this?"

Prusik kept her eyes down, concentrating, trying to formulate words that wouldn't come.

"No, Roger, sir, not at all. My actions were predicated on late-breaking information and forensic evidence discovered at a condemned building at thirteen seventy-one Hawthorne Boulevard in Delphos, apartment 3C. I called you. I tried to tell you on the phone, sir, at the time of the discovery." She spoke louder to address Howard, who was still on the call. "Bruce, if you want to check out the apartment, we can—"

"Check it out?" Thorne tossed another paper her way. "Why don't you check this out first? Please explain, Christine."

Prusik scanned the face page of the Weaversville District Court's stipulated bail order, which was dated earlier that morning.

"You mean the terms of Claremont's bail release?" Prusik's heartbeats ratcheted up.

"You know damn well what I mean!" Thorne's forehead bunched up. "Howard has confirmed already that you were instrumental in this. That you assured Prosecuting Attorney Gray he had the full backing of the bureau to release the suspect. For God's sake, Christine!"

"Roger, if you'll give me a moment to explain, I can. We've uncovered critical new information on a Donald Holmquist, Claremont's twin, that will answer all your—"

"Then you'll have no trouble explaining this to me!"

Thorne flung a third document over the desk edge, which Prusik snatched midflight. It was an APB for David Claremont, now at large, who was wanted for three murders and the kidnapping of Dr. Irwin Walstein, a court-appointed psychiatrist who had gone missing from the Claremont farm following a scheduled medical appointment earlier that same day.

Prusik gasped. She took a chair, speechless.

"Since you're at such a loss for words, I'll talk. Effective immediately you're relieved of duty. I'm suspending you. Consider yourself on paid leave for now. Be thankful—I could have your badge for this, permanently. The lab team is being notified as I speak that you are off the case. They don't follow your orders anymore."

Thorne removed his glasses. "Whatever your reasons, they're unimportant now. Save them for your administrative discharge hearing."

Prusik swallowed hard and then somehow found her voice. "The reason for Claremont's release on bail—there's a perfectly logical explanation if you'll let me. It's important that I explain."

"Explain?" Thorne shook his head and snorted in disgust. "You had no business pulling a stunt like this, Christine. Signing a directive, speaking on behalf of the department on such a high-profile matter. *Releasing a suspected murderer?* Really, there is no explanation that will suffice." His face was red with heat. "'The complete backing of the FBI'—have you gone mad? You're lucky I'm not firing you on the spot. As it is, my hands are tied now. There's nothing more I can do for you."

He meant Washington knew. He was following their orders.

"For your information, your Sheriff McFaron is part of the dragnet combing the southern Indiana area for Claremont right now. Am I correct, Bruce?" Thorne spoke directly into the speaker pod on his desk.

"I just got the call," Howard's voice came back. "He said he's checking out someone down his way that identified Claremont from the police sketch."

"Your hands may be tied, sir, I grant you that," Prusik said, steeling herself, "but that still leaves open the matter of Donald Holmquist's being at large. Eisen and Higgins ran background checks on his history."

Prusik planted both hands on the front edge of Thorne's desk. "I've got the goods, Roger. The physical evidence is an eye-opener from hell. David Claremont is no more responsible for Dr. Walstein's disappearance than he is for those girls' deaths. Holmquist is our man, sir. And…" She stopped short of telling him about the feather under her windshield wiper, realizing how ridiculous that would sound to Thorne. "And he's on the move."

"An interesting theory, Ms. Prusik." Howard's voice over the speakerphone was grating. "Especially since we've already obtained a set of Claremont's prints from the doctor's syringe that was found on the barn floor at the Claremont farm."

"Fingerprints prove what? That Claremont may have been present? He lives there. And, besides, by my estimation, those are most likely his twin's prints on that syringe, not Claremont's. The friction ridges and whorls of Donald Holmquist's are a very close match. Too close to exclude without running a bilateral print comparison of them both."

Prusik held up the APB fax Howard had sent Thorne. "I challenge you, Bruce, to show me one bit of corroborative evidence that you've taken from the Claremont farm incriminating your suspect. So far, nothing you've sent to the lab even remotely ties Claremont to any of these crimes."

"Excuse me," interrupted Thorne, "but there's an outraged community calling for my hide, demanding an answer from the FBI for authorizing Claremont's release. The fact is, Special Agent Prusik, you're officially relieved as of this moment. End of discussion."

"You should know, sir," Christine said, holding her ground, "that on the night of Claremont's arrest, a report was filed with our Indianapolis field office by a Mrs. Henrietta Curry. The woman saw Holmquist riding on a bus bound from Chicago to Indianapolis. She sat next to him for over three hours, sir. We lost track of him once he arrived in Indianapolis, but I'm sure that very soon we'll be able to confirm he subsequently traveled to Weaversville. He's within our reach, sir."

Thorne smiled bitterly, shaking his head. "You're really something," he said. "You don't know when to let it go, do you? You never have, Christine." His expression turned dead serious. "The local deputy charged to watch the Claremont farmhouse saw

Walstein's car leave," he said. "He logged in the doctor when he first arrived at the Claremont farm, nobody else. A half hour later he noted the doctor's car leaving. And now Claremont's missing, just like that. The prints on the syringe corroborate more than mere presence at the scene, Christine." Thorne thumped his forefinger on the desk. "You should have known better than to pull this kind of stunt! His prints are all over the hypodermic!"

Thorne's secretary poked her head in. "Deputy Commissioner on line one."

"That'll be all." Thorne shooed Christine away.

The security guard shadowed her as she walked back to her office and stood conspicuously outside her door while she collected a few personal things. She moved as slowly as she could, trying to sort things out in her mind and formulate a plan. The true killer remained at large. In spite of present circumstances, she must find a way to navigate or another girl would surely die. She had to get in touch with McFaron.

She closed her briefcase and tried to phone Eisen and Higgins but with no luck. No doubt they were all down in the conference room being filled in by Howard over the speakerphone there.

Margaret stuck a pained face in the doorway.

"I'm so sorry, Margaret. I had no right getting you involved like I did. None. Please don't tell me you've been put on leave, too."

"Oh, pooh." Margaret waved it off. "This will blow over, and I need a good vacation anyway."

"I'm so, so sorry." Prusik ducked her head and futzed at her desk.

"Oh, I almost forgot." Margaret stepped into the office and closed the door. "Your flight to Crosshaven—it leaves in ninety minutes." She held out a plane ticket.

Prusik looked up, puzzled. "You don't understand. I've been taken off the case."

"Don't you remember? I reminded you after Sheriff McFaron flew back. Mrs. Greenwald, the scout leader, called to confirm.

It's all been arranged, Christine. The Brownie troop is expecting you to speak to them at their Echo Lake State Park outing this afternoon."

Prusik flopped back in her chair. "I can't go now." She massaged her temples. "I've been put on administrative leave, probably on my way to being fired. I can't very well show up as an example of professional success."

"So you're not going to honor your commitment to those little girls?"

Prusik raised her head, caught off guard by the older woman's crustiness. "I've been relieved of duty, Margaret. Even if I wanted to go, I couldn't. They've practically fired me, for Christ's sake!"

"Woe unto you—flustered FBI agent cancels speaking engagement to a group of hopeful Brownies." Margaret's scorn was unmistakable. "Aren't you forgetting that *I* was actually the one who signed your name to that directive?"

"Yes, under my orders."

"What are all those young hopefuls going to think when they hear that the professional agent who was going to come speak to them didn't because she was taken off a case and then was too embarrassed to look them in the eye?" Margaret looked almost as disturbed as Thorne. The older woman leaned forward. "Look, it may be none of my business, but I overheard you speaking to Special Agent Eisen. Don't let these coots bully you, Christine. Not when you see things as clearly as you do."

Prusik pressed her lips together and swallowed hard. "Thanks," she said after a moment.

She shoved the plane ticket inside her jacket pocket and picked up her briefcase. "Someday very soon we'll have a nice long talk over some stiff drinks."

"A car's waiting downstairs." Margaret motioned her hand toward the door. "Now get to it, Special Agent."

* * *

Prusik walked out of the building that had been her life for the past decade, tossed her case on the backseat of the waiting car, and asked Bill to take her to the airport terminal. It relieved her that he just smiled and nodded, meaning he hadn't heard yet that she hadn't authority to even issue instructions to be driven to O'Hare. And he was good enough at reading signals to know she wasn't in the mood for conversation. Which was good, because she didn't want to have to outright lie to him. Telling him the truth would only get him in trouble.

Her cell phone vibrated. Dr. Katz's name flashed across its display. "Yes, Doctor?"

"Something's been bugging me ever since you left my office about this dichotomy business between the man who is doing the killing and your suspect who is not and who may share the same genes."

Judging from the doctor's focus to task it was clear he hadn't been given word of her being relieved of duty, either. "I'm listening."

"Extreme abnormal behavior such as you described may be part of a broader progression."

"What are you saying?"

"Christine, something severe is lacking. A person who removes the organs of his victims most certainly is experiencing a tremendous state of emptiness—a void—which is all consuming. These visions of David Claremont's, if the transposition phenomenon is at work, probably mean that they know the other exists by now. If so, the killer knows that his brother has been arrested. It's been on TV, the radio, all over the newspapers. This could change things dramatically, escalating out of control. I'm not sure I mentioned it to you in our last conversation, in cases of metabolic brain disease, there is a higher than expected concordance among monozygotic twins in more than one study."

"Meaning exactly?"

"One twin may trigger the other into performing these despicable acts. You said yourself you haven't evaluated the suspect properly. I certainly haven't. We don't know the full extent of his pathology. It's a troublesome unknown. I advise you to proceed with caution."

"Look, Doctor, it is my expectation from your mention of this twinning bond that Holmquist—the name of our killer—will seek out his brother, in earnest—"

"Yes, yes. But that's just the point, my reason for calling," the doctor interrupted her. "It has to do with you. You were Claremont's arresting officer?"

"Howard technically was, but yes, I interviewed Claremont."

"He knows your name, what you look like, and probably has a fair idea where you work. It would be easy for this other twin, the presumed killer, to find out about you should he make contact with Claremont. You represent a real threat to him, Christine. I'm concerned for your safety. You're heading into unknown territory, assuming we're not just talking poppycock."

Christine swallowed hard. The killer *did* know about her. The feather under her windshield wiper, hidden until she'd turned the wipers on, proved that.

"I'm just on my way to a speaking engagement," she said, preferring to ignore the threat of the feather for the moment. She was uncomfortable enough as it was concealing from Katz the truth of her present status with the bureau.

"Keep your line open. I may want to call you back again. You're a good egg, my dear. Don't go out on a limb without backup. Promise me?"

"I promise. Thank you, Doctor."

For an instant she flashed on the service revolver tucked away under a sweater on the closet shelf in her apartment, but said nothing to Bill. There wasn't enough time to collect it and still make her flight. She'd have to make do on cunning and gut instinct. It had gotten her this far.

* * *

Dennis Murfree met Prusik at the Crosshaven airport at three thirty. The troop meeting was scheduled for four thirty at Echo Lake State Park, a good thirty- to forty-minute drive, according to Murfree. The old rattletrap accelerated poorly. Passing through Crosshaven, there was no sign of the sheriff's Bronco in front of his office. Ten miles farther south, Murfree cut onto a secondary dirt road. It was nearing four o'clock.

Prusik replayed in her mind Katz's call and was touched that he had cared enough to call. What if he called Thorne afterward and found out the truth of her dismissal? How humiliating. She shook her head. The whole situation was an unmitigated disaster. After she spoke to the Brownies, she'd have to find a way to get someone to listen to her.

Suddenly, the car engine chuffed. Murfree goosed the gas pedal a few times to no avail as it slowly died.

"Must be flooded," he mumbled. They glided to a halt along the gravel roadside. He whined the starter motor a few times without success.

"What seems to be the problem, Dennis?"

"It acts up sometimes." He scratched his bald crown. "First time today, though."

After a few more unsuccessful attempts he lifted the hood. The wretched car, Prusik thought. Her watch read 4:05 p.m. "About how far is it to Echo Lake?"

"Better part of five miles yet." He stayed hunched over the engine, fiddling and wheezing. "Give or take."

Prusik tried McFaron's number. Still out of the area. Restless, she pondered the wisdom of making a run for it. She grabbed her purse and cell phone.

"Listen, Dennis, I've got to make this speaking engagement. The girls are counting on me. If I start out on foot, any possibility that someone'll pass by and give me a lift?"

Murfree looked up and blinked a few times. "It's possible. I wouldn't go counting on it, but it is definitely possible. People do drive by."

Christine nodded, her mind made up. "OK. Do me a favor and notify the sheriff's office." She gave him a twenty-dollar bill and started jogging down the road. "Keep the change."

"Yes, ma'am. Sorry about…" But he was talking to the wind, watching Prusik's short locks disappear around a bend, shaded by the dark boughs of overhanging hemlock. He decided he'd wait a good fifteen minutes for the flooded engine to clear. In the meantime, he could pass along Prusik's message. He radioed the sheriff's office on his two-way, using the police frequency.

"Murfree's Cab Service calling. Mary, you there, darling?"

CHAPTER TWENTY-SEVEN

The radio dial spun, stopped, and spun again. The driver was searching the airwaves the same way Claremont liked to. To Claremont it seemed as if he himself were driving, but he was pretty sure he wasn't. In fact, he was pretty sure he was crammed uncomfortably in the backseat. The car smelled new; there was something ominous about it. The whole thing wasn't right. The ringing in his ears made him feel uneasy, too; he wasn't exactly sure why. He couldn't seem to move other than to blink. He couldn't see out the windshield, either. The shadows of trees whizzed by overhead as the car bounced heavily over ruts.

The dial lingered on an old rock tune. *Break on through to the other side.* Claremont hummed the refrain, a favorite of his. He heard it being hummed from the front seat, too, the driver lightly tapping the steering wheel now.

The song ended. Claremont recognized the DJ's deep-throated voice. The radio was tuned to WTWN, the station for the twin cities of Weaversville on the Indiana side and Metamora, which straddled the Illinois banks of the Wabash River. It was the station he liked, too. The DJ read the daily calendar of announcements.

"Quilt show down at Cave Springs Baptist Church has some mighty fine bed throws to see. Doors open to the public at two o'clock sharp, folks."

After an ad break for Henderson Galoshes came a news flash announcing the escape of the suspect David Claremont. The driver flicked off the radio and tossed the green tweed rain hat he was wearing down on the passenger seat. He twitched his neck left and right and vigorously vibrated a forefinger in his right ear, reaming it out good, the same way Claremont dealt with an itch. The man blinked with enough force to dance his cheeks up and down, which triggered an identical tic in Claremont. It was as if an invisible cord were stretched between them. But something wasn't right. Claremont's churning stomach told him so. Still, he couldn't take his eyes off the hands that played freely over the top of the steering wheel, pitter-pattering and then constricting around the grip. It was also a habit of his.

That bitch FBI agent thinks she knows it all. The unspoken words streamed into Claremont's head, words he couldn't control, words that made no rational sense. The man up front was having himself a little interior chat. *Where to go next—Paoli, Blackie, or back to Delphos?* The clamoring in Claremont's head became deafening.

The driver tilted the rearview, glancing over a pair of gold-rimmed glasses that rode low on his nose. He gave Claremont the once-over. Squinted harder. They were familiar-looking glasses; Claremont had seen them before, the same wire rims. *Dr. Walstein's!*

Claremont's throat went dry. He *hadn't* imagined anything. He hadn't been crazy. It *was* this other person all along. Claremont's mind raced down the years, the chain of puzzling events, the minor gaps in time that had seemed so bewildering. He remembered riding in the backseat of his father's truck when he was a youngster, then suddenly starting to gag. He'd banged on the passenger door, signaling his distress. His father stopped along the dusty shoulder. David had felt an inexplicable rawness in his throat from something hard to swallow and a peculiar sense of being punished—abhorrent feelings he now realized had come from the man driving the car.

The driver made a silly face, kindling a return smile across David's own—the symmetry of it sent pinpricks showering across his chest and back. He made a move to sit up, but something was preventing him. He concentrated on the ache, the only thing he could do. Somehow he had to make the bastard stop. But how?

He focused between the front seats on a notepad holder fastened to the dash with handsome printing along the top edge: Irwin Walstein, MD. His eyes grew wide. *Walstein's car! The doctor's wire rims! His tweed hat!* He fought to hide his labored breathing.

"What did you do to the doctor?"

The driver's mouth drew to a razor slit. "Me? You mean what did *you* do, don't you?" He tightened his grip around the steering wheel. "He was calling out *your* name in that barn as I recollect." He poked one forefinger into the roof liner to punctuate his point.

"It's you, brother, not me, splashed all over TV and the radio. Them who sow thorns will not reap roses." The man blinked vigorously for emphasis. The hollows of his eyes burned back at Claremont.

"He's in the trunk," he added matter-of-factly. "Ain't going nowhere. Neither are you, brother."

Painful cramps knotted David's calves as the car jounced hard over washboard dirt. They were traveling fast, taking a back route. A muffled tweet intruded. The driver reached across the seat and punched open the glove box. Louder tweeting sounded.

"Well, looky here—a police scanner," he said. A transmission was in progress, something about an FBI woman on foot to Echo Lake. An agent named Prusik.

"Copy that. I'll report it to Sheriff McFaron," the dispatcher said. "Over and out."

The driver gunned the motor and met David's eyes in the rearview mirror. "What's that you say?"

Claremont hadn't said a thing, but he'd recognized the agent's name.

"Don't lie to me. She's the one after you about all them girls?" Without warning, he turned and lunged over the seat.

"You been talking to that FBI lady about me?" His hot breath hit David's face. He wasn't watching the road or giving a damn about where the car might be headed. "Don't think I'm not onto you, brother. Like white on rice."

He quickly checked out the windshield, then flung himself right back into Claremont's face. In the split second it took, the man's face had morphed from fury to joy; his cheeks stretched upward enough to reveal the ends of yellowed teeth. For the moment he was a changed man.

"Ever get so you can barely hold on to the wheel? Nearly wreck yourself before even getting started?" he said, giddy as a kid. He rapped Claremont's shoulder with the back of his wrist as if nothing bad had come between them.

"Nothing like gaining the upper hand, is there, brother?" The man twisted his neck this way and that, loudly cracking vertebrae, then rubbed the back of one arm hard enough for David to hear. "Get that prickly-pear skin all over you just thinking on her running through the woods."

His words knifed through David's gut. Sweat coursed down his cheeks. "Leave me alone!" he screamed. "Leave them alone!"

The driver leaned back over the seat and grabbed Claremont by the throat. "How many other coppers did you tell? Huh? Just that FBI woman? How many?"

He released Claremont and accelerated the car around a bend. They were headed east, toward Echo Lake, on another mission. Claremont worked his wrists behind his back, digging the twine through his flesh till it stung. He had to find a way to stop the visions from ever happening again. He had to find a way to stop the killing.

The car slid to a stop, and the demon was upon him again, as if sensing Claremont's growing determination. His fingers cinched tightly around Claremont's larynx.

"You was supposed to be dead already, Mother said. She told me you was dead." Now he was pinching off Claremont's air. "You were planning this all along, weren't you? Planning to bring me down."

Claremont's eyes rolled back. The light faded. When he regained consciousness, heaving raspy breaths, he arched his neck, gulping precious air. The car's ceiling panel swirled with dots. The driver's words loomed large—David was supposed to be dead, his mother had said.

"Sometimes I don't think you get my meaning at all." The driver spoke in a halting voice. "Like I wasn't sorry or something. Like I didn't try harder. To be more like you."

Claremont stared into the sad face of his twin, all signs of anger now drained away. The man seemed closer to mournful than to getting even. And closer to Claremont than anyone else on earth.

"We got our troubles, don't we?" A tear crept out the corner of the man's eye. He sat forward in his seat, resolute for the moment, content with his final assessment. As if no truer brotherhood existed.

A disorienting sensation—old familiar ground—suffused Claremont's mind with a diplopic effect—as if he were experiencing double vision. He saw himself muttering up front, knowing it was this other, and yet, at the same time, from somewhere deep inside, Claremont's very own shame was directing him to open his mouth. The driver turned, stretched over the seat. Obediently Claremont sat up. Without a word said between them, the driver fingered out of his pocket a small stone and placed it on Claremont's obliging tongue.

* * *

Twenty-three six-, seven-, and eight-year-old girls were chasing one another on the mowed lawn in front of the Echo Lake Recreation Center building. Quickly they were gathered and shuttled inside by chaperones. Arlene Greenwald, the scout leader, was taking no chances after learning of the manhunt for the escaped David Claremont. She was comforted by the fact that the ranger's cabin was directly across from the rec center. All the same, she had called the girls' parents to discuss whether to reconvene the outing some other day. The scout leader checked her watch—half past four—and wondered why Ms. Prusik hadn't yet arrived.

The girls gathered in the center of the room for the troop's regular announcements. Except Maddy, who leaned against the back wall, away from the group, inching her way to the door. She slipped outside and walked down to the water's edge. The peaceful solitude was soothing. Ever since her sister, Julie, had died, she couldn't stand to be around other people, except her parents. She crouched by the shore, observed a bullfrog disappear underwater and become a flattened image of itself. Out farther, fish were biting through the mirrorlike surface, feeding.

Maddy wandered along the lake edge, gazing at her reflection. A narrow foot trail entered the woods circling the lake. She took it without a thought. Her ninth birthday was a month away. Big for her age, the girl had her father's stocky build.

"There you are!" Arlene Greenwald, the scout leader, panted up behind her. "I thought we'd lost you."

The scout leader tugged Maddy by the hand. "We'd never have found you in those old woods." She blinked down at the girl. "Let's go join the others, shall we?"

Maddy didn't say a word. She pulled free, not liking being tugged by the woman. She marched ahead of Mrs. Greenwald and rejoined the others, who were already sitting cross-legged in a circle on the floor, playing a guessing game about nature.

"Who knows what kind of bird of prey sits in the trees surrounding the lake, waiting to dive down and catch a fish?" one mother said, moving her arm like a swooping bird, scanning a sea of Brownie faces.

Hands went up all around with attention-getting grunts. Maddy twisted her neck from side to side; she didn't want to play.

During a singsong she asked to go to the bathroom, and a chap-
erone followed her to the door marked for ladies. Maddy's eyes
focused on an outside window with a frosted pane next to the
sink. It was a double-hung style, just like the kind her father had
installed in their house last year. She turned its center latch and
lifted it open all the way. A waft of lake air slipped up her nostrils.
Without a thought she hoisted her leg over the sill and lowered
herself to the ground, drawn by the quiet tranquility of the lake's
coves.

A late-model black sedan bearing MD plates slowly motored
past the picnic area and disappeared along the service road.

Maddy went back to the lake trail. A few feet into the woods
it turned darker. The other girls' singing reverberated off the still
waters. Between tree trunks she glimpsed the one-story brown
building, now nearly a football field away.

She stepped over a muddy spot in the trail with deer tracks
through it. Just ahead a small creek fed into the lake. Her eyes
wandered up the creek bed, which contained only a trickle
now—a vestige of what it had been during the springtime flood,
which would have concealed the rocks that lay dry and exposed.
A dribble of water spilled from a limestone overhang, challeng-
ing the girl to climb higher. She hopped from rock to rock, her
arms extended for balance, completely oblivious to the gathering
of Brownies now out of sight several hundred yards behind her.

The jumble of rocks in the bed grew steeper. She found hand-
holds, careful not to slip. Catching her breath, Maddy crested the
waterfall and looked out across the lake, and for the first time in a
long time she experienced a sense of triumph.

A shrill cry tore open the silence. Too loud for a birdcall—
too human sounding. The anguished cry was repeated, this time
as a perfect high-pitched echo coming back across the lake, the
sound of someone choking. It wasn't right. Goose bumps raced up
Maddy's arms. A dragging sound drew nearer, made her crouch
behind a tree stump. She noticed a road ahead.

It grew quieter again. There was no more gasping. Gaining courage, Maddy cautiously rose, holding her breath as she did. Her own heartbeats filled the girl's ears—nothing else. Had she only imagined it?

The sound of someone rolling in leaves, rolling and groaning, made the young girl freeze. Her eyes focused on a stand of evergreens near the place where it leveled out. The noises didn't sound like fun; someone was in trouble, maybe needing help.

She skirted the evergreens, keeping a safe distance from whoever was moaning. The immense girth of an old beech tree stood blocking her view at the edge of the dirt road. A sign was nailed to it, a direction sign. She'd seen it out the car window before arriving at the lake. It read: PICNIC AREA ¼ MILE AHEAD.

A man's bloodied face slid into her view, propped against the tree trunk with the sign. His shirt and pants were torn and dirty, one cheek scraped raw. She'd never seen anyone in such an awful state before. Had he been attacked by some wild animal? The man's eyes were fixed, not really looking at her. He seemed very distressed. Maybe he'd been lost in the woods overnight, or had broken his leg? Maddy's father always warned her about wandering off. Crosshaven's woods were plenty notorious for kids getting lost or hurt or worse, like Julie.

The man's stance shifted awkwardly. He scraped his shoulder along the tree trunk for support, grimacing and twisting. His arms were restrained behind his back. Suddenly his hands popped free. The man rubbed his reddened wrists. He dropped to his knees, his head sunk down. Maddy climbed the rest of the way to the road, emboldened by the apparent emergency.

"Mister, are you OK?"

His head bobbed, and he closed and opened his eyes once. "Better...you leave." His chin slumped back to his chest. "Go... quick..."

Maddy didn't budge. "Who hurt you? Do you want me to get help?"

The man jerked his head from side to side, as if expecting someone's return. A motor rumbled closer, crunching and spitting gravel sounds of a car rapidly approaching. Its running lights shone through the trees up ahead.

The man tumbled to the ground and he rolled down the embankment toward her. Maddy leapt backward. Her Brownie cap fell off as she plunged through the leaves, not caring about the noise she was making. She didn't have time with the car braking hard behind her, the car door slamming. The hurt man's cuts and bruises had spoken loud and clear: GET OUT!

* * *

It was after five o'clock, and the sky grew noticeably dimmer along the narrow forest road. Prusik had developed a bad blister on her right heel. She chided herself for running off like she had in a brand-new pair of oxfords. The blister was tiring her right leg, with no sign of the lake in sight. Worse, no one had driven by to flag down.

She dug her hand into her coat pocket and tried McFaron's number again. The low battery symbol blinked on. She grumbled aloud to herself. She couldn't believe it: limping with an excruciating blister in the middle of nowhere with a dying cell phone. Up ahead through the trees, the flicker of headlights caught her attention. The distinct whir of a car motor approaching—someone was coming her way.

"Finally. Now we're getting somewhere."

The wash of the car's beams illuminated the gloomy woods. A moment later they shone brightly in her face. She shielded her eyes, holding the FBI badge out. The car slowed. She hurried to the passenger side. The driver leaned over and pushed open the door.

"Your timing couldn't be better," Christine said, clambering inside the vehicle and pulling the door shut. She gingerly pulled off the back of her right shoe where it had rubbed unmercifully.

The driver accelerated hard. "You Ms. Prusik? FBI?" He spoke from under a dapper wool hat with a pull-down brim, an Irish tweed sort.

"That's right, Special Agent Prusik," she responded, taking in the man's profile. All she could see clearly was a side view of his lower face—the rest of his face was concealed behind the hat—but the driver's chin and jawline were David Claremont's. Her heart began to hammer in her chest.

The man's shoulders were slightly askew—lower on his right—meaning there was some degree of curvature to the man's spine. His driving posture slouched toward the left. He held the steering wheel firmly with his right hand while propping his left elbow on the window ledge, resting his head against his left hand—all of which suggested right-handedness, not like Claremont, who she'd verified was a lefty. During her interview of Claremont, Prusik recalled that he had sat canted to his right side, another facet of left-handedness. She squeezed her pinkie in the tightening ball of her fist.

"Who contacted you? Was it Sheriff McFaron's office?" Prusik said in her most assertive voice. She was good in an interview room, but in the confines of a speeding car with a killer, she was clearly not the one in control.

"Yes, that's right, the sheriff's office. Didn't mean to get your credentials wrong, Special Agent. They sent me out looking for you as soon as they heard." The man's speech had a boldness and confidence totally absent from the man she'd interviewed in the Weaversville Police Station.

"So you were in contact with Sheriff McFaron?" she demanded to know, feeling increasingly uneasy. How could this man—Donald Holmquist?—know who she was and where she'd be?

"That'd be him all right."

He hadn't really answered her question at all. No acknowledgment either way, which told her that she was in great danger. Christine scrubbed her fingers through her hair. She needed to buy herself time.

"Then you must know I'm expected at Echo Lake State Park for a speaking engagement with the Brownie troop. I imagine they'll be looking for me by now."

"A woman's work is never done," he pronounced cryptically.

Christine distinctly heard neck vertebrae cracking as the driver twisted his head toward her, then away—a quirk she recalled seeing David Claremont do at one point during the interview. "I appreciate your coming to look for me," she said as casually as possible. "How close are we to the picnic area?"

The driver gunned the motor in response. They were careening back through forest tracts she'd spent the better part of an hour limping past.

"Just a ways ahead." He levered a forefinger up off the top of the steering wheel, pointing forward. "There's a shortcut that leads to the lake quicker."

"Yeah." Prusik forced a chuckle. "I know all about your short-cuts down here."

"Not like the big city, is it? With plenty of people around to help out when you need it," the man said almost gleefully.

Prusik blinked in surprise at this second cryptic remark, some kind of inward code of his, or implied threat. She decided to take a calculated risk. "Say listen, you know your brother, David, has become quite a celebrity in the media? I think your story is worth hearing, too."

The car gained speed, passing an intersecting road Prusik recalled seeing a half hour before. Her mind raced. "Are you sure we haven't missed the turn?" she asked, saying "we" to sound less threatening. "We could turn around back there?"

He swerved a little too rapidly around a bend; gravel dinged beneath the car. "Hardly," he said, then uttered in a deeper voice, "Mother always said, as you make your bed, so must you lie in it."

The man's odd manner of expression sent Prusik's blood pumping. His driving too fast and going the wrong way did, too. Her throat went dry. Pulses from her amygdala crowded her head as they had in the stuffy interview room at the Weaversville jailhouse. She opened her mouth to speak, but no sound came out. She had found the man she'd been hunting for. Or he had found her.

She steeled herself, focusing out the windshield on an invisible vanishing point in her mind, envisioning the hypnotic quiet of the lap pool. Taking stroke after stroke, her arms pulling her through the water, her flutter kick steady, keeping her abdomen taut with each breathful of air. Maintaining steady her pace, a V-shaped wave rippling off her bathing cap, Christine Prusik touched down in her calm place.

"Speaking of your mother, Donald"—she took a brazen leap of faith—"what would she say if she knew that you still wet your bed? I've been up to your room in Delphos. But you know that, don't you? Quite a mess you've made of the place." Prusik watched the man's hands jam tightly together, scrubbing across the top of the steering wheel.

"What do you think your mother would say about your soiling the mattress like that?" Prusik pressed. "A man your age still soiling *her* mattress, I mean *really*."

Holmquist's lips were quivering.

"And I won't even ask whether she'd approve of what else you're doing—of what you've been canning up these days."

The car slowed. The man's head slumped down in shame.

"I don't think she would approve at all. That would definitely be a big no."

"You better just hush," he said in a small voice.

"OK, Donald, we'll just drop that line of conversation for the moment. According to St. Mary's Hospital records, you were the first born." He shot her a mistrustful look. "That's right. That would make you the older brother, Donald, the man of the house, seeing how your father disappeared. Don't you know that being the big brother is a responsibility? It means you're supposed to set a good example for your younger brother, even if David's only a few minutes younger."

"I said hush, now!"

She couldn't risk stopping, even if it meant treading danger-ously into unknown territory, as Dr. Katz had warned her against. "Now I know for a fact David doesn't kill and eat people. I know you know that, too. Am I right, Donald? You two have already met up? Haven't you, Donald? Have you seen your brother today? Maybe even before today?"

Holmquist's face was perspiring heavily. He looked confused, panicked, trapped. Just as she had felt only moments before.

"What did big brother Donald accomplish today? Huh? Did you treat your kid brother right? Take him under your wing the way Bruna would've wanted you to?"

The man hit the brakes hard enough to rock Christine for-ward off her seat back. She heard something shift in the trunk, a dull heavy thud.

"So you've got David tied up in the trunk, Donald?"

"Don't say I didn't warn you, FBI lady." Before she could think what to say next, a shower of blue sparks stung her chest, bringing sudden darkness.

* * *

McFaron high-revved the Bronco. He'd received word from his dispatcher about Murfree's cab stalling and Christine run-ning off. He'd hightailed it from the Sweet Lick Resort in Cave Springs, Indiana, normally a thirty-minute ride that he'd made in less than twenty. Earlier that afternoon, he'd heard from Brian Eisen, who'd passed along information about a call from Lonnie Wallace, a groundskeeper at the Sweet Lick, to follow up on. Wallace had looked at a picture of David Claremont and said that it looked almost exactly like an odd-duck freelance sign painter who Wallace hadn't seen in nearly a month and who'd skipped out on finishing a job. A man named Donald Holmquist, who Wallace suspected for the recent theft of a Sweet Lick Resort vehicle.

It bothered the sheriff that he couldn't reach Christine. Tapping her cell phone number still indicated no signal was available. Why hadn't she waited for him to come pick her up, as he'd promised Howard he would once her departure from Chicago had been discovered? The spot where Murfree told Mary he'd stopped was only five miles from Echo Lake, he figured. Maybe Christine had left the phone in the cab with her briefcase? Turned it off to preserve the batteries? He doubted she'd do either. He anguished over the impulsive move, her running like that.

A large black late-model sedan, a Chrysler, sped by McFaron in the opposite direction. The sheriff made out the silhouettes of two people in the front seats and no one in back. He hadn't passed any other cars. The sparkle of the lake appeared in and out of the trees. The sun was low over the treetops, shimmering on the lake. It was well past five thirty. A minute later he skidded to a halt behind a maroon van. Kids were huddled around several women, crying.

"Sheriff!" Mrs. Greenwald rushed forward. "Sheriff, come quick! It's Maddy Heath. She's gone missing! Her friend Rachel saw a disheveled-looking man on the shoreline trail who looked like the one on TV, the one wanted for..."

The scout leader hesitated, as so many children were within earshot. She pointed toward the trail sign.

"I should have known better. I found her earlier straying from the building, walking down to the lake." The woman covered her mouth. "I should have known."

"MADDY!" A high-pitched scream echoed off the steep-sided lake. Three Brownies, in unison, screamed the missing girl's name again.

McFaron dashed toward the woods, unclipping his holster. At the trailhead he withdrew his .38, checking that the chambers were fully loaded. It had been six months since he'd fired his weapon—and that had been at the state police range. He'd never fired a gun at anyone before, not even aimed one; his two-year stint in the army had not involved any actual combat.

He moved down the muddy trail, alert to movement, brandishing the weapon in a cautious stance. A hundred feet down the trail a figure stumbling forward sent the sheriff into a crouch. Was he too late? A man limping badly came into view behind spindly second-growth yellowwood trees along the lakeshore. He was laden down, carrying something, speaking in a halting voice.

The man approached, sideways now, passing over some deadfall, hefting the girl in a chest carry. McFaron saw her feet dangling. The girl's face was slumped against the man's chest, expressionless. She was missing a shoe. It was too dangerous to risk taking a shot.

McFaron looked around for a good ambush spot near the trail. There was none other than the birch trunk he was leaning against. He extended his thumb and levered back the firing pin, careful not to touch the trigger.

CHAPTER TWENTY-EIGHT

An uncomfortable tickling beneath her ribs brought her around. The car was idling beside the road. She was slumped against the passenger door under the man's weight. A pungent salty odor— it was his breath, she realized, coming from very near—turned her stomach. Prusik cracked open her eyelids enough to see Holmquist, heard the glove box pop open and him rummaging through it. Something was jabbing her side, lower down than before. He was prodding her abdomen, his eyes wide open now in an expression of wonderment. A small groan escaped him.

"Get off of me!" In a command burst, Christine shoved her feet hard against the floorboards and repositioned herself upright.

Holmquist stayed put, grasped her by the arm. "You going to hush now?" He waved the menacing electrode prongs of the Taser close to her face, the telltale high-pitched whine of the device reaching full power. "You didn't tell me about your little surprise."

She raised her free hand, acquiescing, realizing she'd been rendered unconscious by his tasing her once already. The flesh near her collarbone still stung from it. What surprise was he talking about?

He resumed a driving position and floored the vehicle before she could even think to open her door. She wiped away drool from her lower lip, feeling dizzy and sore and foolish for not having a firearm on her as required by the bureau. As a forensic anthro- pologist, she usually conducted interviews in the presence of armed personnel and, therefore, had rarely felt compelled to lug one around herself.

"Mind if I listen to the radio?" He flicked it on without waiting for her answer. A special bulletin broadcast interrupted a song. "Breaking news—this afternoon the search for David Claremont led police to Echo Lake State Park, where the man was successfully apprehended—"

The man turned it off and chucked his hat into the backseat. In the green glow of the dash she recognized the full profile, that same prominent zygomatic arch, overhanging browridge, the hollowed eyes—David Claremont's. Prusik sucked in a breath she couldn't seem to release. Her heart threatened to gallop out of her chest. His overpowering her physically had proved a setback.

He turned his head toward her. "Spot that feather I left for you?" he said, brimming with overconfidence. "You and that cop poking your noses around? I wasn't too happy at first, finding someone snooping in my house, but once I knew it was you..." He nodded and grinned as if that explained everything.

"Donald...please...I won't..." Prusik's tongue balled in her mouth. Whatever imbalance had caused him to tase her now seemed forgotten, judging from the man's nonchalance. Prusik realized that with a psychopath, little things like understanding how someone else knows who you are or what you are doing or even why you are doing it are unimportant, nothing to worry about.

"Seen you up at the podium in front of all those fancy people dressed for the occasion, too. Yep. I was there, Special Agent. You and me go back a long ways." A smile broadened across his face. "Cat kind of got your tongue, huh? Just like it did when you saw that wild man of Borneo back there at the museum? Our friend with the stone." He chuckled like a parent somehow indulging a child.

Prusik's mind started spinning wildly. He'd been there. He'd seen her reaction to the display case.

"See, that's what I like about you. You and me, we understand. We're alike that way."

"What do you mean we're alike, Donald?" She tried to sound conversational. "I don't go around killing innocent people."

He cackled. "You do have a sense of humor, don't you, FBI lady? You're *just* like me. That's why I been leaving those presents for you like I been doing. The first girl, she only got a regular stone, but that was before I knew there was someone else out there like me. And it was you, a copper!" He cackled again. "But no use cryin' over spilt milk."

Prusik felt sick. He'd been leaving charm stones in his victims' throats for her to find.

"You ran out the room because of its power, didn't you?" Holmquist lifted his hand from his shirt collar and dangled something. "See? I know you."

Prusik didn't dare look up. The fact he'd had her on his radar from the beginning had her floored. She clenched her knees, tried summoning her vanishing point through the windshield: the lap-pool lane, coursing through the smooth waters, rolling her torso from side to side, rotating her arms up overhead, and knifing down through to complete the rhythm of her swim stroke. This time she couldn't visualize it. She couldn't grasp anything beyond feeling like a cornered animal.

She focused her attention on the blank pad of paper stuck to the dashboard. It was a small prescription pad conveniently adhered near the instrument cluster, above where an ashtray is usually located. Printed across the top of the pad she read the name: Irwin Walstein, MD. The thud in the car's trunk when Holmquist suddenly braked flashed through her mind. She had an urge to speak, but her throat constricted as if it might seal off. She gathered herself. "What about Dr. Walstein?"

Holmquist twisted his hands around the steering-wheel grip, shrugged. "You mean Claremont's doctor?" He twisted his neck right and left, cracking the vertebrae like Prusik's father would crack his knuckles. "Did unto him as he'd have done unto me." Prusik fought to find calm. She had a terrible urge to leap from the moving car, with the idea that she would tumble and run. But she couldn't, not with the car doing fifty. She'd be knocked unconscious—if not from the jump, from his finishing her off at the edge of the road. Stick with plan A, she told herself: stay calm, keep him distracted, somehow get to a public place, and do it quickly.

Prusik flashed on his fingers prodding along her abdomen when she lay semiconscious a few moments ago. "What did you mean by my 'little surprise,' Donald?"

He cast a quick glance at the rearview mirror, then returned his eyes to the road.

"Let's talk about this stone business. The power they have, as you say."

Holmquist was listening. She noticed him shoving his tongue against his cheek, or maybe he was chewing on something inside his mouth.

"I'm an anthropologist, you know." Prusik gritted her teeth, determined to maintain level, that calm space in the heat of battle that she'd practiced during her FBI basic training. "I did summer research a long time ago in Papua New Guinea. Saw carved stones just like yours."

He nodded slightly, an acknowledgment of sorts.

"It's been puzzling me—the stones, and their significance to you."

Holmquist turned toward her, his face oddly displaying a cheesy grin. "Why? You wanting another all to yourself?" he said in a low voice.

His lips parted. Between his teeth was something hard: a shiny sliver that glistened with saliva. A charm stone.

Prusik squinted to read the fuel gauge. From her angle, it looked nearly on empty. If the car rolled to a stop, she'd make a dash for certain. She slipped off her shoes, preparing. She rubbed the bottoms of her heels against the floorboards.

"What'd you do that for?" he said. "Take off your shoes?"

"I…they hurt." She felt herself winding back up; her heart knocked against her blouse. "How's the fuel?" she blurted out.

"Enough to last till Blackie."

Prusik groped with her hand down between her seat and the passenger door. She felt inside her purse and coughed hard at the same time as she punched the memory button for McFaron's cell phone number, praying it would connect through to him this time. She didn't dare look down and risk losing her one chance. She had to assume the call went through.

"Donald, why are we turning north onto the state high-way?" She enunciated as clearly as she could. "Isn't Echo Lake in the opposite direction? You said Blackie? Why are we headed to Blackie when they were expecting me at Echo Lake more than two hours ago?"

They passed under a large green sign indicating five miles to Crosshaven's airport, where she'd landed only hours ago. *Why is he headed back to Blackie?*

"Take a left at the Crosshaven airport ramp, would you?" she said brusquely. "I forgot my bag at the counter."

His right hand descended at lightning speed and squeezed her thigh painfully hard. "Nice try, copper. You won't be needing no bags where you're going." He returned his hand to the steering wheel and tapped out a lively rhythm.

Prusik's heart vibrated like the wings of a hummingbird, threatening to dart right out of her chest and buzz off into the night. His confidence was ratcheting up her fear. So was the shiny sliver of stone he'd displayed between his teeth. Why had he asked her if she wanted another? She flattened her sweaty palms against her thighs, fighting to pull herself together.

The outside lights of the interstate gas plaza north of Crosshaven appeared up ahead.

Numb from adrenaline rushes, Prusik was devoid of any fur-ther desire to struggle. Just the way he wanted her. She thought of the nature programs she'd watched on television as a young girl. In the slow-motion chase of a cheetah after a gazelle, the cheetah would lunge, swiping the legs out from under the graceful animal, then hover nonchalantly over it, with no need to hold on to it. Hovering was enough to keep the poor animal frozen in place as its own nervous system conspired against it. Prusik had pounded the floor in front of the TV screen, urging the fleet-footed gazelle to run: "Get up, go! Get away, you can make it!"

Now, she was like that downed gazelle—feeling that same frozen-in-place terror, that same inward collapse as if an invisible but palpable electric current had hooked up between Holmquist and Prusik, predator and prey. He looked at her. She caught a faint flicker of retinal red in the passing lights of an oncoming car.

"Don't try any funny business, if you catch my drift," he said, as if reading her thoughts.

Prusik gripped the door handle in her right hand. She'd bail if she had to. But first she must steady herself.

The rumble of a vehicle approaching fast from behind caught Christine's attention. Headlights flooded in through the back window. A large SUV veered closer into Holmquist's lane, trying to head him off, clipping the front panel of the doctor's car and sending it fishtailing onto the soft shoulder in a cloud of dust. Ahead, the SUV's tires squealed, got hung up on the lip of the pavement, and careened sideways too fast over loose gravel. In an instant it was airborne on an angle and cleared the steep embankment. Christine winced as she watched it slam into a freshly plowed field and come to rest on its roof.

The sedan's front tires were spinning freely, suspended over the deep irrigation ditch ten feet below the road's shoulder. Holmquist flung open the driver's side door and dropped down into the ditch out of sight, thrashing among the weeds. Beyond the ditch, Christine could hear the whirring sound of a spinning tire fade—the flipped vehicle. She made out the shape of it and read, upside down on the door panel, the large letters: CROSSHAVEN SHERIFF'S DEPARTMENT.

Christine flung open her door and slid down into the steep irrigation drain, grasping handfuls of weeds to steady herself. She slipped onto the scummy tiles lining the bottom of the excavated channel, enveloped in sudden darkness. Without her .38 Special, being trapped in the dark ditch with Holmquist wasn't an option. She clawed her way up the opposite side and reached the plowed field. The loamy dirt felt good under her bare feet. The sound of splashing came from the ditch behind her—Holmquist was getting away.

Christine plodded awkwardly through the deep plowed soil, her arms outstretched for balance. The Bronco lay resting on its roof at the edge of the field. She reached through the busted-out driver's window and with two fingers palpated the sheriff's carotid artery, checking for a pulse. It was strong.

"Joe," she whispered, gently squeezing his arm. "Can you hear me?"

McFaron didn't respond. She felt along his gun belt and pulled the Maglite from its holder. She flicked it on. McFaron's face was bloodied. His eyes fluttered.

"Check Claremont." He winced. "In back."

Prusik shone the light across spare rubber boots and an emergency first-aid kit that had broken off its holder. Glass shards from the busted-out side windows glinted under her beam. "He's not there. He must have been thrown clear." Christine aimed the beam around the sides of the truck and spotted a set of fresh footsteps that led across the field. She traced the light in their general direction, but there was no sign of the man.

McFaron's eyelids closed again. She feared that moving him would cause him more injury, so she didn't unfasten his seat belt. Prusik retrieved his service revolver—all six chambers were loaded.

The radio transmitter suddenly blared from the dangling mike cord. "Sheriff McFaron, this is Mary, over."

Prusik grabbed hold of the mike. "Mary, this is Special Agent Prusik speaking. There's been an accident about four miles north of the interstate gas terminal, in a field bordering the northbound lane of the state highway. Sheriff McFaron is hurt, semiconscious. We need an ambulance and police backup ASAP. Donald Holmquist kidnapped me this afternoon and has now escaped on foot. He's killed at least three Indiana girls that we know of."

Christine waited for Mary's acknowledgment and then took off along the field toward a small stand of second-growth poplars, holding the sheriff's gun barrel high. Nearing the trees, she dropped into a crouch beside the embankment, listening for signs of movement. The horizon glowed beyond the trees. Less than a minute later the edge of a full moon appeared over the crest of a hill, perceptibly brightening the landscape. A branch snapped. Something moved up ahead in the thicket that bordered the field's edge—the shadow of someone ducking behind a trunk. Donald Holmquist or David Claremont?

Christine held the gun steady and trained the powerful Maglite beam from tree trunk to tree trunk. She felt certain it was Holmquist hiding there. Claremont would surely have revealed himself or said something. She pressed forward through the weeds, aiming the gun chest-high, continuing to sweep the beam from left to right. The killer was probably eyeing her already, planning his next move. She illuminated one trunk large enough to hide a man and stayed hidden in the weeds.

"Donald Holmquist, this is the FBI. Come out with your hands up. You're under arrest for the murders of Betsy Ryan, Missy Hooper, and Julie Heath."

No sound came back in return but her beating heart. She approached slowly, remaining low on her haunches. Stopping under the gloomy canopy of the largest tree, she shone the light slowly around the grove.

"Stand clear, Mr. Holmquist, with your hands up!"

Prusik drew back the firing pin. For the first time, *she* felt like the hunter. She was a dead shot—her marksmanship had been best in her class in the FBI training program—and holding the gun helped compose her.

"Holmquist, this is your last chance. Give yourself up now." The words came to her automatically. "I will shoot to kill if necessary."

A branch cracked overhead. Holmquist was airborne over her, his arms outstretched. Prusik fired once at the man's midsection. The sudden force of his falling body knocked her to the ground. Both the gun and flashlight came out of her grasp. He was on top of her, panting loudly—she'd wounded him.

"Nice shooting, FBI lady," he managed between heaving breaths.

Prusik jerked her knee up into the injured man's crotch. Holmquist cringed but didn't relax his hold, pinning her by the wrists. His face drew near hers.

"You won't be needing to shoot me full of holes no more." Clasping both her wrists in his left hand, he jerked up her blouse, prodding, palpating her abdomen, as if getting a measure of things. She was amazed by the wounded man's strength.

Summoning her rage, Prusik strained her neck muscles upward and bit down on Holmquist's chin with everything she could muster, lodging an eyetooth deep into his flesh. He groaned, slapped at her cheek, clawing, searching for purchase along her jawbone. Prusik bit down harder, scraping chinbone, willing the strength of her entire body into her tooth hold.

She freed one hand and grasped the stone dangling from his neck. With a furious jab, she drilled the charm stone inside the killer's ear, twisting it for maximum effect. He flopped off.

A squirt of adrenaline was all that seemed to be necessary to clear his mind and send him scrambling off across the field. Prusik frantically patted the weeds, searching for and finding the gun and the light.

She stood gazing in the direction Holmquist had taken. The moon suddenly dimmed, cloaked behind a passing cloud, as if conspiring with him. Precious seconds had passed.

She knew a gunshot wound in the stomach was mean. A web of major arteries and veins fed through a man's midsection, and the chances of a .38's slug passing clean through were next to nil. The loss of blood would be substantial.

The full moon appeared again, hanging over the treetops, orange as a mango. Out in the open, it was easy for Prusik to pick out Holmquist's footsteps in the plowed soil. She hoped that she'd spot the injured man crumpled on the ground, but only uninterrupted plow lines met her gaze.

From the distance came the wail of police sirens and a strand of shimmering bubble lights. The imminent arrival of backup buoyed her confidence. A small rise in the field sloped suddenly away. Prusik kept her head down, the barrel of the gun straight ahead in a lowered position. Her left hand clutched the Maglite. She passed down the gentle slope without realizing that she was now hidden from the view of anyone on the state road.

Just ahead of her, a darker smudge marred the tilled expanse. A leg moved in the furrows—Holmquist's. Prusik warily approached the downed man. From a good ten feet away she shone the light into his face—no response. His shirtfront was heavily stained with blood. She moved in, tapped his leg with her foot. Still no response.

She lowered the Maglite. Holmquist came alive, thrashing and kicking the light out of her grip. He was on his feet and charged her. Christine lost her balance and fell to the ground.

"Get away from her!" A body lunged in from the side, separating her from her assailant. "Get away from her, I said," her defender roared in fury. The two men struggled on the ground.

Christine got to her knee and drew a bead on the man who lay beneath her rescuer. "It's OK, sir," she said to the man in a tattered shirt on top of Holmquist. "I'm an officer of the law, Special Agent Christine Prusik. Please get off the suspect."

The men continued to struggle as if they hadn't heard hear. Amid grunting and moaning and bellowing came tearful accusations from both straining figures—had she heard right?

Prusik fired a shot in the air. "Get off the suspect, sir! That's an order!"

When her rescuer hesitated, Holmquist threw him off. Then he hobbled unsteadily toward the dark edge of the field. Prusik didn't give chase this time. Holmquist wasn't long for this world, and she was exhausted to the bone. Between heaving breaths, the man on the ground said, "Please, ma'am, don't shoot him."

Prusik immediately recognized the voice. "David?"

He raised his hand in acknowledgment. "Please don't shoot my brother."

Prusik lowered the gun. Her arm trembled badly from the strain of combat. "I owe you an apology, David."

Claremont's eyes drifted back out over the field, following his brother's haphazard footsteps. "I'll stay with him till the law comes. I promise."

"Forgetting something, David? I am the law. A .38 slug tore through his midsection. He won't get very far." She measured Claremont's ragged state. "You were thrown clear in the car wreck?"

He got to his feet, fidgeting his hands. "I'm sorry for not helping out before. I was afraid I'd get shot in the mix-up." As Claremont spoke he gazed intently in the direction Holmquist had fled, wringing his hands, caught in a maelstrom Prusik could barely begin to fathom. In the illumination of the cool moonlight, his face gave the appearance of a man who bore too much of the world's weight upon his shoulders.

"I should go, Ms. Prusik. I need to find him." Claremont started off in the direction Holmquist had loped.

Christine wiped a few clods of dirt off her suit pants, too drained to stop him. Claremont's anguish—and it was nothing less than anguish—was excruciating to witness. What agonies of the deep had the twinning bond dredged up? What loss must Claremont be feeling as the life drained out of his mirror image?

Christine shook her head, trying to clear it. She couldn't remember the last time she'd cried, but she felt perilously close to tears. Bursts of laser-like light illuminated the western sky from what she estimated to be fifteen or twenty police cars just out of sight over the rise. She gazed east, in the direction that Claremont had taken, then turned and headed back toward the state road.

CHAPTER TWENTY-NINE

The sun rose to the noisy cries of red-winged blackbirds aggressively defending their territory. The feisty birds flicked their wings amid a cacophony of cackles. It had rained hard the night before and steamy mist was rising from the ground everywhere, making it look like a battlefield on the day after.

The front tires of the rental car spun in the muck. McFaron put it into park. He'd get stuck if he drove any farther into the muddy field. His new four-wheel-drive truck was on order, and he wouldn't have it for at least another week. The farmer who'd wakened him at four thirty that morning had insisted he come immediately. An early riser for years, the sheriff had elected not to stir Christine, who had spent the night at his home in Crosshaven. She'd looked exhausted after the press conferences yesterday and all the back-and-forth faxes and calls between his office and hers in Chicago.

McFaron usually enjoyed the peaceful quiet of morning, a quiet that today was broken by the pesky birds raising a commotion near a hedgerow less than a mile from where the Bronco still lay totaled. Something was upsetting them. He removed his knee-high boots from the back of the car, a staple of the sheriff's equipment kit. His left arm was in a sling, the tendons in his shoulders badly strained from the accident. He followed the farmer's footprints, as the man had said to. It was difficult keeping his balance, pulling each boot free, wincing each time he had to jerk his bad arm to keep from falling. He huffed from the workout. Peepers trilled from a manmade pond. As he passed by it, the chorus abruptly ceased, silenced by the sucking noises of the sheriff's rubber boots.

Where the hell is it? The sheriff scanned the perimeter of the field. The blackbirds were relentless, dive-bombing the massive hedgerow. They made up in spitefulness what they lacked in size, the sheriff thought. It surprised him the birds didn't budge as he neared. His eyes followed one bird as it swooped down upon another, then rose, joined another, and another, until dozens were rising and falling in a mad boil high in the sky above the dense, sprawling bush. He trudged closer. A man suddenly appeared, as if waving at him. But he wasn't moving.

For a brief moment, McFaron tensed. Then he continued forward more slowly, stopping short of the first thorny tentacle a good ten feet from where the man's body was entangled. It wasn't a pretty sight. The man's hand was hung in an upright position, hooked through the index finger by a vicious-looking thorn. In his gaping mouth, the man's tongue was bloody with peck marks. Still, no matter how loudly the birds protested and jabbered, the man was immovable, quite dead, his eyelids gouged out.

McFaron recognized the brown Woolrich shirt David Claremont had been wearing when the sheriff had placed him under arrest at Echo Lake. The man was no longer wanted by police. In fact, he'd helped save Maddy Heath and Christine. In the eyes of the public and the law, he had transformed overnight from psychopath to hero.

Now, though, the hero looked like a freakish scarecrow. A blackbird hopped angrily across the dead man's chest. Other birds swooped low over the sheriff's head, raising a fuss as if he were the next menace to barb.

It hurt to see Claremont's body in such a tormented state. McFaron felt badly that he'd told the state police to resume their wider search of the area when daylight broke. As it turned, not such a good idea. It crossed his mind too that the troubled man must have panicked gripped by some darker inward traverse that only an identical twin could know. Like losing a part of himself maybe, even if the other was a deranged killer. The scene was too gruesome for McFaron to ponder any further.

McFaron flashed a shot with his camera, sending the birds skyward. The farmer who'd found Claremont was right. It would take a chain saw to carve through the murderous thorns to extricate the body. And it was downright weird his being caught up in thorns just like his brother Donald Holmquist had been less than a mile from this spot.

* * *

The unfolding events at Echo Lake State Park and the farm field north of Crosshaven had miraculously altered things back in Chicago. Prusik still needed to complete and file her report, but Thorne had canceled her administrative disciplinary hearing as well as the special trip to Washington he'd planned for Bruce Howard's promotion. Thorne had even apologized to Prusik, who surprised herself by not asking more from him over the phone. She hadn't felt the need to.

McFaron drove her to the Crosshaven airport. They waited in the car by the small concrete terminal building. Prusik focused on an incoming dot that was growing larger in the sky. It was her plane, the last flight to Chicago that evening.

They sat silently watching the plane drift in; its landing gear descended, and it touched down in a flourish of reversing engines.

She hadn't felt right since last night. She chalked it up to exhaustion. Closing her eyes and leaning her head against the headrest, she murmured, "Ever notice, Joe, how one way or another life catches up with you?"

"Beg pardon?" McFaron pressed his hand over hers on the car seat and gave her a puzzled look.

She quickly withdrew her hand. "I haven't told you...I need to tell you..."

"What's wrong, Christine? What do you mean about life catching up with you?"

She fumbled her hand into her purse, wrestled out the pill canisters, and held them to his face. "This is what I mean. Benzodiazepines for panic attacks. Beta-blockers to help slow me down enough to sleep."

"It's understandable. This has been a very stressful case."

Prusik leaned her head back and tossed two down dry. "You don't know the half of it, Joe." Her voice sounded strangely deep.

The sheriff looked at her questioningly. Beads of perspiration formed on her forehead. Her cheeks were blotchy red. "Are you OK, Christine?"

She forced herself upright, feeling blanched and tired. "I want to show you." She softened her gaze and, without looking, lifted up her blouse, exposing the long purple scar along her left side.

McFaron looked from the scar to her face and back to the scar again. Its lower edge bore a dark scab, a recent flesh wound. He wondered whether it may have been caused from her fighting with Holmquist, but he didn't ask.

"You know I did graduate research in Papua New Guinea, right, Joe?"

He nodded.

"I don't know what drove me to it. I don't know what I was thinking, what got into my head. Christine's big plan. Go off to a foreign land on her own and study deviant behaviors in remote highland villages. Discover whether or not there are any remaining survivors of a feared clan called the Ga-Bong Ga-Bong. They were cannibals, Joe. I wanted to study cannibals. I wanted to see if there was any hereditary component to their behavior, or if it was all cultural. I wanted to see if they were proof positive that psychopaths exist among primitive peoples."

She squirmed uncomfortably in her seat. "I was out by myself one afternoon. Miss Bukari, my key informant, watched me leave the small village." As she spoke, the high-pitched operatic scream of a palm cockatoo traced through her head as if she were, back there again, her sight clouded by the interminable haze and her skin a greasy saline paste.

"I knew the Ga-Bong clan was treacherous. But I went down that forest path alone anyway, knowing full well the danger. I was out of my league, Joe. Out of my mind when I think of it now. I had no business leaving on my own without village or government support."

McFaron nodded. "You do tend to do things that way."

"The point is, at the time I really knew nothing about aberrant psychology. I'd only read some academic treatises—my knowledge was all conceptual. I was fresh bait wrapped in sweat-drenched khakis. I was a marked woman."

"Why do you say that, Christine?"

"I hadn't a clue. I brought it on myself. There I am deep in the Trans-Fly region, a week's riverboat ride out of Port Moresby, thinking, I'm smart. I can handle this. What an interesting, original dissertation this will be. And now I pay the price." She closed her eyes. "The bits and pieces, the flashbacks. The panic attacks. Triggered anytime anywhere. This case. The similarities."

"What similarities? What happened?"

She looked directly at Joe's face. "I didn't hear him coming. His feather mask, the lanyard around his neck, the stone hanging from it. I was slopping around on riverbank mud..." She hesitated. "His knife, he cut me..." She gently traced her fingertips over her blouse along the abdominal scar, then wiped away the building sweat on her brow with the back of her hand.

"You don't have to—"

She held up her hand. "His mask came off sideways in the struggle, revealing a white-haired man, old as my father for chrissakes." The sour smell of his breath, the charm stone dangling in her face—the memory ignited in her as if it were yesterday. It caught her off guard, but she pressed on.

"I kneed him. Tumbled into the river. Thank God for that. The one thing I did right. The only reason I'm talking to you today is that man's advanced age. It was the Ga-Bong father, not one of the notorious sons, who had tried to shove a stone in me." Her words came out with growing conviction. "But I outswam him and the rest of his hateful world that day."

McFaron shook his head in disbelief. "This case must seem like some kind of weird unfinished business for you," he said softly. "I'm so sorry, Christine."

"Part of the time it *really* did." She gazed out the windshield. "No question about it." Her face eased. The medication was taking hold. "I swam downstream for what seemed like hours. I have no idea how I made it with that wound. I came to a dock full of people wearing trousers and shirts, peacefully standing. They were waiting for the ferry. Everything seemed so damn normal, so uneventful." She drifted in a daze.

He massaged the back of her neck.

"That feels nice." She sighed. "Your hand on my neck, I mean." Prusik looked directly into McFaron's eyes. "I'm finished with the FBI, Joe. You're the first to hear it. Finished."

McFaron bridged the transmission hump and cradled her in his arms. "Don't decide today. Think on it. You've done a fantastic job, Christine." He kissed the top of her forehead. "You went out on a limb, and you stuck it out until the end. I'm damn proud of you for it. Not to mention a whole troop of Brownies who have you to be thankful for."

Christine slumped back in her seat, her eyes suddenly blurring. Her stomach felt queasy. For a moment her gaze out the windshield caught on two twinkling stars. In a tired voice, she said, "I don't know, Joe."

She stared up at the encroaching night sky. "Like two galaxies—always looking as if they're going to collide, but they never do. In fact, they're not even close. But millions of light-years apart, just like us, Joe." She blinked away tears. "We may look like we're touching, but we're just as far apart—my limitations, my parents' limitations."

"Look," McFaron said, taking her hand. "I've spent the larger part of my life holding in my feelings. It's led to nothing but sorrows. Face it. Things never happen the way you want. And you can't save everyone. Sometimes it's all you can do to save yourself. Being here with you, I think to myself, wouldn't it be a shame if we didn't have our chance to collide?"

At that she looked up at him. McFaron said, "All I know is how good you make me feel. I don't want to lose that."

Without saying another word she kissed him, and they held each other close until the sound of the prop wash of the nineteen-seater as it roared down the runway had become unintelligible, distant droning. The last flight for Chicago had gone.

Christine looked up at McFaron and smiled weakly. "Looks like my report to Thorne will have to be a little late. Again."

"Looks like it will," Joe said, kissing her earlobe. "But I'll be happy to help you out any way that I can, Special Agent. Maybe we should get on that right now." He stopped his nuzzling abruptly and pressed his palm against her forehead. "Christine? You're burning up."

The special agent didn't respond. Her face was flushed, and she'd broken out in a sudden sweat that dampened her hair and temples.

"Christine?"

She attempted to move, winced, and doubled over with pain.

McFaron accelerated down the airport exit road and radioed ahead to the regional hospital twenty minutes away.

* * *

Christine stirred. The repeating beep of a monitor overhead measured her vital signs. An intravenous line was taped to her right arm. Out her hospital window was a vast field of stubble corn. She pressed the remote device by the bed rail that alerted the nurse's station.

"So, Ms. Prusik, how do you feel this afternoon?"

Christine attempted to sit upright.

"No, no." The nurse gently patted her patient's hand. "You must lie still, or you'll pull out your stitches. Let me get the doctor for you." The young nurse had a dark complexion and long dark hair braided in a bun. Christine read the nurse's name on her ID pin. Miss Rodriguez.

She strained to read the labels on the hanging bags of fluid that fed into her arm: one was a fairly strong antibiotic, the other a steroid compound she was unfamiliar with. A thin man of a young age entered the room, probably a greenhorn resident fresh out of med school, she thought. His head was shaven as clean as his face. He was dressed in a green gown and green booties, a stethoscope casually yoked around his neck. He smiled down at her. "How's my first-ever FBI agent patient feeling today?"

"Please tell me you're not a doctor?"

"Well, I was the surgeon on call last night when Sheriff McFaron brought you in," he said while scanning her chart. "So I guess that counts for being a doctor."

"Surgeon? Did my appendix burst?"

The young man stopped looking at her chart and studied her for a moment. "Your appendix did not burst. You had an infection. Caused by this." The doctor withdrew a vial from his gown pocket and handed it to her.

Prusik instantly identified the dark stone figurine—it was the same sliver that had been poking between Holmquist's teeth in the car. Her heart started to pound. "Where'd it come from?"

The doctor leaned on the edge of her bed and lifted the sheet. "If you don't mind, I need to see how you're healing." He pulled back a piece of sterile gauze, inspected, and mumbled some instructions to the nurse on redressing the wound. He checked the monitor recording her vitals.

"I'm waiting, Doctor."

"I removed that stone object from a subcutaneous layer in your abdomen. You sustained a penetrating trauma, I'm not sure how exactly. Fortunately for you, it had not perforated your abdominal wall. Your infection would have been much worse if it had."

A wave of panic passed over her: Holmquist leaning across her side of the passenger seat, her shirt pulled up, exposing her abdomen, and his finger rubbing back and forth across her scar. He had slit open her scar then and inserted the stone while she lay unconscious after being tased.

The monitor overhead beeped rapidly. The doctor ordered the administration of a sedative. Massaging the top of her hand, he said, "I understand you were attacked? My assumption is—"

"Please, Doctor, hand me my cell phone. I need to call someone. It's very important. Please."

She punched Dr. Katz's speed-dial number and asked the doctor and nurse to leave her room until she completed the call.

"He didn't kill me. Didn't shove it down my throat. Why not, Doctor?" She started right in as if the conversation in her head had been going on all this time with Dr. Katz.

"Perhaps it's something you said?" Katz replied. "You provoked him maybe? Caught him off guard the way you like to do, Christine?"

She went back over her chaotic car ride with Holmquist. "I remember the charm stone jutting between his lips. He told me he'd been at the museum when I...when I tried to give a speech. I told him I did research in New Guinea." She was fuzzy about everything that had happened that day. It all seemed a jumble to her now.

"You see!" Katz said. "You connected with his interest in these things."

"If I could *see* I wouldn't have called you."

"Christine, you told me yourself how over the millennia the indigenous Papuan people had inserted these carved stone figurines into the dead out of respect for their ancestors. You said

Holmquist had stolen these stones from the museum. He knew of that practice. He did this out of respect for you."

She brushed her hand over the surgical dressing. Somehow Holmquist had found her old scar. Prusik did know that charm stones were often placed in the abdominal cavities of the dead by their clansmen. In the warped mind of a psychopath who crushed girls' necks and inserted stones forcefully in their busted-out airways, where was there any room for respect for the living? It didn't add up.

"Respect? That's awfully far-fetched, Doctor. It's not Holmquist's profile."

"Aren't you forgetting another significant factor that makes your circumstances especially unique?"

She closed her eyes and let out a long sigh, comforted by Katz's voice in spite of their unsettling conversation. "Of course, I realize David Claremont is part of this equation."

How exactly, she couldn't fully comprehend, although Eisen had reported back yesterday, before she fell ill, how the museum security tapes from the spring and summer data banks captured a remarkable sequence. On three separate occasions—each time within twelve hours of a visit by Holmquist to the Oceania collection—David Claremont had passed the same camera points leading to the same exhibit of charm stones. From the videotapes at least, there was no proof of an actual reunion between Claremont and Holmquist. Had David "seen" the museum display? Or had his own fascination with collecting and carving stones brought him there on its own right? If the result of a vision, it would explain David's sudden unexplained departures to Chicago. He was acting on a compulsion to find the missing part of himself, this other who also liked stones, but who did such abhorrent, unimaginable things with them.

The museum tapes had also shown that on the evening of the gala, among the handful of casually dressed nonpaying guests, in attendance no doubt thanks to the museum's free Tuesday night policy, one stood out: a young man wearing navy-blue work pants and a stained Carhartt jacket. His face was never fully visible under the shadow of his baseball cap, but his stance and his gestures and his gait were unmistakable.

"We have no idea how Claremont, the good twin, may have influenced your killer's thinking in the hours before their deaths." Dr. Katz's familiar voice brought her back to the present. "This is not a straightforward profile, Christine. It's as much about a man's soul—two men's souls—and the search to fill a void inside as it is about a twisted psyche."

"Maybe you're right." Christine sighed.

Katz made a spitting sound—Prusik figured he'd chewed off a piece of the ragged end of another ballpoint. "Maybe I'm right, maybe I'm wrong," he said between spits. "I explain nothing. I can only put to you possibilities for what might be at work here. This is a strange case, sure. Genes alone can only explain so far. Claremont's adoptive parents prove that a good environment does make a difference. Of course, we know very little about your killer's childhood experiences. You must rest, Christine. Congratulations for proving to them all what a fine forensic scientist you truly are."

"Thank you for saying that, Doctor." She said good-bye to Katz, but her mind continued to whir. The thought of Holmquist pushing a charm stone inside her body made her queasy. Was her scar what he had meant by her "little surprise"? Did he think they shared something in common? The idea was revolting.

And Claremont. His anguish as he had followed his brother into the night had been so palpable that remembering it, Christine could almost feel it in her own body. Had he felt his own life draining away as well? Losing a synaptic link that had existed since before birth, since the womb, since a cleft in a single egg had split them into two? It all represented a planet of grief Christine could not fathom. And then Claremont's ending up in the thorns, just like his brother? Christine shuddered. Had poor Claremont found the thorns, or had the thorns found him? She had read how confounded and despondent one identical twin could become upon learning of the sudden death of the other. The loss of someone who truly understands, knows what you are going through without having to be told anything at all would be a devastating blow. Even if the someone was a monster. Poor David Claremont. He'd tried his best, but he'd never stood a chance. She ached in her gut at the thought.

A nurse entered and adjusted her IV drip, and soon, mercifully soon, Christine closed her eyes as the sedative took hold.

* * *

Sometime later, McFaron whispered, "Hey, partner," his fingers tapping the top of her hand. "What are you doing?" The sheriff placed his trooper hat at the foot of her bed. "Sleeping the whole day through?"

"There's enough room for the both of us in this bed," she said, inching over as best she could. Suddenly there was nothing she wanted more than the feeling of his solid frame next to hers.

He leaned over and they kissed. "You're not just saying that because of these drugs?" He jiggled the metal IV stand.

"Probably, but since when does that ever stop a big sheriff from taking advantage?" He leaned back down and cradled her as best he could with his one good arm. She wrapped her free arm around his chest, holding him close.

"I was so afraid of losing you, Christine," he said softly. "I don't ever want to lose you."

"Oh, Joe, I don't want to lose you, either. I know I'm not always a very nice person. And I'm sorry for not being straightforward with you, and for doing something that could compromise you, and…"

"Shhh," he said. "That's enough of that kind of talk." He pulled back and kissed her fingers gently.

"Joe." She gazed at him and couldn't imagine a kinder, truer man. Tears were beginning to spill down her cheeks. "I've been wrong about so many things. What I said about our galaxies colliding? I think...I think maybe they can. If you still want them to."

"I still want them to, Christine," he whispered, and his smile suffused her entire being with a sense of contentment.

She sighed and nestled into him, drowsy again. Today was a reprieve, a welcome one. She was thankful to be alive. She had survived, and so had Joe, and so had whatever future was in store for them together. And for the moment, that was good enough.

EPILOGUE

A shriveled leaf twisted on a stalk in the unobstructed breeze over a vacant field of corn stubble. Rain fell in dribs and drabs. The air surrounding the Blackie Nursing Home was acid to the taste though the Lincoln strip mines were a good five miles away.

The tip-off had come from the day nurse, who'd overheard Earl Avery, one of the Blackie home's patients, chuckling and talking about his two boys being famous while watching a TV news story on Claremont and Holmquist. The nurse later confirmed it by poking around Avery's bureau drawer and finding four old letters addressed to him from a Bruna Holmquist pleading for him to send her money to support his two sons—Donald and David.

A cable TV van jerked to a halt across the road from the visitors' parking lot. A WTTX TV news team scuttled across the back lawn toward a side door the alert day nurse held open. The video cameraman handed her a hundred-dollar bill for her troubles. A tall newswoman wearing a sharp-looking tan pantsuit with a bright-turquoise silk scarf followed in next. Last through the door was the backup grunt carrying an extra tape player in case something went haywire with the direct-link satellite feed.

Silently, the nurse led them down the hallway, and they slipped unnoticed into room 29. The cameraman flicked on the bright halogen lamp, aiming it squarely at the eyes of the sixty-one-year-old bedridden coal miner. Avery's eyes fluttered open.

The newswoman began her routine—"Testing, one, two, three, testing"—and the cameraman gave her a nod.

"Lights are good. Sound's ready," he said. "You're on in three, two, one…"

"Good evening, ladies and gentlemen. This is Marguerite Devereux reporting to you live from the Blackie Nursing Home in Blackie, Indiana. We are in the room of Earl Avery, a bedridden coal miner recently confirmed to be the biological father of both David Claremont and Donald Holmquist. Holmquist is the serial killer of three girls that we know of, and is also responsible for the death of a psychiatrist who had treated Holmquist's identical twin brother, David Claremont. Police shot Holmquist in a cornfield a week ago, later finding his corpse caught by thorns, in what appeared to be an attempt to escape. In a macabre twist, Claremont, the twin, was found dead a day later, his body similarly entangled in a thornbush."

The newswoman turned her attention to the miner. "Mr. Avery?" She shook the old man's arm. "Can you hear me?"

Avery's head was propped on several large pillows. His eyes opened and he gazed straight ahead. The newswoman leaned over his bed.

"Marguerite Devereux from WTTX TV Indianapolis. I'd like you to answer a few questions for our audience."

With his pronounced cheekbones and bushy eyebrows, the old man had the same pronounced cheekbones and bushy eyebrows of Claremont and Holmquist. Take away the white color of his hair and a few extra lines and it was the same lump of clay.

"I understand, Mr. Avery, that you are the father of David Claremont and Donald Holmquist. Is that true?"

A faint smile revealed the worn edge of deeply yellowed ivories.

"Jenny Sprade, age eleven, disappeared almost ten years ago from the coal-mining camp where you once worked. Penny Simons, age thirteen, disappeared two years before that."

Devereux's intuition was on overdrive. She had no proof against Avery other than guilt by genetic association—if his son Donald Holmquist was a vicious killer, so could he be. "Could you please tell the girls' still-grieving families and the rest of our viewers whether you know anything about their murders? Mr. Avery?"

Avery began a cough he couldn't stop. He stared at a glass on his bedside table.

The newswoman noticed. "You'd like a drink?"

She steadied the man's hand as he slurped down water. "What about it, Mr. Avery? Do you know the police just found their remains in an abandoned shaft on the Lincoln Mines properties?"

The newswoman had his attention. Avery's eyes were locked on the svelte figure under her suit jacket. Another coughing spasm erupted, black lung disease in its final stages. She gave him more water.

"Mr. Avery, what about Jenny Sprade and Penny Simons, the dead girls? For the sake of their families—they have a right to know what happened to their loved ones." She leaned in closer to him.

Avery's mouth sagged wide. He was barely able to take in air through lungs scarred from years of inhaling coal dust. His eyes brightened as the cameraman shifted position for a closer shot.

Frustrated, the newswoman let the mike dangle. In a whisper, she said to her technician, "You said he'd talk. What's the deal?"

Avery's head suddenly came off the pillow. "Sure as a vein of coal pissing gas will blow," he said and slumped back, heaving for air in great rasping gulps.

The newswoman didn't blink an eye at the man's pained expression. She was too perturbed.

"I take it you're admitting you know something about these killings? It's only a matter of time before police forensics will prove it."

The old miner grinned, showing off his teeth to the camera.

The newswoman looked frazzled. "Cut," said the cameraman, stopping the shoot.

Devereux heard a button clicking—Earl Avery was signaling the nurses' station with a remote device.

"I'm sorry. This is in violation of home policy." The head nurse filled the doorway, and her tone left no room for disagreement. "You must all leave immediately."

The nurse took Avery's pulse. An oxygen mask dangled from a nearby hook. She repositioned it over the patient's nose and mouth and adjusted the flow gauge on the tank.

After the nurse and the TV people had left the room, Earl Avery sank back deeper into his pillows and let his mind wander. Bruna—he could remember picking her up at a bar in Chicago. A big girl she was, with a Scandinavian accent. Plain, but with a body on her that immediately made him hungry for it. And right after she'd swallowed the last of her suds, he'd done the gentlemanly thing and asked if she'd like him to walk her home, and she'd said that she would. He'd taken her down a deserted side street and shoved her up against a brick wall, having his way with her. He'd been surprised to wake up later with a lump on his head. Bruna was gone, and that was the end of it. Until the letters began arriving from her in her broken English. Ridiculous, whiny letters begging him for money so she didn't have to give up one or both of their sons for adoption. The letters stopped, and he'd more or less forgotten about her. Why he'd bothered to keep any of the letters he wasn't sure, but he'd liked the idea of having sired sons.

With a trembling hand, Avery reached for the glass of water on the bedside table. He gulped a mouthful, spilling it down his chin, his thoughts drifting further back. It was late summer, just like now, and he was seventeen. It was hot. He liked that, even though he worked on a farm and spent long hours stacking hay. He was laying up bales for the winter in a three-story loft. From the open bay where the chain pulley swung to hoist the pallet, he saw her—the nubile young daughter of a neighbor farmer in a flower-print dress that flowed prettily. The tight-fitting bodice showed off her slim waist. The way her body moved inside the frock sent him tumbling down the wooden steps and out into the hazy August air.

Avery smiled, the pleasure of the memory never failing him.

She wandered into a cornfield, slapping the long green leaves of a second planting tasseled in full bloom, and disappeared down a row, taking a shortcut home. He followed her into the corn as if pulled by a ring in his nose, pushing aside the leaves and thick stalks in the fading heat of the day. Walking faster, two rows over, he caught glimpses of her flowery dress. For several minutes he trolled behind, waiting till she was farther along into the maize. Gradually, he drifted deeper into the sweet-smelling crop abuzz with bees going from tassel to tassel.

His skin began to crawl as if covered in a swarm of ants. Breathing shallowly, he was stricken, his eyesight shrinking. He dropped to one knee. Everything had gone dark. He scratched at the ground, as if searching for his lost sight there, heaving on all fours with his face in the soil, sucking up dirt. Then slowly the light returned, and with it a new craving.

Clumsily he crashed down stalks, fearing he'd lost her for good. He jogged madly, crisscrossing the rows, crushing the corn, until, fifty feet away, still ambling with her hands outstretched, gently catching the broad-curled leaves, there she was. He could hang back no longer—the hunger had rooted in him. He ran recklessly, and she let out a cry as she turned and saw him thrashing behind her. He lunged, tackling her, punching out her air. Circled his arm around her face. She bit him hard, and still he felt nothing but joy, searching and finding the smooth seam of her jawbone. With the same tremendous force that he used to jerk the hoist chain, he snapped her neck sideways, hearing it pop. Becoming all his. He felt so alive lying over her still-warm body, with the smells of the corn and the deep black soil effervescing.

He carried her body a great distance, into a forest, to an old limestone cave he had discovered. Carefully, he climbed down the steep entrance. Hunched over her body in the dim light of the passage, he opened out the blade of his pocketknife with barely enough strength, he was trembling so. He worked the thin carbon steel below her rib. And he feasted. With each bite, he grew stronger, enabling him to lift her afterward to the edge of a deep vertical shaft in the cave. Seconds passed after he'd tossed her before he heard the dull thud of her body hitting rock.

When he'd emerged from the darkness empty-handed, the daylight had been too much. He'd stumbled, fracturing his ankle. The memory of it now, in his hospital bed, pained his leg immensely. But oh, the pain had been worth it. The pain had been very much worth it.

ACKNOWLEDGMENTS

I am grateful to my wonderful agent, Elisabeth Weed, for taking me on and investing her time and patience in me, and never losing enthusiasm believing in this book. She kept the project moving forward and got me to the finish line. Thank you so much, Elisabeth! And thank you, Stephanie Sun, for your cheerful assistance. I cannot thank enough my dear editor, Nan Gatewood Satter, for getting me to Elisabeth and for her keen eye and commonsensical judgement; she challenged my plotting and rooted out awkward expression, and minded those p's and q's in the otherwise silent world of authorship.

Senior Acquisitions Editor Andrew Bartlett's enthusiasm for my writing made it happen. And thanks to the whole Amazon Publishing team: Jessica Fogleman, Jacque Ben-Zekry, Leslie LaRue, and Reema Al-Zaben, who deserve high praise for their professionalism, competence, courtesy, and, above all, for making me feel like a true partner on their team. Particular praise is due Kate Chynoweth for her fresh laser eyes that scrubbed the book while helping lift the story to a better place. Thank you, Kate!

Pat Sims and Chris Noel gave much-needed feedback in the book's early stages and challenged me to reach to a higher place.

To my sister, Susan Richards, a gifted author herself, who believed in my writing from the get-go with all her heart and cheered me on to never give up. I am deeply grateful, Sooz! To Nathaniel, Marguerite, and Evan: I am privileged as their father because they have taught me so much about myself; without them

I would have been denied my greatest gift—to demonstrate to my children what dogged determination, love of work, and believing in one's self can bring.

And above all to my wife, Cameron, who never doubted me or had a cross word all those hours I spent writing in the attic; I am forever blessed.

ABOUT THE AUTHOR

Lloyd Devereux Richards was born in New York City and traveled extensively in Europe, Africa, and Central America before attending law school. He previously served as a senior law clerk for an Indiana Court of Appeals judge, researching and writing drafts for dozens of published opinions, including the appeal of a serial killer sentenced to death. A father of three, he lives with his wife, Cameron O'Connor, and their two dogs in Montpelier, Vermont. *Stone Maidens is* his first novel.

Made in the USA
Las Vegas, NV
12 February 2023